The Walking People

MARY BETH KEANE

PENGUIN BOOKS

PENGUIN BOOKS

UK | USA | Canada | Ireland | Australia
India | New Zealand | South Africa

Penguin Books is part of the Penguin Random House group of companies
whose addresses can be found at global.penguinrandomhouse.com

Penguin
Random House
UK

First published in the US by Mariner Books, 2009
First published in the UK by Michael Joseph, 2021
This edition published by Penguin Books, 2021

001

Copyright © Mary Beth Keane, 2009

The moral right of the author has been asserted

Typeset by Jouve (UK), Milton Keynes
Printed and bound in Great Britain by Clays Ltd, Elcograf S.p.A.

The authorized representative in the EEA is Penguin Random House Ireland,
Morrison Chambers, 32 Nassau Street, Dublin D02 YH68

A CIP catalogue record for this book is available from the British Library

ISBN: 978-1-405-95001-5

www.greenpenguin.co.uk

MIX
Paper from
responsible sources
FSC® C018179

Penguin Random House is committed to a
sustainable future for our business, our readers
and our planet. This book is made from Forest
Stewardship Council® certified paper.

TO MOM AND DAD

*or, as they will be known by the time they
read this, Mamó and Daideó*

How perilous is it to choose
not to love the life we're shown?

– from 'Badgers', Seamus Heaney, 1979

Prologue

At exactly 6:16 on a Friday morning the front attendant at Champion Parking Garage looked up from the nine-inch monitor of his television screen and watched Michael Ward steer his car onto the lot of the construction site at the corner of Thirtieth Street and Tenth Avenue. This one is always first, the attendant thought as he strolled over to stand under the fluorescent light at the garage entrance. When Michael looked over at him, the attendant nodded. Michael raised his arm and nodded back. It was getting close to a shift change for the sandhogs, and as he did every morning of the five weeks the attendant had been working at Champion, he watched the cars arrive in the hope that there would be too many and some would be forced to come over and park with him.

If there was nothing good on television, the attendant sat, peered out across the faint dawn light, counted the sandhogs' cars as they parked and then the men inside them as they got out, stretched, disappeared behind the sixteen-foot aluminum fence that marked the boundary of the site. The guys who shuffled and reshuffled the cars downstairs had told him that the sandhogs had been working across the street for years now, but from where he sat there was no sign of what they could possibly be building. As he watched Michael attach the club to the steering wheel of his little red Corolla and then circle the car to make sure the doors were locked tight, he remembered Mr Zan from the business office telling him that they were digging, not building. They were digging down, down, down below the city, below the subway tunnels, below the riverbed all the way over on the East Side, below Roosevelt Island, below Queens. 'Take the highest building you've seen since you came to America,' Mr Zan had said. 'Now pretend it stretches down instead of up. That's how deep they

I

dig.' When the attendant asked why, Mr Zan shrugged, threw up his hands. Who knew? In America they dig just to keep busy.

The sun, risen now for twenty minutes, had not yet reached its arms across the city to the westernmost stretch of Thirtieth Street. Michael Ward angled his wrist to catch the dim light and narrowed his eyes to read his watch. He had forgotten something, he felt sure of it, but he couldn't remember what it could be. It was a feeling that kept stopping him lately, like a tiny, nagging hair that kept brushing his skin but he couldn't find. He stood in the middle of the parking lot, hoping it would come to him, and then, after ten seconds of stretching his mind back to earlier that morning, to Greta in the kitchen, to the lonesome curves of the Palisades before rush hour, he abruptly wondered why he'd stopped walking. He looked down to find his lunch hanging from his fist in a plastic Pathmark bag – one roast beef sandwich, one Granny Smith apple, one banana, two slices of brown bread, one can of ginger ale, two bottles of water. As usual, Greta had wrapped everything neatly, even the soda can, which she'd covered in two layers of tinfoil. 'Keeps it cold,' she said almost every morning when she showed him what she'd packed. She'd learned the trick back in 1969, the year their oldest daughter, Julia, started kindergarten. Julia had come home one afternoon and told Greta what she'd seen in the other lunch boxes, and Greta had been wrapping soda cans in tinfoil ever since. After thirty-seven years working underground, Michael didn't have the heart to tell her that down in the tunnel it wouldn't get a chance to get warm, foil or no foil.

Everything else he would need for his shift was in his locker. The code to his lock was written on a small piece of paper in his wallet – Greta's idea, and a good one. He'd had to go to that piece of paper quite a few times in the past months. Recently he'd forgotten that the code was in his wallet and had had to use a sledgehammer to break the lock. The guys on his shift had joked that he'd need another reminder – on the back of his hand or pinned to the steering wheel of his car – to remind him where the reminder was. Standing motionless in the half-empty lot, he recited the numbers quickly: 26 right, 3 left, 9 right. But the nagging feeling was still there, as if someone had stolen part of his morning and he couldn't figure out which part was missing.

A low-grade buzz still sounded in his ear from the blast of the day before, and he cupped his hand over the side of his head as he started walking again. He pressed hard with his palm and tried to suction the noise away. When this failed, as it had failed fifty times already that morning, he jammed his index finger into his ear as far as he could, hoping to steady the vibration. With his finger working its way deeper, he glanced over at the hoghouse, which was lit up on the outside by a tripod of industrial floodlights. It reminded him of a school play he'd seen once. Which of the kids was performing? He couldn't remember. He couldn't remember the story either, but there was a handsome American barn painted red with pure white along the eaves, and that barn was in the background of every scene, lit up like Christmas by the lights at the foot of the stage.

'You might be sad,' Greta had said after dinner the day before. 'Last days can be sad, you know.' He'd laughed, nearly had to spit his tea back into his mug. Then that morning she'd all but asked if there would be a farewell party. The things she came out with sometimes. And yet, once he'd navigated the car through the local roads of Recess and finally hit the Palisades, he couldn't get the possibility out of his mind. Not a cake or balloons or that kind of thing, but something. Not many had lasted as long as he had. As he did every morning – winter, spring, summer, and fall – he'd rolled down the car windows to breathe in the Hudson as it flowed south to meet the Atlantic. He'd seen a lot of rivers in his life, but this one was mighty. Broad, solemn, abused, the Hudson was a special case. In the years when he'd worked the overnight shift, he would insist to anyone who challenged him that it was the Hudson that carried him home each morning. When his eyelids refused to stay open and the dust that rimmed them burned as he blinked it away, he would position his hands on the steering wheel, let the speedometer fall to sixty, and follow the sound and smell of the river.

Keeping his focus on the low-slung and windowless building that was not a building, really, but a simple shelter, a runty eyesore stuck in among the brick and brownstone of the much taller buildings that surrounded the site, Michael knew he wouldn't be able to tell if anything was unusual, not from a distance, not with the ringing in his ear.

Still, the hoghouse looked quiet. He laughed, the sound breaking up the steady crunch his new loafers made on the gravel. It was a thing Greta would say: that something looked quiet. Once, at a benefit dance in the Bronx, she'd spotted an American woman they'd both known when they first came to America, a woman they hadn't seen in almost forty years. Greta had rushed up to the woman and said, 'Is that you? Here at the dance?'

The world knew New York as the city that never sleeps, but it seemed to Michael that there was an hour each morning, maybe less than an hour, maybe only fifteen minutes, that were so singularly still and silent that those minutes stretched out until they felt like an hour, when there were no cars on the avenue, no horns, no dog walkers, no one hosing down the sidewalk, no one sweeping, no heels clicking, no brakes squealing, no nine-to-fivers weaving in and out of pedestrian traffic, because there was no pedestrian traffic, not yet. The commuter trains were just beginning to trickle in. He'd passed only a dozen or so cars between the George Washington Bridge and Thirtieth Street, and now, as he continued the walk from his car to the heart of the site, despite the damn ringing in his ear, he would be willing to swear he heard the Hudson lapping up against the pilings two avenues away.

He looked again at the plain off-white structure that housed the lockers, the showers, and a small table they called the breakroom even though it wasn't its own room at all, only a corner inside the larger room. As he got closer, he told himself to smile, to shake a few hands. Not smiling and not shaking hands, instead turning red and nodding, letting them see that he was touched by their gestures, would make him the mickey for the entire shift. After too, at the union picnics and memorial services and all the other occasions that would keep bringing them together. Maybe they'd even had a joke trophy made for him. There were shops that did it. His son, James, had one with a baseball figure on top of a toilet paper roll. Across the gold plate it said FOR ONE POOPER OF A SEASON.

Now, as he went for the knob of the hoghouse door, he agreed with Greta: a cake wouldn't be unheard of. Who else had been working as a sandhog since the very first day the water tunnel project

4

began? Even when the construction contract passed from company to company and the work site moved from borough to borough, Michael moved with it. Who else had lasted thirty-seven years? No one he knew. Twenty, yes. Thirty, sometimes. More than thirty, barely ever. One of the wives might have suggested it, might even have volunteered to pick it up and run it over at the end of the shift. Yes, cake was a possibility, but it was his locker he prepared himself for as he pulled the door wide, and them playing cool until he opened it. One of the young guys had been down in the tunnel with a camera a few weeks back. Maybe they'd had a photograph blown up and framed.

Inside, nothing seemed unusual. The showers were on and the air in the long room was thick with steam and the smell of soap. Half a dozen muck-covered rain slickers hung from the hooks that ran across an entire wall. A row of steel-toed rubber boots, also covered in muck, were lined up underneath. If he'd told them once, he'd told them a million times: rinse your gear before you rinse yourself. It was easier. It was more logical. But no, he thought, day after day they just peel off and head for the showers, and later, when the muck gets on one of their nice clean shirts, they curse like the devil. Then their wives curse them again when they get home. He walked farther into the room and saw two men from the overnight shift sitting at the breakroom table, the television on low. They'd already changed back into civilian clothes, the teeth of their combs visible on their damp hair. In an hour, when they finally reached their homes, they'd strip once more, down to their clean undershirts and shorts, and try to sleep out the day while their wives and children tiptoed around the rest of the house, reminding each other to talk in whispers.

'How's it goin', Ward?' one of them asked. Michael nodded, stood and watched what they were watching for a minute, and then made for his locker. One of them snakes that pops out, he thought. Or something that makes a loud noise. They were always riding him for his hearing.

Finding he needed the reminder after all – damn it altogether, but that was strange, didn't I just now have those numbers in my head? – Michael removed the small piece of paper from his wallet and, after reading it, turned the dial of the combination lock. He fiddled with the latch for a moment, then lifted the little metal handle and pulled hard so the door wouldn't stick in the bottom corner. There were his boots, his thermal socks, his work jeans, his flannel work shirt, his yellow rain slicker, his hard hat, his flashlight, his fold-up ruler, his nail clipper, all arranged as they'd been arranged in similar lockers all over New York City for the past thirty-seven years. He stared at his things for a moment, then unbuttoned the top two buttons of his blue shirt – a golf shirt, Greta called it, though he'd never picked up a golf club in his life – and pulled it over his head. He unzipped his khaki pants. He slipped off his new loafers. He hung everything but the shoes on two hangers where they'd wait for the next eight hours. Limb by limb he put on his work clothes, rough and stiff from industrial strength detergent and years of fine gray rock dust embedded in the cotton fibers. He pulled on a pair of white kneesocks, then the thick gray thermal socks. May or December, the weather was always the same in the tunnel.

With ten minutes to go, he was at the shift check-in board, flipping the tag under his name so it was red side out. He looked over at the midnight shift board; no red tags meant that they were all up top. All up top meant there hadn't been any problems. There were three others from Michael's shift already in the steel cage, including Ned Powers, a sandhog for twenty-nine years and Michael's closest friend. They waited for him. 'Losing your step, Ward?' Asante, one of the power guys, asked. 'It's your last day so you figure what the hell, they can fire me?'

'Greta was up. Wanted me to take my vitamins. Am I late?'

'Ward, wait just a second,' Powers said as he stepped out of the cage to stop Michael from stepping in, and to the engineer who operated the lift he said, 'Hold it a minute.' He clapped a broad hand on Michael's back and steered him toward the hoghouse.

'What's happening?' Michael asked. It could be now – a party when he least expected it.

Ned pointed down at Michael's feet and then said loudly, so the others could hear, 'I know you said you don't plan to do a lick of work today, Ward, but I don't see why you have to ruin good shoes just to stick it to us.'

Michael looked down and blinked. There were his double-socked feet shoved into his new loafers. One step into the tunnel and he'd be ankle-deep in muck. The two waiting in the cage laughed as Ned said gently, so only Michael could hear, 'Go on, now, Michael. Get your boots. Put those shoes in your locker. Will I go with you? No, you're grand. All the commotion of last day, isn't it? Makes a person lose his head.'

Michael hurried back to his locker and, not wanting to fiddle with the lock again, grabbed a spare pair of boots from storage and left his loafers on a bench. When he finally got back to the cage and the engineer latched the door, the steel platform swayed above the hole for a moment and then with a loud groan began to descend.

The men looked down through the darkness at the murky light more than six hundred feet below. It was a woman's department, Michael decided, goodbyes and gag gifts and that kind of thing. It made sense for nine-to-fivers, office workers, where there were rooms you could have a little party in and desks you could decorate. But in the tunnel? Maybe he'd been watching too much television lately. It was just that one of the Jamaicans had retired in February, twenty-five years in the tunnels, and they'd made a to-do out of it, passing around a card everyone had to sign, chipping in for a gift certificate to a restaurant uptown.

The cage picked up speed. 'One hundred,' Powers shouted. Michael heard Powers say something, saw his lips move, but wouldn't have known what was said if he hadn't taken the same ride five, sometimes six, days a week for almost four decades. Despite the damage to his ears, he could usually tell if someone was shouting at him over the roar of the machinery. Human voices were weak compared with so many other sounds, but often, when someone yelled over the machines, there was something in the pitch, some quality added to the noise that did not quite fit, and that made him look up. Other men had made the same discovery, and no one could explain it. Down below, when the machines were off, the men's shouts ricocheted inside the tunnel, hitting the dead end and bouncing right back like a rubber ball thrown hard against a wall. When the machines were on – the shaker, the mole, the muck train, the conveyer belts, the pumps, the fans – they filled the tunnel with sound in a way that felt almost physical, and was physical, actually, when the ground began to tremble.

'Two hundred,' Powers called after another thirty seconds. What little daylight had begun to creep in at street level disappeared entirely. At four hundred feet the dim light at the bottom of the hole became brighter, though it remained hazy, as if Michael were looking at it through the oily gauze left on his car windshield after a rainy commute, truck after truck kicking up grit and greasy puddles from the road. At five hundred fifty they were nearly there. At six hundred twenty-five feet the cage came to a stop. As always, the journey had taken just over three minutes. The exposed bedrock wept constantly, big, wet tears that fell in heavy drops or streamed down the rock face in rivers. The air was dense with moisture and dust. The thermometer read fifty-five degrees. The men stepped out of the cage and walked the last twenty feet down the wet aluminum staircase, single file, each making sure to hold tight to the railing.

The week before, Michael heard the walking boss yelling at one of the new guys that only a fucking moron would walk across the bottom of the shaft – hard hat or no hard hat. It took years for the new guys to be as careful as they had to be, and it usually took a tragedy to make them cautious. Once, in 1988, a man on Michael's shift was passing across the bottom of the shaft with his hard hat tucked under his arm when a socket wrench fell from six hundred feet above and cracked his skull as neatly as if someone had gotten him from behind with a cleaver. Every year on the job brought a new tragedy. And then, only a few months ago, there were the stories out of West Virginia, newspapers left open in the breakroom, articles tacked up to the board, novenas said before each shift for nine consecutive shifts, men who hadn't set foot inside a church since they were children, who'd never been south of New Jersey, bowing their heads, clasping their hands, asking God to save the coal miners, to protect them and their families, just as they felt sure those men in West Virginia would ask God to protect New York's sandhogs if the tables were turned.

The men left their plastic lunch bags and mini-coolers on the damp and mold-freckled picnic table that had been lowered into the hole six years before. They boarded the mining train – a single car, no doors, no roof, like a ride you might see in the littlest kids' part of an amusement park – that would take them to the dead end two miles away. As Michael took his seat, he reminded himself that it was his last trip to the end of the tunnel. It didn't feel like his last time; it felt like every other time, no better, no worse. As the train began to move, he saw that someone had used the chalk meant to mark drilling points to draw a huge yellow sun on a dry section of the rock face. Drawing on the rock was common, and if you picked a good spot it might last for days before being erased by the constant dripping and the wet air. Farther down the tunnel were more drawings: a shamrock, the flag of the Dominican Republic, a series of stick figures. Strung along the mesh wire that covered the sides of the tunnel was the occasional lightbulb. As one bulb flickered and then went out, Michael thought about his first day, and how he thought he'd last just a few weeks. The job was in the Bronx then, in Woodlawn. It was good money, he and Greta kept reminding each other at the time, but the money meant far less when he went down the shaft for the first time and realized he'd have to arrive in the dark, work in the dark, eat in the dark, finish his day in the dark, drive home in the dark. And when he arrived home he was too tired for supper, too tired to talk, too tired to touch Greta for weeks at a time or even to sense her body curled up against him all night long until the alarm went off again and he discovered her behind him, the small spoon holding the big.

Throughout his shift, Michael kept searching for some part of his day to feel different, kept waiting for a feeling to come over him as it had some others who were surprised to find themselves torn about leaving. As always, the mud below sucked him deeper while the mud above kept dripping until it ran down the sides of his hard hat, down his cheeks, his neck, under the collar of his shirt. What was there to miss? Not the muck, these men insisted, not the work, but the strange life lived so many stories under the sidewalk, too deep and dark even for the city's rats. For a lot of men, it didn't hit them until the very end that the job they'd done for so long was actually important. They were the men who were building the new water tunnel – number 3. Tunnels 1 and 2 – dilapidated, vulnerable – were built more than a century earlier and could fail at any moment. They were already leaking, crumbling, propped up and patched so crudely that Michael couldn't see how a disaster had not already happened. Failure of the first two tunnels before number 3 was complete meant that there would be no water for eight million New Yorkers. No water to drink, to bathe, to boil for tea, to put out fires, nothing. 'Any moment' was the phrase that had been used for decades to describe the impending disaster. These men were so busy scrubbing behind their ears, cleaning their fingernails, washing the filth off their skin so as not to be embarrassed when they re-entered the world at sidewalk level that they never took the time to stop and think: this project is crucial to this city's survival, and I am a part of it. Michael wasn't one of these men. He'd known all along how critical the new water tunnel was and how that need was, in a way, the city's biggest secret.

By the time Michael took the train back to the picnic table and ate his lunch, listened to the usual arguments about whether it was better to work fast or work slow, about which shift did the least work, about how many of them probably had silicosis, about whether or not there would be a strike, he decided he just wasn't the sort of person who got affected by things like leaving. After lunch, he and Powers had to weld five large pieces of rustproof sheeting together. It was a difficult task because of the position of the sheets – mostly overhead – and because the seams had to be absolutely perfect or they would leak. As they worked the blowtorches back and forth across the edges of the metal squares, applying constant temperature and speed, the sparks rained down around them like fireflies flaring, disappearing, flecks of light erupting in an arc over Michael's head, over Powers's head, and landing somewhere behind them. Taken together in the otherwise dark tunnel, the storm of light and the blue glow of the torches' flames seemed like a celebration.

It didn't hit him that he wouldn't be back, didn't honestly become a circumstance he felt for certain, until the very end of his shift when he took his turn on the buster. The muck train went out with the bulk of the rocks, but the men had to use the buster to break the bigger rocks into smaller pieces before loading them onto the conveyer belt that would bring them up to street level. Michael sighed as he approached the buster, bigger than the jackhammers used at street level. He braced himself for the noise, as loud as dynamite explosions even through his earplugs and his one buzzing ear, and he was surprised all over again at just how loud it could get. And then there was the actual shaking, the lights trembling against the tunnel wall, his joints, his neck, the disks of his spine, his brain vibrating inside his skull. Fuck this, Michael thought. I should get them the cake, not the other way around. I should get the lady in the store to write on it FOR THE GUYS WHO HAVE TWENTY YEARS TO GO.

At 3:00 P.M., as the rest of the men made their way to street level and a hot shower, the walking boss kept Michael back. 'It'll be impossible to replace you,' the boss said, and shook Michael's hand until Michael felt he could be back on the buster. Behind him, he could hear the cage begin the ascent to the street, and he knew it would be at least fifteen minutes before it returned. By the time he finally got to the hoghouse, rinsed off his slicker and boots, rolled up his muddied clothes, put them in a black plastic bag, retrieved his loafers from the storage room and took a shower, only Powers was around. Michael tried not to be disappointed, but he couldn't help but think they'd all left unusually fast.

'Will we go for a pint?' Powers asked. Powers was two years younger than Michael, and was the only person, aside from Greta, Michael had known since he first came to New York. They never went for pints after work. They were tired. They were hungry. Greta expected Michael home. He and Powers saw each other often enough outside of work. Powers, who was from Mayo, was first drawn to Michael because he heard he was from Galway. When they first met, Powers had asked Michael what town he was from, what village. He knew every village in Connaught, he claimed, or at least the ones worth mentioning.

'We moved a lot,' Michael had explained. 'But I liked Greta's place. If I could pick a place to be from, I'd pick there.'

'Moved a lot,' Powers had repeated, drawing his eyebrows together. The year was 1963, they were both working as furniture movers, and Michael had not yet considered how he'd answer the question from other Irish. Ned looked at his new acquaintance for so long that Michael scolded himself for not taking Greta's advice, for not just making up a place and sticking to it. And then Powers had nodded, a single, conclusive dip of the head and thrust of the chin, putting an end to some dialogue he was having inside his own head. '*An Lucht Siúil?*' Powers had asked.

The walking people. Travellers. Wanderers. Tinkers. Thieves. *An Lucht Siúil* was a country person's way of putting it. They were all walking people now, Michael had considered pointing out. They were all travellers. Instead, he crossed his arms and waited for whatever Ned would say next.

'I understand completely,' Ned said finally. And then: 'We're all Americans now anyhow, isn't it true?'

Now, decades later, Ned waited for Michael to make a decision about going for a pint. '*An Lucht Siúil*,' Michael said out loud, shaping the sounds to fit the old language. Michael had been thinking of home a lot lately, and now, remembering the Irish for what he once was, his thoughts tripped away once more. Greta said he'd been talking about ponies in his sleep, but Michael knew he'd been awake on the night she referred to. Daydreaming at night, he guessed, though he couldn't remember ever dreaming so vividly. He'd been instructing Greta to pull out the pony's wisdom teeth so she could be sold as a two-year-old, and he only realized how little sense he was making when Greta said, 'Wake up, Michael. You haven't any ponies in America. Wake up.' He'd lifted himself on his right elbow to look at her, and she'd lifted herself on her left to look right back. They'd been through every phase of their lives together, and that night, for the first time, it felt as if change was in the air again. Greta could feel it too. He could tell by the way she watched his mouth and waited for him to speak. She seemed different to him that night, apart from him in a way he'd never felt before, and he felt a chill run through him that he couldn't understand. Greta, who he'd known since childhood. Greta, the girl who'd seemed so hopeless back then and who never would have believed herself capable of making the life she ended up with.

'I met you fifty-one years ago,' he had pointed out after doing the calculation in his head.

'Lord,' Greta had said, finally turning her eyes away from his face and letting her head fall back on the pillow. 'Don't tell me you're getting sentimental.'

'A quick one,' Ned Powers urged his friend now, and Michael was pulled back to the present, to the city, to the construction yard that was busy with the arrival of the afternoon shift. 'For myself, really, or else I'll have the guilts all summer that we didn't make a fuss over you.'

Michael smiled. 'Do I seem like the fuss type to you?'

'Well, you never know now, Ward. You just never know. Come on, you'll be bored silly in a week's time.'

So they went up the street to The Banner – south for three blocks along Tenth and then a left onto Twenty-seventh – and had exactly one pint. When they finished, the froth still sliding down to the bottom of their empty glasses, they stood, lifted their chins in the bartender's direction, and walked back to the lot at the site. They shook hands, and at four-thirty in the afternoon they said good night.

PART I

1956–1957

One

At home in Ballyroan, in the single-story cottage that stood beside the sea, in the bed she shared with her older sister, eight-year-old Greta Cahill woke before dawn to a sound that was not the ocean, was not the animals bawling into the wind, was not a slammed gate, a clanging cowbell, or the rain beating on the gable. The sound was different, it was a first, and to hear it better Greta pushed the layers of blankets away from her shoulders and sat up.

'You're letting in the cold,' Johanna said into the dark without whispering, and tugged at the blankets Greta had pushed away. As they struggled, a faint whiff of salmon stopped Greta's hands. She had forgotten that part of last night's catch was lined up on a shallow tray and resting in the emptied top drawer of the dresser she and Johanna shared. Greta pictured the six flat bodies in a neat row – tails to the back, heads to the front, all split along the backbone and buried in salt. The smell was barely noticeable so far, but Greta knew that in a few more hours the delicate tang of the drying fish would be like an itch inside her nose that could not be scratched. The salt would pull the water from the salmon's river-logged bodies, and it would be Johanna's job to drain the brine with Greta looking on and their mother standing behind saying, 'Are you watching, Greta? Are you seeing how your sister does it?'

'Christ,' Johanna said, and pressed her face to her pillow. Greta knew what her sister was thinking. Last night, late, after listening to the usual activity at the back door and then in the kitchen, and after following the tsk-tsk of their mother's slippers as she scurried around the cottage to the other hiding places, Johanna had sat up in bed just as Lily opened their door and said she'd not have any fish in her room, thank you very much.

Holding the tray flat so the salt wouldn't spill, Lily had set the lantern on the floor, placed the tray in the drawer, and reached over to give Johanna a lug. Smart, fast, her hand fell from the dark space above their bed and caught Johanna square on the cheek. There were salmon in drawers all over the cottage and in the highest cabinet of the press in the hall.

Now Johanna flipped over to her back as Greta worked to identify the sound that had woken her. 'There was blood left last time,' Johanna said. 'She says they're all cleaned, but –'

Greta put her hand over Johanna's mouth and held a finger in the air. 'Listen,' she said. Then Johanna heard it too. Greta could tell by the way her sister's back went rigid and her head lifted from the pillow.

'What is it?' Johanna asked. 'A horse and cart,' she answered herself a second later, and jumped out of bed to go to the window. 'Coming fast.' It was bouncing violently on the stones and dips in the road, the wood of the cart splintering as it slammed against the iron hitch. For a half second here and there the world went silent, and Greta cringed in expectation of the airborne cart landing with a clatter. The racket grew louder as it came closer, rolling toward their cottage like thunder, like a stampede. The bedroom window didn't face the road, but Johanna stayed there, hopping from foot to foot on the wood planks of the floor as she peered through the gray-green light. Just as Greta was about to shout for their mother, they heard the crash, an explosion of wood coming to a sudden halt against stone and hard ground, followed by the everyday sound of a horse galloping away.

'Tom,' Greta heard Lily say on the other side of the wall. 'Get up.'

Johanna opened the door of their bedroom and the cold of the hall swept into the room just as cruelly as if they'd stepped directly outside.

'You stay where you are,' Big Tom said when he emerged from his bedroom and saw Johanna. 'Don't make me say it twice.' He walked over to her, looked over her head to Greta, who was still in bed, and then to every corner of the room. 'And keep that drawer well closed.'

'It's something to do with the salmon,' Johanna said when he left, still hopping from foot to foot. Greta didn't understand about the salmon, so she didn't answer. She suspected that Johanna didn't understand either but liked to pretend that she did.

In another minute Lily came out, tying the belt of her long cardigan, and told Johanna to either get back under the covers or get dressed. 'You too,' she said to Greta. She lit the paraffin lamp in the hall, twisting the

knob to raise the wick and make the yellow flame higher. The boys –
Jack, Little Tom, and Padraic – were already outside with Big Tom;
Greta could hear the low hum of their voices traveling on the heavy air
of dawn. As her much older brothers, they existed for Greta as a unit, all
roughly the same age – twenty, nineteen, eighteen – all tall, black hair,
black stubble on their cheeks by the end of each day. The only thing that
kept them from being three identical spokes on the same wheel was Little Tom, who was born with his top lip attached to the bottom of his
nose and something wrong with the inside of his mouth.

Greta squinted to find Johanna. 'What's happening? Did Mammy
go out too?' She felt for the lump of wool stockings she'd tied and left
beside her bed the night before, and then for the navy cardigan that
hung alongside Johanna's at the back of the door. 'Johanna?' she said,
turning around and stretching her neck toward the shadowed corners
of the room. 'Are you there?' She felt a draft from the front door opening and closing, and she heard the other doors in the cottage shaking in
their frames.

'Well, look it –' Big Tom shouted from outside a moment later. His
voice was big, full of tobacco, turf smoke, and crushed seashells
whipped up by the wind. 'Get inside, girl. Lily! Get this child inside!'
Lily had just plunged her hands into the water pail in the kitchen
when she heard him and rushed out of the house to catch Johanna,
who'd taken off in a run across the yard to the field, where a woman's
body lay in the grass.

'It's the tinker from yesterday,' Johanna shouted as Lily hooked her
around the waist and pulled her back toward the house. 'Greta,
remember your tinker from yesterday?' Johanna kicked as she was
pulled. She put both heels into the dirt and drew tracks.

Greta stood framed in the open cottage door, pulling the sleeves of
her cardigan over her hands. It was the kind of day that wouldn't get
any brighter, gray upon gray in every direction. She could feel the
dampness on her skin, weighing down her clothes and making her
shiver. She put her knuckle in her mouth and began to suck.

'Greta?' Lily said. 'Come in now, will you? Like a good girl? Like
two good girls, you'll both wait by the fire.' Lily blessed herself.
'Lord to mercy on the poor woman.'

'It's an awful day to be dead in a field, isn't it, Mammy?' Johanna said, her breath ragged, the heat of her body coming through her sweater, cutting through the cold and the damp so that Greta could feel it as her sister brushed past, flicking her hair this way and that as she looked back and forth between her mother and the field, where Big Tom had gone down on one knee to lift the woman into his arms.

'I'd say so, love,' Lily sighed. 'Greta, take them fingers out of your mouth.'

Ballyroan sat at the very western edge of Ireland. Once, when the book man came to the Cahills' door selling volumes on all subjects, he'd taken Greta on his knee and told her to find her village on the map he unfolded and unfolded until it was the width of their kitchen table. When she couldn't do that, he told her to find Connemara. When she couldn't do that either, he used his finger to find Galway for her and covered the whole west of Ireland in the process. She was surprised to learn that at the end of all that ocean that began at the end of their lane was a piece of land a hundred times the size of Ireland, and that someone over there might be standing at the end of her own lane and looking back toward her.

At the start of the Second World War, the village of Ballyroan consisted of seven families, which came to just over fifty people spread over one square mile. Conch, the closest town, was four miles inland and not a single person lived on the bogland or in the fields that stretched between Conch and Ballyroan, leaving those seven families alone, except when the children went to school or the people from town rode their bicycles out to swim in the sea or for some other equally isolated purpose. Big Tom often said that living in Ballyroan was like living on an island, except better. In every direction was water, but unlike the islands that sat out in the ocean like the backs of whales, Ballyroan had a freshwater river running through it. Not a stream, mind you, but a river. Fast, deep, full to the brim with fish if you knew the right places to look. It was because of the river that the Cahills never had to leave. Not when the Normans came, not when Grainne O'Malley ruled the clans and the seas, not even during the potato blight when the people either fled or turned into shadows.

'Because of this,' Big Tom always said at the end of this familiar speech, and held up his fishing net.

'Put that away, you fool,' Lily said when she saw him at it. Sometimes she would grab it out of his hands, gather it up in her arms until it was as small as she could make it, and carry it out of the kitchen to a hiding place only she and Big Tom knew.

But by 1956, despite centuries of gathering seaweed from the high sea ledges, drying it, giving it to the children to chew or keep for the flower beds, despite generation after generation of the same families driving cattle, footing turf, churning butter, bleeding the fall pig from the ceiling rafter of a dark back room before covering him with salt the size of hailstones and closing him up in his barrel, despite all the narrow headstones sticking out of the fields like milk teeth, five of the seven houses in Ballyroan were abandoned, their windows boarded, their inhabitants gone to England or Australia or Canada or America. Every one of these families said they were certain they'd come back one day, once they had their legs under them, once they'd put aside a little money to bring back home and start again, and when that day came, could they please write the Cahills to take the boards off the windows, light the fire in the kitchen, let the air and sunshine in.

Greta assumed that these families did not have a net like her father did, or they wouldn't have had to leave. According to the man on the wireless radio, all of Ireland was leaving for England and America, all except the very young and the very old. It seemed a simple thing, a net. Such an ordinary piece of daily life – like a bucket or a spade – and Greta couldn't see why people wouldn't just go out and get one.

In the only other house left in Ballyroan lived Mr Grady. Mr Grady's house stood exactly one mile north of the Cahills, and considered together the two houses were like signposts marking where one entered and exited Ballyroan. Big Tom said that no one ever wrote to Mr Grady, and when Greta asked why, Big Tom said it was because Mr Grady was a miserable son of a bitch. Lily didn't like Mr Grady spoken ill of in the Cahill house. She said it would bring bad luck. Sometimes she included Mr Grady in the bedtime prayers she said with the girls, and when Big Tom said she should pray for the net and the salmon as long as she was praying for Mr Grady, she said that would bring bad luck too.

If there were still seven families living in Ballyroan in 1956, the travellers might have decided to keep going to a roadside farther away. They came to Conch at roughly the same time every year, after the Ballinasloe Horse Fair in October, and stayed until the middle of December. Greta and Johanna had seen them there when they went to town for Mass or errands, which they weren't allowed to do alone if the tinkers had set up camp. They had passed the brightly colored barrel-top wagons, their hands clenched firmly in Lily's fists. But by 1956 the travellers had worn out their welcome in Conch. They were run from town, run from the outskirts of town, run up the western road toward the coast, where the townspeople didn't have to pass their damp clothes drying in the bushes, their collection of tinker tools scattered in the grass, their gypsy stews cooked in open view, their made-up language no one could understand. Ballyroan was a compromise that had been reached after name-calling, fist fighting, denial of entrance to pubs and shops, spitting on ancestral gravesites. The travellers were run all the way to the ocean, where that October they lined up their wagons, set up their tents, built their fortresses of plywood, cardboard, scrap metal, and oilcloth, and lit their fires on that particular high sea ledge for the very first time. It was an easy walk from there to Conch, where they could spend the days going door to door begging or offering their services or stealing, depending on who was describing it.

The morning before the traveling woman landed in the Cahills' field, she'd come to their door and knocked. 'God bless all here,' she'd said when Greta answered. Big Tom said that tinkers were without religion. They only pretended when they came to Catholic homes. They had rosaries in their pockets and the string of the scapular peeking out above their collars just like country people, but it was all a trick where a tinker was concerned. Lily said they were born into their lives the same as anyone, and if Big Tom had been born in a tent by the side of the road he wouldn't know any different either.

'I'd know enough, no matter where I was born, not to go around begging instead of going out and doing. They'll pull the hay from our haycocks to make their beds, and they'll turn their animals into our fields at night.'

'And what harm?'

'And then after that the whole lot of them will come pleading at the door for the clothes off our backs. What harm? And them with more money than any of us with their goats and donkeys and ponies.'

'I've come across a few good ones, is all I'm saying. There's bad ones and good ones just like country people. You think you're perfect, Tom Cahill? Think of what we sell from this house. That's right. Now think of people who might say we're no better than the tinkers.'

Greta had opened the door for the woman, and though she shouldn't have been surprised – Lily had said they'd start at the two Ballyroan houses before they headed into town – she couldn't remember what she was supposed to do. Lily was in the kitchen with her bucket of heads and tails, her fingers sticky from pressing the salmons' bellies and sweeping aside with her cupped hand all that oozed out, when she saw the woman walking down the coast road toward their cottage. She had immediately started cleaning up and shouted to Greta to open all the windows in the cottage as high as they would go.

'God bless.' Greta echoed the woman's greeting, and opened the door wider.

'Is your mam at home?' the woman asked, taking two small steps into the hallway so that Greta could shut the door. She was about the same age as Lily, Greta guessed, except rougher-looking, lined in the face the way leather gets when it's left outside too long. She was wearing an orange scarf wrapped around her hair and a heavy black shawl over her dress. On her feet were thick wool socks stuck into sandals that had once been white. Lily came out of the kitchen wiping her hands. 'Missus,' the tinker said.

'Greta,' Lily said, 'go make the tea.'

The woman, whose name turned out to be Julia Ward, stayed for almost an hour. Big Tom and the boys were out cutting turf; Johanna had taken the bicycle into town to sell the eggs, deliver the salmon, buy flour, tea, sugar. Julia undid her shawl to reveal a heather gray cardigan unraveling at the cuffs, a navy blue skirt. Over everything she wore an apron turned backward, so that the pockets were facing inward. The woman reached under the apron and drew out a small bag that glinted in the light of the lamp. The little purse was covered with buttons, brooches, beads from broken necklaces. Julia took out needles, pins, spools of thread, a comb, a smoking pipe, asking as she arranged everything on the table if there was anything Lily needed mended. Lily avoided the question as she cut slices from a loaf of brown bread, the same as she would for a priest or a visitor from town. Greta touched the little purse, ran her hand over the flashes of color that quivered when she moved it. Julia looked at Greta when she touched it, looked from Greta's face to the purse and back, then spoke to Lily.

'If it's not sewing you need I have a husband who does good work with a soldering iron. Will I look in at your kettle or your saucepans?' She looked around the kitchen.

'Drink that down,' Lily said as she walked over to the small table next to the fire. She brought back the bundle she'd wrapped. Half a loaf of bread. Butter coming through the paper. A jam jar filled with flour. She left it next to Julia's cup and saucer.

'The one working in the bog by the low road – is he yours? With the mouth?' Julia asked. 'I've seen it before, and I know there's a way to cut inside his mouth and his nose to make the lip fall down to where it's supposed to be.'

'He has his own way. He does as well as you and I. His two brothers understand him and he's a lovely writer and writes down for us whatever we don't understand.'

'And what about that child?' Julia asked, nodding toward Greta. Greta was listening to their conversation only vaguely as she held her teaspoon in her hand and relished again and again the sound of the purse tapping out a miniature racket on the kitchen table as Julia sifted through it. 'Is she in need of a tonic?' The woman leaned in close to Greta's face. 'She has a kind of a look.'

'Don't mind her,' Lily said, and for a moment both women looked at Greta in silence. 'That's our Greta.'

'Is she – ?' Julia asked, touching the side of her own head.

'She has her own way, like Little Tom has his way. She was nine weeks early when she came.'

'How many have you in all?'

'Ten in all. Five alive. So she's either the youngest of ten or the youngest of five, depending on how you look at it.'

Lily noticed Greta peering over at her, peering with that look she had so often, her features drawn together in a clump at the center of her face, her neck stuck out ahead of the rest of her body. Greta the Goose, the children often called her, and Lily lifted her leg to kick anyone she heard at it, whether that child was a Cahill or not.

'We love her,' Lily said, and watched the clump at the center of her youngest child's face relax into itself again. Large green eyes, freckled nose, round cheeks, and perfect chin. Not as pretty as her sister, but still a good-looking girl when she wasn't making herself the goose. 'Greta is my pet. Aren't you, love?' Lily said, reaching across the table to take Greta's hand and kiss it. Greta knew this was her reward for being home when the others were not. As far as she knew, Lily had never called Johanna her pet. She'd never given Johanna a squeeze when no one else was looking and whispered that she was the best girl.

Julia rummaged inside the purse once again and drew out a square piece of paper, which she folded, twisted, and tucked until it became a flower. She put the flower in front of Greta.

As Greta examined the flower, they heard a bicycle coming up the path, a skid of gravel outside the front door. Julia looked quickly at Lily and then pushed her chair back from the table, stood, took the bundle of food Lily had wrapped, and tucked it under her shawl.

'They wouldn't give me brown sugar in Finnegan's,' Johanna announced as she opened the kitchen door. 'But I –'

Julia dipped her head in greeting and then moved toward the door.

'Missus,' Johanna said, still winded from the bicycle. As she struggled to catch her breath, Lily and Greta both, each in their own way, guessed what she was going to ask. The boys had been up to the sea ledge to size up the tinker camp and report to Big Tom how many were in the group. They'd returned home with a full account: seventeen travellers in all, plus three piebald ponies, four dogs, five goats, two donkeys. Two of the young ones, Padraic mentioned, looked about the same age as Johanna. And then there were babies they hadn't bothered to count.

'Are you the mother of the two young ones in the group?' Johanna finally asked. 'About my age? A boy and a girl?'

'Johanna –' Lily warned.

'The twins,' Julia said. She kept her hand on the handle of the door and spoke to Johanna over her shoulder. 'I didn't mark the day they came. They're gone eleven, I'd say.'

'Twins,' Johanna said. She nodded and clasped her hands together, as if to agree that this made sense.

'A tinker for tea!' Johanna said when the woman had left and she had time to comprehend the empty cups, the crumbs on the plates. Lily went to the back room to continue the work that had been interrupted. Johanna turned to Greta. 'Were you here talking to her the whole time?'

Greta told her about the purse and all the colors and all the things the woman had offered to do. Mending, soldering, milking, how she had a collection of tonics back at the camp, ways to turn gray hair brown, ways to fix a sore back or a sore leg, even Little Tom's mouth. She showed her the paper flower.

Johanna had pulled Greta close to hear the news and now leaned away from her, sinking back in her chair as if she'd eaten too much at supper. 'What do you think they do up there all day and all night? The young ones, I mean.' Greta could feel her sister's excitement and knew first in her stomach, then in her throat, then in her mind what was coming next.

'We have to go there,' Johanna said.

That night, once they were sure their father and brothers would not be going down to the river with the net, and after they heard the creak of their parents' bedsprings on the other side of the wall and counted to one hundred, Johanna threw off her blankets and reached for her sweater. She pulled on a pair of kneesocks and stepped into the short lace-up boots that had once been Padraic's and had been carefully preserved by Lily until Johanna's feet grew big enough. Greta, who was without shoes or boots at the moment, was next in line to be brought to the shoe shop in Conch. 'Before winter,' Lily always said, and at night she would have Greta lie on the floor with her feet on Lily's lap so Lily could rub them.

'Either come or go but decide right now,' Johanna said to Greta as she laced the boots.

'Doesn't Pop hate the tinkers?' Greta asked.

'He buys buckets off them,' Johanna said. 'He says some tinkers make buckets that can last forever. And he bought a horse off one once. But it died the next week. You remember. He said they had it well timed.'

'But does he like them or does he hate them?'

'Are you coming or not?'

'Is there a moon?'

'There is. A three-quarter one, and it's a clear night.'

'But what will you do when you get there? They'll be asleep in their own beds.'

'You mean in their tents.'

'In their beds in their tents.'

'They mightn't have beds in the tents.'

'They must! Straw beds, I mean. What about in the wagon?'

'They might have beds in the wagon, but only for the old ones. Only one or two could sleep in the wagon. I'd say it's strictly tents for the young ones.'

Greta sucked her knuckle as Johanna lifted the latch on the window. With one quick heave she shoved it all the way up. She waited a minute to hear if the sound had woken the house; then she put one leg through, straddled the window frame for a moment, and fell onto the grass outside.

'You almost broke it with your boot,' Greta whispered with as much ferociousness as she could muster. Then she grabbed her sweater and did the same.

Outside, Greta's stockings immediately wet with dew, they crept around the back of the cottage and swung wide toward the road. Johanna took the lead, fearless of rabbit holes and the ankle that might break if she stepped in one, while Greta stumbled after with her arms and head held in front of the rest of her body. 'Come on, you goose,' Johanna said, mimicking her sister's style of walking and then shooting ahead.

When they got to the road, the way was easier. Greta could feel the incline begin under her feet, and her body leaned naturally into it. Up they climbed, keeping the ocean to their left, its roar always mightier from the high sea ledge. Both girls held their hands to their heads to keep their hair from flying in the wind. They walked until the road became flat again and curved slightly away from the ocean. Then they saw it at the same time: the flicker of a campfire in the distance.

'Listen,' Greta said. She stopped walking. The sound of a harmonica glided through the dark to where the girls crouched by the side of the road. Then: 'I have to pee.'

'So pee,' Johanna said, and edged forward to get a better view. There were three dark silhouettes sitting by the fire and two smaller silhouettes skipping in circles around them. One of the wagons, its door propped open, was pulled up close to the fire. Johanna whispered that there was an old man sitting on a chair inside.

Greta pulled up her nightdress and tried to pee but found she couldn't. 'Let's go now,' she said, feeling the urge come back the moment she stood up.

'Wait. I see the twins. I don't see your woman from today.' Johanna was crawling to get closer; Greta hung back and kept her focus on the white of Johanna's legs. She pushed the overgrowth away from her face and arms. She looked up to find the moon, which was slowly disappearing behind a cloud. She heard the first strains of a fiddle joining the harmonica and wondered if, had they stayed in their beds, the wind would have carried the music all the way down to their bedroom. Then the music stopped.

The young girl who'd been skipping called out something in the tinker language, and the three adults around the campfire stood and peered into the darkness. One, a man about the same age as Big Tom, picked up a plank of wood that was lying on the grass and walked toward them. He lifted it, poised to swing. Kneeling on the wet grass, Greta covered her head with her arms and folded over so that her forehead rested on her knees. She held her breath.

Johanna stepped out into the road as if she were out on her usual midnight stroll. 'Good evening,' she said.

The man stared at her, then noted Greta just behind. 'The two girleens from down below,' he called to the others.

'Lookin' at what?' the tinker girl asked, running up to the man and standing behind him. The man threw his plank of wood into the grass. Just then the young boy who must have been the girl's twin came up quietly to observe.

'The cat can look at the king,' said Johanna, putting her hands on her hips.

'Johanna!' Greta pleaded as she slowly stood up. She could hear people moving in the long grass, the pop and crack of the fire. Johanna didn't flinch. The wind came up off the water, wrapped her nightdress around her legs, whipped her long hair around her face, and still, she kept her hands on her hips. Greta, expecting more of the Ward clan to materialize out of the darkness with their planks of wood, took her one remaining cool nerve and used it to turn herself around and run back the way she came. She moved as fast as she could, keeping her left hand on the low wall that ran all the way down to the Cahill gate.

She went around to the bedroom window and heaved herself in headfirst, using her hands to walk forward and dragging her legs after her. She pulled off her wet stockings, gave her feet a quick rub with the washcloth, crawled under the covers, and prayed that Johanna had survived. She listened for her parents on the other side of the wall and decided that if Johanna wasn't back in five minutes she would wake them. She counted to herself. She gave Johanna another five minutes.

One whole hour later, Johanna's head and shoulders came through the window. 'Christ, Greta,' she said. 'Thanks a million.'

'Where have you been? You could have been murdered.'

Johanna took two long strides to the edge of the bed. She pulled on the string of her boot and casually loosened the laces. 'I sat by their fire, and then the boy one walked me to the gate. They go back and forth all the time in the dark. You wouldn't believe the places they've been, and some of them younger than us. Dublin, Cork, Manchester, Liverpool. Can you imagine?'

Greta listened as Johanna paused after each place she named to give each city its own particular due. The way she said Manchester was different from the way she said Liverpool, and Greta knew that her sister had already walked down their streets, imagined their people, dipped into their shops, and plucked things from their shelves to have wrapped and tucked into shopping bags. Johanna hugged her arms around her body as if trying to gather these places closer.

'Julia – your one from today – must have been somewhere. She was the only one who didn't show herself.'

'Good night,' Greta said, pulling the covers and tucking them under the far side of her body so that Johanna couldn't pull them away.

'His name is Michael, by the way. Michael Ward. The one who walked me.'

'Good for him.'

The next morning, just after cock's crow, Big Tom carried Julia's body from the field and brought her to Johanna and Greta's bed. Greta pressed up against the wall as he passed, and the woman's shawl brushed Greta's face. It had the same muscular smell as the animals, and it reminded Greta of how she liked to rest her cheek on the cow's warm flank when she milked. Lily explained that Johanna and Greta's bedroom was the only choice, with the three boys crowding the front room, and she couldn't very well go in Lily and Big Tom's room with the pile of clothes to be washed in a heap under the window. They couldn't very well put her on the kitchen table or on the floor of the hall. Greta took the news quietly, not minding the recently dead woman in her bed but feeling like she should mind, or would mind soon. She watched from the hall as Big Tom placed the woman over the covers and held her in a sitting position while Lily wrapped a bandage around her forehead and then a clean cloth over the pillow. They laid her down, and Lily arranged her legs, skirt, apron, shawl, hands. The woman's hair had come loose, and at first Lily gathered it together and tucked it under her head. Then she fanned it across Greta's pillow.

'Look at the length of it,' Johanna whispered.

'Don't talk about the dead,' Lily warned as she reached forward and put her fingers under the dead woman's chin and gently pushed her mouth closed. She took her hand away, and the woman's jaw fell open. Lily reached forward again and, keeping her hand on the woman's jaw, looked around Greta and Johanna's room.

'Bring me something,' she said to Johanna. 'Cut off a strip of the flour sack.'

Johanna disappeared and quickly re-emerged with a strip of burlap. She handed it to Lily, and Lily wrapped it around the woman's face, starting under her chin and tying the strip off with a bow at the top of her head. When Lily took her hand away, the woman's mouth stayed closed, and Greta, stepping closer to the bed for a better look, thought the woman's face looked like a package, or like a picture in a frame.

'Are you sure she's dead?' Greta asked. The woman seemed to be peering at them from behind lowered lids, peeking at them in the sly way a person might peek if she were only pretending.

Lily placed her hand over the woman's eyes. 'Go bring me two coins from the cup over the fire.'

In the kitchen, after they'd done as much as they could for the woman, Big Tom and the boys prepared to go up to the campsite. Johanna begged to go with them. She whinged, she moaned, she followed Lily around the kitchen. She pleaded with Big Tom; she looked desperately at her brothers, but they shrugged and looked away. She stamped and threatened to follow them. She pulled on Lily's elbow and promised to do anything in the world Lily wanted if she could only go up to the camp.

'That's enough now, Johanna,' Lily said. The men were putting on their caps. 'You'll see them when her people come down. It's not a day for gawking and asking questions.'

Johanna calmed down. 'Do you think they'll all come? Will she be waked here?'

'They have their own way. We have to see.'

As the men were leaving, Lily walked with them as far as the front gate and told her husband the dead woman's name. Big Tom looked at his wife as if her knowing the tinker's name was more surprising than waking up to find a tinker dead in his field. Then they turned right and walked up the wind-battered coast road, four across, up past the high sea ledge, until they came to the camp.

The ground of the camp was strewn with half-burned sticks, bits of paper, and feathers. In the middle was the dark ring of an extinguished fire. A few feet away was another fire, this one blazing, and next to it a woman bottle-feeding an infant. A man with a sharp red face to clash with his red hair put down the bucket he was making and stepped forward. As the Cahill men stood there looking around, the man recognized them first by their coal black hair, then by their number, four together – three young, one older – and then by the one with his mouth pulled up into his nose. The little imp of a thing from the middle of the night might have made up a story. He hadn't liked the way she cast her eye around the shadows, peeked into the wagons whenever someone went in or out, and now the consequence of his hospitality had come calling.

'I'm looking for the husband of Julia Ward,' Big Tom announced.

'I'm Dermot Ward,' the red man said. They rarely had country people in their camp, so to have four at once, and so soon after the strange midnight visit of the two girls, drew every traveller in the group away from what they were doing. Julia had gone in the late evening of the night before to perform what she called women's work on a woman named Mary. Last name not given. It was the reason they'd left the Ballinasloe fair a day early. Mary had sent word to her sister, who'd married a man whose brother had married a tinker, settled her in a house near Tuam, but could not get her to abandon her tinker ways.

Dermot Ward didn't mention any of this to the four men who entered the camp. He never liked the idea of Julia's women's work when it brought her down certain roads as opposed to others. They had set up lovely in Ballinasloe, showing their beautiful piebalds to the world, visiting everyone they knew and hadn't seen since the last horse fair. There were ponies to be swapped, marriages to be arranged, fabric to be traded for tools, tools traded for swag. Then, out of the blue, Mary's sister's husband's brother's wife had come knocking. Helping conceive a child was one thing, but this – country people didn't know the value of a child, and now their clans were scattering all over the world. Dermot felt that just because Julia knew more about babies than anyone – making them and otherwise – didn't mean she had to go running. Not for money. Not for all the tea in China. Julia saw it differently.

Dermot crossed his arms over his narrow chest. 'You live in the cottage closest to the water. Both waters. At the bottom of the slope.'

'We do,' Big Tom said. Then he took off his cap, and the boys did the same.

Greta wondered, the whole time her father and brothers were gone, where a tinker is buried, where a tinker is married, where a tinker puts a tree at Christmas, what happens when the rain comes lashing and the campfire is put out. Lily told her she was as bad as Johanna with the endless questions, and didn't she ever notice the little chimney pipe coming out the top of the barrel-top wagons? They have little potbelly stoves inside, just like some people have inside houses. There are ways to keep the campfire going in the rain. In the winter they build shelter tents and they're as warm and dry as a house. Warmer, even. Drier. Yes, they might have tables and chairs. Not grand ones, but still. The Cahills didn't have grand ones either. Yes, they have plates and cups and saucers. Yes, they have decorations. Pictures in frames. Yes, the children have dolls. Why wouldn't they? What's there to making a doll except sewing a piece of cloth up the side and stuffing it with feathers? Two buttons for eyes, yarn for hair. No, Lily had never been inside a wagon. No, she didn't know why they didn't just build a house and settle. No, she didn't think the children went to school. No, she didn't know how they took their baths.

Lily started baking as soon as the men left. She kneaded the last of the flour, the new milk, eggs, yeast. Greta greased the tins, going over the corners so that the bread wouldn't stick, not so much that it might burn. The draft from the kitchen door whipped around Greta's ankles, under her skirt, and she wondered how much worse the tinkers had it in their tents. Did they have rags stuck in every crack and crevice like the Cahills had in their house? With every big rain the Cahill roof leaked in the same spot: the boys' bedroom, to the left of the window. The water ran down the wall in thin streams, and when it happened in the middle of the night, Greta would wake to the sound of them swearing, furniture being pushed, Lily and Big Tom rushing in to help. Catching the water would be easier if it came down from the ceiling somewhere in the middle of the room; they could just place a bucket underneath and watch it fill. The way it streamed down the wall in a river, twisting and turning according to the hills and valleys in the plaster, made it impossible to collect in a bucket, and the boys had to take turns standing on the chair and holding a towel at the source. When they held it at one spot, it would burst forward a few inches away. If they managed to hold it in two spots, there would spring a third. That part of the wall was dark with mold, the dried rivers extending down from the ceiling like fingers on a giant handprint, as if someone had reached down from the sky or out from the ocean and taken hold of the house, tried to lift it from its frame.

The days after the leaks were always the same, Big Tom with a plank of wood and a collection of nails held between his teeth, one of the boys on a ladder outside. Jack swore that the whole side of the house was so damp that if they pushed, really dug their heels in, dropped their heads between their shoulders and gave it everything, the wall would come tumbling down. 'I wouldn't risk it,' said Big Tom.

The Cahill men were back in less time than it took Lily to bake one brown bread. Dermot Ward was with them, plus an older man, Julia's father, and Michael Ward, the son who'd walked Johanna home less than twelve hours earlier. The three travellers followed the Cahills with a horse and cart, making sure before they left to sweep it out and line it with fresh hay and a clean sheet. The horse, when it passed the field where the woman had landed, stopped to sniff the air.

'Where is she?' Dermot asked as he strode into the cottage. Michael and his grandfather hung back and stood side by side without touching. They seemed unwilling to enter past the front hall.

'I'm sorry for your trouble,' Lily said as she opened the bedroom door.

Dermot stood over the bed, put his hands on his wife's cheeks. He lifted her arm and let it fall back onto the blanket. He turned and pulled the curtains apart, then lifted Julia's head from the pillow and inspected the bandage. They'd passed the pieces of splintered wood on the road.

'A stone, I'd say,' Lily offered. 'When she landed.'

'The horse was spooked,' Big Tom said from the doorway. 'It was charging like the devil with the cart behind it and took off full gallop after the crash, harness and all.'

'Took off,' Dermot repeated in a dull tone. 'That horse was never spooked in his life.' This wasn't true and Dermot knew it. Still, he stood to his full height, which was not as tall as Big Tom or any of the boys, and with his windburned face he looked at each of them one by one. He stood as a barrier between the group and Julia. It was the women's work, Dermot knew. The discovery was made and she'd gotten chased. A gunshot probably, aimed just over her head.

'He might wander back,' said Lily.

'Unless someone already has him caught and stabled,' Dermot said.

'There's that, I suppose,' Lily said.

Big Tom crossed his arms over his chest. To Greta he looked the way he did when he caught one of the boys resting instead of working, or whenever they saw Mr Grady passing on the road.

Dermot turned his back on Big Tom and spoke only to Lily. 'She had great nature for people, Julia did.'

'She did, of course. Anyone could see it.'

'And she mentioned you yesterday, the food you sent.'

Big Tom looked at Lily, who kept her eyes fixed on Dermot. 'You can leave her if you like,' Lily offered. 'It's no bother. You can send the women down to wash her body.'

Dermot made a little grunt, like a laugh smothered before he could let it go, and otherwise ignored the offer.

'Boys?' Lily said when she saw that he'd made up his mind. She nodded at Jack, Padraic, and Little Tom.

'Leave them,' Dermot said. He put his fingers to his mouth and sounded a sharp, short whistle. A moment later Michael and his grandfather appeared, and Greta felt embarrassment light up in her belly when she realized that the boy was seeing his mother dead for the first time. We shouldn't be here, she thought, looking at the tall silhouettes of her brothers, her father, the softer shape of her mother, and Johanna beside her, buzzing with energy even when completely still. Dermot embraced his wife from behind, locking his arms around her chest. He nodded at the old man and the boy to take hold of her legs. Without hesitation they lifted her. Michael kept his chin up, and his lips were white from being pressed together so tight. Only when he squeezed past her brothers did Greta realize how small he was. Dermot said something in the traveller language, and the old man shifted over to help the boy.

They laid her in the back of the cart just as she would lie in a coffin. Michael tugged at the sheet, which had gotten bunched to one side when they arranged her. He tucked the loose straw underneath, and then he climbed in next to his mother. The older men climbed in front.

'I'm sorry for your trouble,' Greta said, relieved that she'd thought of the right thing to say, and stood on her tiptoes to reach the boy's hand. Michael sat up straighter but didn't look at her.

'Can we go up?' Johanna asked, turning her big eyes on her mother.

'Hush!' Lily said. Big Tom put one rough hand on top of each girl's head and steered them both inside.

The travellers waked Julia for two nights, and on the third morning was the funeral. How word spread along the tinker channels was impossible for Greta and Johanna to figure out, but spread it did, because people began arriving within two days. There were a few wagons, but most of the mourners arrived on foot. Johanna and Greta washed with their minds on the road, they swept with their minds on the road, they chopped and scrubbed and milked and churned thinking only of the road. No chore was completed. Even the boys turned their attention to the activity on the hill, laying down their hayforks to watch the spectacle pass. Only Big Tom was indifferent.

'You know why tinkers wander?' he asked at tea. 'Because they made the nails for Jesus' cross and now this is their punishment.'

'Have they not paid their debt?' Johanna asked. 'Jesus died a long time ago.'

Little Tom said something in his mushy style, shush-shush-shushing it out to Jack and Padraic for translation.

'Some say they descended from the ancient kings of Ireland,' Padraic said, and Greta wondered if Little Tom had read that in the book he'd borrowed from Mr Boyle the thatcher. It was a big book, and most nights he read it at the table while the others talked.

'You see?' Big Tom laughed. 'That's the kind of trickery they give out about themselves.'

Johanna had been quiet since Julia's body was taken away, and Greta followed her from the henhouse to the hay shed to the stable, waiting for her to suggest a plan, expecting at all moments to have to convince her not to do anything silly. When the funeral procession began and the strangers made the long walk from the camp to the old Ballyroan cemetery, where the priest from Conch was waiting with one hand on his Bible and the other on his pocket watch, Johanna turned her head away from her work, but didn't even walk to the gate. When it was over, the woman's body packed tight under the mound of dirt, the visitors journeyed back to the camps they had left, and the only travellers left on the hill were the original seventeen, minus one.

In bed that night, the girls stayed awake long after they tucked their hot-water bottles in at their feet.

'I thought it was a nice life,' Johanna said, speaking to the ceiling in the dark. 'But it isn't, is it? They put three planks of wood across two barrels and that's where they laid her. I saw it myself. And I saw them, Michael and his sister, Maeve is her name, crawl out of their tents on their hands and knees the morning of the funeral, Michael in a dark suit, Maeve in a blue dress, and both of them brushing off their knees and the palms of their hands. They sat on upturned buckets by the fire. An old one came out of the wagon and ran a comb through Maeve's hair. They were baking bread in the ashes, and when it was ready the visitors pulled it apart with their hands and all the time there's herself on the planks of wood and no one paying her any heed. I waited for it to rain, I thought definitely it's going to rain, and what would they do if it had rained, I wonder? Would they have wrapped her up? Thrown an oilcloth over her?'

'When did you go?' Greta asked.

'Michael looked over at her the odd time, but that Maeve – she was talking and laughing, part English, part Irish, and part that language they have, and miming something the others had to guess.'

'I didn't notice you go.'

'Oh, I went early, early. She had you in the back room with the you-know-what. I was back before anyone missed me.'

'Did they see you?'

'Maeve saw me. She gave me a good long look, but otherwise didn't take any notice.'

Greta tried to imagine the body laid out in the rain, stiff like the animals get when they wander off and die and a few days go by without finding them. She thought of the boy Michael who'd helped carry his mother away, and what it would feel like to have no mother at all. It seemed worse for him who had to sleep out in the cold and the rain than for the children in town who had lost parents. They might be missing their Mammies but at least they missed them from warm houses, tucked inside warm beds. She imagined Johanna crouched in the brush where she could see it all, her bony knees tucked under her chin. 'They won't come back after this,' Greta said. 'They won't want to be reminded.'

'Strange,' Johanna said. 'I was just thinking the opposite. Now they're tied to this place and they'll come like clockwork. You watch.'

For some reason Greta couldn't think of, she pictured the orange bog grass that stretched from their cottage all the way to Conch, and how it was interrupted here and there by cuts made by slanes and the triangular stacks of damp turf left to dry in the wind. She remembered a story she hadn't heard in a long time. Before she was born, a local man had cut into the bog and found a pig, still pink, still whole, as if she'd sunk into the moist ground only the day before. Men came from Dublin, from Galway, from Cork and decided that pig had been there for hundreds of years. They took it with them to one of the universities, where Jack and Padraic claimed it went on to have a better life than anyone left in Ballyroan.

It was a miracle, some people still said. A sign from heaven to remind them that they don't know even a quarter of the secrets the universe holds.

Two

On the day Julia Ward died in the Cahills' closest field, Greta had been going to school for a little more than two months. There were laws about schooling, Lily knew. Laws that had been in place since she was a girl, but like most laws, they seemed to apply to other places in Ireland, places where the heavy salt wind didn't rattle the houses and cut swaths through the land. Reading and writing, of course, Lily was all for it. The rhymes of Mr Yeats, the island stories of Mr O'Flaherty. Those were the things that kept people company their whole lives. The boys had gone until they were twelve, and it had done no harm. Adding, subtracting, multiplication tables. Yes, yes, yes. But Irish? And history? Those things could be taught at the table at home. And there was the added complication of Greta being Greta. She was, Lily had long ago decided, like a new calf who couldn't find her feet. Sometimes Lily wondered if she'd done anything unlucky when she'd carried the child. That Johanna had lived and was so strong was a miracle, and she'd tried to do everything the same with Greta. But maybe she'd made a mistake after Greta was born, laid her on her left side instead of her right, fed her from the same spoon she'd used to feed herself. Foolishness, Lily had always thought, but when she looked at Greta, she worried.

Lily held Greta at home for two years. The first time, Greta was five going on six, and no one noticed. After Johanna left in the morning, Greta followed Lily around the house, chattered away to Shep, who barked back like he had something on his mind, played mermaid in the swimsuit a distant cousin had sent from England, even when it turned cold and Lily made her wear it with thick wool stockings and a sweater. She hummed, she tried to skip stones on the river like her brothers, she helped Lily chase crows from the yard. Sometimes Lily came upon her whispering to herself, asking questions in one voice and answering in another.

'Who are you talking to, Greta?'

'My name is Mrs Fishburne and I've come all the way from America.'

'Oh, excuse me. What part of America?'

'The furthest part.'

'And did you come by sea or by air?'

'Ahhh . . .' Greta dropped Mrs Fishburne's expression of exhaustion. 'What do you mean by air?' she asked in her own voice.

'In an airplane. Did Mrs Fishburne fly in an airplane, or did she come on a ship over the ocean?'

'Which would make you more . . .' Greta raised the back of her hand to her forehead and fluttered her eyelashes.

'Ship, I'd say. Takes a fortnight, and you might be seasick. And the airplane is very dear. Then again, I'd say Mrs Fishburne is very rich, is she?'

'She is, of course, but she came by ship anyway. The ocean was rough, and we had one man go overboard.'

'And did anyone save him?'

'No one noticed but me, and by the time I got to the edge of the ship he'd gone under the water so I thought the best thing was to leave him in peace, poor bugger.'

As Greta played, Lily slipped in lessons. She'd hand Greta two spoons and ask her how many she had given her. Then she'd hand her three more and ask how many she had then. When Greta graduated from spoons, Lily used eggs, of which there always seemed to be a limitless supply. Eventually she just told Greta to figure out the sum in her mind. 'If Padraic gives you seven sweets and Jack gives you ten, how many do you have?' Almost always, Greta got the answers right.

It was more difficult to teach letters and sounds. Sometimes Lily wrote the letters out on a piece of newspaper and they sounded them out at the kitchen table. Greta didn't like doing this, and she pressed her head against the table and closed her eyes. She cried sometimes, and other times she was all affection, throwing her arms around Lily, snuggling against her, doing her Mrs Fishburne voice and waiting for Lily to laugh. When there was a bit of chalk and the weather was fine, Lily wrote the letters in huge print on the side of the stable. Greta was better at the stable lessons than the inside lessons, but she always did best when they sounded the words out without writing anything down. B as in box, button, bull. D as in duck, dog, door. And what about when the sound is inside the word? Not at the beginning? Stubborn. Handle.

After the second time Lily kept her at home, Sister Michaela of the convent school rode her bicycle to Ballyroan. It was late June, and the school year was about to end for the other students. It occurred to her recently, Sister Michaela said to Lily, that the youngest Cahill was almost gone eight. She pulled Greta toward her in the kitchen and looked into her face.

'How's Greta today?' she asked.

'Grand, Sister. And yourself?'

Sister Michaela turned to Lily. 'This one's as ready as she'll ever be. And' – she released her grasp on Greta's elbow – 'it would be a way to show herself in town as independent. You have to consider that part of it as well, don't you? You never know who might be in need of a girl, a live-in to help with the things Greta can help with. Does she understand about cooking and cleaning? Do you trust her with an iron? With so many gone to England now the old ones need looking after. Isn't that where a girleen like Greta would be a great relief to someone? It's an opportunity, really, as long as she's capable.'

'I trust her the same as I trust myself,' Lily said, and stood to add more turf to the fire.

'Well then,' said Sister Michaela. 'I'll mark her in for September.'

Lily nodded as the nun stood and gathered her things.

'I might as well take my other business while I'm here. Save the girls from walking it into town.'

'Oh, yes,' Lily said, forgetting about Greta as she hurried into the back kitchen, stepped on the stool, reached up to the top shelf, and moved aside two empty jugs, a stack of tin cups, a jar of sugar, three folded tea towels. She removed two whole cured salmon and wrapped them in brown paper.

The moment the nun left, Lily decided that the lessons she had given Greta were not enough. There had to be more if the girl was going to enter school in a matter of months. Instead of allowing Greta to follow her all day, instead of allowing her to chatter away in her collection of voices, Lily decided it was time to give her some responsibility. She waited for Big Tom to announce that it was dry enough to cut and lap the hay, and then she started Greta on delivering tea to the men: bread, crisp salmon skins fried in butter, tea in a thermos with sugar and milk. She gave the girl some warning.

'Tomorrow you'll have a big job,' she told Greta, and spent the rest of the afternoon explaining about men and their stomachs, the hard work they do, how they depend on their sustenance coming across that field at the same time every day, how everything the Cahills had depended on that delivery. After the hay was cut, it had to be dried for three or four days if the weather stayed clear, then a day of shaking it out with the tips of their hayforks, another day turning it over so the air and sunshine could touch the damp underside. Another day of drying, and then it had to be raked, cocked, brought mound by mound down to the hay shed, which had a roof four times the height of the cottage.

'If they don't eat, they won't have the strength to work. And if they don't get it all done before the next big rain, then what? Can I trust you, Greta?'

'Yes, Mammy.'

'Can I count on you?'

'Yes.' Greta pushed her hair out of her face and looked at Lily with those big green saucers of eyes. Pretty, yes, when she wasn't twisting her features into a scowl. The nose a bit long, granted, but lovely skin, lovely coloring. The hair, black like Johanna's but wilder, a lot like Big Tom's when he had more of it, hair that defied gravity by curling out of her scalp and straight up into the air.

'Will you tie it?' Greta asked.

'What?'

'My hair,' Greta said, pulling the curls straight with her fingers. 'I can feel you looking at it. Will you tie it back?'

'That's another thing you're old enough to do, Greta.'

The next morning, Lily put everything for the men in an old canvas satchel. 'You know where Hurney's old field is? The one over and beyond? Well, go on then. They'll be hungry waiting, so off you go.'

It started like this every morning for a week, the men in a slightly different place, Lily giving slightly different instructions. Greta, her face pinched up as if she were working on a puzzle, would nod for her mother and set off. Lily would work around the kitchen for a while, then go stand out at the gable to watch Greta try one direction and then another, her head stuck out ahead of her, the bag of food held out as if at any moment she might place it on a table. She would strike out full speed and then come to a halt, stay frozen for a few moments, then turn a few degrees and strike out again. 'Go on!' Lily would shout across the distance. 'They'll be waiting.' Then she'd return to the kitchen and wait.

'You goose,' Jack or Padraic would say when one of them found her, and then they'd lead her back home by the hand. If it was Little Tom who came, he would give her a little shake before pointing, almost with anger, toward the direction of home. He'd look at her, point, then look back with his eyebrows raised before marching her all the way back. The times when Lily came, she appeared before Greta in the mist like an apparition. 'Just what do you think you're doing?' she'd say, and pinch the lobe of Greta's ear as she led her back to the road. A few times, she was kind when she came and only squeezed her daughter's hand. 'Greta,' she'd say, just once, as if they were at the end of a long conversation.

When Lily had Greta back home, she led her to the chair by the fire and told her to sit down. 'When I send you out to the fields,' she'd ask, 'what do you be thinking of?'

'Of Mother Goose,' said Johanna once, listening from the wings. It was a Saturday, and Johanna was mad because she wasn't allowed to ride her bicycle into town to see her friends. 'Is that it, Greta? Little Robin Redbreast sitting on the rail, niddling his head and wiggling his tail? Is that why you niddle-naddle your head and wiggle-waggle your tail?'

'Keep quiet, you,' Greta said to Johanna.

'One more word and you'll be sorry,' Lily said to Johanna, and turned back to Greta. 'What do you be thinking of?'

'Of the men,' Greta said. 'And how Pop gets if he doesn't have his tea.' The tea. The thick slices of molasses-smeared bread, all still in Greta's satchel. Lily knew enough to continue sending food with the men in the morning so they wouldn't go without their midday meal.

After a few weeks, Greta learned a few tricks. She walked along the low stone wall for two hundred and twenty-seven steps, her head cocked to the right to better hear the sound of the ocean; then she was on the bridge, four steps up, four steps down, back to the road and the wall for another thirty-eight steps. When the wall ended, she made a sharp left turn into the field, the sound of the ocean behind her. She walked straight for fifty steps or so until she hit another low wall. She climbed over it, stamping on the nettles as she did, followed that second wall to the right for thirty steps, and then came the final, most difficult part – a walk into the great and shimmering expanse of amber and blue if it was sunny, dull and gray if it was not – until she heard her father and brothers talking or the sound of their forks being plunged into the hay, the hay lifted and tossed to the top of the waiting pile, settling with a sound so soft and light, fainter than any other sound Greta had noticed so far, fainter than the sound of fabric on fabric as Lily tied the belt of her apron and pulled it tight. She heard things other people didn't.

At the end of the hay-making week, Big Tom told Lily that he was afraid Greta would get lost in the bog one day, sink into one of the soft holes like the pig from five hundred years ago. 'A girleen like that has to stay close to home,' he said. 'There are some in every family, aren't there? Ones who can strike out on their own and even go off to England, and then there's ones who never leave and shouldn't leave and that's just the way it is. You should see the cut of her when she comes across the field at us. She's all arms and neck, and why does she stick her neck out like that? And the expression on her face like she's surprised to see us, and then she stands there looking around herself like she's waiting for instructions. You know what Jack figured out? She's dead tired! Johanna would be up and back twenty times in the time that one takes to come once, and not a bother. I say from now on, keep her close to home.'

Lily hushed him. 'Keep your voice down.'

'I had an aunt once who left our place to live outside Oughterard in a flat. She came every Saint Stephen's Day and would sit at the table with her mouth hanging open so far you'd nearly see what she had for breakfast. Then she'd go laughing at nothing and shushing at nothing, and then she'd close her eyes and nod off for a few minutes before jumping up and announcing that she had presents waiting for her at home. There's a woman who should have been kept at home.'

'How many times do I have to hear about this aunt?'

'Well now, Lily, remember that girleen when she first came? So red, and the size of her! No bigger than my fist, and not a peep out of her, only those big eyes looking around at everything. All I'm saying is why go trying to change her and turn her into Johanna? Sending her on errands and sending her to school. She's not Johanna and never will be and that's what God made her and that's the end of it.'

'All you're saying and saying and saying and saying. Enough.'

Going to school, for Greta, was a little like leaving the stone wall that showed her the curves in the road and striding out into the twinkling expanse of field and fog. She and Johanna walked together to and from, but once there, they were separated, Johanna in the back half of the room, Greta in the front. Johanna with her friends, Greta with her head down and her hands folded in her lap, praying that the teacher, Mr Joyce, wouldn't call on her. Mr Joyce, Big Tom often said around the house, was from Cork, born and raised in the city, and the smell of manure in the country made him sick. To pass the time on her first day, Greta tried to count how many of her classmates wore shoes and how many did not. She could tell by the sound they made walking up the aisle when they were called up to the board. Johanna said that Deirdre Sullivan's feet were blue and would never be right again. Lily had wrapped and double wrapped Greta's feet in strips of oilcloth and promised as she tied the strips off, 'Before winter, love. Before winter, and you'll be doing a hard shoe across the boards.'

During Greta's first week she was terrified by the scratch of the teacher's chalk as he wrote on the board and the turn of his heel as he scanned the room. The letters and numbers he drew were much smaller than the ones Lily had drawn on the side of the stable. Johanna warned her that he wouldn't go long without calling on her, and urged her to start thinking of the answer before he called on anyone. 'Greta Cahill,' he said finally, his pointer stopping at Greta's desk. She had been in school for three weeks. 'Can you step up, please?' Greta turned to look for Johanna's dark head way in the back. The older students were given their own set of problems, and thinking that Johanna might not be listening to what was going on at the front of the classroom, Greta pretended to sneeze.

'Have you been paying attention?' Mr Joyce asked. Greta turned and took a step toward the board. She gripped the piece of chalk he placed in her palm.

'I have to ask my sister something important,' Greta said.

'Ask her later,' Mr Joyce said.

'It has to do with a calf born this morning. You may not understand, sir, about the animals.'

'You've three grown brothers at home, Greta. Step up and finish this problem now, please.'

With her nose almost touching the board, Greta moved her head along to follow the marks he'd made. Then she made matching marks: a long line, a short line, a curved line, a dash. She slashed this way and that until she'd taken up as much space on the board as he had. Then she put the chalk down on the ledge and went back to her seat.

'Greta,' Mr Joyce said after a moment of silence, 'can you explain yourself?' Greta heard the drawer of his desk open.

'She can't help it,' a voice called from the back, and Greta turned to find the dark shine of Johanna's head rise up among the lighter heads around her. 'She's not being fresh.' Another long moment of silence, and Greta felt Mr Joyce inspecting her all over, the way her hands were folded, the way her legs were crossed at the ankles in the place where her stockings had fallen and bunched. She turned her head left and right, shifting in her seat to hear what else Johanna would say, but that was the end of it, and the next thing Greta heard was the switch being returned to the desk drawer.

On the way home from school that day, Johanna told Greta that she'd lied to Mr Joyce and that Greta had to try harder. 'How many times does three go into fifteen?' she asked.

Greta counted on her fingers. 'Five with none left over.'

'How many times does four go into sixteen?'

'Four.'

'And how many times does seven go into twenty-one?'

Greta thought for a moment. 'Three times.'

'That's all the questions were, Greta. Why didn't you just write the answer instead of making all those marks on the board? He thought you were making fun of him.'

'Was he very cross?'

'You better cop on, Greta. I won't speak up again.'

'But Johanna –'

'Don't but Johanna me,' Johanna said, then hugged her bag to her chest and ran ahead.

She'll wait for me at the crossroads, Greta told herself. She'll wait for me at the bridge. It was getting dark fast. Greta moved to the left side of the road and kept close to the wall that would lead her home.

In December, just before the school closed for Christmas holidays and almost two months after the tinkers left Ballyroan, a dentist came to the convent school to examine its forty students. By this time it was widely known that Greta smiled and nodded at things that didn't call for smiling or nodding, and that she had a way of walking as if she were leaning into a strong wind. When Mr Joyce posed questions to the lower levels, he passed over her, calling on students he'd heard from three times already that day.

The dentist came all the way from Galway City in a long blue car that the boys couldn't keep themselves from running their hands over. It was parked outside the gate, and Mr Joyce had to keep going over to usher them back onto school grounds. When he had everyone in one place, he asked the students to line up single file, youngest to oldest. Greta was placed toward the middle, and she immediately heard whispers travel up and down the line and an unfamiliar voice commanding them to stand still. Two of the mid-level boys took off running across the yard and launched themselves over the gate, which Mr Joyce had locked. Before he could say a word, another two followed, sending a brief titter up the line. 'Next,' the dentist said now and again. 'Step up.' Greta couldn't hear anything except breathing from the remaining students. Those who'd had their turn were shuttled somewhere else, back to the classroom, perhaps, or told to go home early. Every once in a while she heard a sound she couldn't identify, like a pebble dropped into a wheelbarrow. The closer she got to the front of the line, the quieter everyone became. When she was three people from the front, she saw the tin bucket on the ground next to the stranger. She saw the stranger in his long white jacket lean back and forth between patient and bucket until the line moved again and again, and then it was Greta stepping up.

'Open,' he said, pressing his thumb against Greta's chin and pushing his fingers inside her mouth. 'Wide.' He pushed on each of Greta's teeth, then tapped and scraped them with a metal instrument. He prodded her gums with something sharp. He shone a light into her mouth and pressed on her tongue until she gagged.

'Name,' he demanded. Greta told him. Then he did something she hadn't heard him ask anyone else on the line to do.

'Greta, if you wouldn't mind, please walk twenty paces in the direction of the gate and then turn back and face me.'

Greta turned and did what she was told. At pace fourteen she turned her head to look for Johanna, but at sixteen she turned back, remembering Johanna's warning that she wouldn't speak up again.

'Now, Greta,' the dentist called above the buzz that had ignited up and down the line. 'How many fingers am I holding up?'

Greta didn't answer. She could see the line of her classmates, one after another in varying shades of gray and blue cardigans, not a bright spot in the bunch. She could see the whitewash of the schoolhouse behind, the shape of the outhouse, the smudge that was the bell, but there was no way she could make out how many fingers the dentist was holding up.

'Take ten paces back toward me. Now tell me how many.'

Greta took ten steps. She smiled. She pulled at her dress, brushed the hair from her face. 'Now come back and stand in front of me, where you were before.' Greta walked back to him as quickly as she could. She stood as close to him as she'd been when he was pushing his fingers inside her mouth. She saw the first three fingers of his left hand held up, the other hand behind his back.

'Three,' she announced. He took a notebook and pencil out of his pocket. He made a few marks on the page.

'You need glasses, Greta. With a strong prescription. They will help you see things that are far away.' He stopped writing and looked up. 'Hasn't anyone ever told you that you need glasses?'

Greta didn't say anything, and as she stood there, he put his hands on either side of her head and pressed on her left eye, then her right, with his thumbs. She stumbled as she took a step back, blinking at the bright white feathers now floating all around.

'Is it your mother you have at home? And your father? And do you ever notice either of them writing a letter? Or reading one? Good. Do either of them ever take the bus into Galway, and do you ever go along? Yes or no, please, Greta. No? Well there's a first time for everything. Isn't there? You'll have to see this doctor in person. He's an eye doctor. You understand?'

'The bus to Galway, yes.' Where is Johanna? Greta thought.

'Give this to your mother. It's the doctor's address, and at the bottom is my name, so you can tell him I sent you. I also made a few notes.' He pressed the paper into Greta's hand. 'It won't cost anything. Tell your mother that too. Tell her everything I said.'

Greta folded the paper in fourths as she walked away. When she got beyond the front gate of the school, she sat on the road, opened her bag, and tucked the note neatly between the pages of her book. Behind the rushes she could hear the creek flowing over the rocks. Father Mitchell had glasses. Greta got a good look at them every time she received Communion and their faces were mere inches apart. They seemed yellow in color and always made him look as if he had just stopped crying. Mrs Norton, who owned one of the two shops in town, also had glasses, but hers were two little half-moons that sat at the tip of her nose. Mrs Norton's Greta could accept. Father Mitchell's she could not.

'What's the story?' Johanna demanded, breathless from running to find Greta. 'What was he on about? Did he pull any teeth on you? No, you're grand. I can see that for myself. Me as well. Did you look in the bucket? You'd think they'd cover it up with something. Johnny Sullivan looked as green when he saw it! I watched him glance down, and then what did he do but put his hand right over his mouth. Trish had a mouthful of blood, and she spit it right on –'

Greta handed her the note, and Johanna snapped it open.

'Glasses?' Johanna said.

'Does it say anything about whether they'll be yellow like Father Mitchell's?'

'No, nothing like that. I think you're supposed to go to Galway.' Johanna refolded the note and handed it back to Greta.

'That's what he said. To Galway to see a doctor, and then the doctor will give me glasses and I'll be able to see.'

'Can you not see?'

Johanna leaned in close to Greta's face, then leaned away, in and out to look at Greta's eyes up close and then from a slight distance.

'When Pepper went blind his eyes went red and swelled up. And he wouldn't come out of the stable if it was sunny. Remember him rearing up on Pop?'

Greta rubbed her eyes.

'Now, Greta. Mammy will want it to be just the two of you to save on bus fare, but tell her you want me to come. You will, won't you? Tell her you're scared and you need me.'

'I will not!'

'Well, I'll be left home, then. You would do that? At Christmas? You and Mammy off looking at the shops and the lights, and me at home listening to the wind?'

'I won't say I'm scared. I'm not scared.'

Johanna shrugged and began walking. 'Might not happen anyway. You know who'll have something to say about this, don't you?'

Lily didn't know what to think. The girls had come home and given her the note as if they were making a formal presentation. Greta offered it on her open palm, and Johanna stood next to her, watching the note pass from Greta's palm to Lily's fingers to the table, where it was opened and the creases smoothed flat.

'Glasses,' Johanna summarized as Lily read. 'For Greta.'

'We're supposed to go to Galway,' Greta said. 'To see a doctor. Does it say?' she asked, standing on her tiptoes and looking over her mother's shoulder.

'I can't make heads nor tails of most of it,' Lily said. 'It's mostly to the doctor in Galway. There's just a little bit at the top to me.' She turned to Greta, took her by the wrists, and pulled her so that she was standing against Lily's knees. 'Can you not see, Greta? I mean, I know we tell you don't squint and do your neck like the goose, but can you not see?'

'I already looked at her eyes to see do they look like Pepper's,' Johanna said.

'I'm not blind,' Greta said.

'Look around here now.' Lily shooed at Johanna to back away, give Greta some room. 'What can't you see?'

'Mammy, how can she tell you what she can't see?' Johanna said.

'She knows what I mean.'

'I can see the kitchen for a start.'

'What in the kitchen?'

'The table, four chairs, the fire, the window, four pipes on the mantel.'

'Can you see the four pipes on the mantel?'

'Well, I know they're there. I put them there this morning.'

'But can you see them?'

Greta walked over to the mantel and stood on her tiptoes. In that position she was just tall enough to rest her nose on the ledge. In front of her, no more than two inches from her face, were the four pipes, and beside them the box of tobacco.

'I can see them,' she said.

'Mammy, will we go to Galway?' Johanna asked, rocking back and forth from heel to toe.

'You? Can you not see either?'

'You wouldn't go without me, Mammy. Now listen, I'll do anything –'

Big Tom and the boys came in just as Johanna's begging reached a pitch that Big Tom couldn't stand. 'Calm yourself, girl,' he said, and swiped one of the pipes off the mantel before collapsing into one of the chairs. He scratched at his face, then sucked on his pipe in short, quick puffs until it got going. To Greta, the sound of him getting his pipe started always sounded like a person kissing his or her own hand before blowing the kiss away. Then the boys went at their own pipes, and there were kisses flying all around the kitchen as Lily filled them in about the dentist and the note and the doctor in Galway.

'And what's wrong with her?' Big Tom asked. 'Useless at finding her way at doing things unless she's shown a hundred times, but nothing a doctor can do that her own family can't. The best medicine is like I said – keep her close to home.'

'Peel the potatoes,' Lily said to Johanna. 'We'll talk after dinner.'

'I can't. Please. I can't do a thing until I know.'

'You should listen to your father, Johanna, and calm down.' Lily took one of the boiled potatoes in her hand and peeled off the skin. With each dark piece of skin that fell away, the white inside was revealed in a cloud of steam. Greta had tried to peel a hot potato once, but she burned herself, and Lily had made her feel her hands and compare them to her own. Greta's were soft and smooth; Lily's were as rough as Big Tom's, thick with calluses and scars.

When Lily was finished peeling the potatoes, she sat on the stool by the fire. Because the kitchen was small and the table seated only four, the family usually ate in shifts: Big Tom and the boys first, Lily and the girls directly after.

Greta thought the discussion would be put off until after they'd all eaten, but suddenly, from her perch, Lily announced, 'We'll go to Galway. The girls and I will go and we'll see what this man has to say.'

Johanna clapped her hands. Greta dropped down to a stool opposite her mother and wondered what other people saw when they looked at things.

'A bloody waste,' Big Tom muttered, and the kitchen was filled with the sound of forks and knives against plates and teeth.

The Galway bus came through the Conch crossroads every Tuesday and Thursday, and the journey took two hours. There were some regulars – people who went to Galway once every few weeks to settle up business – but most of the people who went were what Lily called once-in-a-blue-moon types, like themselves. On the Thursday before Christmas, Lily, Johanna, and Greta walked the three miles to the crossroads with a bag of sandwiches and waited for the sound of an engine in the distance. Greta was wearing shoes Lily had bought from a woman in town whose daughter had grown out of them, and Johanna was annoyed that she had boys' shoes and Greta had girls' shoes. To distract them, Lily told them that she could count on one hand the number of times she'd been to Galway. After half an hour they heard the bus approaching. When it appeared, Lily stepped out into the road and held up her hand.

Greta and Lily shared a seat. Johanna sat by herself across the aisle and looked out the window. There had been a lot of talk about Pepper in the days leading up to their journey, talk Lily tried to hush. Pepper was a fine, strong horse when Big Tom bought him, but after a few months his eyes went red and rimmed with pus. That lasted a few weeks; the boys took turns washing his eyes in salt water. Nothing helped. Then he started getting skittish about the sun. He shook his head at every noise, however slight. Then he lost his balance, began to trip and run into things. By the time they had him for a year, he was completely blind.

Lily had asked them how they could compare a girl to a horse, and Jack and Padraic (and Little Tom, by nodding at whatever his brothers said) insisted that Pepper used his eyes just as people use theirs. Didn't horses have eyes to see out of? Didn't Pepper start in with that head-shaking, looking-around-himself routine, and didn't that remind her of Greta a bit, with the neck and the arms and keeping her head cocked to the side?

'Look it,' Johanna said. She had her finger pressed to the glass. They'd been on the bus for over an hour and all Johanna had said up until now was that everything looked the same. Finally she noticed something different, and Lily hopped across the aisle to see. There were poles planted in the ground every hundred feet or so, and at the very top of the poles were thick black wires. 'Electricity,' Lily said. Every day on the radio there was more talk of electricity. The cities were electrified. Large towns were electrified. Soon all of Ireland would be connected in one enormous grid. Big Tom said they could keep their electricity where it was. He for one did not want to worry about being burned alive in his bed.

The bus came to a stop, and the driver got out to help an elderly passenger board. Outside at the crossroads, someone had tied a bull to one of the poles. As Johanna and Lily watched, the bull lowered his ugly head, bunched his massive shoulders, and pulled at the rope that held him. As the animal strained and lurched, a hundred thousand sparks rained down from above as if a bundle of hay had been set on fire and thrown into the wind.

Galway was filled with people, everyone squeezed into a space so tight that Greta and Johanna didn't see why they didn't spread out a bit. Because it was nearly Christmas, the streets were also full of lights and wreaths with red ribbon bows. Two steps out of the bus station, Greta found herself on the sidewalk, surrounded by strangers. Next thing she felt Lily's hand take hold of her arm and steer her to a doorway. 'Don't walk into people, and don't leave my sight,' she said. She tried to take Johanna's hand, but Johanna shook her off.

'You'll hold my hand, girl, or the three of us will get back on that bus and go home.'

'I'm old enough.'

Lily turned back to the bus and started walking, pulling Greta after her. Johanna lunged forward and slipped her hand into her mother's. 'Lovely,' she said. 'See?'

The three of them made their way past Eyre Square and turned onto Shop Street. One street turned into another as people crisscrossed from side to side, stepped around the threesome, walked close to the storefronts or the curb to let them pass.

'Twenty-seven Market Street,' Lily said, dropping the girls' hands for a moment to pull her shawl tighter around her shoulders. 'Be on the lookout.'

The night before, Big Tom had pulled out his old map of Galway City and shown Lily where they'd have to go. The names of streets, he warned them, could be difficult to find. Sometimes they were up on the sides of buildings, sometimes down at your feet. Sometimes an address was on one street, but the door to get in was on another street around the corner. What he'd failed to mention were the cars and the trucks that would be there, pulled up against all the curbs, rolling down the street one after another like a long caravan. Mixed into all of it were the horse-pulled carts and people loaded down with bags and newspapers. Lily pointed out a donkey with a creel full of turf being led down a side street, a car close on its heels.

Market Street was a side street, less crowded, so Lily dropped their hands and let them walk ahead. Johanna hopped from window to window, calling back information about shoes, dresses, hats, flowers, until she stopped at the window of a bakery. The vents were open to let the steam out, and the smell of fresh bread and sweet glaze pulled them forward. Even Greta could see the muffins and cakes smeared with white frosting or berry red jam. Johanna didn't even have to ask. 'First things first,' Lily said. 'I'll think about it.'

The door to 27 was plain, not as grand as Johanna and Greta had imagined. Inside the street door was a list of doctors with corresponding office numbers, then another door. The threesome walked up four flights of stairs until they came to office 4W. 'Go on, girl,' Lily said to Greta. 'What are you waiting for?'

Inside, Lily told the secretary why they were there and handed her the note the dentist had sent. The secretary disappeared to the back room, and Johanna planted herself by the window to watch the people passing on the street below. After a few minutes a young man came out of the back room. 'Greta?' he said, turning toward Johanna briefly but then deciding on Greta. 'Would you step in, please? Are you Mrs Cahill?' He came forward to shake Lily's hand. Lily introduced Johanna, and the three of them followed him into his office.

'You're having trouble with your vision,' he said as he positioned Greta by an X painted on the floor. Greta nodded as he pointed toward a chart on the wall and told her to read off the letters. After the very top line, Greta recited letters at random.

'Whatever trouble she has isn't new,' Lily said. 'She's been the way she is since the day she was born.'

The doctor had Greta read off the letters with her left eye covered, and again with her right. He made her look into the ceiling light and try not to blink as he squeezed two drops into each eye. Greta couldn't stop her eyelids from fluttering, so he did it again. 'That should do it,' he said after a third try. Greta's cheeks were wet and streaked dark yellow with the drops that had failed to hit home.

'I'm staining her eyes,' the doctor said. 'It makes it easier to see if there's any kind of surface damage. Ulcers, for example.' He held Greta's eyes open with his first finger and his thumb. 'She'll blink it away after about an hour.'

'I see,' Lily said. Pepper had had yellowish pimples and burst blood vessels in his eyes.

The doctor led Greta to a special chair and fitted a device on her head. Greta looked through a pair of frames while he slid different pieces of glass inside, asking her to look back at the chart after each try. When he settled on one he liked, he told the three Cahills to wait outside. The secretary gestured toward the long, dark sofa and Lily and Greta sat close together on one side of it. Lily waited until the secretary turned back to her work, then she licked the corner of her sleeve and rubbed at Greta's yellow-streaked cheeks. She licked, rubbed, licked, rubbed some more. Johanna stood by a shelf on the other side of the room and examined the different objects on display. She picked up a snow globe and shook it. 'Chicago,' she announced, and held it up for her mother to see.

After a half hour, the doctor came out to the waiting room and handed Greta a small hinged box made of wood. Greta opened the box and saw immediately that it was lined with blue material that Lily said was satin. There in the bed of satin sat a pair of glasses held in place with two clips. Not as small as Mrs Norton's from the shop, but not as yellow as Father Mitchell's.

'Go on,' Johanna said. Lily hushed her.

Greta put the glasses on and pushed them up to her nose. They slid down. She pushed them up again.

'Show,' Lily said, and Greta turned to her.

'Well?' Greta asked.

'Well yourself,' Lily said. 'You're the one wearing glasses. What do you think?'

That's when Greta noticed that the world looked slightly different. Objects loomed large and seemed to curve in space. She reached for her face, but the doctor stopped her.

'You must keep them on. This is important. Even if you feel sick. Even if you get a headache. Keep them on. It'll take a little while to get used to them. Come back to see me in six months.'

Johanna reached over and straightened the glasses on Greta's nose. The frame was black and heavy enough to hold the thickest glass in the doctor's case, and Greta could already feel where the new weight would press down behind her ears and become sore. Next to Johanna, Greta could see the window, the bottles on the ledge, blue and yellow, one with the color purple coming out the top. On the secretary's desk were a teacup and saucer.

They stopped at a hotel called The Bay. Johanna swore they'd eat their sandwiches later, that they wouldn't go to waste. Greta was most concerned with keeping the glasses balanced on her nose. The hotel had separate entrances for lodgers and diners, so they didn't get to go through the lobby. The girls wanted to know how much it would cost to sleep there and how many nights did people stay, and why didn't they sleep at home, and if they're so far from home what brought them away when it was so close to Christmas.

They ordered tea and three cream cakes. Greta thought it was just like a ceremony, almost like Mass, the way the man came over first with the plates, then with the forks and knives, then with the teacups and saucers, then with the teapot, then with the plate of three cakes. It was like what the priest did when he went over to the little gold door, took out the dish and closed the door, walked the dish over to the altar and took the lid off, and held the sacrament up in the air before breaking it into pieces and putting a piece in everyone's mouth. By the time everything was laid out, there wasn't an inch of table left to spare. Twice, Lily reminded them that she could have made the same tea, the same cream cakes in her own kitchen in Ballyroan. She could make them better, actually. And cheaper. They had the eggs and cream and butter themselves. She was about to say it a third time when she heard herself as if from the next table and stopped. She took off her shawl and folded it neatly over the back of Greta's chair. 'Plenty of heat in this place, isn't there?' she said, and licked the tip of her finger.

The streetlights had all come on by the time they left the hotel, but Lily said there was no rush on them. They'd paid for the bus fare, so why not see what was to be seen? Except for when they sat down to eat, Greta had been holding Lily's hand since they left the doctor's office. She'd also given most of her cream cake to Johanna. As they walked, she kept touching the bridge of her nose with her free hand. 'You'll get used to them,' Lily said, then suggested they go to the cathedral. That way they could sit, light a candle, Greta could calm down. Lily remembered the bridge from the last time she was in the city, and knew the cathedral was just beyond. They had almost made it when Greta pulled her hot hand out of Lily's, walked over to the curb, put her other hand up to stop her glasses from falling off, and vomited. She froze for a moment, a thick rope of drool stretching down between her mouth and the puddle at her feet. Then she sat down on the curb and began to sob.

Lily rubbed her back. 'Isn't it a great day, Greta? You'll be able to see everything very soon. No more Greta the Goose.'

'Please,' Greta said, reaching for the glasses. 'Mammy, please.'

'You're meant to keep them on.'

'Mammy, Mammy, Mammy,' Greta chanted as she breathed in and out, rocked back and forth.

Johanna said, 'Could she take them off if she keeps her eyes well closed? I mean, as tight as tight can be? That way she won't be looking at things the old way. It'll be like when she's asleep. She can't wear them when she's asleep, can she?'

'Five minutes,' Lily said. Lily and Johanna sat down on the curb beside Greta, and Greta handed her glasses to Lily. 'Ten Our Fathers,' Lily said. 'And make sure you keep them well shut.' They nodded their heads to pray. Lily kept a close watch on Greta as she rattled off the familiar words. Greta had her head between her knees and was mumbling the prayer over her sobs.

Johanna, who sat on the other side of Lily, could also concentrate on two things at once. The prayers came so naturally she could recite any one of them without even hearing what she was saying. She made her lips move, and the words came out, but her mind remained in the city. 'Our Father, who art in heaven, hallowed be thy name . . .' She watched the skirts and shoes go by. She watched the wheels of the cars. She could see the spire of the cathedral. In the other direction, she saw where one busy street intersected the other. She glanced down at the river, black now that the light had faded, and watched the outlines of the merchants selling their wares along the quays. She saw the piles of potatoes, fruit, carrots, parsnips. One woman sold dolls, one sold clothes, sweaters, wellies, fishing gear, hard candies, soft candies, chocolates, Christmas cakes. At the very end was an old woman beckoning people to step in and have their fortunes told. Another stood under a streetlamp and hawked paper flowers. Johanna strained her eyes as much as possible, taking in the woman's weather-beaten coat, her bare feet stuck into sandals despite the cold.

'Greta!' Johanna said, hopping to her feet. She half walked, half ran to the other side of the bridge, down the narrow, blackened staircase, down to the river and along the quay. She took in the telltale shelters, cardboard and sheet metal. She took in the people's haphazard dress, layer upon layer upon layer. She noted the grub boxes outside the flaps of the tents. She took in the windburned faces, the black toes, black fingernails. She watched the flap of a tent being pulled open from the inside and saw a boy climb out on hands and knees. She watched him brush off his knees as he made his way down to one of the merchant booths. She observed the older man say something to the boy, something sharp by the way the boy's back straightened up.

'Johanna!' Lily called as she watched Johanna's head disappear down the steps. Greta, her eyes still squeezed shut, her glasses still in Lily's care, stumbled after her mother, feeling for the edge of each step with the toes of her new shoes, listening to the river lick the pilings. Greta pulled back when Lily shouted again. 'Mammy,' she said, 'you're shouting. And I've my eyes closed.'

'Where the hell has she disappeared to?' Lily dropped Greta's hand and walked ahead. 'Wait here,' she commanded.

Greta stopped walking, dropped her hands to her sides, stood perfectly still. The way the wind pushed her this way and that, the way the water rushed over the rocks just a few feet away, she felt that she could have been standing in the middle of her own back field, except for the rattle of the occasional bicycle and the buzz of voices. She counted to one hundred. She raised her arms and reached as far as she could in front of her; she reached to her sides. The voices faded, and even the water seemed to grow calmer.

'Hello?' she said. Her voice came out as a squeak, barely a whisper. She cleared her throat and took a breath to try it again.

'Hello yourself,' said Johanna, her voice landing like a hammer inside the circle Greta had imagined for herself.

Greta opened her eyes. There was Johanna, white electric light from the lamp over their heads reflected in her ink black hair, and beside her a young tinker boy with wide brown eyes and shoulders unusually broad for a child of eleven. He was standing with his feet wide apart, like his father had done in the Cahills' hall when Jack, Little Tom, and Padraic had stepped forward to help with the body. Johanna was holding his hand.

'It's Greta, is it?' he said.

'You remember Michael Ward, don't you?' Johanna asked.

Three

Unlike their solitary spot on the sea ledge in Ballyroan, in the city the Wards were just one among many caravans. Tents and horse-drawn wagons lined the riverbank and rose out of ditches as if a new city had been built overnight. As Lily rushed across the busy street in search of Johanna, she remembered that the tinkers came to Galway at Christmas because there was money to be made. There were holy pictures to be hawked to the pious, wreaths and beads sold to the festive, fortunes told to the desperate who had no family, no faith, only a little droplet of hope that 1957 would be better than 1956. As she rushed down the stairs from the bridge, she could see their campfires dotting the banks like torches lighting the way. Few settled people would walk all that way along the river, pass tent after tent, observe the eyes peering out, and not feel the blood drain out of their faces. She tried to see which direction Johanna had gone, and imagined the tinkers looking up to watch as the settled girl came running toward them, waving, her hair flying behind her like a flag.

Later, as the bus approached the crossroads in Conch, Lily was still too angry to speak. Anger at Johanna for running off, for never listening. Frustration with herself for not making clear the dangers of the city before they got there, for not telling them there was a difference between giving the poor crathurs butter and flour and a bit of work and actually going to their camps, trying to make friends. Then she felt panic – what kind of girls were these? So brazen, so fearless. That boy was sound enough, but the way his people had stood outside their stalls and watched them had given her chills. Then she felt a surge of love; thanks be to God nothing had happened to the girls. There they were, swinging their legs in their seats, heads swiveled toward the window so they wouldn't have to look at Lily. Greta was fading; Lily could see it. She had her glasses on, but her eyes were closed. She had her arm looped in Johanna's. Then Lily was angry all over again. Never in a million years would she have dreamed of running off on her own mother.

'Are you going to tell Pop?' Johanna asked once they'd gotten off the bus.

'You think I'd keep a secret from your father?' Lily said.

Johanna shrugged. 'You didn't tell him Julia came that day until she died and you had to tell him. You don't tell him half of what you give to the tinkers in town. I saw you push a coin into a woman's hand last year and from the look on her face I'd say it was a big one.'

Lily felt her blood rush to her cheeks. With the short winter days, it had been dark for hours. The bus could still be seen in the distance, its electricity-bright inside lighting the fields on either side. Lily reached out and slapped Johanna across the face. She thought about slapping Greta too, but she was afraid she'd break the glasses. Johanna turned away, and Lily slapped her on the side of the head, catching her on the ear. She reached over, got a good grip of the girl's skirt, lifted it, slapped her bare legs. She slapped her and slapped her, the cold night bringing an extra sting to both Johanna's legs and Lily's palm. Greta stood by, sucking her knuckle, gasping back long sobs.

'That's the end of it now,' Lily announced finally, and struck out in the dark toward home. Greta rushed up beside her and grabbed her hand. By the time they'd covered the three miles, Lily didn't see any reason to tell Big Tom what had happened.

Winter turned into spring, and with spring came the water bailiff. Big Tom had a routine he did every year where, without warning, he would put his finger over his lips and shush everyone around him. If he was eating, he'd put his fork down and go over to the window. If he was milking, he'd stop mid-pull. In the spring of 1957 he clenched his pipe in his teeth, stomped across the kitchen, and threw open the back door. 'Do you hear them?' he demanded, asking Lily and each of his children one by one. Just like every year, they fell for it, if only for a few seconds. His expression was serious, his voice grave. 'By God, I can hear them, and my ears are a lot older than yours.'

'What is it?' Johanna asked. The boys had already caught on.

'Now, Tom,' Lily said, hurrying over to the window. 'It's bad enough as it is. I don't think we need a performance.'

'Oh,' said Johanna, and sat back. 'I know.'

'Greta,' Big Tom said, 'close your eyes now, girl, and listen well.'

'The hens. Is it?'

'Now that you've got glasses, have you forgotten how to use your ears? What else?'

Greta listened, but couldn't hear anything. Big Tom was grinning, everyone was looking at her. The routine was vaguely familiar, but she couldn't remember the answer. She took off her glasses, and just as she had them folded and safe on her lap, she heard the water bailiff's bicycle coming up the road. She knew it was the bailiff by the loose gear that hung down and clanged against the spokes of his front wheel. The bailiff's arrival signaled only one thing.

'The salmon,' Greta said.

'By God, I never lost faith in you, girl,' said Big Tom, laying his hand on her head. Greta flushed, felt loved. But still, it was confusing. Mr Joyce said that the water bailiff was supposed to guard the river against people who would take the fish, but Big Tom looked forward to him every year. It was as if the salmon waited patiently at a starting line way downstream until they heard the bailiff's bicycle, which they understood as the signal to take off. Big Tom and the bailiff were friends – Greta often heard them talking in the field behind the cottage. They'd been in the same primary class. Big Tom often mentioned the nine children the bailiff had at home, and how much it costs to feed such a family, and to mention it so often meant that they must be friends. But then sometimes when they passed on the road they acted as if they didn't know each other at all.

Big Tom and the boys managed the odd catch in the late summer and early autumn, but spring was the real salmon season. According to Lily, there were poets who said that to see the rivers of Connaught in the spring and early summer was to see water turned to silver. On a clear day the fish caught the sun like thousands of mirrors just below the water, and once in a while, out of impatience or determination to get ahead, one would burst out of the water and shoot into the air, arcing against the sky before diving in again. They were so crowded and the water rushed so quickly that sometimes one of the fish would get trapped against a rock and pounded by the impact of the water and its fellow salmon until it died, sometimes slipping back into the water, sometimes left on the rock to dry in the sun and the wind.

Every spring, the water bailiff unlocked the little hut on the bank of the river and swept it out. He set up his wireless, turned the old stool right side up, and got a long stick to knock down the cobwebs. He leaned his shotgun against the wall.

According to Big Tom, the Ballyroan portion of the river was the best. The salmon were drawn to the blackwater pools, deepest where the river ran behind the Cahill cottage. Where the river ran near town was too public. Too public for what, Greta didn't know. For fishing, she supposed. So many people talking and walking around on land would scare the fish away. And maybe where the river ran near town there was no good spot to fish at night, when it was quiet enough to trick the fish. She also wasn't sure why, when Big Tom and Jack discovered someone from Conch fishing in the Ballyroan section of the river one night, they'd come home in a panic and discussed it at the table all night.

'When he says the Ballyroan part of the river,' Johanna informed Greta in the spring of 1957, 'he means Mr Grady's part.'

Greta took this information and added it to all the other bits she'd collected about water and salmon and fishing and rights. She tried to read Lily, but that made her even more confused. Sometimes Lily seemed dead set against taking fish from the river, but once in a while, usually after supper – when there was nothing to do until bed except talk and Big Tom went on about how it was everyone's river and plenty in it to go around, and no person had the right to own the river no more than they had the right to own the sea or the air – Lily nodded along and made no attempt to stop his talk. Plus, no one was more excited than Lily when Tom and the boys caught a big load. And yet each night when Big Tom fetched the net and the boys readied themselves to leave, she tried to talk them into staying home. She was afraid of something, Greta realized in 1957. It was the first time she knew that her parents could be afraid of things.

In the Grady family, river rights were handed down from generation to generation like the Belleek jug that sat on the Cahills' kitchen mantel.

The bailiff's shelter was like a miniature house, so small that if Jack, Little Tom, and Padraic held hands, they could make a circle around it. Just big enough for the bailiff to escape the rain, Big Tom said. The point, after all, was not to be comfortable, but to be on the lookout for poachers. On the nights when the bailiff did not come, Mr Grady took his shotgun and his electric torch and walked up and down the banks of the river himself. Greta had collected enough information to know that these were the nights when Big Tom and the boys had to be most cautious.

Greta once asked how Mr Grady expected the bailiff to know what was happening at every point he was supposed to be guarding. No man could see what was happening miles upstream, and in some places the river was very wide.

'It's impossible to know,' Johanna said. 'That's why they get away with going with the net. And the bailiff is Pop's friend. Don't you remember us delivering to his wife the odd morning?'

'Shut your mouth about the net, girl,' Lily said, her eyes wide and serious, her teacup paused between the table and her lips.

In the Cahill house, the punishment for taking salmon from the river without permission was not discussed. Johanna thought it was likely a money fine, and at eleven years old the idea of money had just come into focus. It was one thing, she had recently started to see, to have enough to eat because your own land and animals provided food, but when it came to things that you had to buy in a shop, things you could get only by handing over notes and coins – that was a different story. Greta – who by 1957 had accepted the idea that what her father did with the net at night was not allowed – thought the punishment must be something more severe. 'They'll take him away,' she speculated as she and Johanna, awake in bed, listened to their father and the boys get ready in the kitchen. 'Lock him up. Not just him, but the boys too. They all do the net, not just Pop.'

'Who will lock him up? Mr Grady?'

'Not Mr Grady. The authorities.'

'What authorities? The *gardai*?'

'I don't know. But it has to be something besides money.'

'But isn't money bad enough? Where would they get it?' Johanna lowered her voice. 'They don't have any, you know.'

Greta considered this. 'Maybe it starts with a money punishment; then, when you can't pay, they lock you up.'

Johanna turned over this possibility in silence. It was almost midnight. After a few minutes they heard the back door close and Lily moving around the kitchen by herself. It was a cold job, and none of the men bothered with waders. They had a long-established system and worked quickly and quietly. After midnight the four walked through the back field until they reached the river; then they turned and walked upstream to shallow water. Big Tom carried the net. Jack carried the shotgun. Little Tom walked slightly ahead, Padraic slightly behind. Once they reached the shallow stretch, Little Tom and Padraic crossed the river in silence – no splash from their boots, no gasp when the ice-cold water soaked through their pants and touched their skin – and two on one side, two on the other, the four walked downstream. Then, when they reached Big Tom's favorite blackwater pool, Big Tom took hold of one end of the net and threw the other end across. Once the two across the river had hold of the net, they were able to circle the pool of fish, catch them in their beds. Jack's job was to keep his back turned on his father and brothers and stare out into the fields and the dark riverbanks, the shotgun clenched in both hands. Johanna had seen it once. Greta had heard them describe little bits and pieces of the scene so often that she felt she had seen it too.

Greta also wondered if she, Johanna, and Lily would be punished for taking care of the salmon once the men got it back to the house. It was their job to clean and salt the fish. Too much or too little salt and the fish would go rotten; just the right amount and they could last for weeks. Lily always took a few out of each haul and hung them inside the chimney to soak up the smoke of the fire. These were Big Tom's favorites, but to Greta, the chimney fish always tasted of turf.

During the spring, summer, and autumn they ate fish at every meal. Salmon and eggs, salmon and toast, salmon and potatoes, salmon stew, salmon chopped up and mixed with flour and eggs and fried into little cakes. In addition to stuffing themselves full of it, Johanna and Greta also had the job of delivering the salmon in and around town. It was a somber operation – Johanna as the bearer of the fish, Greta as the companion charged to make conversation, keep everything light, swing her arms alongside her sister and appear to the world as two girls out for a walk. Johanna stowed the fish in the bag she used when she went in to sell eggs, and they went only to the houses Lily trusted. There were two bed-and-breakfasts in town, and one small hotel with a restaurant; the girls delivered salmon to these places as well. Jack and Padraic took the horse and cart to deliver to places farther away, places miles down the coast road, where people from England came in the summer and stayed in the single large hotel in the area or the private bungalows that lined the beach. Greta wondered if people could smell the salmon in their hair and their clothes, just as she had smelled earth and animals on the shawl of dead Julia Ward. Big Tom insisted that fresh fish didn't give off any odor, yet their cottage was swollen with the smell, and each night they cleaned little flecks of pink flesh from under their nails and off their jumpers. Lily put fresh wildflowers in every room. She grated orange peels and boiled cloves. They slept with the windows open and took turns watching out for Mr Grady on the road.

In town, even the people who didn't buy from the Cahills knew what they were up to. Greta heard it in their voices when people said hello, good morning, what a wonderful day for a walk. Most seemed happy to see them, as if she and Johanna were just after playing a big joke and everyone was on the verge of applauding.

'Them eggs have a strange shape to them, Johanna Cahill,' Mr Doherty said with a wink as they passed one day, and then he laughed and laughed as they quickened their pace. 'You must have very unusual hens at your place.'

'If you're interested in buying these unusual eggs,' Johanna shouted back, 'speak to my mother.'

Greta had also noticed that there were one or two who were not amused to see them, who stood at the half doors of their homes, arms folded, to watch them and see whose house they'd visit next. Mr Cox, whose wife was sick with a disease that made her tremble so much her daughters had to hold her down during Mass, said quietly one morning as they passed, 'Tom Cahill is a thief and will go the way of thieves.'

Greta felt her legs go weak and her heart begin to beat very fast. 'What did he say?' she whispered to Johanna, though she'd heard perfectly well. Without answering, Johanna took her by the wrist, and they ran the rest of the way.

Big Tom said that if people weren't buying from the Cahills, they were buying from someone else. A few had the courage to go out with their own nets, and to these, Big Tom said, he wished best of luck. No one had access to those blackwater pools like Big Tom. The Cahills had been taking fish from the river since before Big Tom was born, before his father was born, and before his father as well.

Each spring, when the bailiff first knocked on the Cahill door, it sounded to Greta as if he and Big Tom were reading from cards, the way they do at school when they put on a performance. The two men had the same conversation every year.

'Now, John,' Big Tom said when the bailiff came to the house in the spring of 1957. 'I know what you're after and I'm telling you, you won't find what you're looking for here. It's Grady who has the idea in his head.'

'Sure, I know it, Tom. And I also know that river is big and full to the brim. There's enough fish in that river to feed all of Ireland. And how are the boys?'

Big Tom shrugged, reached up to pry something from between his teeth. He clamped his hand on the man's shoulder. 'Can I get you anything? A drop of *poitín* on this cool night?'

John Hogan looked around, and as Greta listened and Johanna watched from the cracked kitchen door, the house seemed to hold its fishy breath.

'I would, if it's in it. Mind you, just a drop now, Tom.'

Mr Grady was another story, and when any of the Cahills saw him coming on the road, they were to tell Big Tom or Lily immediately. If someone in the family was out, whoever was home was to tie a handkerchief on the knob of the front door as a warning. Jack and Padraic could handle themselves, and Mr Grady never bothered with Little Tom. He liked to get the girls, alone if possible, and there was an often-repeated story about Johanna, at four years old, announcing to Mr Grady what a fine, big fish her Pop had caught the day before – how if the fish had feet and were to stand up, he'd be almost as tall as herself. Big Tom had had to give up the net for weeks.

Lily tried to keep the girls away from him, but they had to go to school, their chores took them far from the house, and there were plenty of opportunities for Mr Grady to catch them on their own. Lily accepted this and worked on Greta in particular.

'What did you have for supper last night?' Lily asked. Mr Grady would never start so bluntly, but it was an exercise. First, Lily warned, he might make conversation about what he ate the day before. He might even mention that salmon were in season.

'Rabbit,' Greta said.

'And lunch?'

'Only a piece of brown bread.'

'And did I see your father and brothers go out the house late last night? No trouble, I hope?'

'Last night? Sure they were asleep in their beds from eight o'clock on.'

'Good girl, only don't blink so much. And don't fidget with your hair. And don't you dare put that knuckle in your mouth when he's talking.'

Greta's sight wasn't perfect, but it had improved tremendously. After only a few weeks she'd stopped feeling nauseous. She'd even stopped putting her hands to her face every few seconds. Despite her improved eyesight, Lily knew that people still saw something wrong with Greta, as if they'd decided something about her so long ago that a change as simple as glasses could do nothing to alter that opinion. The old goosiness had not disappeared. At nine, Greta walked and sat and listened the way she always had, out of habit. The heavy black-rimmed glasses added a kind of last stroke, a final ingredient to the whole concoction. People thought she was slow, simple, and Lily knew this was why, out of all of them, Mr Grady would want to put his questions to her; like most people, he thought Greta was too innocent to lie.

One morning in late spring, just after dawn, Mr Grady surprised Greta as she was walking from the henhouse back to the cottage. He came up behind her and wished her good morning. He smiled as she looked around, confused about where he'd emerged from. Coming up behind her that way meant he would have walked through the fields, waded through the stream, marched through the soft and muddy ground between his place and theirs. She looked down at his wellies, which were splattered with fresh mud. He was a small man, not nearly the size of her father, and his shadow barely outstretched hers. The brim of his cap was pulled so low that all Greta could see of his pale face was the ginger-colored stubble on his cheeks and throat.

'Did I scare you, Greta?' he asked, stepping in front of her so she had to stop walking.

'No, Mr Grady. Fine day.' She took a few steps to her left, pretending to look at something on the ground. She hoped her mother would glance out the window and see them there. Lily and Johanna were inside, draining the brine, removing the bones that came away easily and piling them in the pot to save for boiling. 'What brings you down our way?' she asked. On several occasions Greta could recall, and even more that she couldn't recall but had heard recounted, he'd been angry enough to walk straight down the Cahills' lane and knock on their front door. He'd shouted at Big Tom, demanded payment for use of his property and for taking away business that rightfully belonged to him, but as far as Greta knew, he'd never sneaked through the fields and popped up in their yard with a smirk like the cat who got the cream.

'Where's your father?'

'Him and the boys went to the crossroads to meet Mr Devine's bull.' They'd filed off that morning with two young cows that had never calved. Greta knew that they would wait by one of the abandoned cottages until Mr Devine arrived and Big Tom gave him money for his bull to hop up on the cows' backs. Greta also knew that sometimes they had to wait a long time for the bull to be ready to hop up a second time. Lily had sent her and Johanna to give him a message once, and they arrived as the bull was beginning to twitch and pace. Just as the bull leaped and the cow staggered forward, Big Tom had roared at them to go away. 'You know what they were doing, don't you?' Johanna had crowed as they raced home.

'And your mother is inside?' Mr Grady asked.

'Yes.'

'And Johanna?'

'Inside as well. Well, now that I think of it, they might have gone around front. My mother wanted to have a look at the whitewash.

There's mud up to the eaves. Will we walk around front and I'll get her for you?'

Greta took a few steps toward the front of the cottage, but Mr Grady stayed put.

'Is it chores they're doing inside?'

'It is, of course. Pop and the boys will be back soon.'

'And what kind of work could they be doing that they'd need to pull the curtains?'

Greta glanced over and saw that the curtains in the kitchen and the back room had been pulled since Mr Grady had come into the yard. Greta smiled. 'Now, Mr Grady, why don't we go around front and I'll get Mother.'

'No, Greta. I think we'll walk to the back door and you'll tell her I'm here to see her about something.' His pale face had become flushed. His voice lost its cheerful, gloating tones and sounded like a chord pulled too tight.

'Will you wait here while I get her?' Greta lowered her voice and in a volume barely above a whisper said, 'She might not be dressed.'

As Mr Grady looked at her, Greta fought the urge to push her glasses higher on her nose. She realized that she was chewing her lower lip, and she stopped. She smoothed her skirt. She concentrated on staying perfectly still. 'She wasn't feeling well yesterday, and she'd be very cross if I –'

'Go, then,' said Mr Grady. 'I'll wait here.'

Greta walked across the yard as if someone else were in charge of her limbs. She glanced around, as if observing different things in the yard, a casual task, off to fetch her mother. When she reached the back door, she pushed it open halfway, then slipped inside.

'What does he want?' Lily asked. She was standing behind the door. Johanna was sitting on the stool.

'To talk to you.'

'How does he seem?'

'Different,' Greta said. 'Something . . .'

'Christ,' Lily said. She took off her apron, smoothed back her hair. 'Stay here,' she said to the girls.

'Why didn't ye hide everything?' Greta asked once Lily had left.

She waved her hand over the rows of salmon, mounds of rock salt, piles of bones, scales, heads, and tails covering every surface.

'I don't know,' Johanna said, throwing up her hands. 'I told her. "Into the drawers," I said, and made off with a tray, but she was just like a statue watching out the window. I asked her what will we do, and she didn't answer. I pulled the curtains myself. I don't think she would have done it.'

'The drawers are full up already. That might be why she got funny. Under the beds would be better – just until he went.'

Observing through the slice of space between the curtains, the girls watched their mother walk across the yard and give Mr Grady a big smile. She patted his arm. She pointed out something in the henhouse behind him. He didn't turn to look, and at one point, as he was speaking, he looked so cross that Johanna wondered aloud whether he was going to spit, and if he did, what their mother would do. Greta heard her mother's soft, calming tones ride gently over his angry ones. It was her shushing voice, the one she used whenever she held a baby. Mr Grady wasn't having it, and after a few minutes he pointed at Lily, his finger so close to her face that if she nodded, he would have touched her nose. Even after she turned away and walked back to the house, he stood there staring at the back door, as if deciding whether to push his way inside.

Johanna gave up her stool when Lily came back in, and the three of them were silent as they waited for Mr Grady to leave. Johanna watched at the window while Greta sidled up closer to Lily and threaded her fingers in her mother's thick hair.

'He's gone,' Johanna announced finally. 'He just turned up the coast road.'

Upon hearing the word, Lily dropped her shoulders and let out a long breath, as if she'd been holding it the whole time she'd been talking to Mr Grady. She inhaled deeply, then let it go again.

'Now,' she said after she'd collected herself. 'No sense getting your father with all the work he has to do. You two finish up here.'

'Are we still going to town, myself and Greta, with the ones that are ready?' Johanna asked. 'Every house along the north road is expecting us.'

'No. Today I'll bring them myself.'

The boys and Big Tom did not return for their midday meal, and if Lily had not predicted that this might happen, Greta would have worried that Mr Grady had taken his angry face and his pointing finger down to the crossroads. Unlike Lily, Big Tom would not have used his soothing voice. The boys would have taken places beside Big Tom, arms folded, as Mr Grady's red face went scarlet.

'How much are the salmon worth?' Greta asked Johanna some time after Lily left. Johanna was fixing the hem on one of Lily's skirts. After stowing the new fish in the places left vacant by the ones Lily had brought to town, they'd parted the curtains and opened the windows, letting in the flies and the gnats along with the fresh air. They never handled money when they delivered the fish in town; Lily took care of all of that separately.

'Enough,' Johanna said, rooting through Lily's box of thread to find the closest match.

'What do you mean?'

'Enough is what I mean. Enough to have to take them from the river in secret and sell them in secret, so what do you think? Enough to make Mr Grady look like he was going to blow steam out of his ears.'

'But maybe he just doesn't like Pop.'

'Well, he doesn't like Pop, but don't you know the bailiff keeps a shotgun that Mr Grady gave him? And on the nights when he doesn't come, Mr Grady walks up and down the river himself with it?'

'To shoot someone?'

'Greta, it's time you copped on, don't you think?'

'That's what I'm trying to do, Johanna. And Jack takes a shotgun too, doesn't he? And we know he's not going to shoot anyone.'

Johanna rolled her eyes.

'You don't know either. Why don't you just say you don't know, instead of pretending all the time that you know everything.'

'I know that this is the way it is. Always has been. Always will be.'

'So, is going with the net the same as if Pop and the boys went over to Mr Grady's house and busted in the door and took his money and whatever they could put their hands to and then went and sold his things in town?'

Johanna pulled the needle through the fabric, pulled it up, up, up over her head as far as she could reach. Then she leaned forward as if she were giving it a kiss and snapped the thread with her teeth. She tied off the stitch, smoothed the edge of the skirt across her lap.

'Well?' Greta asked.

'I'm not talking to you,' Johanna said.

Since walking away from Mr Grady in the yard, Lily had felt a tremor in her body that she couldn't manage to still. Her hands shook, her knees shook, her heart felt out of rhythm. Twice on the way to town she'd had to stop pedaling the bicycle so she could get a better grip on the handlebars. One of those times she'd been tempted to walk down to the ocean, unwrap the dead fish from their brown paper packaging, and throw them all into the Atlantic. She pedaled fast through the crossroads without even lifting her hand to her sons when they shouted hello. She'd been pleasant to the man, but in return he'd pointed his finger in her face and raised his voice. A man who does that to a woman, to a neighbor, to a person he knows full well he'll have to pass in the road for the rest of his life, doesn't care anymore, and this thought made Lily breathless. When she looked at him, she'd seen hate, and she also saw that his hate had been handed down to him alongside the river. His father had hated Big Tom's father, and his grandfather had hated Big Tom's grandfather, and while she was seeing all of this, she also pictured Johanna and Greta looking out the window at her to watch what she would do.

That night, Lily waited until the house was asleep to tell Big Tom that Mr Grady had been to visit and that he'd been more angry than she'd ever seen him. The girls had been buzzing around Big Tom all evening, looking at him, looking at Lily, asking with their expressions whether he knew. Lily ignored them. It was better to wait and get him alone, in private, in their bedroom. It was an off night, and when Big Tom said he planned on getting a big sleep, he meant it. He refused to open his eyes.

'And?' he said.

This, Lily thought, is the man I married. Ten pregnancies, five children mostly grown.

'And he got Greta.'

At this Tom opened his eyes and turned toward Lily. 'And?' he said.

'Stop saying *and*. Greta was brilliant, no worries there, but he told me he knows all about the hotel and the B and B's. Private houses are bad enough, but he said the other business went over the line. And he said that when the county official came to pay him for what they take upstream, he was told the stock was low. He said it was like stealing money from his pocket.'

Big Tom grunted.

'He's serious, Tom. He's had it.'

'Well, I've had it as well. Did he ever think of that?'

Lily kicked off the covers and sat up. Tom saw things in black or white, always had, but there had to be a way to explain to him that feeling she had when Grady's face was in front of her. She'd grown up in Ballyroan just as Tom had. She knew it was no sin to take food from the river God gave them. Even before she and Tom married, her family took the fish the Cahills gave to them and were grateful to have it. But there was a difference between her and Tom; Lily was scared, and Tom didn't know what it meant to be afraid of anything. And the situation in Ballyroan wasn't the same as it had been when Lily and Tom were children and there were enough people around to protect and defend the Cahills. Lily had never missed having neighbors as much as she had that afternoon when Johanna first spotted Grady in the yard.

'He's in the right, Tom,' Lily said. 'It's time to stop now, before this gets any worse. He'll do like the man in Clifden who started getting water bailiffs from the north or from some other part, paying their whole wage himself and giving rewards for what they can discover at night, and then where will you be? The system he has now is a fool's system, and he knows it. Someone from Conch will turn in Tom Cahill? After shaking your hand in town for the past forty years? It's a laugh, actually. And he's through.'

'I'm through as well.'

'Jesus, Tom –' Lily stopped, reversed, began again more calmly. 'We could make up the loss somehow, couldn't we? What if we sold a piece of land? We hardly use that back-road field Gibbons sold you before they left, and it's hard to get to.'

Big Tom was quiet for so long that Lily began to feel a nugget of relief crack open in her chest and spread along her limbs.

'Sell it to who?' Big Tom said finally.

'Well, I don't know. We'd have to figure that out.'

'Lily, sometimes I wonder about you. Gibbons gave me that field for less than we make selling eggs in one month. Who would take it except for me? Useless, rocky land – it's a wonder the cows haven't starved. We need that river, do you understand? We need what that river brings in.'

'Well then,' Lily said, 'look at those Dennehy boys who went off to Germany to work in a pottery and how well they're doing. Or the boys could do half years in Manchester, back and forth. It's not the same as going to America, where we'd never see them again. You don't need all three of them here. They could take turns coming and going.' Lily paused, let her eyes follow the slight crack in their bedroom ceiling where it ran from the top of the window to the door. She took a breath. 'You're forgetting that it's his right. It's his river, his fish.'

'No, Lily. You're the one who's forgetting.'

The next afternoon, the loose gear on John Hogan's bicycle clanged like an alarm as he sped along the coast road, then turned down the Cahills' lane. Lily and Big Tom had headed off together earlier in the afternoon to settle up accounts, Lily hoping to mark an early end to the season, Tom seeing it only as a routine collection of payment and orders. John Hogan hopped off the bicycle before it came to a complete stop and took a few fast skips alongside before abandoning it to the dirt. Looking left and right, he rushed to the Cahills' door and pounded.

Inside, sitting with legs crossed and facing each other on their bed, Greta and Johanna froze their game of *fidchell*. They pushed the small board under one pillow and swept the empty spools they used for players under the other pillow.

He waited, pounded again. 'It's John Hogan.'

'Will we answer?' Greta whispered. This was unexpected. Before leaving, Lily had told them to stay inside and if Mr Grady came back, to ignore him and keep the doors locked tight. No one said anything about the bailiff.

Johanna put her finger over her lips and shook her head. Like the night months before, when they went spying on the tinker camp, Greta fought the urge to pee.

Outside, the bailiff gave up and circled around to the back of the house. He pounded on the back door, and the sound, that much closer than the front door, made Greta jump and clap her hand over her mouth.

'Will he bust through the door?' Greta asked. Johanna shook her head more vehemently than the first time and scowled, as if commanding Greta to stop asking questions.

The pounding stopped. The girls heard footsteps crunching the gravel at the side of the house. John Hogan poked his head into the stable. He whistled into the hay shed, squinting in the shadowy darkness. There, he spotted the three boys, fast asleep and half buried in hay.

'Lads!' he shouted, taking hold of Padraic's boot and giving it a shake. 'Where's Big Tom?'

The boys, groggy, stared at him for a moment and then sprang into action, Jack and Little Tom tumbling down from the highest mounds of hay and landing on their feet. No one answered the man.

'Fair enough,' John Hogan said. 'But pass him this message. I've been let go. Grady's got two men from Roscommon coming to take positions along the river, starting tonight. Former guards, both of them. No ties to Conch or to Ballyroan, you understand? You tell your father from me. Tell him to think hard on it, and I'll say the same to the three of you as well.'

Big Tom and the boys stayed away from the river for two weeks. Big Tom was like a thunderstorm trapped inside the small cottage, stomping around in his heavy boots, his expression a dark cloud the rest of the family stayed away from. Lily restrained herself from pointing out that her prediction had come true, that the fool's system had been put to bed. In the evenings Big Tom stood at the gate and watched for the two strangers from Roscommon to pass his door. He never laid eyes on them, and after a few days he concluded that they must be getting lodging from Grady as well. This made him even more angry.

The boys, on the other hand, were delighted. Instead of sleeping, they took their pipes to the shed and talked away the long daylight hours left after coming in from the fields. Twice they walked to the crossroads and caught the van to Oughterard, where the local parish hosted dances on Friday nights in the month of June. They stumbled home at two and three in the morning, complaining of the van's many stops but also keyed up over the girls they'd met, who'd danced with whom, who'd seen the culprit who spiked the punch, who'd witnessed the bloody fight that rolled into the cemetery. They clammed up when Greta came around, and more so when Johanna came, because she demanded details of the girls' outfits, hairstyles, the music that was played, the names of songs, the order of the songs, and so on. She begged to go with them next time, and they swore they'd never bring her.

On the first of July, Big Tom decided enough was enough. The day was overcast, and the night would be the same. 'There will be no moon tonight,' he said to Lily at supper, and the boys exchanged looks. 'It'll be black as tar out there, and I know the fields and the riverbank like I know the rooms of this house. So do the boys.'

'And so does Grady, and knows you'll be looking for a black night like this one,' Lily said.

'Grady knows this land as well as I do? My eye. I hear that river flowing all day and all night. The river on one side, the ocean on the other. East and west. And every rock that lies between.'

'And can Grady not hear the water from his place?' Lily asked. Big Tom glared at her. After dinner he went as he always did on river nights to lie down for a few hours.

Also as always, he told one of the boys to wake him just before midnight. 'We'll do it a little different tonight,' he said before leaving the kitchen. 'We don't need three on the net. If we have to, we'll take a smaller catch. Padraic, you take the second shotgun and go wide with Jack. Make sure you clean it, and clean it well. Little Tom is the strongest, and the two of us will handle the net.'

The boys nodded, taking the change in stride. Lily had gone quiet and was holding on to the arms of her chair. Greta looked at Johanna and saw that she'd noticed too. Lily stared blankly at her husband, then at her boys. Then her gaze ambled across the room and rested on Greta and Johanna. She jumped into action, standing so abruptly that her chair hopped backward. She rushed across the kitchen. 'Out!' she shouted at the girls. 'To bed!' She followed them into their room, and for the first time in years she helped them out of their clothes, yanked off their shoes. She plucked Greta's glasses from her face and pulled her sweater roughly over her head.

'It's only gone half eight,' Johanna protested. 'It's still bright out.'

'You're hurting my ears!' Greta cried as Lily pulled and pulled, Greta's head caught in the head opening.

'I'm sorry, love,' Lily said. She tugged gently, and the sweater gave way. She tucked them in and had to lie half on top of Johanna to reach Greta for a kiss. After kisses she sat at the edge of their bed, and the girls pretended to fall asleep. With her eyes closed and Johanna's warm breath brushing against the back of her neck, Greta let out a long yawn.

When all three heard Big Tom's snores come from the other side of the wall, Lily left them.

At a quarter to twelve Little Tom opened the door to his parents' bedroom. When the light from the lantern didn't wake his father, he went and touched his shoulder. Lily was in the kitchen making tea.

After dressing, Big Tom joined the boys in the kitchen. The curtains were pulled tight, and the room was lit by a single lamp, the wick lowered as far as it could go without the flame going out. If Lily had her way, they'd get ready in the dark, but no, Big Tom would never agree. Lily put a steaming mug in front of him, and he slurped it down. The two shotguns waited side by side at the back door. At midnight Big Tom fetched the net from its hiding place and told the boys to shake a leg. Lily stepped outside the back door and was relieved to find the sky as inky black as Tom had predicted. The night was warm, and the air was very still.

'There'll be a big rain later,' she said as they brushed by her. The boys kissed her cheek one by one.

'Don't wait up,' Jack said.

'We'll be back in an hour,' Padraic said.

Jack walked about twenty feet ahead, Padraic twenty feet behind. As they disappeared into the darkened field, Lily watched Padraic look left, look right, pointing the shotgun in whichever direction he was facing. He'll make himself dizzy, she thought, and was tempted to call out to him. When she looked again, he was gone. She went back inside, blew out the lantern, and lit a single small candle. She placed the candle on the floor in the corner farthest from the window.

At a quarter past, Lily heard the girls talking in their bed. At twelve-thirty she heard their bare feet slide along the worn wood planks of the hall floor. She listened to the kitchen door creak open, inch by inch.

'Don't tell me you're both up.'

'Couldn't sleep,' Johanna announced, pushing the door open all the way and flopping down in Big Tom's chair. Greta sat in front of the cold fireplace. She almost asked if they could build a fire, but then she remembered.

At one A.M. Lily went to stand watch at the back door.

At one-fifteen she walked out into the yard as far as the hay shed and peered out into the empty darkness. After a few minutes she pressed forward, walking past the stable to the wall that marked the boundary of their first field. She saw a light in the corner of her eye and turned to find the lantern she'd snuffed out an hour earlier bobbing toward her. When the girls reached her, she snatched the lantern away and gave them each a pinch. 'I could kill you both,' she said, but instead of extinguishing the flame, she put the lantern on the ground and pulled the girls close. She decided to give Big Tom and the boys another fifteen minutes, and if they weren't back, she was going to take that lantern and march straight down to the river. She'd yell for them if she had to. She'd have the girls yell too. Damn them to hell anyway. She'd call the *gardai* if she had to. She'd wake all of Conch.

If they'd been caught, Greta reasoned, the *gardai* would have made a racket dragging them away. There would have been shouts. They'd have heard Mr Grady's voice cut through the dense night air. Big Tom would never go silently; he would have cursed and sworn, and the boys would have done the same.

'What in the world is keeping them?' Lily whispered.

Then all three heard a pair of thunderous cracks, one call and one answer, and the night was split in two.

Years later, Greta would still not know whether she actually remembered the second half of the night or if she'd merely visualized what she'd been told. The picture she pieced together looked as if it belonged inside one of those toys she'd once seen in Norton's shop. While Lily was shopping, she'd picked up the toy, looked through a peephole, and seen what looked like fragments of a stained glass window, and when she turned the dial, all the colors and shapes collapsed and came together again, collapsed and came together, constantly turning into something else.

The two blasts were soon followed by real thunder and rain so heavy it pressed down the nettles and the long grass. Big Tom was dead. That was the first thing that soaked in, though Greta would never be able to recall the moment she knew, if she'd still been standing out by the wall or if she'd made it back home with Johanna before realizing what had happened. Sometimes she remembered Lily telling her in the kitchen. Sometimes she remembered listening on the other side of the kitchen door as the boys recounted the story for Lily. Sometimes she was sure that no one ever told her; she simply knew.

It was a funny thing, in a way, with all the shotguns that had been present that night – Jack's, Padraic's, and those of the two strangers – Big Tom had drowned in his own river. Grazed by a shot meant only to scare him, he stumbled and fell. The rush of the water carried him for about thirty feet, until his head became wedged between two rocks. Unaware that their father was in trouble, one of the boys – which one was a secret they decided not to tell – fired back at the strangers but missed, instead finding the chest of Mr Grady, who was observing the capture of the poachers from a few yards away. In the spot where Big Tom died, the water was two feet deep.

The boys carried him home, laid him on his bed, pulled off his shirt, loosened his belt, touched and retouched his face with the backs of their hands. And this Greta was sure she remembered firsthand: when they pulled off his boots the river poured out and ran to every corner of the room.

PART II

1963

Four

More than two hundred men and women, old and young, pressed elbow to elbow in the Conch town hall. The collective heat from their bodies and the dampness of the unseasonably warm day steamed the two windows of the long, low-ceilinged room that faced west onto Sky Street, where another two hundred people waited, some from as far as forty miles away. Inside and out, the people were silent. Even the floorboards had stopped creaking as soon as everyone found a spot. The people who gathered had already worked a full day, had their supper, had their tea, and now they waited together for the daylight to disappear. Most of the heads were turned west, as if a stern look might goad the last of the sun's rays to get on with it, get out of the way.

'Here they are!' A man standing on the top outside step shouted over his shoulder into the crowded room, his voice sparking life into those who'd begun to let their minds wander as the blood pooled in their tired feet. The crowd, which had arranged itself to take up every bit of spare space, silently agreed to split down the middle as the pastor, the county councilor, and the local director of the Electricity Supply Board passed down a narrow center aisle. The crowd stood on tiptoe to see them.

The ESB representative reached the small raised platform first, then stood aside and gestured to the priest and the councilor to precede him. When they took their positions, he joined them on the platform and cleared his throat to address the crowd. The people outside surged forward to hear.

'It's been a great honor getting to know so many of you over this past year, and on behalf of the entire board, I wish the people of Conch, and the outlying homes, much happiness and prosperity. It has brought me particular pleasure, in this post-development phase, to continue bringing light to communities beyond the reach of the initial push. One day very soon, all of Ireland will be electrified.'

He stepped back as the crowd, believing the time had come, applauded. The priest raised his hand to shush them, and like dutiful children, they dropped their hands to their sides. The county councilor cleared his throat and thanked the supply board for its speed and efficiency. The ESB man smiled, pretended to wave his words away. A muffled cough sounded from the middle of the room.

The priest stepped forward next and read a short passage about light and darkness from the Gospel of Saint John. He shook holy water on the rust-spotted switch box that had been temporarily set up for the occasion. It had finally grown dark, and the priest signaled to the men in the far corners of the room to extinguish the paraffin lamps.

'Father?' the ESB man said. 'The honors?' All eyes in the room were strained to make out the dark shadow that was the priest reach over to the box and move the ceremonial switch from the bottom to the top. A half second later the room was filled with bright electric light. The electric gramophone clicked to life, and the first notes of Rosemary Clooney's voice were overwhelmed by thunderous applause, stamping, shouting.

Outside, the shop windows and arc lamps lining the streets had also lit up, and at the outermost edge of the crowd, Greta looked over at Johanna and then at Little Tom and announced that she could see them as clearly as midmorning. She took off her glasses, which were almost identical to her first pair of six years earlier, and the brightness remained. The streetlamps buzzed, and for a moment Greta panicked, thinking that they might not be safe to touch. Before she could mention it, a young man grabbed hold of one of the poles and swung around and around, calling out for everyone to look at him, look at him, he was an American film star. A girl about his age caught his elbow and told him he was making a bollocks of himself. The dancing that had begun inside was beginning to spread to the people in the street, and the same young man who'd been swinging on the lamp grabbed Johanna's elbow and spun her around. When he released her, she came back to Greta and announced that she could count every single freckle on Greta's nose.

The three Cahills celebrated with the crowd until two o'clock in the morning, and then they collected their bicycles from outside the post office and headed back to Ballyroan. The light appeared to dim as they got farther from town, and by the time they reached the sharp curve in the road, they were in total darkness. Greta tried to estimate how many times in her life she'd walked or cycled that road in the dark, but on that night, it seemed so much darker. Johanna weaved back and forth, cutting an unseen pattern with the treads of her bicycle wheel, and talked nonstop about electric irons, electric cookers, electric clothes-washing machines.

On the radio that morning, there had been a man talking about the ten-year plan. The man had joked that the ten-year plan was now, in 1963, in its thirteenth year. The Electricity Supply Board had finally closed in on its goal of one million poles, seventy-five thousand miles of power lines, one hundred thousand transformers. From above, Greta thought, with all the crisscrossing of black wires and the haphazard placement of the poles, Ireland probably looked like a fish caught in a net.

The next morning, Johanna and Greta tried to explain to Lily the excitement of the night before. The music, the noonday brightness of the streets, the food cooked on electric cookers and lined up on tables.

'There was tea?' Lily asked.

'Oh, loads,' Johanna said. 'Everything you can think of.'

'Did anyone have the tea?'

Johanna looked at Greta. 'Anyone who was near, I'd say. We didn't want to fight through the crowd. They made it in a five-gallon thing, and people said it boiled up in no time.'

'Why are you asking about the tea?' Greta asked, and watched as Lily pursed her lips and bent to stoke the fire. Johanna sat in the chair beside Greta, who could feel her begin to buzz like the arc lamps of the night before. She pressed her knee against Johanna's under the table.

'It's just like Big Tom said,' Lily said finally. 'Here come the poles and the wire and the switches and a monthly charge to do the things we've been doing for a thousand years. It's a rent, is what it is. It's tricking people to sign up to pay rent. Wasn't there a woman on the radio last week saying that the electricity lit up the thatch and set fire to the whole town?'

Little Tom knocked on the table and shook his head. He placed his hand over his mouth and said something. Greta couldn't quite understand it, but she guessed.

'A rumor,' Greta said, looking at little Tom for approval. He nodded, sat back in his chair. Greta remembered the program now. She had rested in the kitchen for a moment between trips to the well and found Little Tom listening to the radio. 'They did a whole program on the things people think about electricity that aren't true.'

'Mammy, if you could only just see –' Johanna said.

'I've been around a lot longer than you, girl, and there's things I don't have to see to know.'

'You'll get used of it,' Greta said, taking her mother's hand and squeezing it. 'We all will.'

'Used of it or no,' Johanna said. 'It's coming. This week. We've waited six years for this, and I can't talk about it for one minute longer.'

Lily stared into the fire as Johanna stood up, stalked across the room, let the kitchen door slam shut behind her. Greta dropped Lily's hand and felt along the cool and clammy wall until she came to the little plate that marked the place where a cord would soon be plugged in. The wall was damp to the touch and would be more damp, the ESB canvasser had said, if they were to take a hatchet, hack away at the plaster, and get at the pulp that was within. 'Like sponges, these western cottages,' he'd said. 'And there's the salt to worry about as well.' He'd taken his first two fingers, run them along the wall, brought them to his lips, and licked. He'd smacked his tongue against the inside of his mouth. 'It's an island, this place,' he'd said then. 'Water on every side. Did ye ever think of that?'

The canvasser came for the first time about a year after Big Tom's death. He arrived in a van, and when he opened the back door of the van, a whole shop's worth of appliances was revealed: electric irons, churns, a machine that could milk four cows at once, a plug-in kettle, a cooker, a big cylinder that could pump water from the well all the way into the kitchen of the cottage. Jack and Padraic had been in Australia since the week after Big Tom's funeral, so it was left to Little Tom and Johanna to listen to the presentation, follow the man around the house to learn where the lines could enter and exit, how they'd run through the walls. They walked out into the fields and picked out places the poles could go without getting in the way. Inside, Greta stayed with Lily as she peered out from between the curtains and asked what was going on. The man explained how it worked – the connection fee, the wiring fee, the calculation based on the square footage of the house, the barn, the stable. He multiplied by some percentage that meant they were far outside the main grid, subtracted the small government subsidy, divided by twelve.

Too dear, Johanna told him, and they turned him away. They turned him away the next year as well, and the next. Next thing they knew, it was 1962, and since the people of Conch had voted to get electricity for the whole village, the Cahills could be absorbed into the local grid for a much-reduced price.

The three Cahill children made their case to Lily. 'Look it,' Johanna had said, opening her hands, palms up, in the way she did when she was going to say things only once. 'Without Jack and Padraic, it's the only way we can keep the place going. Tom can do the work of three men with the help it will bring. Think of it, Mam. We can pump water right up to the house. No more trips to the well. No more carrying those heavy buckets.' Little Tom rubbed his thumb against his first two fingers to remind her to talk about the cost.

'And it pays for itself after a while,' Johanna added. 'For a start, look at the battery for the radio.'

'Don't tell me what to look at,' Lily said. 'I want no part of it. We'll be electrified in our beds. And what happens when Jack and Padraic come back and they don't like it?'

Johanna threw down her hands and let out a long sigh. She raked her fingers through her hair. Greta knew what was coming, so she moved over to sit next to Lily.

'They're in Australia,' Johanna said. 'They've been in Australia for six years.' Her tone said that these two brief sentences were the beginning and the end of that particular story.

'And it's time now for them to be coming on home,' Lily said.

In the first few months after Big Tom's death, it seemed to Greta that her mother had gotten very old. She held herself differently, her back bent like an old woman's. Her lips became chapped and got so raw that

87

they cracked and bled when she ate or spoke. She was tired all the time and took long rests in the middle of the day. She didn't like going to town anymore, and when she did go, she didn't like talking to people. After a while, time began moving in the other direction, and although Lily appeared older, it seemed to Greta that her mind was getting younger, as if she couldn't understand the world and needed her children to get her out of bed, force a washcloth under her arms. The only time she appeared to be happy was when a letter arrived from Jack or Padraic. When their letters came, she would call out the back door for any of them within earshot and tell them to drop whatever they were doing to come hear. 'We'll write back straightaway,' she'd say, putting a biro and piece of paper in front of Greta, who was now as good at writing as Johanna and had far more patience for it.

At first it seemed to Greta as if Lily were satisfied by the boys' descriptions of Canberra and Melbourne and the work they were doing on the roads there. She watched her mother nod at any positive news, as if they could see her, and how she brought her hand to her collarbone if she thought they were leaving something out. At the time, it had seemed the smartest thing for the boys to leave, and quickly. A *garda* had come asking questions at Big Tom's funeral, and the possibility of Grady's son coming from England to investigate what had happened choked Lily in her sleep. As they were hemming and hawing about whether they should go, she told them that shortly before he died, Big Tom had decided that this would be his last season of taking the salmon from the river, that he was going to find work on one of those foreign fishing boats where they spent four months on, four months off, and that the boys should either do the same or find work somewhere else. They listened closely, and they knew that even though it wasn't true, this was her way of telling them to go.

But Grady's son had not come from England to press charges, and the *garda* who had come asking questions the day of Big Tom's funeral had not returned. In the papers, they called Mr Grady's death an accident. By the time it became clear that the boys would not face any trouble, they'd already reached Melbourne and the childhood friend who promised them work.

School went by the wayside after Big Tom died and the boys left.

Greta followed Johanna's lead. If Johanna got up and went to school, so did Greta. If she stayed home, so did Greta. Neither Lily nor Little Tom nor Mr Joyce seemed to notice either way. It seemed silly to both girls to be reciting poems in Irish while at the same time wondering if Lily would get up the energy to take in the wash, if Little Tom would remember to check on the day-old chicks. The girls went off and on for a few years, but then quietly, without discussion, when Johanna was fourteen and Greta was twelve, they stopped going entirely. There was never a last day. They just went one Wednesday, and as it turned out, they never went back. To make up for it, they began buying a newspaper whenever they went to town, and they took turns reading out loud after they'd cleared the supper dishes. Ever since getting glasses, Greta had had a far easier time with reading and writing. She could write a good letter to her brothers in a faster time than Johanna, who never had the patience to sit and describe all the things the boys might be interested in. Johanna, however, was still a better reader. When Greta read out loud, she concentrated so hard on pronouncing the words correctly that she often read a whole passage without having the slightest clue as to what she'd just said.

Although Johanna said that school was mostly a useless waste of time, Greta missed it now and again. She liked the plays they put on at Christmas and the little chocolate eggs at Easter. She liked the stories about how Ireland used to be divided up among kings, though she could never figure out if that was real the way Pádraig Pearse was real or if it was a made-up story like Cuchulain the Hound of Ulster. During the day Lily looked at them sometimes as if she couldn't quite put her finger on what was wrong with the picture she was seeing, but she never said a word.

It wasn't that Greta thought putting electricity in the house would be easy, but she hadn't thought about how much it would take, how many men it involved, the lorries carrying long wood poles, the huge wheels of wire like giant spools of thread. The men who worked on the poles wore funny-looking boots, gloves, hard hats, and big belts around their waists. It took seven of them to put the poles upright. Little Tom did most of the wiring inside the cottage, working from the pamphlets the ESB had mailed to him when they finally reached an agreement. Johanna helped him, reading certain parts out loud, turning the pictures around and around until they figured out a way to get it right.

One week after the ceremony in Conch, on an overcast day that never got any brighter than predawn, Little Tom ushered Lily into the kitchen and pulled out a chair for her to sit down. At his signal, Johanna switched on the light, and the room was as bright as it had been that night on Sky Street. Lily blinked in the sudden brightness and looked around. She turned her face away from the glare of the lamp. She squinted up at the ceiling and, after a few seconds, stood up to take a closer look. Without warning, she snapped into action, grabbing the broom from its place behind the door and tearing at the cobwebs with the bristled end. It was the fastest her children had seen her move since Big Tom died. When she was through with one corner, she worked over toward the next, then the next, leaning over whatever furniture she couldn't push out of the way.

'The man said we'll get used to the brightness after a few days,' Johanna said. 'This is sixty watts. There's seventy-five watts and ninety if we want it brighter.'

'Brighter?' Lily took a last swipe at the ceiling. 'This place is a disgrace. First thing tomorrow you girls are going to dust every square inch.'

Yes, Greta thought. Give us chores. Lift our skirts and give us a slap.

'And don't even think of doing a thing until you do,' Lily added as she ran her hand along the nicks and scrapes on the arm of the chair where she had just been sitting. When she finished inspecting the kitchen, she seemed taller. She untied her hair and retwisted it so it was neater, tighter. That's it, Greta thought. Take us by the ear and march us through the fields back to the main road.

When the electrification of Conch and the outlying areas was complete, the owners of the few B and B's that the Cahills had once supplied with salmon got it into their heads that their business would turn around. Word would get to America and England that the far west of Ireland now had hot water running in every faucet and electric blankets in every room. One place, a B and B that called itself an inn, advertised in town for kitchen help. One month after the electrification of Conch village, Johanna spotted the ad, removed it from its post, folded it in fourths, and tucked it into her pocket. That night Greta and Johanna washed their hair, dried it at the fire, scrubbed themselves in the basin, pressed their best skirts and blouses. The next morning, they cycled the ten miles along the coast road to the six-room inn and presented themselves to the owner, Mr James Breen, who, after introducing himself, didn't have the slightest idea of what to do with them.

'We saw your advertisement,' Johanna said. 'We're looking for work.'

Mr Breen nodded, looking back and forth between the two girls. 'Ah . . .' he said, rubbing at his temples. He hadn't expected anyone to turn up so soon. He decided he should give them a tour of the guest rooms, then stopped himself. This was not how his wife would have done it – his wife who had run the place for eleven years and then up and died on him just as things were going to turn around. A thought came to him.

'Experience?' he said. 'Do ye have any experience in hotels?' He directed his question at Greta, who deflected it to Johanna.

'No sir, but we've been cooking and cleaning our entire lives, and we're good workers.'

'Brilliant,' he said. 'Will I show you the kitchen? We have an electric cooker. Are you familiar?'

'Of course,' Johanna said, ignoring the nudge Greta gave her. They had a cooker, but had used it only a handful of times. Johanna's tone implied a level of expertise that made Greta nervous.

Mr Breen led them to a small dining room with four tables, through a swing door to the kitchen. 'We'll have a test, will we?' he said. 'To see how this will work? There's all the makings here of a full breakfast, so why don't I see how you do, one at a time, and then we'll eat and talk a bit more.'

Johanna was already rolling up the sleeves of her blouse. Two minutes later she had the skillet sputtering. She cracked an egg, halved a tomato, diced a potato, sliced pieces of black pudding, laid four bangers next to the eggs. She remembered to fill the electric kettle and plug it in. Fifteen minutes later she plated a hot breakfast. Twenty minutes later Greta had cracked two eggs onto the skillet and let pieces of the shell fall in. She tried to pluck them out but burned her fingertip, which she popped into her mouth and sucked as the eggs bubbled. When she flipped the first egg, the yolk broke and ran across the skillet. She was afraid to do the same to the other, so she watched it cook until it was fried hard. The potatoes were cold. She forgot the tomatoes and the tea.

Mr Breen was kind about it. He said he was sure that Greta was a fine worker, but in fact he had only one kitchen position open, and she might be more suited to a housekeeping job, something quiet, out of sight, less demanding. Greta agreed, and waited for him to tell her when she could begin such a job. 'Unfortunately,' he said, 'we have nothing like that available at the moment.'

'Do you have anyone making up the rooms now, Mr Breen?' Johanna asked.

'I do it myself,' he told her. 'It's only the kitchen where I'm pure useless. To be honest with you, the rooms don't get much use except for the summer, and even then . . . It's really the kitchen that stays busy all year with the coast traffic. There's lorries going up and down all the time now and not many places to stop for a hot meal. And I still have a working farm here, you know. Half working.'

'But with the crowds you're sure to get soon, do you not think you'd need more help? Someone to serve the plates? Someone to clean up? Sweep? Dust? Someone who would work for, let's say, two quid a week?'

Mr Breen rubbed his temples again. The crowds. The radio had been promising crowds for years now, and he was sure, just as Mrs Breen had been sure, that it was only the electricity that was holding them back. Now even that obstacle was behind him. He leaned back in his chair and rested his hands on his belly. The girl had done a power of a job in the kitchen, and looking at her, he wondered if she'd take the job only if there was something for the other girl as well.

He looked at the other girl, the way she looked back and forth between the older girl and himself. She'd hardly said a word, and he wondered if there might be something just a touch wrong with her.

Just a touch, mind you – nothing that would keep her from doing a good job making up the rooms, but perhaps not someone he'd want greeting the guests and bringing them their tea. It was the way she held herself, a bit awkward, and the way whenever she looked at anything, she turned her whole body to face it head-on. She was looking at him now, peering out from behind a quarter inch of glass, and she had turned in her chair so that they were practically knee to knee. For the second time that day, Mrs Breen seemed to walk into the room without showing herself, just to whisper in his ear.

'I haven't asked anything about yourselves,' he said. 'Where are ye from? What's your name? How will you get here and back every day? Lateness is something I can't tolerate, not in this business.' He looked at them closely, first the older, then the younger. 'What age are ye anyway?'

Johanna took his questions in order. 'We're from Ballyroan. Our name is Cahill. We've three older brothers, two in Australia, one at home. We've good bicycles we can use every day. If we're late, you can dock us. I'm twenty, and Greta is eighteen.'

Greta's head snapped up, and Mr Breen caught a look of panic pass through her features. He guessed they were more like eighteen and sixteen. It would be easy enough to find out if he asked in Conch, but he didn't mention any of this, and he had to will himself not to smile at the girl's boldness. The name was familiar, and he knew there was almost no one left in Ballyroan.

'All right then, girl. You've talked yourself into a job. Into two jobs, in fact.' He glanced at Greta. 'I like a clean slate, so let's start on Monday, and we'll do the weeks Monday to Sunday from this point forward.'

Johanna was too elated to go back to the cottage, so just where they should have turned off onto their own little road, she veered left and down to the ocean. She couldn't stop the numbers from streaming through her thoughts: three pounds a week multiplied by fifty-two weeks of the year, plus possible tips in the summer, a possible extra bit for Christmas or for doing a good job, and in a year's time she'd have something substantial. Plus the eggs and the odd jobs she did around town, mending and fetching errands for some of the old ones. Greta followed her sister, bouncing and rattling on the bumpy ground, finally hopping off the bicycle and walking it almost to the waterline. By the time Greta caught up, Johanna was already in her bra and underpants and striding out into the water until it was knee-high, hip-high, chest-high, and then her dark head disappeared. The sky and the water were the same slate gray, and Greta shivered as she picked up Johanna's clothes and moved them out of the water's reach.

At home, Johanna told Lily and Little Tom the news, and Greta described the dining room with the little bud vases on each table, the napkins folded like party hats. They expected Lily to be happy, but she listened in silence, her face stony. When they were finished telling, she began with the questions, one after the other, as if she'd finally woken up after a long sleep. What kind of man was James Breen? Was there a woman of the house? Did he have children? Was business really expected to get better? Were there any other people around? Did he talk to either of them alone, or always together? Why did he hire two if the advertisement asked for only one? On and on, her questions poured forth, one on top of the last, so that they could barely answer one before she'd already moved on to another.

'Mammy, I don't understand you,' Johanna said. 'You should be delighted.'

'I want to understand it first,' Lily said. 'James Breen is no more to me than a stranger in the road, and you'll be scrubbing his kitchen and sweeping his floors.'

'For a price,' Johanna said. 'For good wages.'

Greta could tell that if Johanna let herself say another word, there would be an argument in no time.

'We thought you might have known him . . . from before,' Greta said. 'Did you and Pop not deliver out that way?'

'Not to any James Breen,' Lily said, but there was a note in her voice that trailed off. 'There was a Frances Breen. A big sort of a woman. She had a B and B, now that I think of it, an inn, they called it. With a ritzy-sounding name – not at all suited for the place I'm thinking, oh, what was it anyway? I doubt anyone ever stayed there. It looked as if it might topple over headfirst into the waves.'

'That's the one,' Greta said. 'It's called Silk of the Kine.'

'Exactly right,' Lily said, clapping her hands together as if she were dusting them off. 'Now, you tell me why they couldn't have called it Breen's, like the Walshes have Walsh's and the McDonoughs have McDonough's. No, your father didn't like them people. Didn't like them at all.'

Each day when the girls were at work and Little Tom was out of the cottage, Lily did something she never thought she would do. She went into the kitchen and turned on the electric light. It was strange the way the new light ate up the brightness of the fire and made it smaller. After a few weeks she went to the back room and had a look at the electric cooker. It was an odd-looking thing, with metal coils and grates. She switched it on and watched the coils turn from gray to red. She held her hand above it and felt the heat pushing against her palm. Eventually she filled a pot with water and put it on top of one of the reddened coils. Nothing happened at first, but then slowly, after a few minutes had gone by, she saw the telltale bubbles begin to form at the bottom of the pot and slowly rise to the surface. They rose faster and faster, and next thing she was looking at water in full boil. She threw the water out the back door and did it again. The next morning, she put butter in the skillet and fried an egg.

What the children had promised seemed to be coming true. Little Tom, poor devil, was doing a power of work on his own, and Lily could see with her own eyes how those plug-in gizmos had picked up the load that Jack and Padraic would have carried if they'd been home. They worked faster than a person could work, actually, and more often she saw Little Tom smoking his pipe out back, something he hadn't had time for since Big Tom died. So far, none of the cows had been scorched or electrified. Neither she nor the children had been burned to a crisp in their beds. One morning, almost four months after the electricity was hooked up, Lily was suddenly sorry she hadn't gone to the ceremony in Conch that night. The regret hit her without warning, as if she'd wandered into a pocket of cold air. Greta had begged her, had pulled her by the arm and told her they'd come home early, and she'd enjoy herself, and there'd be nothing like it again, nothing like the first time. Johanna, as was her style, asked her only once and, when she refused, did not ask again.

Lily knew that they thought she hadn't noticed a thing in six years, and she could understand why they would think that. It would be difficult to explain even if she wanted to. Most days life seemed like a pantomime, like one of those drawn-out plays the nuns made them act out at holidays, all parts scripted and assigned. The girls moved in circles around her, and Little Tom in a big circle around all of them.

The girls thought she didn't notice anything anymore, but they were wrong. She noticed everything: that they'd stopped going to school, that they never went to Mass, that their underclothes were stiff with salt from swimming in their skivvies, that Johanna now cursed like her brothers, and that Greta had begun a hobby even Johanna didn't know about. Greta had begun collecting things and keeping them in an old biscuit tin under their bed. Silly things, really – an old thimble, a rusted key that didn't open anything, a few buttons, a few beads, a hair clip, a prayer book, a yellow rubber ball, a tin of hair pomade, a tea sieve, and one surprising thing: a brand-new compact with a mirror inside. It was shiny, pristine, with a mother-of-pearl finish and a hidden button for popping it open. Inside, in addition to the mirror, was a small circle of pressed powder, many shades too dark for Greta, with the manufacturer's tissue still pressed to the top. It was nicer than any cosmetic Lily ever had, and she wondered where Greta got it, how much she'd paid for it, and why, for God's sake, she had spent that kind of money for a shade that didn't match her skin. At first Lily thought it must have been Johanna's, but no, it was there with the rest of Greta's things. It was a small discovery, but it was the first time Lily had felt surprised since Big Tom died. So little Greta, that goose, wanted grown-up things. It was time, Lily supposed.

Every week Greta spent at Mr Breen's hotel, she noticed a new thing she liked. Sometimes they were physical things – the white towels, the blue-and-white-checked tablecloths, the little bud vases she'd noticed on the first day – and sometimes they were just ways of doing things. The tea, for instance. At home they always threw everything in together, the leaves, the water, the sugar, the milk, and heated it up on the fire. Mr Breen put his leaves in a tiny sieve about the size of a chestnut, then lowered the sieve into the hot water. He let it steep, then removed it and stirred in a bit of sugar, a splash of milk.

'So the idea is to never let a leaf loose in your cup, is it?' Greta said.

'You're pure genius, Greta,' Johanna said.

Johanna's job was no busier than Greta's, despite Mr Breen's talk of coastal traffic. He was apologetic. 'Soon,' he promised. 'An off week, I'd say. It's a blessing, really. This way you can settle yourselves before the crowds start coming.' He seemed so sorry about it that Johanna worried that she'd misunderstood, that he was going to pay them only if people came. But at the end of that first week she got her three pounds, Greta got her two, and he promised a busier second week.

Over the next few weeks they saw a total of two dozen people, none of whom stayed overnight. Once, they got four ESB men who were there to see firsthand the progress that had been made in the west. Mr Breen sat with them as they smoked their pipes and talked about the threat of an unusually wet spring. Johanna sat in the kitchen for three hours, trying to decide whether she should clean up or whether they'd talk long enough to want another round of eggs and rashers.

Then one morning, after Johanna finished mopping the kitchen floor and was dumping the wash water outside, she spotted a woman walking up the road toward the inn. She was carrying a small suitcase in one hand, and the other hand she kept on her head to keep her hair in place. She was lopsided with the weight of the suitcase, and every few feet she came to a dead stop, switched the case from one hand to the other, wriggled in her shoes. 'Greta,' Johanna said, nodding toward the road. Greta immediately went upstairs, unlocked the biggest and brightest guest room, put fresh sheets on the bed, and plugged in the electric heater. She ran a damp cloth along the windowsill and along the baseboard. By the time she got downstairs, the woman had taken off her long tweed coat to reveal a pink corduroy dress, long sleeved, with a collar like on a man's shirt, buttons from top to bottom, and a wide navy blue belt cinching it in the middle. Mr Breen had not yet appeared.

'Hi,' the woman said when she saw Greta. 'The bus driver said there would be vacancies? I hope so, because it's nasty out there and these shoes are killing me. This is April? I'd hate to see January around here.' She paused as she looked at Greta. 'Stupid, wearing shoes like this. I knew it too, and I wore them anyway.' She put one foot forward to show Greta what she was talking about: dainty round-toed navy blue shoes with a narrow heel about an inch and a half high. She laughed. 'Well, now that you know I'm desperate I guess you'll go ahead and bump up the price.'

Greta could hear by the creak of the floor that Johanna had come up behind her. She looked over at her, but Johanna seemed as thrown off as Greta. The woman was looking back and forth between them. 'Is it a bad time?' she asked. 'You could direct me somewhere else.'

'Not at all,' Johanna said finally, moving swiftly across the room to take the woman's bag. 'We've plenty of room. Make yourself at home. Pull yourself right up here – Greta, move that chair closer to the fire, will you? Take those shoes off, Missus, if you like. We don't mind. I'll fetch Mr Breen and he'll –'

'It's Miss, actually, but you can call me Shannon. Named for the river.'

'Is there a river Shannon in America?' Greta asked.

Shannon smiled one of those pure white one-hundred-watt American smiles. 'No, honey, your river Shannon. Never heard of any other.'

In the kitchen, after taking the woman's suitcase upstairs, Greta pulled on her sweater to run out to the stable in search of Mr Breen. 'Well, for fuck's sake,' Johanna said as she took an inventory of what they had in the way of food. 'You never know what the day will bring, do you? A Yank in Yank's clothes and a Yank way of talking with a face like the map of Ireland.'

And as she ran across the stretch of grass behind the inn, over the patch of gravel, around the derelict barn, down the little hill to the stable where Mr Breen was working, Greta wondered what kinds of things Shannon carried in her little case.

Supper was chicken, killed by Mr Breen, cleaned and cooked by Johanna. Shannon went to her room for a rest beforehand, and down-stairs, Greta suggested that they bring up tea. Johanna was up to her elbows in blood and feathers. 'I'll bring it myself,' Mr Breen said cheerfully, then looked off, as he did when something was occurring to him. 'Will I? Or will you bring it, Greta? Will she be indisposed, do you think?'

'The Lord save us, Mr Breen,' Johanna said. 'She's already had two cups in front of the fire. I'd say she'll live the next three-quarters of an hour without.'

'Right,' said Mr Breen. 'Let's leave her in peace then. Lovely. Exactly right.'

Shannon didn't want to eat alone, so she asked the three of them to sit with her. Mr Breen declined, citing unfinished business in the stable, so Greta and Johanna sat and heard all about the place in New York City called Queens and, inside Queens, a place called Woodside. It sounded like a busy place, at least as busy as Galway City, plus a train that ran above the streets that you had to climb a long flight of stairs to board and that brought you straight to Midtown, whatever that was. Straight to the Statue of Liberty, Greta guessed. Shannon didn't seem the least bit like the fussy Yanks Greta had heard about secondhand and thirdhand when she went to Conch on errands and stopped to listen to stories about so-and-so's third cousins who'd come from Boston or Pittsburgh to find their roots. Greta, like most people who'd never met a Yank in person, assumed that all of them complained of the cold or the damp, or said things like there's a spot on my knife, I don't take sugar, I prefer my potatoes mashed, and that kind of thing.

'Are you on your holidays, then?' Johanna asked.

'Not exactly. More like business.'

'Business here?'

'In Conch, actually. Do you know it?'

'In Conch?' Greta said, and looked over at Johanna, who ignored her.

'Well, actually, in a little place called Ballyroan. It's a few miles outside of Conch, right on the ocean. About ten miles up the coast from here. That's if the bus driver had it right.' She described the place she was talking about, and the strange quality of the whole afternoon was made stranger hearing local words coming out of Shannon's mouth: O'Hara's Bridge, Boreen Thomas, Gavin's creek.

'Pardon?' Greta said again. She stopped herself from kicking Johanna under the table.

'Do you know it?' Shannon asked. She put her fork down and leaned back. 'You two should get into poker, you know that? With those faces?'

'What age are you, if you don't mind my asking,' Johanna said.

Shannon sat up tall and pretended to be grave, 'I am twenty-eight years old. And you?'

Greta watched Johanna consider her answer and could tell by the set of Johanna's mouth that she'd decided on the truth. 'Seventeen,' Johanna said.

'I'm fifteen,' Greta said. 'We're sisters.'

'And who do you know in Ballyroan?' Johanna asked as she propped her elbows on the table and leaned forward.

'I don't know anyone,' Shannon said. She drummed her fingers on the table, pretended for a few seconds that that was as much as she was going to tell. 'I can see I'm not going to get away without divulging everything. It's not so interesting. My mother and father were from there, and I was born there, and now my mother has died and she wanted to be buried there. Anyway, so here I am. No, please, it's okay. Really. She was sick for a long time. You know how people say sometimes it's a blessing? Well this was one of those times. The arrangements have been made, and she'll be buried the day after tomorrow.'

'I'm sorry,' said Johanna, breathless.

Greta stopped herself from asking where they put the dead body on the plane.

Lily remembered the O'Clery family well, particularly Shannon's mother, who was expecting Shannon around the same time Lily was expecting Jack. They were one of the first families to leave, and after that the departures kept up at such a heavy rate that at the time, Lily felt she could really miss only the ones who'd left most recently. To miss everyone at once, to look up and down the road at the boarded-up houses nearly swallowed by grass, and to think of every single person who used to live in Ballyroan would be too much.

'What are they to us, Mammy?' Greta wanted to know. 'Relations?' Johanna wanted to know too, from the look on her face. Shannon O'Clery must have made an impression. Yes, Lily told them, the O'Clerys were related to the Cahills, just as all of Ballyroan was related, with the exception of Mr Grady. Not first cousins, of course, not second or third. Not once removed, twice removed, or however the sequence worked. Just related, which meant that their parents and grandparents had lived in the same place and had helped each other.

It was understood between Johanna and Greta from the moment they left the guest to her room and mounted their bicycles to start for home that Shannon would end up staying with them. She had no bicycle, the bus went only twice a week, and those navy blue heels proved that this was not a person who was going to walk ten miles to a funeral. It was a shame, taking Mr Breen's one and only overnight paying guest away from him, but when the time came, he actually seemed to feel that a burden had been lifted. 'Go on,' he urged, not knowing Shannon had already accepted the invitation. There was a man in Conch with a Ford, who would come fetch her and drive her out to Ballyroan for a small fee. Mr Breen arranged it.

The girls arrived at the inn just after dawn, served Shannon breakfast, and sent her off. She was hesitant when she realized they wouldn't be with her, but they assured her that they'd be along later and that their mother had been looking forward to it all the night before.

Lily kept lookout from the front window of the cottage, and when she heard an engine, she made her way up to the coast road so the Ford wouldn't have to turn down the Cahills' narrow lane to be scraped by brambles. Little Tom had already moved his few things to the hay shed, where he'd sleep probably more comfortably than he did in his own stuffy room. The girls would move to his room, and Shannon would take their room, which was the driest and brightest in the cottage.

'Well, welcome home,' Lily said as the car door opened, embracing Shannon the moment she stepped out. Shannon returned the embrace and felt in danger of tears for the first time since stepping on the tarmac of Shannon Airport and smelling turf and manure and all the things her mother had told her smelled so good, although Shannon had never believed her. She'd not known where to wait for the coffin, so she stayed by the plane and ignored the drizzle until finally a teenage boy approached to say that they'd received the shipment that had accompanied her and it would arrive in Conch by airline lorry in two days' time.

'The shipment?' Shannon had asked. 'You mean my mother?' She had not meant to embarrass the boy.

'Yes,' the boy said as his ears grew inflamed. 'The body. Your mother.'

'Now,' Lily said as they made their way up the path, 'I wasn't much of a writer, but I thought of your mother often over the years. You're a good girl to bring her home. Did she ever mention me?'

'Oh, yes,' Shannon said. It wasn't a lie, exactly. Whenever her mother mentioned Ballyroan, she meant the people there as much as the landscape, and though Shannon couldn't remember her mother mentioning Lily Cahill by name, she did talk about the cottage closest to the ocean, with the river cutting through the back field. It was like an island, in a way, her mother had said, with the ocean in front and the river curving around behind. Shannon smoothed her skirt across her lap and for the second time in two days drew from the local words her parents had braided into their lives in Queens. Words that, oddly, made sense in that crowded place, where everyone, every single day, talked about home, and where home always meant somewhere else.

Greta came to two conclusions after sorting through Shannon's bag. First, Shannon would be leaving fairly soon after the funeral. She hadn't brought enough clothes to stay longer, and everyone knew that Yanks wore different clothes every day. The second was that there must be nice shops in Queens. Shannon had a few scarves that felt slippery and cool when Greta reached them at the bottom of her case. She had lipsticks, creams, powders, silk stockings. She had a bag that said BAMBERGER'S across the front, and inside that bag Greta found two necklaces, one of round wooden beads painted black, the other a thick silver chain. She had a silver cuff bracelet. She had a clear plastic case that held a pair of black eyelashes – two half-moons next to each other, the same distance apart as real eyes would be, making the box look as if it were sleeping. She had two bottles of nail polish, one clear, one cherry red.

Sitting on her own bed with Shannon's things spread in a half circle around her, Greta listened once more to make sure no one had come back to the house early. She thought she heard a knock at the front door, but she dismissed it. A few seconds later she thought she heard a man call out, but she decided it was her imagination: Little Tom was out driving the cattle from an upper field to a lower field, staying close to the herd in case one of the cows began calving and needed him to wrap his strong arms around the calf's legs and pull it out of her. Lily had announced at breakfast that she was taking Shannon to town to introduce her to people who'd known her parents, and the three younger Cahills had looked up from their bread and butter and tried not to look too surprised. Greta only half believed it until she saw Lily take her change purse from the box over the fire and wrap her shawl around her shoulders. Soon after they left, Johanna had gone down to the ocean for a swim.

Greta began lining Shannon's things up in the order they would re-enter the case. The balls of the wood necklace clacked against each other, the glass bottles of the nail polishes clinked. She shouldn't have done it, opened Shannon's case to look at everything, but there it was, and the house was empty, and what harm was it? Shannon had so many pretty things Greta wondered if she'd miss something small. Maybe one of the scarves; she left it to the side. Shannon would think she took only two from America. She'd think, Did I take all three, or did I leave that royal blue one on my bed at home?

'No!' Greta said out loud, and quickly pushed everything back into the suitcase, including the blue scarf, making a sloppy job of it at first but then willing herself to calm down, go slower, do it right. Shannon was a guest, here for her mother's funeral, and for all Greta knew, she might have saved for months for those scarves. Might have gotten them as a gift from her mother right before she died. Might have borrowed them for the trip and then have to explain herself when she got back to America. Greta shut the suitcase, fastened it, stood it on its side under the window, where she'd found it. As she stepped back, glad she'd come to the right decision, she thought she heard something again. She froze, tried to think of a reason she could give for being in Shannon's room. As she looked around, she noticed that she'd forgotten to return a small hairbrush to the case. She cursed silently and tried to stay still. Yes, there were footsteps along the side of the house, and then the singular sound of the back door brushing against the gritty floor as it was pushed open. Greta waited, listened for a clue that would tell her which one of them had come back, but whoever it was was being very quiet. Just as she began to doubt that she'd heard anything at all, she heard a man's voice again, not Tom's, calling out as if to announce himself. As quietly as she could, Greta reopened Shannon's case, dropped the brush inside, and moved as far away from it as the small room would allow. She opened the bedroom door and slipped into the hall. Just as she was about to call out, hopeful that it was just Johanna back from her swim – ravenous, cold to the bone, moody that the temperature had dropped – but at the same time sure that it was not, she heard the sweep of the door again and footsteps running fast around the side of the house.

Half an hour later, Johanna did come back; she burst through the back door in her damp clothes, her lips blue and trembling. 'Guess what?' she said as she pulled off her shoes and socks and dropped her long wool cardigan to the floor. She hung her sopping underwear in front of the stove. She peeled off her skirt, her blouse, her undershirt, until she was completely naked. Greta was not used to seeing her sister's body in the light of the kitchen's north-facing window, and the sight of the gooseflesh on Johanna's skin made Greta shiver. 'We have a Peeping Tom.'

'You're making it very easy for him,' Greta said.

'Not here. Down at the water. Someone standing there watching me. A man. I only wanted a quick dip but I couldn't get out of the water until I was sure he was well gone.' She picked up the afghan from its place on the back of Big Tom's chair and wrapped it around her shoulders. 'They haven't come back yet, have they?' she asked. Greta shook her head, rolled her eyes. A little late for that question, now that they would have seen all there was to be seen.

'Did anyone come round here? Any strangers?'

Greta hesitated and then chose the easiest route. 'No,' she said.

The coffin arrived in Conch just as the airline promised it would, and from there it was transferred to the hearse that brought it to Ballyroan.

They all went to the funeral, plus five of the old ones from Conch. It was quieter than most funerals, and all Greta could think about as she stared at the gleaming wooden box was how far it had come. First the place inside New York City called Queens, and inside Queens a place called Woodside, then the hospital, then a memorial service in America, then a trip to Idlewild Airport, then thousands of miles across the Atlantic, then Shannon Airport, then the long ride to Ballyroan.

Johanna, Greta, Lily, and Little Tom all noted to themselves that Mrs O'Clery was buried next to Julia Ward. They also noted that on Julia's grave was a bundle of fresh wildflowers, but of the four Cahills, only Greta and Johanna looked at the bundle – it was dewy, as if the flowers were still rooted in the ground, not a wilted one in the bunch – and thought of the strange man standing on the shore. Privately, Greta also thought about the sounds she had heard from their own back room. On the other end of the graveyard, up at the highest point of the sloping land, where a single tree had grown bent in the wind, lay Big Tom.

As they walked back to the house, Johanna fell into step beside Shannon and looped her arm through the older woman's arm. Shannon found all this attention from Johanna flattering and thought it was funny that the girl seemed to have the impression that Queens was an exotic place. After days of Johanna's questions and requests for more stories, Shannon realized how little her mother must have known about America before leaving Ireland. Many days, at home in Woodside, it was all Shannon could do to get up in the morning, press her uniform, get herself to work at the medical clinic on time, and get out to the bars and the community center once in a while to catch up with her girlfriends and meet a few guys. All of that, plus classes at the community college, had seemed like a lot, yet her mother had done all of that and more in a place that must have felt totally foreign to her. Thinking of Queens, now that her mother was buried, made Shannon eager to get back. What would she be like now, she wondered, if her parents had decided to stay? She couldn't imagine mustering up Johanna's energy in this lonely place, but she didn't see herself much like Greta either. Poor Greta, who, most days, didn't quite seem to know where she was.

'Will we walk up to the sea ledge?' Johanna asked. 'The wind is calm, and you must go once before you go home.'

Shannon followed Johanna's lead as she powered her way to the top. Greta tried to catch up to them, but Lily took her wrist and leaned on her all the way back to the cottage.

'What do you think they're talking about?' Greta asked as Johanna's and Shannon's silhouettes got smaller and smaller.

'Not the price of eggs,' Lily said as she eyed the backs of the two girls. 'Not the weather either.'

'What then?' Greta asked. But she knew. America. What people did for work and what kind of dinners they ate at night and where they drove in their cars. Johanna had been greedy for stories of Shannon's life since the moment she'd stepped into the inn.

'Come on,' Lily said. 'I'm dying for a cup of tea.'

Just before Shannon left, she dipped into her suitcase of slippery scarves and clacking necklaces like Santa in his sack. She had planned on staying at a hotel the whole time she was in Ireland and had not planned on thank-you gifts. 'It's not much,' she said as she handed Lily a small bottle of perfume. She doubted Lily would ever use it – a twelve-dollar bottle of Chantilly from Gimbels – and she'd gone back and forth that morning in the room they'd given her over whether Lily would even realize how nice a gift it was. If Lily was anything like Shannon's mother, the bottle would sit on Lily's dresser gathering dust for the next two decades. She gave Johanna and Greta each a scarf, red with small white polka dots for Johanna, solid royal blue for Greta, who, upon accepting, said, 'You gave the two prettiest away.'

'I have nothing remotely masculine,' Shannon said in Tom's direction, and smiled as his windburned neck and cheeks turned a deeper shade of red. 'And this,' she said, handing a card to Johanna. 'It's my address and telephone number in New York should you ever come to visit. Any of you.'

She imagined the card propped up on Johanna's dresser like the perfume on Lily's – to be looked at and admired but never used.

Lily swept in and kissed Shannon on the crown of her head. She squeezed the girl's hands together until the knuckles cracked. Greta was about to shoo her mother away, tell her to leave the poor girl alone, when she noticed Johanna still holding the small white card in both hands like the priest holds up the Communion wafer. 'Go on,' Greta said, nudging her sister with her hip. The rest of them were already outside, walking toward the black Ford that would bring Shannon to the bus. 'I'm going,' Johanna said, shoving the card into the pocket of her skirt and hurrying outside.

Later that evening, as they sat in a circle of light cast by the sixty-watt bulb, Lily said she'd miss Shannon, that the girl was a breath of fresh air, and wouldn't the girls miss her too? Yes, thought Greta, there was certainly a hole left behind in Shannon's absence – a big hole that had taken a place at the table, pulled a chair right up to the fire, and was shaped just like America.

Five

Michael Ward noticed the bicycle on the caravan's first day in the Burren, before they had even set up camp. It had a white frame, which was unusual, and handlebars set wide so a rider could pedal without leaning forward. The chrome fenders were shining and the black rubber tires clean, as if the bicycle had dropped from the sky just to twinkle and catch Michael's eye in the late evening sun. It leaned against the mud-splashed gable of the first pub they'd seen in many miles, and Michael knew that wherever Dermot chose to camp would be within easy distance of this pub. An Bhoireann could not be crossed in a single day. Not by the old ones. Not by the ones who were too small to keep up but too heavy to carry. There were no trees in the Burren, few pastures, no bog, just slabs of limestone as far as the eye could see. Dermot claimed that there were rivers hidden beneath the bald landscape, that they flowed underground through caves and tunnels. As Michael walked, he tried to listen for the water rushing beneath his feet.

The Wards were on their way from Ennis to Kilkee, where one of their women would be married and handed off to her husband's people. Sometimes new husbands or wives joined up with the Wards, sometimes the new couple went to the in-laws. It was all a question of need, and in this case, the husband's people needed more women. The bride-to-be was young, only fifteen, and Dermot said that circumstance alone would be her dowry. Maeve had also gotten married at fifteen and now, three years later, had two girl children. Sometimes Michael watched Maeve and wondered what life would have been like as a girl. They had shared their mother's womb, swam in there together for nine months, split everything fifty-fifty, and then when the cards were revealed, he came out a boy and she a girl. The two little ones roared at her all day and, when the older one could walk, toddled after her as if she were attached by a string. Maeve had gotten fat. She wore her skirts too tight, too short. Their mother would have had plenty to say about it, and about the way Maeve once left the younger baby on the ground, where she rolled off down a slope, under a wooden fence, and could have been stomped by one of the grazing cows if Michael had not seen the empty blanket lying in the grass.

Michael had been through the Burren only once before that he could remember. The campsite was a short stretch of earth and wind-eaten grass cordoned off by the government in an attempt to keep travellers off the roads. As Michael looked off into the distance, the limestone clints and grikes backlit by the setting sun, he realized that this might be the last stretch of grass for many miles, and when they started moving again, it would be up to the animals to find knots of green at the side of the road.

Normally, Dermot did not like to stop at these camps. He didn't like the particular designation, the poles set up special for tethering animals, the stones already arranged in neat circles to hold traveller fires, a well to the back of the site with the hand pump painted red in case they would miss it. 'Only one half step until they've pushed us into flats in Ennis,' Dermot usually complained, but this time he whistled to the boys who'd gone ahead and used his thumb to jab the air, just once, in the direction of the camp. 'Two nights,' he said to Michael as he took off his cap and rubbed his head.

It was evening, almost completely dark, and within five minutes of turning off the road, the youngest boys had already set to work milking the goats. The women with infant children sat down on the sparse grass and unbuttoned their blouses as they pulled their babies into their laps. The oldest woman of the group – Grandmother, they called her, though to most of them she was a great-aunt – continued her work on a piece of lace for the bride-to-be. The rest of the women peeled potatoes and carrots. One woman unwrapped a large section of smoked pork loin from the grub box and began dividing it into portions. As they prepared supper, they discussed what would have to be done once they arrived in Kilkee. There was a wedding cake to be made and the ingredients to be begged. For fifty guests they needed two dozen eggs, two pounds of sweet butter, eight cups of sugar, and five pounds of flour just to make the inside of the cake. For the frosting, ingredients would have to be bought. And they'd have to protect these ingredients as they gathered them. The little ones would take spoonfuls of the sugar and pour it onto their tongues if they knew no one would catch them. Michael, who was far too old for such theft, had been caught and boxed for eating a spoonful of sugar as recently as his sixteenth birthday. Then there were the cake decorations: colored paper flowers, enough satin ribbon to circle the base of each tier. As the women fretted over what they might be forgetting, they also discussed how in their day a wedding cake always meant a fruitcake, which could be made six months ahead and tucked into the bottom of a trunk until the wedding day came. Not anymore. The young ones now had their heads turned by shop windows that displayed pure white three-tiered cakes that looked like they'd blow away in the wind as soon as they met with the blade of a knife.

In addition to planning the ingredients they'd need, the women also reminded the bride-to-be of the things she absolutely musn't forget, just as they'd been reminding her since the day the arrangement was made. Go on, laugh at your old aunties, they told her, but mind you do what we say. 'First,' Grandmother said, taking the girl by the wrist and pulling her close to the sharp angles of her face, her breath like the dank bottom of the grain barrel, 'you'll eat the oatmeal with your husband before any celebration begins. No matter what's going on about you, you'll eat it, and well salted too, for the salt and the oatmeal together is what protects. They're pure useless on their own, you see. Three big spoonfuls of it, and then carry on. Him too. It'll be your first duty as a wife. Second, if there's dancing — and I never saw a wedding where there wasn't — mind you keep one foot on the ground all the time. If you were to jump or hop or do any sort of thing where both feet are off the ground, like if he lifted you up in the air — some husbands do it without thinking, though his people should have him warned — or if one of your brothers should swing you. Fairies love all beautiful things and nothing so much as a bride. Don't smirk at me, girl. You're not too big for a slap on the mouth. Not today, not any day while I'm alive, married or no, are you too big for a slap. You think I'm blind as well as slow? I survived this long because I am wise. As you, please God, will be wise one day. Third, remember not to sing, even if you love the song, even if everyone else's throat is burst from singing . . .'

Michael looked at the bride-to-be, a second cousin, and wondered if she knew what this wedding meant for her. She would be lashed to her husband's people just like a new animal bought at the fair. He stood and strolled away from the light of the fire to where he'd tossed the tarp he'd sleep on. It was a clear night so far, and he decided to chance the weather until morning without building a tent. The rest of the men were busy constructing their low shelters, and as Michael watched the others tap long stakes into the hard earth, lug jugs of water from the well, talk, stir, chop, feed, he wondered if any of them had ever lain awake at night and thought about settling.

There were eighteen in the group now, including the babies, and for supper they divided among three separate fires. 'Soon it will be your wedding we're off to,' Dermot said to Michael as he tucked his fork and knife into his pocket and took his wedge of pork in his hand. 'Did you hear me? Don't you want a warm body next to you at night? Don't you want someone when the wind finds a way beneath the tent flaps?'

Michael knew he was only teasing. Men got married later than women; Maeve's husband was thirty-one. Lately, Dermot's teasing had touched on everything related to females. What kind of shape did Michael like in a woman? What color hair? At every question, Michael shrugged and Dermot laughed. Marriage was practical, Michael knew. It was the way things were done. But for a long time now he had been wondering where a partnership left a person chained more tightly to the camp and to the wagon. Dermot spoke of the travellers' life as if theirs was the only way to live, as if they were the only ones who truly saw the world because they were up to their necks in it, not only when it was dry and fair but also when it was wet and miserable. To Michael it felt like all they ever did was go round and round, with fair days few and far between. A few months back, on the way from Bantry to Kinsale, the caravan had passed a construction site – three identical squares dug into the ground, three wood frames, and two men pouring wet cement from buckets. And just like the gray splatters that had already hardened on the toes of the workers' boots, the concrete foundation would also harden and become an anchor for these structures, keep them from being blown away in the wind. It would be easy to build a house like that, Michael had thought as the group passed by and the two men stopped their work to watch them, and the thought had prodded him forward like an iron taken from the fire and pushed into a goat's flank. Also like the hot iron, the thought marked him, and later, when Dermot shouted for him to hurry up, Michael flinched.

In the morning, Dermot decided they should send a letter to the husband-to-be, letting him know they'd be a few days delayed. Bitty Ward, who'd married Dermot's brother, was the only one among them who could read and write, but she wasn't around to put the letter down for them. Dermot guessed that she'd walked up to the closest house with two of the other women in hopes of getting flour and eggs. The Christmas month in Galway was the only time of the year when traveling children went to school. Officials came down to the riverbank, asked the adults for the names and ages of the children under fourteen, and then directed them to a schoolhouse on the other side of the river. Each year, Dermot Ward went mad at the idea and forbade his children to go. They could already add up what was in the cash box. Why should they go to a goddamned schoolhouse all day to be called names and told all the things that are wrong with them? Before she died, Julia had always found a moment to speak softly to Dermot, to assure him it was no harm for the children to go learn a few things. But after she died, Dermot stood his ground, and Michael was sorry for it. He liked sitting in the schoolhouse. He liked the warmth of the stove, the huge pot of porridge the teacher made for them, the passing around of bowls and spoons. In school, they learned about letters and making words.

Dermot usually gave Bitty money to buy a paper whenever they passed a shop, and at night she would read it to them around the fire. Another few Christmases, Michael believed, and he'd have been able to tell what the sheep and donkey were saying to each other in the comic that ran on the back page.

'Michael,' Dermot said, 'let's go to that pub and see will anyone write a letter for us.'

Dermot came up behind Michael to hurry him as he splashed his face with water and changed into a fresh shirt. 'Quick, before the women ask us to help hang up the wash.'

As they walked the two miles back toward the pub, Dermot with his arms crossed over his chest and his hands tucked into his armpits, as comfortable as if he were stretched out on soft ground, Michael with both hands shoved deep in the pockets of his trousers, Dermot told him about a girl he would meet at the wedding. Dermot had never seen the girl, but she had a motorized camper she'd bought with her own money, and she was looking for a husband. Her father had a painting business – houses, fences, signs, wagons – but had all daughters and needed a young son-in-law to help. The girl was twenty-two and had already been engaged, but that had fallen through for reasons Dermot said Michael should find out.

'I'm only eighteen,' Michael said. Surely, all that jabbing around the fire the evening before about his wedding being next was only teasing. Only the same old teasing that had been going on since he was twelve. Everyone knew that males married older than females. His older brothers had not married until their late twenties. Michael's pace slowed, and Dermot's slowed beside him. Michael looked at his father and saw that his eyes were closed. He had once told Michael that he could sleep while he walked, because his feet knew to follow the road. Michael had tried it and ended up slipping on a fresh cowpat.

'There's no right age for marriage. You marry when the time is right,' Dermot said. He opened his eyes. 'You might see that motorized camper and decide now's the time.'

'I won't,' Michael said, and Dermot smirked, threw up his hands.

'You're handsome, you know,' Dermot said, as if he hadn't heard Michael's protest. It was something he'd been wanting to point out to the boy for some time, in case he wasn't aware or in case he didn't know it was important to some women. 'I'm not good at seeing these things myself, but the women talk, and it's a point they've agreed on. And you know as well as I do what it means when the women agree. Michael Ward is easy on the eyes.'

Dermot looked over to see how Michael had taken this news about himself, but they were just coming up to the ruins of a stone fort they'd passed the day before, and Michael stopped to look. The day before, it had seemed a natural part of the landscape, as permanent as the limestone and the rivers flowing under their feet. But now Michael could see that there was logic to the arrangement. Choices had been made by men, not nature. There was a hole, three feet wide, three feet deep, that could have been a cooking pit. There were mounds of stones piled here and there around the periphery of the site, some arranged in intricate and intentional patterns, and Michael knew that these were burial cairns. There was a long slab of stone set upon two smaller ones, which could have been an altar.

'This has been here since Brian Boru,' Dermot said, stepping carefully around the crumbling walls. He picked up a smaller stone and cracked it against another.

A thousand years, Michael thought as he tried to imagine the fort as it must have been once. He had long ago stopped asking his father how he knew things, never having been to school, never having read or written a single word. 'I know because I have eyes to see and ears to listen,' was all Dermot would say. And then he would ask, as he had asked before, 'You think something has to be written in a book to be true?' Michael went over and stood in the center of what looked like the foundation of a small building – a dwelling for people or for animals – and thought about how even then, even in this place, so old and hard it didn't even look like the earth anymore, people had felt the need to build four walls and a roof to lie down in at the end of each day. They remembered their ancestors, whose graves were marked with stones set into patterns. And when they were far away finding food or fighting battles, they thought of a single place on the face of the earth, a specific place with walls of a particular thickness, land of a particular slope, and when they spoke of this place, they used the ancient word for home.

Julia Ward hadn't wanted to settle any more than her husband, but she had sympathy for the travellers who tried it. She wished them well. And when they failed, she welcomed them back and never held it against them. She also saw more similarities between country people and travellers. Michael recalled being on the road with her one day and seeing two men stop their work to pull bottles of porter out of a cool bog hole. There were no houses nearby, no bicycles, and Julia told Michael that the men must have come over the mountain from one of the bog houses on the other side. 'God bless the work,' Julia had called out to them. 'God bless,' they'd answered. When they passed again, the men had built a small fire and were eating their supper. 'Well, look it,' Julia had said. 'Everyone does what they have to do in this world, don't they, Michaeleen?'

Since Julia's death, the caravan had avoided that part of the country where she was buried. Dermot didn't want to camp out in that direction anymore, didn't want to pass the place on the road where she'd died, didn't want to see those people who had taken her into their cottage and propped her up on a bed and watched his every move as he removed her from the dwelling and took her back to the camp. Also, he pointed out, that sea ledge in Ballyroan was too remote, too far from the village, too abandoned to make a living. If Maeve wondered about their mother's grave – whether it had grown over with weeds, whether the headstone was still standing straight – she never mentioned it. Dermot neither, and perhaps, Michael thought, they carried Julia around with them in other ways. They didn't think of her grave, because that was only her body, only the skin she walked around in. And maybe that marker by the high sea ledge in Ballyroan meant no more to them than any other place they'd been. Maybe his father, who'd known Julia longest after all, recalled his wife equally in every place they'd been together. But since 1956 Michael couldn't forget that his mother was not in all of these places. She was in one place, in Ballyroan. By dying, she'd made herself a country person.

What could be so difficult about settling, Michael had been wondering since seeing those houses built on the Kinsale Road. Not difficult for other people, but difficult for travellers in particular. There were places that had been hard to leave, so what would have been so difficult about deciding to stay for good, building a house, planting a field, seeing the seasons in one single place? Dermot always said it had to do with blood, with something very basic inside them that had nothing to do with the brain or the human ability to reason things out. It was outside of reason. It was just the way things were. A cousin of Dermot's, Peter Ward, had tried settling and had lasted for two years. When he came back to the camp, he said that every night when he went to bed, no matter how cold or wet it was outside, and how grateful he should have felt, and how his wife had gotten used to storing her dishes in the press, and her sugar and flour on the kitchen counter, he always felt as if someone had gotten a rope around his neck. And oftentimes, in the middle of the night, in his warm bed and his dry clothes, he woke up with a feeling that someone was standing on his chest, tightening the noose.

But I'm not like the others, Michael thought as he walked alongside his father. 'Go on, boy,' the older men would urge when they went to the market and he set up his smithing tools. He was supposed to call out to passersby, draw people down to the stall with his voice, but he was no good at yelling and calling. Sometimes he opened his mouth and drew a long breath, but when he went to speak, he didn't know what to say.

The pub was empty except for the bartender, who stopped what he was doing the moment they entered.

'Lost?' he asked, and then glanced over his shoulder to a door that led to a back room. Michael could hear plates being stacked, something heavy being dragged across the wood planks of the floor.

'Never,' Dermot said as he claimed a stool. He ordered two pints, and the bartender waited until he'd put his coins on the bar before he brought them over. Dermot didn't like asking favors of country people, but when he did, there were certain rules he always followed. First, show them they can trust you, which was why Dermot put his money on the bar. Second, show them that you don't trust them, which was why he waited until the man brought back his change before taking his first sip. When he was younger, Michael used to wonder how people always seemed to know right away that they were travellers. Now he guessed it was just something in the way they carried themselves, tired from all the walking. From the back room a second man emerged and wiped his hands on his shirt as he watched Dermot tip his glass to his mouth.

'I wonder can I ask you a question,' Dermot said to the bartender once he'd drained his first pint. 'Do you have any kind of knack with writing?'

'Why? You need a letter put down?' the man asked. Dermot put another coin on the bar, and the man went to the back room and came back with a biro, one sheet of paper, an envelope. He placed them in front of the man who'd earlier emerged from the back. 'Will you put down a letter for them, Ethan?' Ethan shrugged, rolled up his sleeves, licked the tip of the biro, and tested it on the back of his hand. Dermot pushed his glass away and straightened up on his stool as if he were preparing to address a large crowd. He cleared his throat. 'To Mister Liam Costello who is to marry Miss Aoife Ward,' he began. When Dermot finished his dictation, he told the man to address it to the post office in Kilkee. 'Right there on the front, just put the word Hold,' Dermot instructed, and looked closely at the letters the man drew, as if he were making sure.

On their way out, the letter sealed, stamped, and left on the corner of the bar for the postman, Michael noticed the bicycle again. It leaned against a different wall but was just as clean as it appeared the day before. 'Lovely looking bicycle,' he said to Dermot.

'Careful, boy,' Dermot said.

'Careful what? I'm just saying.'

'Well, now you've said, so get on with it,' Dermot said, and with his hands tucked under his arms, he started for camp.

That night, after a supper of oatmeal and currants, Dermot brought up the girl with the motorized camper once more. Michael's cousin's husband, Malachy, was at the same fire, and he said he'd seen the girl a few times. Good-looking, he said. Blond. Good hips. Another cousin at the other side of the fire said he knew the girl too, and what's more he'd seen the camper.

'Will you make an offer?' Malachy asked Dermot.

'We'll see what this lad has to say about that once he meets the girl,' Dermot said, winking at Michael. Michael swallowed what was in his mouth and felt the warm spoonful slide down his throat to his belly. Then he stood and scraped the rest of his oatmeal into Malachy's bowl. The night air smelled like rain, and he set to work building his tent.

Later that night, Michael heard rustling outside his tent and lifted the flap to find his father stretched out on the damp ground. 'We need turf,' Dermot said without moving. Michael raised his eyebrows and thought of the last bog they'd passed, more than twenty miles back. 'That place,' Dermot said, referring to the house that had earlier turned Bitty and the other women away. 'They'll have it somewhere.'

'Now?' Michael asked. There was a harvest moon, yellow and close. In answer, Dermot jumped to his feet and brushed off his backside.

He waited in the road as Michael pulled on his boots, stretched his jacket tight over his thick sweater, and just managed to get the button in the hole. The moon made a bright path of the road, and Michael shook the sleep off his limbs to match his father's pace. It was the hour of night when the world always seemed haunted to Michael, their ponies turned to kelpies, their women turned to banshees, and Dermot, paces ahead, collar pulled tight against the back of his neck, was the spirit who spit and hummed and picked his teeth with his longest fingernail.

They found the turf shed just a few yards away from the house, and Dermot reached under the rusted, sagging tin roof that came up to his chest and passed piece after to piece to Michael. From somewhere in the dark hills behind the house a sheep bleated, and another answered. 'We have enough,' Michael said when he could hold no more, but Dermot untucked his shirt and filled that too. The turf was damp in Michael's arms, and he wondered if it would be dry enough to burn so soon. 'Enough,' Michael said again when he saw that Dermot was still reaching for more. He thought of the day in Achill when the *gardai* came to arrest Dermot for stealing eight lobsters from the fishermen's traps. It was before Julia died – how long before, Michael couldn't remember – and they'd all feasted on the lobster with butter and salt. After, her lips still rimmed with butter, Julia had walked circles around the wagons, asking aloud why he hadn't stopped at one or two. Michael had driven his tongue into the gaps between his teeth as he watched her, hoping to find one last piece of fish.

As they walked home, careful to keep close to the ditch in case any-one should pass, the moon so bright above the empty landscape that it was easy to imagine they were alone in the world, Michael decided to ask the question he'd been thinking of asking now for many weeks. Dermot was humming in low tones, and Michael waited until he stopped and then took his chance.

'What if I wanted to settle?' he asked. He felt a piece of turf slide out of his arms to the ground, but he ignored it. He hadn't meant to blurt the question out like that. He meant to bide his time, to raise the subject gradually over several months. But then Dermot had thrown off his plan with talk of a blond girl with a motorized camper, and he felt that the question couldn't wait any longer. Sometimes the dream of settling seemed like an idea that had just come to him, a seed blown in the wind that had landed and taken root. Other times he could look many years back and remember Maeve accusing him of wishing for a bed in the country houses they passed, wishing to go to a settled school, wishing for a barn and a field of his own. After Julia's funeral so many years ago, after all the mourners had left, Michael had crawled into Maeve's tent to tell her about the cottage by the river, the short hall with doors that led to different rooms, the smell of bread coming from behind one of the doors, the windows that allowed a person to look out onto the world from the inside. Even then, Maeve had been offended by his admiration for the cottage and had asked if he thought he was too good to do as his people had always done. And though he'd denied it when accused, as he had denied the same accusation since then, he knew he had wished for those things, or at least wondered about them, felt curious enough to want to try them.

Now that he'd said it, he pushed on. 'No, don't say anything. Listen. What if I wanted to get one of those little attached houses and try it? I'm serious.'

'Michaeleen,' Dermot said. 'No more than a country person can become a traveller, a traveller cannot settle. It's been tried! You think you're the first that's liked the look of those government houses? And it's failed over and over and over and over. First, your people have been travellers for a thousand years. Did you hear what I said? Second, you think people won't see you as a traveller just because you live in a house?'

'But why would I care how they see me, as long as I live in the house and earn my living and come home at the end of every day?'

'Michaeleen, you're my son, but you're no more than a newborn sometimes. Worse. You're like the foal who thinks he's a stallion. Now' – he stopped to get a better grip on the tails of his shirt – 'I won't hear this again.'

Then I won't ask again, Michael thought, and instead listened for the water flowing through the caves carved out of the earth below them and beside them, untouched by sun, untouched by a moon so close it seemed the earth had spun out of position. He imagined the gaping mouths of the caverns, guarded by sharp and craggy teeth. He smelled rain in the air and wondered if the underground rivers ever overflowed their banks.

When morning came, the women decided it was too wet to leave. The rain lashed down like it was blown straight out of the ocean, and when Michael licked his lips, he tasted salt. The rain and wind were blowing from the west, so Michael drove two stakes into the ground and draped their heaviest oilcloth across like a sail. On the east side of the stakes, he moved the stones of the ring closer together and then laid down a grid of sticks, five one way, five the other, the way the women laid the reeds before they wove baskets. When the grid was three layers above the damp ground, he went to the wagon that carried his tools, drew out four short planks he'd been saving, and leaned these planks over the turf and kindling so the rain would slide down and away. Holding a plastic tarp over his head, he crouched in front of the fire until it grew big enough to warm him. Once he was warm enough to get wet and cold again, he set out for a walk.

When he got to the pub, the bicycle was in the same place it had been when he pointed it out to Dermot. After a quick look around, without any real plan, he gently kicked the back tire. He took hold of the handlebars and kicked the front tire. He lifted the bike and bounced it against the ground. He reached down, spun one of the pedals, and listened for a healthy tic-tic-tic as they whizzed around and around. He looked behind him at the door of the pub and then in front of him at the miles of limestone, its weather-polished surface gleaming in the rain. He expected someone to shout at him, ask what he was doing with a bicycle that was not his, but there was no sign of the bartender from the day before, no sign of the man called Ethan who'd written their letter. I'll just test it, he thought, swinging his leg over the crossbar.

The seat was the perfect height for him, and without allowing himself to think, he put his head down and pushed the pedals. After a while the pub disappeared; the Burren became an ocean of hardened rock. He cycled as hard and as fast as his lungs and legs would allow. Village after village fell behind him like a curtain that had been yanked aside, and the same for field after field. Uphill, downhill, the smell of seawater came and went as the road bent toward the ocean, then away again. No one stopped him, no one shouted after him, and by the time he slowed down, sweat-soaked and lungs burning, he'd reached Galway.

Outside Galway City, more than forty miles from the pub where he began, he rested under a tree in an empty field. The rain had stopped hours before. He could see the lit-up windows of a house just beyond the field, but it was growing dark, and no one would be out again that evening. He could go back, catch up with the caravan as they were leaving, or take his time and catch up with them in the Midlands in a few weeks' time. He wondered if they'd hear of the stolen bicycle, if the man in the pub would go marching straight up to the camp looking for him. His stomach rumbled, and it dawned on him that he was alone, without money, without food. It rumbled again, and he fell back on the old wisdom: when there's no food to quiet a hungry belly, go to sleep and eat in your dreams.

He woke the next morning to a crick in his neck and a sharp pain in his side. He pissed against the tree he'd slept under, making sure to keep the thick trunk between himself and the house beyond. After buttoning his pants, he raked his fingers through his oily hair. He folded the blackened cuffs of his shirt so that they were hidden beneath the sleeves of his jacket. He put his fingers in his mouth and did his best to clean under his fingernails by biting and licking away the grit. He broke a twig off the tree to finish the job. He ignored the uncomfortable dampness of morning dew in his clothes and walked the bicycle up to the house. Begging was women's work in his clan, but in others, where women were scarce or unwell or too busy, it sometimes fell on the men to go out. He'd watched Maeve long enough to know that the trick was to offer a service – mending, hauling, handiwork – but that was only to show they weren't lazy and if the country person gave them something for free, that was his own choice. He observed the house from a distance and then up close. It was small but well kept, with fresh whitewash, decent curtains in the window. He expected a woman to answer, so when a young man came to the door, a boy, really, younger than Michael, his plan went out the window.

'Howaya,' Michael said, friendly, as if they'd met before. The boy raised his eyebrows and waited. It was sneaky, Michael knew, pretending to know the boy, acting familiar. Country people already thought travellers were too sneaky. Honest and straightforward was best. 'I'm starving,' Michael said, and immediately regretted his choice of words. Travellers also had a reputation for exaggeration. 'I cycled all day yesterday, and I've another day of it ahead. Can you spare any bread?'

The boy looked him up and down. 'Did ye sleep in the field?'

'It's just myself.'

'Is it a tinker, you are? Traveling alone?'

Michael surprised himself. 'I'm no tinker,' he said, smiling, 'but I suppose I have all the markings. I been on the go for so long without a shave or a change of clothes. I'm from up Conch way, from Ballyroan.' He stopped, but the boy was still looking at him. 'I was robbed. I was lucky to get away with my bicycle.'

The boy nodded, held up his hand for Michael to wait where he was standing. Michael heard a low voice from inside the house, also male, and then he saw the boy cross the hall into what must be the kitchen. He left the kitchen door open and Michael could see the boy's elbow and forearm reaching for an empty jar. He saw the boy's knee bend as he dipped the jar into a milk bucket that was out of sight. When the boy came back, he was carrying half a loaf of brown bread and a cut of pork along with the house-warm milk. 'The ole one's having an off day,' the boy said, passing off the items one by one. 'Cancer of the stomach.' When he'd handed Michael everything and they stood there looking at each other, he added, 'My two brothers are out back. They could be here in half a second if I shouted for them. For the ole one. They keep an ear out. Drink up the milk here if you don't mind. It's the last jar.'

Michael bowed his head and thanked him for the food, taking care not to look inside the little house in case the boy saw some kind of want in his expression and misunderstood. He wondered if the boy's brothers really were out back, or if there were any brothers at all.

'And look it,' the boy said just as Michael was lifting the jar to his mouth. 'If you're trying to pass yourself off as a local, you'd better start talking like the west of Ireland. You tinkers have the strangest way of talking. It's from everyplace, isn't it? All mixed up. Just now I heard Dublin, Cork, Donegal, and a little bit of Connemara, all jammed in together. So eat up your bread and mind what I said. Leave the jar whenever you've finished.'

Michael sat on the stone wall at the side of the house and ate every last crumb of what the boy had given him. How old could the boy be? Twelve? Thirteen? Just like a little old man, with his advice and his way of watching. Michael drank all the milk, and after looking around for a place to rinse out the jar, he gave up and left it on the wall, its thin white film clinging to the glass. He walked his bicycle to the road and oriented himself. Behind was the direction he'd just come from, ahead and slightly left was the direction he needed to go if he was really going to go through with it. What was there to go through with? he asked himself as he lifted one leg over the bar of the bike. What was wrong with a son visiting his mother's grave? There was nothing wrong with it, nothing at all, and yet the more he insisted on the rightness of it, the more he feared he'd done – or was about to do – something to his father and to the rest of them that would be unforgivable once he returned. Dermot would tell them, Michael supposed, about what he had said about settling, and they would be disgusted, Maeve in particular, who looked on everything he did as if it were an extension of her own actions.

Back in that desolate landscape, they'd have gathered close around the fire and talked about him all night, how closed he was, how no one ever knew what Michael Ward was thinking, and how he'd probably been preparing himself to leave for many years, planning it, saving little bits of money, and one among them might point out that if this was the case, Michael Ward was far shrewder than they'd ever given credit for. Then they'd think on that for a while, and Dermot would point out that no one knew whether he'd left for good. Dermot would remind them to think back on themselves at eighteen and the foolish things they'd done, the men in particular, and with all the attention Maeve had gotten in the last few years – don't forget things were different with twins.

But Michael hadn't planned anything. The possibility of leaving, of actually, physically, striking out and doing it, had not come to him until that first time he saw the bicycle leaning against the gable. No. In truth, he couldn't really say it had come to him then either. He didn't even understand that he'd left until he'd reached Galway and rested and felt the spikes of hunger in his belly and the dampness the field had left in his clothes. Even now, a day later, headed farther west on the same bicycle, he didn't know whether he was leaving or had left or was just taking a few days out of the routine. I'll catch up with them in the Midlands, he told himself. But like his thoughts on visiting his mother's grave, the more he insisted on one way of looking at the thing, the more false that one way seemed.

To pass the time as he cycled out to Ballyroan, he counted the electricity poles and remembered hearing that those very same poles had once been trees as far away as Norway and Finland. As he closed in on Conch, he expected the poles to fall away, the wires strung through the air to reach their boundary, but they didn't. Where there was one, he could always look into the distance and find the next one, and the next and the next. He skirted Conch village and headed straight for Ballyroan. For the first time in years he thought of those two strange girls who had lived out there the year Julia died, the way they'd watched him, how they'd spied on the camp in the middle of the night, the way the older one asked question after question while the younger one shivered in her thin nightdress and her wet feet before turning and running away. Then seeing them again in Galway just a few months later, the older one greeting him as if they were relations, dragging him along the quay to say hello to the younger one, who once again seemed frightened by her surroundings, as if the action on the pier had come to her, and not her to it. They were lonely, Michael realized now, and wondered why it had not occurred to him at the time.

The road to the sea was shorter than he remembered it, the curves arriving sooner. The abandoned houses were still abandoned, and a few were slung so low and were so wet and black and grown over that they'd become as much a part of the landscape as the mountains and the bog. He had to look twice and say to himself, That's a house, and there, that's another. The thought of needing to eat again soon was growing stronger by the mile, but he kept going, pressing the pedal with all his weight as the road began to tilt up toward the sea ledge. He dropped the bicycle to the ground just outside the flimsy gate of the cemetery. The ground was so uneven that he had to take hold of a headstone now and again as he negotiated the slope and the wet grass. Unlike the cemeteries in towns or cities, here there were no neat rows, no aisles, and to get to one grave, a person had to walk on many others. Many of the headstones were worn down to stumps.

The first thing he noticed when he reached her grave was the thin green film that covered the light stone. He reached out and touched it, rubbing the slimy matter with his fingertips. It was one of the only headstones without a name stamped across the top, and after looking at it for a while, examining how well the mound of dirt that covered her had leveled out, he wondered what to do next. It crossed his mind that a prayer would be the thing, but he'd never prayed by himself without being told, without joining in with a dozen or more other voices. Then he noticed the fresh dirt just beside his mother and the yawning hole beyond. A new arrival expected. Tomorrow, from the looks of it. His thoughts leaped to the cottage by the river and how they were the only family that would still bury its dead in this place.

Up at the top of the slope was a wind-bent and knobby hawthorn tree that looked as if it were pointing back at Ireland. Michael walked up to it, again stepping over grave after grave, doing his best to stay at the edges and take broad strides. He broke a small, leaf-heavy branch from the tree and went back to scrub some of the green veil from Julia's headstone. He rubbed and scratched until he had warmed up again, eventually dropping the useless branch and using the rough tweed of his jacket sleeve. When he had done as much as he could, he walked in a wide circle, gathering wildflowers and then a long blade of grass to tie them together.

It was beginning to feel impossible to go a single step more without eating. Catching a fish might take hours, and he had no line and no net, and the thought of the water when he was already so cold made him shiver and feel sorry for himself. 'Well what do you expect?' he demanded, casting the words hungry, tired, sore, and cold from his thoughts. Then, at the height of his frustration, he had a thought that stopped him. There was another option, one that didn't require getting wet. He half wished he hadn't thought of it, but now that he had, he couldn't turn away. Stomach turning in dread, he got back on the bicycle, which he'd begun to think of as his own, and coasted down the hill to the rocky beach at the bottom. There they were, the rocks he remembered, standing at high tide. And yes, there too were the spots of grayish white covering the rock, covering all the rocks at high tide, a feast of barnacles for the taking. He willed himself to do what he'd seen his father and his uncles do a thousand times. He got up close to the rock, leaned in to examine the little creatures, then pried off a middle-sized one and pulled it out of its shell. Dermot ate them alive, killing them with his teeth and swallowing them down just the same as if they'd been fried in a pan full of sweet butter. But at the moment Michael was about to put it in his mouth, he found he couldn't, and instead he squeezed it between his palms good and hard until he was sure it was dead. He put it in his mouth and thought he felt it move. He spit. If I could get hold of a pot or a pan, he thought. If I could build a fire.

As he called himself every harsh name he could think of and geared up to try it again, he heard a splash. He looked out at the water and saw a person swimming, male or female he couldn't tell, just a pair of pale arms and a dark head. He looked around to see if anyone was watching him and noticed a heap of clothes lying just beyond the reach of the water. Women's shoes. He looked out again at the water, and the person had stopped swimming. Her head bobbed in place, and he couldn't tell if she was just resting or whether she was looking at him. He hurried away.

Back on the road, he could just make out the roof of the cottage where he'd first seen his mother dead. Cahill was their name. What could he do but ask? They would remember him, surely. How many dead travellers had they given shelter to in their day? He turned in on the narrow road, the weeds and bushes pushing in from both sides to a degree he hadn't remembered from before, and he went straight up to their door. He knocked and waited. Knocked again. Waited. Shouted 'Hallo?' toward the side of the house before walking around to the back and knocking again. He gave up knocking and listened. A bolt of nervous energy shot from his stomach to his groin, then up again to the back of his neck. I'll just take something to hold me over, whatever's on the counter. They were decent sort of people and will understand, and I'll come back tomorrow and I'll tell them. He pushed open the door, called out one last time, and, after waiting for a moment, stepped inside.

The door led to a back room kitchen, small, just a counter and a few flimsy cabinets. There was an electric cooker sitting out, an electric teakettle, and a small refrigerator that hummed softly and was so pristinely white it seemed out of place. There was a full loaf of bread sitting out, and when he laid his hand on it, it was still warm. He cut four thick slices from the loaf and smeared butter onto each. He looked for some kind of meat – more pork like he'd had that morning, or cured beef, or salmon. Surely a cottage this close to the river had salmon to bring them through the season, but no matter where he looked, he couldn't find anything. He thought of the hens he'd heard clucking on his way around the house, but he pushed the thought out of his mind. He took four eggs instead, filled a jar with milk. He pushed the swinging door open just a crack and looked into a room with a table, four chairs, a fireplace, and a larger cushioned chair pulled up close to the fireplace, which was now cold. He listened for a moment, then tiptoed across the room. He swiped a book of matches off the mantel and a few pieces of turf from the pile. Once in the back room again, he thought he heard a creak – like a footstep or a door being pushed open slowly, carefully. He froze, his arms full of the things he'd gathered, and he waited, breathing as quietly as his pounding heart would allow. It would be better to call out, he told himself. It would be better to announce myself and say I called out once before. More than once, in fact. His thigh muscle began to twitch. It would be better to put these things back, go round front, and try again.

After a few seconds passed and he did not hear another sound, Michael let himself out the door he'd come in and, crouching low as he passed the windows, ran off into the closest field, careful not to drop anything.

That night, he decided to sleep indoors in one of the derelict cottages. If he hadn't been so bone cold, the heavy iron padlock on the door would have been comical against the rotted wood that flopped open with one kick of his travel-weary legs. Inside was a scene halfway between two worlds. To the right of the door the roof had caved in, letting a generation's worth of weather and bird shit in upon the single bare mattress and single wooden chair. To the left was a table, a mirror spotted with mold but still hanging, an iron pot sitting where a fire would have roared, a broom leaning in the corner. After taking an inventory of the house, everything precisely where the occupants had left it except for the half the weather had claimed, he went out once more to gather more turf from one of the neat stacks at the side of the road, and to see if the old well still had water.

He tested the old well rope and retied the knot that held the bucket. He leaned as far as he could into the dark hole and sniffed. He stood and lowered the bucket, hoping there was enough rope, giving it just a few inches at a time. As he waited and hoped, he spoke to himself out loud for the second time that afternoon. 'Tomorrow I'll go straight over and tell them what I done.'

He heard a gentle slap and felt the rope resist his grip as the bucket filled with water. Fighting his own greed, he forced himself to pull it up early, hand over hand, careful to keep the bucket from banging against the sides.

As he lifted the bucket to his mouth, tilting it too high so that the water sloshed out and ran into his nose, he thought of the girl's name. He hadn't been trying to remember it, but there it was. She must have been the one swimming, head bobbing in the waves, squinting and craning her neck toward shore as she'd squinted and craned that night on the road and again when he'd gone to help collect Julia's body. Yes, in Galway too. Her stained face, her arms stretched out like a child acting the bird, ready to take flight. Greta.

Six

Within hours of Shannon O'Clery's departure from Ballyroan with her single suitcase and her passport zipped into the inner pocket of her purse, it began to rain. It was the kind of heavy, beating rain that usually kept up for only a quarter of an hour before tapering, but that night, and right up until daybreak the next morning, it poured and poured, flattening the brambles and the high grass around the cottage so that it looked like Little Tom had been out there all night dragging the old curragh back and forth. The hedges, too, looked like they'd born a great weight, and the way they'd split down the middle reminded Greta of a man's hairstyle – parted in the center, each half combed away toward the ears. The river, which had already been close to overflowing its banks, rose up over the stones that marked its edges and slid halfway into the Cahills' back field, swelling the ground, causing Little Tom to stand at the back door of the cottage with the lines in his forehead as knit and twisted as his mouth. Twice during the night he'd been out in the storm to check on the cows, the single bull, the mule, the two ponies, the chickens, and the three small leaks that had sprung from the roof of the hay shed. Twice he'd come back, muddied to the knees, more worried and heartsick than he'd looked before.

'It won't come any closer,' Lily assured them. 'To the eye that field looks flat, but there's a slope there where it's stopped. You wouldn't notice except to feel it under your feet when you're walking.'

But after only a few hours respite in the morning, it began to pour again in the early afternoon of the next day, and all day was as dark as midnight except when lightning flashed and the world turned greenish yellow like the water that sometimes pooled in the lanes and the fields. They'd shut off the electricity as a precaution, and the kitchen, lit only by lanterns and candles, seemed to Greta like a photograph from a long time ago. They waited – Little Tom in Big Tom's chair, Lily and Johanna at the table, Greta in the straight-backed chair by the fire, all wondering if what Lily said about the slope was true, if it had ever been tested like this before, if they should prepare themselves for water to come sliding under the door of the cottage and set the furniture sailing.

As they waited – Johanna with her hand to her throat, fingering the scarf Shannon had given her, Greta thinking of hers wrapped in tissue and safe in her dresser drawer – the girls, in their separate silences, also recalled that fresh bundle of wildflowers on Julia Ward's grave and the loaf of bread that had been torn into in the back room. Lily had made the loaf to have the day of Mrs O'Clery's funeral, and she was livid when she saw it half eaten. The girls, who didn't want Lily to know the possibilities stirring in their minds and, at least in Greta's case, didn't know why she wanted to keep Lily from knowing, took the blame. For her part, Lily couldn't get over their greed or their carelessness. It wasn't like them. One half gone, the remaining half was left uncovered on the counter to go stale in the damp air.

Leaving the topic of the bread behind was the one good thing brought on by the rain – a new subject, a new worry, the incident forgotten until, in the late afternoon on the second day of rain, there came into the quiet, darkened kitchen the sound of pounding on the front door.

'Who in the world?' Lily said, getting up and taking a lantern with her. It wasn't only the weather that made a visitor so surprising, it was also the use of the front door knocker. Anyone with any sense would go around back and not be dragging mud all through the house. Little Tom followed, then Johanna, then Greta, all pressed against one another in the short and narrow hall that was colder and damper than the kitchen. Lily opened the door and, without exchanging a single word, ushered the visitor inside.

'God bless all here,' Michael Ward said, his voice just a notch above a whisper as he took in the group crammed before him. He brought the smell of wet earth and smoke into the cottage with him. He cleared his throat. 'Nasty day,' he added, this time at a volume they could all hear.

'You're wet to the bone,' Lily said, taking hold of the sleeve of his jacket and squeezing. 'Have you had a breakdown?'

'A breakdown, Missus?'

Little Tom mimed the steering of a driving wheel.

'He might be on foot,' Lily pointed out. Then asked, 'Is the road washed out?'

'Mammy,' Johanna said, sticking her head into the discussion, 'why not let him in the door so he can sit by the fire?' Greta could tell by the sudden music in Johanna's voice that this person who dripped rain on their floor was the Peeping Tom.

In the kitchen, sitting on the straight-backed chair Greta had just vacated, Michael Ward was instructed by Lily to peel off his jacket and pull up as close to the fire as possible without catching fire himself.

'Do you know me, Missus?' Michael Ward asked once everyone had settled themselves in positions around the room. So far, he'd directed all of his questions and statements only to Lily, but he felt the others looking on, especially the two girls. He couldn't for the life of him remember the older girl's name. There should be more of them, if he remembered correctly. More boys, plus the father. Back then, it had seemed like a family of boys, with the girls sprinkled in for good measure. Now the Cahill cottage was overwhelmingly female – not just because there were three women inspecting him from various corners of the room and the one male presence had retreated to the darkest corner, where he sat and said nothing. There was also a female quality in the fire-warmed air. All that waiting and watching, and the sense that they knew things without being told.

'I do. Not until you took off your jacket, but then, yes. Michael, isn't it? You've gotten very tall. Are ye up the road again? Have ye been here long?'

At that moment Lily remembered the bundle of flowers on Julia Ward's grave. Next to that memory she put the vision of her lovely bread, the nearly full pound of butter it contained, a cup and a half of sugar left abandoned and half stolen on the counter, crumbs all around. It was a puzzle she now realized her daughters had solved days ago. The boy had nice ways when he was younger, not so like the tinkers that you'd recognize him as one of them right away. It seemed the years had brought him up to their speed.

'It's only myself, and no, not long, just a few nights.' No one spoke.

It was unusual to see a tinker so weather-beaten, so desperate for shelter. Tinkers, more than anyone, knew how to handle the elements. But Michael looked exhausted, his skin ash gray, with bruiselike circles under his eyes and a short beard covering his cheeks. He looked hungry too. The hollows in his cheeks reminded Lily of the boy's father, those high cheekbones, eyes drawn just a touch too close together like you'd see on a dog turned mean. But the boy had turned out to be better-looking than his father. To start with, he was taller. Not quite so tall as Little Tom, but still. And he was broader through the shoulders than his father had been. And though his face showed more of his father's features than it had as a child, they were more attractive on Michael. He was, all in all, very nice-looking – aside from his present state of sodden clothes and bloodshot eyes.

The half-collapsed cottage Michael had found that first day had proved impossible to heat. He got a fire going easily, was generous with the turf, pulled in as close to it as he could, but it was no use. It was as though the collapsed half of the cottage sucked the warmth away and whipped it out toward the ocean. While he lost heart over it, he also found himself amazed. A campfire built in the middle of an open field threw off more heat than this neat square in the wall that had been built specially. He found an old piece of cloth folded on a shelf and had the idea of hanging it between the two halves of the broken house to help keep the heat in, but when he went to unfold it – a curtain or a sheet, he couldn't tell – it fell to the ground in tatters. Then he tried building a wall of furniture at the dividing point, but there was only an old table and a dresser, and two chairs that came apart in his hands when he went to lift them. Eventually he had given up and tried to sleep, but sleep turned out to be almost as difficult as trapping the heat of the fire. All night long, and for the next two nights as well, anytime he closed his eyes he imagined the remaining half of the roof crashing down on him. The rotted beams creaked in the wind that barreled up from the Atlantic, and the thatched roof of the intact side sagged lower and lower with each hour of rain. The mirror still hanging on the standing wall and the precise shape of the fireplace now seemed to have lasted through years of neglect only to mock him. All his daydreams about living as a settled person had featured cows at pasture, fields healthy and productive. He'd never thought about how settled people begin – the seeds, the lumber, bringing each cow to the bull to make a herd.

Just as Lily was about to ask what in the world brought him out in this weather, Michael Ward drew a long breath and made his confession.

'I done something I want to tell ye,' he began, and the Cahills leaned away from the sound of the rain to listen.

Each time lightning flashed, Greta noticed, Michael Ward was the only one who did not look to the window. The rest of them turned their heads, stared at the stretch of mud between the cottage and the stable, braced themselves for the clap of thunder that always followed. His presence in their kitchen was not as worthy of their attention as it might have been if the day were clear, or if it had been a regular kind of rain. After the burden of his conscience was lifted, Michael appeared most concerned with finding a new position in his chair, turning himself around in increments, like a pig on a spit. As his damp clothes warmed and slowly dried, the smells buried deep in their wool and cotton fibers were set free and filled the kitchen with more of the outdoor smells Greta had sniffed earlier. In addition to the strong whiff of turf smoke, there also came the scent of something human, more flesh than elements, a body unwashed for more than a week, the underarms of Michael's once-white shirt yellowed with wear. It was different from the cow manure and chicken shite smell the Cahills carried around in their clothes and on the bottoms of their shoes, and although she knew it was a scent that should be scrubbed off him as soon as possible, there was something not entirely unpleasant about it. Every time she looked away, out the window, toward the lightning in the distance or the mewling of the cows inside the stable, the odor drew her back as decisively as if he'd walked over to her and cupped her cheek in the palm of his hand.

Michael's confession was not brief, and it included a description of how he'd cycled close to one hundred miles. Not tarmacked, easy miles, but country lane miles, roots and rocks cropping up out of the ground, the lane sometimes stretching straight up the side of a mountain before shooting around the side. It also included a description of seeing his mother's headstone, catching it just before it became grown over with moss, and how when he got to the Cahills' cottage, he'd knocked and knocked, shouted his presence, walked around the side of the cottage and shouted again, knocked on the back door as insistently as he'd knocked on the front. He remembered them as good people, he said, and when he entered and took something to eat, stole it, yes, to be fair, though he hoped they wouldn't see it that way, it was the only thing he could think to do. He didn't mention trying the barnacles down at the high-tide mark or seeing a girl's dark head among the waves.

'Our father died,' Johanna said sometime after he'd finished and turned a new side to the fire. Thunder clapped, rolled away. Greta could tell she'd been waiting to say it, had started to say it once or twice already but held back until she was sure Michael's story was over. It was a simple statement of fact, the most direct way of bringing their guest up to date. 'And two of our brothers have gone to Australia.' Her concise summary of the events since Michael was last in Ballyroan took a moment to sink in. Greta knew that in laying it out so bluntly, Johanna was also saying that sad things had happened to them as well. He wasn't the only one. And she'd covered for him, a circumstance that was now making Johanna feel deeply annoyed. Without being one hundred percent sure who the culprit was, without knowing if he'd be back, why he'd done it, if he'd do worse, she'd covered for him, taken the blame, and now here he was proving her a liar. Greta too, because as she always did, Greta had tagged along, nodding her support of Johanna's fib in her wide-eyed goosey way.

'Greta was home that day, at the time you said, and didn't hear a thing. Weren't you, Greta?' Johanna asked.

'Johanna!' Greta said.

'Johanna!' Michael repeated, tapping his forehead with his index finger.

'Well?' said Johanna. 'Greta would know if you knocked and called or if you just waltzed in and helped yourself. Greta?'

So Greta hadn't been the one swimming after all. Michael turned to look at her as he felt his explanation fall from his lips to the flames of the fire. Dermot always said that no country person will ever side against another country person in support of a traveller, and Michael wondered if the rule applied to country people like Greta, who surely hadn't seen much or had much to do with travellers and who had a kind way about her. Johanna looked like a different girl from the one he remembered from his last time in Ballyroan, but this younger one, Greta, looked almost the same. She was much taller and looked a bit neater – as if she'd finally grown into the clothes she'd been wearing for years – but in the face she was the same. She looked hard at him before stretching a finger under her glasses to rub her eye, and Michael knew she would tell them the truth.

'Well, girl? Did you hear him calling?' Lily asked.

'I did,' said Greta. 'He knocked and shouted hallo and knocked some more, just like he said.'

'Why in the world didn't you answer?' Lily asked. Johanna asked the same question in the way she uncrossed her legs, shifted, then crossed them again. This was not the story Greta told that afternoon when it was just the two of them in the cottage, part scared and part thrilled at the notion of a Peeping Tom, a full twenty-four hours before they'd notice the flowers on Julia Ward's grave and put the pieces together. Since the funeral, each girl had tucked away her suspicions, knowing the mystery would still be there long after Shannon disappeared. Even after Shannon's departure, after their false confession, after spotting the flowers on Julia's grave, the girls had not discussed the possibility of Michael Ward. Johanna's reason was simple: she didn't want to end up being wrong. And here was Greta saying she'd known for certain all along, had heard him calling, had seen him through the window and recognized him, and had kept the nugget of certainty all to herself.

'I was on my own,' Greta said. 'And it was a strange voice, a man's voice, and . . .' She trailed off, hoping she'd said enough.

'You're a goose, Greta Cahill,' Lily said, but her tone said she approved. Her youngest daughter had some sense after all.

Grateful, Michael Ward turned back to the fire.

The boy made them an offer, and since he was alone, without money, without his entire extended family waiting in the wings to pounce on any sign of generosity, Lily decided, What harm? The western walls of four different fields had crumbled into heaps during the storm and had to be rebuilt. The leaks in the roof of the hay shed would only get worse. A number of trees that dotted the landscape had lost branches, and some had come down completely. Plus all the regular work. The calving season would begin soon, and Little Tom had to go to the fair to sell one of the heifers. Michael could sleep in the hay shed, in one of the dry sections. With blankets, he'd be as snug as could be. It had been quite a while since Lily made a family decision, since she'd stepped into the pantomime instead of just watching from the audience, and the rest of the family felt comforted when she told the boy where he would sleep and what time they ate their meals. It was as if they'd been seated in the wrong chairs for six years and had finally stood up and switched.

To the girls she made one warning, and she waited until both Michael and Tom had left the room: 'If he ever lays a hand where it doesn't belong, you come straight to me without stopping.'

For Greta, Lily's warning opened up a world of possibilities as abruptly and dramatically as if someone had come into the cottage banging a drum. He might lay a hand on them? Or even if he didn't, he might want to? But which of them, and where would he lay it? And what would it feel like, that broad and weathered hand?

At supper on the second evening of Michael's stay, Little Tom tried to ask their guest a question. He pointed his finger in the general direction of Michael's chest and jabbed the air. Greta heard three syllables, understood a long *e* sound in the middle, but she couldn't quite get what he was trying to say. There were words and phrases Little Tom said so often they didn't need repeating, but the guest at the table meant that Little Tom was trying for words the rest of them weren't used to hearing from him. He tried once more, and again all Greta could make out was the long vowel in the middle. Tom tapped Michael's chest, then pointed outside, then looked to Greta for help.

'Your people?' Greta guessed, and Tom sat back, satisfied. 'Where are your people?' Greta asked Michael.

Michael had spent the day reconstructing part of a wall while Little Tom went to Conch to trade hay and turf for planks of wood to lay over the ground where the paths had been washed away. The girls had returned to the inn, where Johanna rubbed the same old rag over the counters in the kitchen and Greta flopped down on one of the guest-room beds and wondered what Little Tom and Michael were doing at home. That morning, as a solution to the mud that would be kicked up by their wheels while they cycled and would surely make them unpresentable for work, they'd decided to pedal with their shoes and socks in their baskets, their skirts folded up and tucked into the waistbands of their underwear for as long as there were no occupied houses along their route and no one would see them. They stopped a mile away from the inn and fixed themselves, but Greta missed a place in the back where her skirt was still caught up and didn't notice until Mr Breen said 'Oh!' at the sight of her cotton underwear and Johanna burst out laughing. Greta resolved on the spot not to speak to Johanna until she apologized, and so far had kept her promise. After the incident, Mr Breen excused himself to go assess his own storm damage, and did not return all day.

'They're in around Kilkee,' Michael said. 'Could be headed for the Midlands by now.'

'You'll catch them?' Little Tom asked, this a bit more clear than the last. Michael needed the question repeated, and Johanna took it upon herself to change it. 'Why'd you leave them?' she asked instead.

'That's not your business,' Lily said.

'Did they ask you to leave?' Johanna asked.

'Johanna, you're being very bold,' Lily said. Now that she'd come back to life, she resolved to put a cork in Johanna's brazenness, her cursing, her temper, her attitude — as if she alone ran the cottage, owned Ballyroan. She was so like her father — that notion of deserving things, of being entitled to say whatever they damn well pleased.

'I just left,' said Michael, his story even more concise than Johanna's summary of Big Tom's death, the departure of the boys. It was so simple, saying it like that. His father, his sister, his aunts, cousins, brothers, and in-laws all went one way, and he went his own way. But looking at the Cahills, seeing himself stuck in with them at the small table, he was all at once desperate that they not think he disapproved of his family's life, that he thought it was somehow less than the life the Cahills were leading, or any other country family for that matter. It was only that it was lovely and warm inside in the kitchen, the fire roaring, the panes of glass a peephole to the world, where you could sit and appreciate but not necessarily pass through. His father, Michael wanted to explain, thought of all of Ireland as his own, but Michael saw every field, every roof, every turn and dip in the road as belonging to someone else. And they were both right.

Greta put her fork down and rested her chin on her fist to better hear what he'd say next. But there was no next he could think of. He left. Story told.

'Just left?' Johanna asked.

'Just got on my bicycle and left.'

'Were they against it? Were they angry, after?'

Michael shrugged. 'I was gone.'

'So you didn't give them any warning,' said Johanna. A statement instead of a question. She understood enough now to fill in the blanks. He'd defied them, gone against their wishes. They'd had ideas about what he should do with his life, about what was possible, and he'd matched them with his own ideas. Giving warning would have only made the process more miserable for both sides. No, the only thing to do was to up and leave. It wasn't that he didn't love them – anyone could see that.

Johanna had high color in her cheeks, and Lily poured her another glass of milk. Gradually the Cahills and Michael Ward went back to their salted potatoes, except for Greta, who continued to stare. There was a question no one had thought to ask.

'Will they have you back if you change your mind?' she asked after watching him shovel a few forkfuls into his mouth.

'They might. But they mightn't either,' Michael said. 'Only one way to find out.'

To try, Greta thought. To cycle all the way back the way he came and ask to be let back in. She couldn't see it happening, not with the way he'd made himself at home at their table.

In bed that night, Greta felt a rare power. Johanna wanted to talk, was busting to talk, but she didn't want to apologize for not telling Greta that her skirt was caught up or for laughing. Plus, she still felt she deserved her own apology for Greta's not telling the whole story about that first day Michael Ward had come around. The trouble was that Greta could wait forever. As Lily liked to say, Greta had a little thing called patience. Lily said the word as if it were a virtue, when really it was the most frustrating quality a person could have. Especially when Johanna was dying to talk and Greta could wait and wait and wait.

'So I was thinking,' Johanna began, holding the bait above Greta's side of the bed, willing her to flip over and engage.

'Hmm,' Greta said, no lilt of a question mark at the end. She was pretending to be half asleep and didn't care one bit that Johanna knew she was pretending.

'Are you listening?' Johanna asked, moving closer to Greta's side, leaning her face toward Greta's neck. She couldn't stop herself. She exhaled a long, hot breath next to Greta's ear and bit her lip to keep from laughing as she braced for Greta's arm to fly around and smack her.

'No,' Greta said, no sign of drowsiness in her voice, no sign that she'd even felt Johanna's breath. After a minute or so, to prove one had nothing to do with the other, she shifted closer to the wall.

Johanna flipped over to her back and sighed. 'Come on now, Greta. I was just having a laugh,' she said.

Greta shot up. 'What about me? Those underpants had a hole, you know. And what if they'd been stained? And what if they'd been riding up? He must've gotten an eyeful. He just about fainted.'

'So what? That man could use a shock. He can barely put a full sentence together as it is.' And again: 'It was a laugh.'

'No it wasn't.'

'Yes it was.'

'I would never have done it to you.'

That was true, but what did that have to do with anything? 'Maybe you should. Then we'd both have a laugh once in a while.'

Greta lay back down and turned to the wall. The conversation was over if Johanna did not do what she had to do.

'I'm sorry,' Johanna said finally to Greta's back.

'You're not a bit sorry,' Greta said.

'I swear to God.'

'You should say you're sorry for swearing to God as well.'

'Ah, but my rule is one apology per day.'

'It only counts if you're really sorry. And you're not. You'd do it again tomorrow if you had the chance.' Greta sat up once more and faced her sister. 'Wouldn't you?'

'No!' Johanna insisted. 'I've learned my lesson. Cross my heart hope to die.'

Greta sighed, tumbled back down toward her pillow, and Johanna knew it was over. She began again. 'So I was thinking.'

'Yes?' Greta said. 'Jesus. Now I have to coax it out of you?'

'I'm getting to it, and here it is. I've been thinking, and I've decided it wouldn't be so hard to go to America and get a job and a place to live like Shannon said.'

It was the moment Greta had been bracing herself for, and now that it had arrived, she couldn't think of a single decent response. The energy pulsing from Johanna's side of the bed lit up the dark room as thoroughly as the electricity that hummed through the wires and the walls. Greta blinked, reached up to adjust her glasses before remembering they were safe on the top of the dresser until morning. Johanna waited for her to say something.

'What about Mr Breen?' Greta asked, but even as the words came out, she felt how feeble they were.

'Don't be thick, Greta. I'd say we're about two months off from being told to hit the road. Sooner, if he gets up the courage. We don't do a goddamned thing all day. Come to think of it, I've been meaning to tell you to be more grateful when you get paid. Get absolutely sickening about it, how much it means to you, and say things like this will keep you afloat for the week, and your family afloat, and bless him a bit and say Mammy includes him in the family prayers and all that. Don't say all the same things I say, so listen to me when I do it. I've been doing it these last few weeks, and he goes absolutely green, but I think it buys us another few weeks.'

'God, you're wicked,' Greta breathed into the space above their bed, already feeling a tightness in her chest about what she would say to Mr Breen in two days' time. So far, they'd spent most days avoiding each other.

'Mammy would never let you go.'

'No, I'd say she wouldn't,' Johanna agreed.

'So?'

'So I thought I might take a page from Michael Ward's book and just leave.'

Greta felt the tightness in her chest spread down her limbs to the tips of her fingers, her toes. She felt heavy, sunk into the mattress, attached to its corners by her ankles and her wrists. She'd need help when the time came to get up.

'You can't just go. There's paperwork.' Greta didn't know exactly what getting to America entailed, but she knew it was complicated. Whenever she'd heard the process described, she felt like pushing the information away with both hands, denying it entrance to her brain where it would only take up room and give her a headache. She was often amazed at how people knew how to do things, which offices to contact, where to show up, what papers were required, and then how they kept all of those things in order, ready to be presented whenever asked. She knew there were trips to Galway, doctor's visits, health certificates. Passport must be applied for, picture taken, contacts made on the other side, a sponsor found, money saved or acquired. It had been complicated enough when the boys went to Australia on short notice, but it was worse now, just a few years later, and going to America was more of a production than going to Australia. Everyone knew that. If you managed to get inside America's boundaries, sometimes it was impossible to come back.

'If so many other people managed to figure it out,' Johanna said, 'so can I.'

The reasoning was typical Johanna. There were many things other people had figured out that Greta was quite certain she couldn't. As she considered what her sister was telling her, she told herself the plan wasn't real yet, just a notion that might pass by morning. It was best to stick to the practical questions: How? When? In answering, Johanna might see that she hadn't thought things out at all, that the actual leap to New York would be far more difficult than anything she'd imagined.

'When are you aiming for?' Greta asked. But before Johanna could answer, Greta added, 'Mammy would be heartbroken.'

'I know,' Johanna said, 'and you'll have a big job consoling her.'

'And what about me?'

'You?' Johanna grabbed Greta at the ribs, managed to tickle her for a few seconds before she twisted away. 'You'll be heartbroken too, but I'll visit. I won't be one of those who goes forever. I promise. And you'll have to be reminding Mammy of that every day.'

Greta saw herself from Johanna's side of the bed, no more capable of wandering outside the realm of the familiar than she'd been as a little girl, one hand sweeping along the rough surface of the stone wall that led her from the farthest field back to the cottage, counting the steps in her head. Maybe she was right, Greta admitted. But it would be nice to be asked. It would be nice for someone to think she could manage it, even if she wasn't sure herself.

'No, Johanna. I mean, what if I want to go too?'

'You go? Now, Greta, please. Don't be silly.'

'Wouldn't you rather have me with you than go by yourself?'

Johanna was quiet, and more telling than her silence was the way her body went still. She quit switching between her side and her back, stopped plumping the pillow, stopped tugging at the nightshirt that always got twisted up around her waist.

Making an offer to go to America with Johanna, hinting at a secret wish to go didn't make the possibility of actually going any more real. It will pass, Greta told herself. Tomorrow she'll have another idea.

'What if I wasn't going alone?' Johanna asked.

'Excuse me?'

'What if I already had someone in mind? Someone who's seen a little more of the world than I have, has been to London, has had all kinds of jobs, isn't afraid of work, who might be willing to strike out with me.'

No, Greta thought. It will never, ever happen. Michael Ward barely knew Johanna, barely knew any of them, had expressed no desire to leave Ireland. Greta had seen him that morning, way off in the distance, as she waited outside the cottage for Johanna to find a rag to wipe water off the seats of their bicycles. He'd been working on the stone wall, squatting to pick up one of the largest stones, getting under it with his legs and then his hips, heaving himself and his burden in such a way that they appeared across the sun-starved fields to be one body struggling against an invisible force, the Atlantic wind, or the suck of the rain-soaked ground. When he turned back for the smaller, gap-filling stones, he took one in each hand, palms up like a human scale, before finding a place for each one.

And the way he talked about oysters caught down around Claren-bridge and Brady Bay, how they tasted of the sea if the sea were reduced to a single perfect mouthful, and how the shells slid and clacked together whenever he added one more to the pile. Greta had listened to his stories at the table, had watched him relax into these memories as he told them, and as she watched him and listened, she felt herself coaxed into forgetting about small worries. This was not a person who would be lured by the train that rushed over people's heads straight to the Statue of Liberty. No, Greta insisted as Johanna's warm legs scissored beside her. No, he would not go. He was not as grown or as travel-wise as he'd seemed at first, when he'd pushed his broad back close to their fire. Sometimes he seemed to Greta even younger than she was, though he was Johanna's age. After being called for supper, he often stood at their back door as if he wasn't quite sure what to do, whether to push his way inside or knock or call out and ask to be let in. But even as she told herself that he'd never go to America, no more than Little Tom or Lily or Greta, she felt the pinprick reminder that he'd already proved his willingness to up and leave everything he knew.

Johanna would not sleep for hours, thinking of America, wondering how Greta could be so calm when her news was so big. And while Johanna ticked off cities in her mind – New York, Boston, Chicago, Los Angeles – Greta, shoulders turned square to the wall, chest rising and falling in what she hoped was a convincing rhythm, discovered that it was possible to be homesick for a place she'd never left.

Seven

Michael Ward felt Johanna's eyes following him, just as he had the last time he was in Ballyroan. She was no better at being sly about it now than she'd been back then, and it struck him after a few weeks that maybe she wanted him to notice, wanted him to approach her and ask if there was something she wanted to talk to him about. They spoke only at supper. He ate breakfast long before her, and she and Greta took their tea at the inn. At supper she always took the seat directly opposite him, and she looked away whenever he glanced up. Sometimes he'd catch her eye as he was passing the carrots or the bread, and he'd get the sense that she'd been looking at him for a long time. Conversation, when she initiated it, was meant for everyone to hear.

'Did you make much progress on the shed?' she might ask. Or 'Did the heifer's fever break?' Questions like that couldn't possibly be what was on her mind when she stood in the lane with her bicycle for thirty minutes, watching him run one of Little Tom's razors down his cheeks, an old, spotted hand mirror Lily had lent him angled to catch the light.

He would answer yes or no, and Little Tom would chime in with his half-talking, half-miming way of communicating; then Greta, who laughed in that childlike way she had at any funny story, would contribute her little bit and, unlike Johanna, never look away whenever he caught her eye.

Lily had taken to sitting in Big Tom's chair while they ate, leaving room at the table for the young ones. She told them that age was claiming her appetite and that the bits she put in her mouth while she was getting supper together were enough to make a meal. She didn't point out that it was easier to see every look that passed between them from the chair by the fire – or what those looks told her. She too had observed Johanna's behavior toward Michael at the supper table and decided that the girl was trying to impress the boy by acting grown up. Lily was more interested in what she observed in Greta, the flitter of flirtation here and there, the way she tried to tame the wilds of her hair. And once, during the boy's first week with them, she'd come to supper without her glasses, claiming she didn't really need them, only to have to go fetch them when it came time to peel spuds. Poor girl doesn't even know to pretend disinterest, Lily thought as she watched her youngest glance at Michael Ward, then down at her plate, then back at Michael even when he wasn't speaking. Lily watched Michael's reactions carefully and decided there was nothing to fear.

When Johanna appeared in the hay shed one night, long after the lights had gone out in the cottage, Michael wasn't completely surprised. 'Hello,' she whispered into the deep cavern of the shed, the hills of stacked hay. 'Where are you?'

'Here,' he whispered back. He'd been sleeping. 'Hold on.' He pulled on his trousers and slid down from his nest in one of the mid-level piles, down to the ground, where Johanna waited. He plucked bits of hay from his hair, brushed it from the seat of his pants. She was wearing a nightdress, with a long sweater over and boots underneath. There was a small space between the top of her boots and the hem of her nightdress that showed pale white skin.

'I have to talk to you,' she said. 'Will we take a walk?'

Michael blinked and stretched, filling his chest with air and reaching as far out into the night as his bones would allow. He counted back and tried to figure out how long it had been since the night Dermot woke him to fetch more turf. Only two weeks, if he'd kept track of his days correctly.

'I was fast asleep,' he said, but she'd already started walking.

They went down to the river, down past the water bailiff's boarded hut, down near the place where Big Tom drowned and the boys pressed the triggers of their shotguns to begin their journey out of Ireland. Johanna stopped at a sloped stretch of grass, leaned over to press her palm against the ground, and, finding it not too damp, sat down and patted the space next to her. Michael looked back in the direction they'd come from.

'Mammy's sound asleep,' Johanna said.

Michael sat.

'She warned us about you, you know. Me and Greta. She warned us you might try something.'

Michael didn't know what to say to that, especially with her looking at him with her nearly black hair loose around her shoulders and smirking like she was daring him to do something. Maybe that's why she'd been staring at him and following him. Maybe she wondered why he hadn't tried anything yet. She was a good-looking girl, dark and fair at the same time. She was tall like her brother, like her father, if Michael's memory served. It was easy to see the shape of her legs under the thin cotton nightdress, and now that she was sitting, the moon yellow and full, he could see the fine hairs on the space of skin above the tops of her boots. This was a girl who swam in her knickers, her skirt, blouse, and shoes left in a heap at the shore for the waves to lap up and swallow. Once, on his second day staying in the Cahills' hay shed, Little Tom had sent him miles down the road in search of a calf gone missing overnight. He never found the calf, but on his way back to the cottage he'd seen them, Johanna and Greta both, cycling their bicycles with their skirts bunched up around their waists, their long white legs folding and reaching and folding again as they pumped the pedals.

Johanna's laughter caught even Johanna off guard and knocked her back on one elbow. She clapped her free hand over her mouth. 'You should see your face,' she said.

He leaned into her briefly, then away, pushing her off balance. 'Did you wake me out of my lovely dreams just to make fun?' He was smiling, glad she couldn't see his face redden. He felt the heat travel from the tips of his ears to his throat to his chest. She threw off her own heat, and he could feel that too. It burned through her nightdress and her sweater and bumped up against the cool night air. This was what his father meant about wanting a body next to him, a soft, warm body to lean into and take hold of. This is what his father meant when he told Michael he was handsome. It was the same as telling him there was no need to be afraid.

Johanna sat up, pulled her nightdress tight over her knees, drew her sweater closer around her chest. She was no longer smiling.

'I want to talk to you about an idea I had.'

What she'd said about Lily warning her and Greta still rang out in Michael's ears. He'd never given her any reason to worry, aside from being eighteen and a boy and a tinker – all things he couldn't help. And Greta! She was as pretty as Johanna, yes, and kinder than Johanna in the way she looked and nodded and never acted as if a person had gone on too long or said silly things, but sometimes she seemed almost as young as she was the last time he was in Ballyroan.

'Go on,' he said.

'I want to go to America. To New York. Well, later I'd go to other places, but to start, New York.'

Michael waited. He got the feeling that she wasn't looking for congratulations, but he didn't know the right question to ask.

'And I thought you might want to come with me.'

'To America?'

'Have you been listening? Yes, to America. You've been to England and seen all of Ireland, and you're just after leaving your family behind and wanting to settle. You can't really want to settle here of all places. Why not New York?'

He was tempted to turn the question right back at her. Why not London? Sydney? Berlin? Why not Ballyroan of all places? Where else could he find land that was like an island you didn't have to row a boat to find?

'With you and Greta?' he asked.

'Greta?' Johanna asked after a moment. 'No, not with Greta. Just you and me.' She was surprised he'd asked after Greta, and she felt guilty all over again that she had not let Greta come with her to fetch Michael from the shed. Greta had woken when Johanna raised their bedroom window and had known immediately where Johanna planned to go. 'What are you doing?' Johanna had asked when she saw Greta reaching for her boots, but instead of answering, Greta had stared at Johanna with those big eyes that seemed somehow bigger whenever she was not wearing glasses. For what seemed like ages, Greta remained fixed over her one unlaced boot, the neck of her nightshirt down over her shoulder. 'He won't go,' she said finally. 'It's useless to ask. He won't leave here.'

'We'll see,' Johanna had said, and was out the window and across the field before Greta had a chance to catch up.

'Are you serious?' Michael asked now. People said they wanted to do things all the time, said they were going to do things, said they had plans in the works, started sentences with 'this time next year,' but most of the time, people were full of it. That's what Michael had figured out. There were lots of people who talked and talked but rarely did.

'Yes,' Johanna said, without feeling the need to go further. Michael believed her.

'Why me?' he asked. He was just curious, he wasn't saying he'd join her, but Johanna turned toward him, bending one knee and tucking her foot under the other, and he could see that she thought he'd accepted.

'Because my mother was wrong about you,' she said, smiling, and Michael knew that whatever her reasons, she wouldn't share them tonight. She'd grown up around brothers; maybe she wanted him around to feel safe, to navigate the streets of New York City as she imagined he'd navigated the streets of other cities. But New York was not like other cities, and she didn't realize that he'd never been to any place except Ballyroan in a group of less than a dozen. He'd never led. He'd only followed, head bent, trying not to wish he were someone else.

Then she leaned over her bent knee, put her hand on his shoulder, and kissed him. Dermot had hinted around this too. Girls who knew what they wanted. Girls who weren't shy. Most times, Dermot warned, he should stay away from these types. Now Michael wished he'd asked why.

He'd always wondered if there might be something in life he was brilliant at but never had the chance to try. For a while it was rugby. Dermot had outlawed the sport for being British. Then it was long-distance running. Then it was swimming – if he could just get a few lessons, who knew what his body might do? That night, the old wonder about untried possibilities rushed back. He discovered he was good at something he'd never before attempted – kissing a girl, tasting inside her mouth, finding a route under the flap of her sweater and between the buttons of her nightdress to her breasts, guiding her to the flat of her back, where he pressed her into the damp ground with the weight of his body. He'd seen similar scenes between the cracks of the tent flaps and had paid attention so he'd know what to do when his time came. Now he realized that his body didn't need instruction; it was reaching and pressing as if he'd had a girl under him every night of his life. She pulled him closer when he lodged his knee between her legs, but she stopped him when he reached for her with his hand.

They sat up, straightened their clothes. 'You should be ashamed of yourself,' she said, and the feeling of not being able to find the right words swept over him as it had all his life when it came time to beckon people down to his stall to see his grandfather's tin pails.

'I thought . . . I'm sorry.'

'Are you sure you're sorry?'

He looked up. She was laughing at him again, pulling a face he guessed was meant to mirror his own: serious, terrified, speechless. She was still laughing as she stood and brushed herself off. They walked back toward the cottage.

'Next time we'll decide when we'll go,' Johanna said at the point where he had to veer off toward the hay shed, and she walked toward the dark window of her bedroom. Michael decided he'd wait until next time to tell her he had no interest in New York.

In mid-July, when Mr Breen finally got around to letting Johanna and Greta go, he opened with a story about seals. 'Girls,' he said, 'you'll appreciate this, living where you do out beyond.' At first Greta thought he was retelling the priest's homily, knowing they didn't often go to Mass. Then she thought it was a story he'd read in the *Irish Times*, knowing they didn't ever buy the *Irish Times*. But no, it was his own story, and one glance at Johanna told Greta that her sister already knew how the story would end. He told them that selkies were the most mysterious of sea creatures, long studied and written about, and the thing that made them most special was the belief among some people – not himself, mind you – that they had human souls. Some believe that on every ninth day the selkies swim to shore, shimmy out of their thick gray-blue skins, rise up on two legs, and become women who walk and talk and appear to the world just like normal women. Greta wondered if he really thought they hadn't heard this legend – being, like he said, from out beyond. But there was no stopping him, and as he spoke, he raised his hand and pointed out the door toward the ocean.

'I'm not a believer, mind you,' he said for the third time, 'but a thinking person would wonder. If it's been written about and talked about for so long by so many people, mightn't they be as likely right as the nonbelievers? Neither side has proof one way or the other.'

Johanna yawned. Greta shrugged. She never thought she'd hear a grown man discuss it so seriously. It was a story told to children at school or before the fire on a stormy summer night. Then again, the legend of the selkie was the reason so many otherwise levelheaded fisherman were against killing the seals, even when they were desperate and their lobster traps came up empty. Mr Breen's face was glistening, as if he'd just emerged from the ocean himself, and he pressed his forehead and his cheeks with a napkin.

'I tell you this, girls, in explanation. Will we sit down? Will I make the tea?' He got up and plugged in the electric kettle. Then he unplugged it, filled it with water, and plugged it in again. He rooted around the cupboard.

'In the tin,' Johanna called. 'Beside the breadbox.' She made no effort to help him and slid down in her chair until her knees were jammed up against the leg of the table.

They all waited in silence until the water boiled, then Mr Breen came back with the pot in one hand and three cups hanging from three fingers of the other.

'You see, I was down at the water yesterday, watching the seals swim and climb out of the water onto that piece that juts out from Harry's Point, and as God is my witness, I heard my wife speaking in my ear.'

'Oh?' Johanna asked, still slouched in her chair. 'What did she say?'

'Will I tell ye? She said "Jim" – she called me Jim – "why do you have those two lovely girls cooped up in that inn to be bored and feeling useless all day when they could be out enjoying the fine weather?" And I thought to myself, good question.'

'Did you tell her you're paying us wages?' Johanna asked.

'Which we're very thankful for,' Greta added.

'Well, she knows that of course,' Mr Breen said. 'And that's the second problem.'

'The only problem, since we solved the first,' Johanna said.

'Did we? We did, yes. Well, as you know, there was big promise of a tourist boom in this part of the country, but we've seen none of it yet, not a bit, and to put it as simply as possible, I just can't swing it until the boom arrives. Ye've been a great help, an honest-to-goodness boost, and I'm sorry.'

'Your wife came back as a selkie and told you to let us go.' Johanna was like the man on the wireless news who said in one sentence what the man before him had taken fifteen minutes to explain.

'No, no, no,' Mr Breen protested, dabbing at his sideburns with his napkin while he let out short barks of nervous laughter. 'When you put it that way . . .' He laughed some more, his body rocking the small table and the lukewarm tea inside their cups.

When it came time to go, Mr Breen walked with them around the side of the inn to their bicycles. 'A departure gift,' he said, handing each girl an envelope with her name printed carefully across the front. They thanked him, shook his hand. Each tucked the envelope into a pocket and waited until they'd cycled out of sight to pull over and open them. Inside Greta's was a card with a picture of the baby Jesus and the word 'Hark!' She opened the card, and a ten-pound note slid out and landed on the road. She trapped it under the sole of her shoe while she read the message:

> Thanks and good luck.
> From James Breen
> P.S. Excuse the Christmas card.

'He gave us the same?' Johanna asked, peering over Greta's shoulder to read her card and spotting the tenner trapped under her shoe. 'Even though I made more per week?' She made a throaty sound that emphasized her disgust, then got on her bicycle and pedaled hard and fast. Greta expected not to see her again until she reached the cottage. It had happened before, Johanna taking off in some private fury, Greta left to squint into the failing light, careful to steer around large stones. But when Greta came around the bend that meant she was three short miles from home, there was Johanna, sitting cross-legged at the side of the road, slapping an impatient rhythm against the wind-scoured ground.

'You know what this means, don't you?' She was calm now, even happy. Something had occurred to her in the miles since she left Greta in the dust. 'This is all I was waiting around for. There's no more wages to be earned here. Not in Conch, not in Ballyroan, not even in Galway, if what I hear in town is true. Nowhere.'

After the first time that Johanna had gone out the window to meet with Michael Ward, Greta had not asked any questions. She woke up each and every time she felt Johanna leave their bed, and she could never fall back to sleep until Johanna was tucked in beside her again. She wondered what they talked about for so long in the middle of the night and if Lily's warning had come true for Johanna. She hated to see them both in the kitchen at breakfast on mornings after these nighttime visits, acting as if everything was as it should be. Sometimes, when Johanna was short with him – if he used the last of the milk or took a second egg – and he reacted as if she'd struck him with a switch – startled, ashamed – Greta wanted to shout at him. But when she tried to think of what exactly she would say, her mind felt too full to pluck out one single thought.

'And did you ever think what would happen to me if I stayed?' Johanna asked. 'The four of us in that cottage looking at each other until we die? No sir. No way.'

'And what about me?' Greta asked.

'Oh, Greta,' Johanna said.

The most recent letter from Jack, written on behalf of himself and Padraic, had said nothing about coming home. They'd met girls, Australian girls, and Jack asked his to marry him. This is what he wrote to tell his mother. He was getting married in a few weeks time, nothing big, nothing fancy, just a few of their friends and the girl's family.

Reading it, Lily knew it wasn't as if he'd thought about asking her to come and, after discussing it with Padraic and the girl, had decided against. No, he simply couldn't imagine that Lily would ever leave Ireland, not for her eldest son's wedding, not for anything. Sitting on the back step with the letter in her lap, alone except for the sound of the dog yipping at a bird down by the river, she envisioned herself packing a suitcase, catching the bus to Shannon Airport, boarding one of those jets that now zoomed daily over their heads, and walking in on the ceremony as though it required no more thought on her part than taking the bus to Galway. They'd faint cold on the spot. She smiled. They'd cry. She'd tell Padraic he was getting a little tight in the belt – he'd been starting down that road before he left – and she'd tell Jack his hairline was just like his grandfather's. Before she left, she'd take the girls into Galway to help her pick out a dress. Pale blue. Periwinkle. Peach. She hadn't been to Galway in years. The girls could pick out gifts for their brother, tokens, really. She wouldn't let them spend too much, and on the way out they'd stop for tea in that hotel they'd been to the day Greta got her glasses and was like a little baby bird who'd been pushed out of the nest.

She folded the letter and slipped it back into the envelope. No, she was sure they hadn't meant to exclude her. And she was just as sure neither of them would ever come home. 'They're right,' she said aloud, looking up at the sky. 'Why should they come back?' She had suspected herself of feeling this way for a little while now, but she had managed to push it away by insisting that she felt the opposite. She said to the empty yard, 'They have cash money where they are, and why shouldn't they stay and find good women and build fine houses for themselves?' For the first time, she wondered if she'd been wrong to keep Little Tom from going with them.

Their situation in Ballyroan was grim, whether the children realized it or not. This is what she hadn't wanted to wake up and face after Big Tom died, and at times she wanted to return to that long slumber, her days a dull repetition of eating, sleeping, one of the girls helping her into the basin, handing her a washcloth, returning again and again with the red-hot kettle, and pushing her knees and shins out of the way while the steaming water poured in. But now that she had managed to step out from under the cloak of Tom's death and take a look around, it was impossible to look away. The biggest problem was that they needed a new cottage. The kitchen was decent because the daily fire dried out the walls, but the rest of the rooms were rotting away. It was getting difficult to breathe, and everything she laid her hand on seemed weighed down with dampness – the furniture, the sheets on their beds, the pictures hanging on the walls. Little Tom and Greta were oblivious; she could see it in the way they talked and went about their chores and flopped down in their chairs at the end of the day, as if those chairs would always be there, that roof always over their heads. Johanna was more aware of the road they were traveling and was the one who pointed out that Conch, their lifeline to the world for so long, was not the same as it was when she was a girl. She reminded them at dinner one night a few weeks ago. 'Didn't there used to be farmers' markets? Fairs? Where has everybody gone to?' Now Conch was almost as quiet as Ballyroan. It was rare to see a group of young people standing together anymore. Shops closed for hours in the middle of the day while the old ones who tended them went home for a sleep.

Lately Lily had developed the habit of shooting ahead in time. She didn't do it on purpose, and she wished she could make herself stop. She'd be doing everyday things, chores she'd done her entire life, throwing grain down for the chickens, pulling the udder of a cow, and her mind would leap ahead twenty years, thirty years. She didn't see herself in these images – dead, most likely, and that sat just fine with her – but the girls and Little Tom, two sisters and a brother stranded in a forgotten place. Little Tom would go completely silent because his sisters always knew what he wanted without having to be told, and the girls would go weird, Greta especially. Johanna would get cranky and let her hair go long and loose like a banshee. She'd take out every little thing she felt on the other two, and they'd take cover when they saw her coming. They would have no husbands, no wife, no *gasúir* running around to populate the place. Johanna would swim in the ocean in her knickers until she was an old woman, with only her gray hair to cover her. They'd make no effort to go to Galway and walk among the people, because one foot in the city would remind them that they'd been left behind.

Michael met Johanna down by the river twice a week for six weeks. At first there was no more word of New York. She'd simply leaned into his arms and played her fingers at the back of his neck. She kissed his mouth, kissed his throat, kissed the top of his chest where she unbuttoned his shirt. Half a dozen times now she'd put her hand inside his pants. She took off her blouse and the thin gansy she wore underneath. She slid out of her skirt and stood in her underpants, turning for him with her hands up in the air like a film star. She let him cup her breasts while he kissed her, and later, when he had more courage, she let him inspect them with his eyes and his mouth. She was always the one to start with the kissing and pulling, and he was always the one to guide her down to the ground, where they could press closer together than they could standing up or sitting. He'd stopped asking himself why she'd picked him, and after the first time, the question had seemed foolish. Who else was there? Like Dermot told him, he was handsome. The women had said so.

Once Johanna and Greta were let go from their jobs at the inn, the nighttime visits to the river were transformed. Michael would place a hand on Johanna's thigh, but she'd move her leg away and remind him that there were plans to be made. He'd move behind her and put his hands on her shoulders, pressing and kneading in the way she liked, but she'd shrug him off and stay rigid until he moved back to his place beside her. She'd made written inquiries about the medical tests they'd have to have done, and she'd written to Shannon O'Cléry asking her to sponsor them. 'The sponsor thing is a bit of a joke,' Johanna explained, already feeling wise to the ways of America. 'She tells the immigration people we'll live with her and that she'll help us find work, but it's really just to get us over there. She'll claim I'm her first cousin and that she has a friend who will give me a job minding her children while she goes to work. But I'm not her cousin, and there is no friend, and once we're there, we're on our own. With both of us working and sharing a flat and splitting expenses, I think we'll be grand.'

Michael decided that Johanna was prettier by moonlight than she was during the day. She had a nice voice, something he hadn't noticed until they started their secret meetings. Her tone was serious, but that voice seemed to ask him to move closer, to put his arm around her.

'Are you listening?' Johanna asked, looking at his hand as though it was a child who'd spoken out of turn. 'How long until you think you'll have enough for the fare? Tom gives you a little something now and again, doesn't he? Have you been putting it away? Do you have anything from before?'

Michael shrugged, shook his head. Tom gave him a pound once in a while, but he was mostly paid with a place to sleep and three meals a day.

Johanna sighed. 'Well, that's another thing to figure out. If worse comes to worst, we'll go by ship instead of by air. It's far less dear.'

And far easier to sneak aboard, Michael thought, thinking how many times he'd watched the foreign ships leave Cobh, the scene a swirling mess of hats, hugs, luggage, tears, families allowed to escort ticketed members to their cabins, even in second class, where the cabins were little more than closets with bunks and strangers roomed together. He could slip on board and crouch in a dark corner until the ship was at sea. Dermot once told him he had a talent for making himself small. Once, on the ferry from Dublin to Liverpool, he'd hidden in a compartment below the thin planks of the wagon floor for eight hours as the ferry carried them across the Irish Sea.

Johanna started every sentence having to do with America with the word *We*. We'll hitch to the airport or to the Galway dock, depending on how we go. We'll stay with Shannon for one month, and then we'll get a flat in Woodside because Shannon said there's a lot of Irish there. We'll get jobs. We'll see the Atlantic from the other side. Michael wondered if he'd let her go on too long to stop her now. She'd be angry. She might even tell Lily about their river visits and make it so Lily blamed him, Lily who had given him a seat by the fire on that wet day and three hot meals every day since then. He asked her if Greta had refused to go with her and if that's why she'd asked him to go instead. 'Greta? In New York City?' she'd asked, as if Greta Cahill and that great city was the most far-fetched combination a person could come up with.

Michael had laughed. 'Am I any more likely to get on there? Are you?'

'Me?' Johanna had said in a huff. 'Worry about yourself. You don't know Greta. Something would happen to her, and I'd always have to be tracking her down and checking on her and helping her with things she can't figure out.' Her voice softened. 'I'll miss her, don't get me wrong. And maybe once I'm settled and know my way, I could bring her out. If she would come, that is. I can't see her straying too far from here, to be honest.'

'I think she's wiser than you think,' Michael said. He wondered how much Greta knew about Johanna's plans. She seemed troubled lately, quiet and attentive. At supper she took everything in, every word, every look, as if she was organizing what she observed and had plans to file it away.

Johanna's portrait of life in America was vivid, tempting, and sometimes Michael forgot that he was ninety-nine percent sure he wasn't going to go. Eighty percent sure. Fifty. And even if he did go to America, why would he want to stop in New York? There were other places to see, much more appealing places than New York City. He imagined New York to be worse than Dublin, with its smells and crowds of people and car horns blaring all day long. Dublin, where no matter how long he stood next to Dermot and listened along with the crowd as his father seemed to sing every Irish song ever written, no one dropped a single coin in his hat. He'd heard of huge tracts of land in the states of Montana and Wyoming and Colorado, places he'd meant to ask Johanna to look up on a map, but couldn't now, not the way she was going on about New York City and using the word We.

'When is liftoff?' he asked, careful to leave out reference to himself.

'October. What do you think?'

'October is my favorite month of the year,' he said, and slipped his hand under the wide sleeve of her sweater, all the way up to her shoulder.

Greta found Shannon's letter among Johanna's things. Inside was a note to Lily, which Johanna had not passed on. Greta read both letters and put them back exactly where she found them. Then she sat on the edge of her bed and looked at the second dresser drawer – Johanna's drawer – for thirty minutes. After thirty minutes she couldn't recall having a single thought except to cycle into town and visit Norton's shop.

In the shop, while Mrs Norton searched the back room for a tin of condensed milk, Greta walked quickly down the middle aisle and plucked a packet of powder yellow stationery and matching envelopes from an upper shelf. She'd had her eye on the set for weeks, thinking how nice the yellow would look against her blue fountain pen and how thick and important the letters she wrote to Jack and Padraic would feel thanks to the heavy stock. She also liked the packaging – the envelopes stacked on top of the stationery inside the handsome navy blue cardboard box, everything tied together with a crisp white bow. She shoved the box under the waistband of her skirt, the bottom corners doubly secure by the waistband of her underpants.

'I'm out, love,' Mrs Norton said as she emerged from the back. 'The only can I have is dented, and I wouldn't risk it.'

'I'll check back this day week,' Greta promised, and walked out of the shop feeling much better.

Poor girleen, Mrs Norton thought as she watched from the window with the dented can of milk in her hand. If only she could lose that peculiar way of walking. If only she wasn't as odd as two left feet.

After a few days went by, Greta returned to the letters, removed the one addressed to Lily, and stored it with her other things in the tin box under the bed. The next day, she took the one Shannon had written to Johanna as well, envelope and all.

Once she made her decision, she left the letters out on the mantel in the kitchen for Lily to find. She propped them up beside the clock, then walked across the room to where Lily might glance up as she came through the back room. No, not obvious enough. She moved them over to lean on their folds against the rarely used lantern. Then she changed her mind again and left them under the sugar bowl on the table. She stood at the entrance to the kitchen and squinted toward the table. She changed her mind one final time and brought the letters straight to Lily's room, where she left them on her mother's pillow.

'Ay!' Little Tom called into the hay shed. He picked a hayfork off the ground and banged the shed's tin siding with the prongs. He coughed, walked back and forth kicking up the grit. Finally Michael Ward woke up and rolled down to ground level, buttoning his pants on the way.

Little Tom raised his thumb over his shoulder to point back at the cottage. Michael looked over Tom's shoulder at the drawn curtains of the kitchen, the smoke issuing from the chimney.

'She wants to see me?' Michael asked. Tom nodded.

'Are you coming?' Michael asked, trying to read Tom's crooked features for a hint of what waited for him inside.

Tom shook his head, used the same thumb to jab the air in another direction. He clapped Michael on the back and walked away.

In the kitchen, Lily was seated in her usual place. He heard no sound from any other part of the cottage, and he guessed the girls had gone out. Or were sent out. Or were forbidden to enter the kitchen with him there. On the table was a bowl of fresh strawberries picked from behind the cottage and a bowl of heavy cream.

'Might as well,' Lily said when she saw Michael looking at the bowl. 'They won't stay forever, and I've eaten myself sick of them. I've been boiling them all morning.'

Michael nodded his thanks and chose his usual seat. He poured cream over the berries and thought of how often they'd almost killed each other over fresh fruit at camp. If someone managed to get hold of a few oranges, they had to split them so many ways that all he ever got was a section or two. Behind him he heard the creak of Lily's chair as she stood, her shoes scuffing the floor as she took the few steps over to the table.

'I have to talk to you, Michael,' she said as she settled herself across from him. She had never sat alone in the kitchen with him before, and she was reminded of the day his mother came with her beady pocket, offering tonics and cures for anything in the world Lily might name.

She pulled Shannon's letters from her berry-stained apron and laid them out flat on the table. Michael looked at them, took in the miniature American flag in the upper-right corner of the envelope, put down his spoon.

'Mrs Cahill —' he managed to say before his lungs gave out, and he fought to catch his breath.

'Michael.' She held up her hand. 'I know my own daughter. Believe me. I'm not saying you've nothing to be guilty for — that I don't know — but as far as the America scheme is concerned, I know who dreamed it up. And she asked you along, did she?'

Michael nodded.

'And you've agreed?'

Michael paused. Lily narrowed her eyes.

'I took you in here, Michael,' she said.

Michael nodded.

'And she planned to go off without saying anything, did she?'

Michael stayed perfectly still, stared at the little square of stars inside the slightly larger square of candy cane stripes.

'She wants you because, brave as she is, she doesn't want to go alone. And you've been places. She hasn't. You understand? Once she gets her bearings, she mightn't be so happy to have you around. That might take two years or it might take six months. I love her. She's my child. But I know her.'

Michael nodded.

'You're still willing to go?'

Michael opened his mouth to speak but didn't know what to say. He never had any intention of going to America until Johanna had started with all the talk of We. Then he'd listened to her for so long, waiting for the right time to tell the truth, that now that it had arrived, he didn't know what he wanted. All his dreams of settling had looked just like Ballyroan. Every single thing about the place was right, down to the hawthorn trees and the rushes and the river stuffed with salmon. But after just a few months he could see why people had had to leave their lovely cottages behind and let their fields turn to scutch. Anything planted risked being torn up by the heavy salt wind. He had no money to start raising livestock straightaway, and even so, he'd have to get a stableful to make enough to live on. He was a stranger in Conch, suspected of being a tinker, and no shop would give him credit. The Cahills couldn't help him for much longer; he could see that. And he was lonely, a condition it took him a while to figure out. After a short time in Ballyroan he began looking forward all day to the supper meal, the passing of plates, the sound of chewing and tearing meat from bone and the steaming potato skins falling to the center pile. Aside from the time spent with Johanna down at the river, it was the only part of his day when he looked other people in the face and they looked in his. It would be worse after Johanna left. Sometimes he wondered what they'd do if he started a campfire beside the hay shed and invited them to visit him there. It would be their own upturned buckets they'd have to use for seats.

'You're not sure,' Lily said. Johanna would run circles around this boy. If he loved her, and she loved him, it might be enough to keep her head on her shoulders, but they weren't in love, that much was obvious. He had sense, yes, but he had no hold on her. It wouldn't be enough.

'If I went . . .' His voice sounded strange to him, choked off, breathless. He cleared his throat and began again. 'If I went, I'd need to get word to my father. I wouldn't like to leave without him knowing. Leave Ireland, I mean.'

It was a practical question Lily had never thought of before. 'How do you . . . ?'

'They keep letters at the post station, and he picks them up whenever he's near. I've an aunt who's a decent reader, and she sounds all the letters out for him and anyone else who gets one. If he thinks a letter might have something in it he mightn't want the camp to know, he asks the postman to read it to him.' Michael paused, let her catch up.

'I see,' Lily said as she reached for a strawberry, scooped out a bruise with her fingernail, and put her finger in her mouth. 'Well, I could help you with that. Couldn't I? You tell me what to put, and we'll work on it together. And in exchange you'd have to take good care of my girl. You'd have to protect each other and help each other no matter what happens. I don't know how it is in America, but here we help each other because we come from the same place.'

For what seemed like the hundredth time, Michael nodded. We come from the same place, he thought, and the space beneath his rib cage hummed like a tuning fork struck with the iron head of a hammer and then, after the clamor faded away, was pressed down on the boards of the wagon to better hear the lowest sounds, the truest pitch, vibrations so fast they sounded like one continuous purr.

'This conversation is between us for now, Michael, and I ask you not to say a word about it until I've talked to Johanna and done a little thinking,' Lily said. 'Go on now and catch up with Little Tom.'

Michael stood, pushed in his chair. 'What about Greta?' he asked. He had not known he was going to ask until he was speaking the words.

Lily leaned back, folded her hands in her lap. 'What about her?'

'Well, she mightn't like . . . She might be lonely after us, after Johanna. I just wonder . . .'

'I have to think about that too. Now go on,' she said, and waved him out of the room.

Michael rushed from the kitchen, lunged across the short length of the back room, barreled through the back door, ran up the lane to the coast road, where Little Tom's silhouette was still making its way.

★

Since handing over the letters, Greta had steered clear of the cottage. After chores, she spent most of her days up at the sea ledge, lying on her back and thinking that maybe after Lily stopped the plan and Johanna wasn't angry with her anymore, they could take the bus in to Galway and walk around. Maybe they could start doing it on a regular basis, and seeing the city so often might get ideas of America out of Johanna's head. They could catch the van to the Friday dances in Oughterard. Lily would be happy to let them go after coming so close to losing one of them completely.

Greta returned to the cottage every evening braced for an explosion. Two weeks went by, and none came. She began to worry that Lily hadn't found the letters after all. Johanna was still asking Michael boring questions in an overloud voice. Lily still sat in her corner and knitted. Only Michael was different. A few times, when Johanna went to the back room for salt or an extra knife or a rag to wipe up crumbs, Greta noticed him glancing at her, as if he were checking on her, confirming she was still there, asking whether she needed his help.

When Lily finally showed her cards, it was not at supper as Greta had expected. It was far later in the evening, after midnight. Johanna had woken Greta by opening the bedroom window, the damp wood catching and groaning in its grooves, and she had one leg out, her body straddled on the sill, when she let out a shriek that woke Little Tom, woke Michael in the shed, woke all of Conch, if Greta had to guess.

'Jesus Christ,' Johanna gasped just before she was yanked by a great strength to the grass outside.

'Johanna?' Greta called, unable to move her body to the window to see was Johanna alive or dead. 'Johanna!' she said louder, a demand this time. The cold draft from the wide-open window swept over her face, filled the small room. She lay still, listening for any telltale sound. She heard Johanna yelp, say something in a sharp voice, and then nothing. Greta took a deep breath and on shaking legs crept over to the window. There was Lily, tall in her long, pale nightdress, like a shee fairy, with her gray-streaked hair whipping around in the wind. She had Johanna by the ear and was leading her around to the back door.

Greta shut the window and leaped back to bed, where she made herself small and whispered what she would say to Johanna, as if Johanna were already beside her. She mightn't understand now, but she'd understand later, when they were both grown up, with husbands and their own cottages, and Greta would remind Johanna of the time she almost disappeared to America.

'Get up,' Johanna said hours later. Greta opened her eyes to daylight and Johanna's face above her, pale, exhausted, and Greta realized she'd never returned to bed. Johanna threw Greta's cardigan across the room. 'Come as you are,' she said. 'Mammy needs to see you.' Greta rubbed her eyes, reached for her glasses. 'Now,' Johanna said, and left the door to the cold hall open when she left.

In the kitchen, Lily was pleasant, fully dressed, her hair twisted up and pinned, no evidence of the scene she'd made the night before. Greta sat down at the table and faced not one but two sets of letters. The originals she already knew word for word: Shannon to Johanna, Shannon to Lily. Laid out beside these was a new set: a second letter from Shannon to Lily and a first from Shannon to Greta.

'I've big news for you, Greta,' Lily said as she reached out to run her fingers through the tangle of Greta's hair. The child had knot upon knot upon knot. 'What do you think about going to America?'

'Johanna going?' This was not the way it was supposed to go. Johanna was to be stopped from going, not encouraged.

'Yes, Johanna. And you as well, Greta. What do you think about that?'

Greta repeated the question to herself, thought of Mr Joyce of all people, how quickly he'd learned not to put questions to her in front of the class. Greta laughed, not her own laugh, but her best impression of a woman's laugh: throaty, full, in on the fun.

'It's a joke, is it?' she asked when neither Lily nor Johanna joined her laughter.

'No, love.' Lily stopped picking through Greta's hair. She pressed her hands against Greta's flushed cheeks, ran them down the back of her neck, settled them on her shoulders, where she squeezed so tight that Greta had to lean forward to get away.

Eight

On a clear October morning in 1963 Lily and Little Tom stood apart on the crowded pier in Galway City as they waved goodbye. There was no dock in Galway for so huge a ship, so the small packet boat made trip after trip carrying luggage and passengers in groups of a dozen. It made for a long goodbye, the ship anchored out in the ocean, the figures on board too far away to recognize but close enough for their mothers and brothers and wives to keep trying. Michael Ward had been one of the first to go over, earning part of his way by unloading the luggage and delivering it to first-class cabins. Johanna and Greta were in one of the last groups, the cash from the sale of the bull in pockets Lily had sewn onto the underside of their skirts.

Johanna had surprised all of them by crying through supper the day before, and she was still sniffling, Lily could see, as the packet moved its passengers away from the pier. Greta hadn't eaten a thing and had spent the night before vomiting into a basin while Lily rubbed her back. 'If you hate it,' Lily promised the girl, 'you can just come home.' Greta promised she would hate it, and why go to the bother of going all the way to America just to come back again and be short one bull? And why couldn't she and Johanna just get jobs in Conch? And so what if there were no jobs in Conch? Couldn't they take the bus to Galway and get jobs there? How could there be no jobs in Galway either? It wasn't possible. But Lily had already decided that the girl would go with her sister, would see a new place, would meet people from all over the world and earn some money for herself. It was like Sister Michaela said that time she cycled all the way to Ballyroan to see for herself whether Greta was ready for school: it was time. She'd given the girl no choice.

As the small boat drifted farther away, Lily could tell that Greta had already lost sight of her. She watched her youngest scan the crowd, the water, her face screwed up as if she'd tasted something sour. She and Johanna were pressed together on the narrow bench seat, Johanna with one hand holding tight to the leather strap of their shared case, the other hand squeezing Greta's, telling her it was fine, if she needed to lean over the side and vomit, then do it, the wake of the boat would carry it away, and no one knew them anyway. It's cruel to send that child, Lily thought. It's heartless of me to make her go. But then next to her guilt over making Greta go was the danger she felt at the idea of sending Johanna without her sister. She watched Greta clutch her stomach and heave and Johanna reach over to stop her from leaning too far over the side. It'll be just like that in New York, Lily thought. They'll be there to pull each other back, speak the language of home.

In their suitcase, thanks to Lily, they had each packed three clean skirts, three blouses, a sweater each, knitted by Lily, underwear, socks, toothbrushes, two clean cotton washcloths, a bar of soap, a single hairbrush to share, a new package of bobby pins. Johanna hadn't wanted to bring anything at all, claiming she'd wear the clothes on her back and start from scratch once she got to America. Greta, at the moment Lily intervened, was headed in the opposite direction and had every single thing she owned stacked in piles at the foot of the bed. Ready for transfer to the case were every old and yellowed gansy, every threadbare pair of underpants, even the old cardigan she wore for milking. After Lily decided on what they absolutely needed, she let them each bring something extra. Johanna's choice: a road map of the United States she'd bought in Galway. Greta: the contents of the old cookie tin she kept under her bed, dumped into an old pillowcase and tied off at the top.

As the packet reached the halfway point between the pier and the ship, Lily could just make out Greta's dark head bobbing with the rhythm of the tide, Johanna moving slightly away on the bench and looking up at the sky. Through the crowd, she saw Little Tom shake his head and then look over at her.

An hour later Lily and Little Tom made their way through the narrow cobblestoned streets back to the bus station, Lily dreading their return to the silent cottage, recalling the chaos of a short time ago, the comings and goings of a full house and herself giving out about tracked mud, Little Tom wondering whether he'd like sleeping in his sisters' room and whether his own room could simply be hacked off from the rest of the cottage, broken up into pieces, and heaved into the ocean. The cottage was sinking in that corner, and maybe taking off that room would free the rest of the rooms from the deadweight.

They were on top of him before they noticed him, Lily's chest square against the pony's flank, the man making a wet, clicking sound with his mouth as he led the animal out of her way.

'Pardon, Missus,' the man said, pulling his hat down over his face and plowing shoulders-first into the crowded byway, the pony walking behind him. From the window of the bus a short time later they saw him again, this time playing his fiddle down by the river, his hat turned skyward like a hand held out palm up. There were no tents down by the river, no wagons either, and Lily remembered that it was October and he should be at the horse fair in Ballinasloe.

'He didn't see us,' Lily said to Tom, who was seated across the aisle. 'He wouldn't know us, anyhow.'

And down by the place where the fresh water of the river rushed up unseen against the salt water of the harbor, Dermot Ward leaned against a bench and ran through every song he could think of about the men of myths, the women who mourned them. Finally, his elbow screaming, his neck aching, his shoulder crying to be let loose, he exhausted himself enough to face the songs he'd gone down to the river to sing in the first place, the old, beaten ballads about leaving for America.

PART III
Letters

November 1, 1963

Mrs Lily Cahill and Tom Cahill
Ballyroan
Conch
Co. Galway
Ireland

Dear Mammy and Tom,

Just a quick line to say we've landed, safe and sound. There was great fun on the ship though not for me as I was sick the whole time and after so many days we're delighted to be on firm ground. Shannon met us and took us for a sandwich and that's where I am right now – standing outside a place called Broadway Delicatessen. We've barely had a chance to look around and see are we really in New York City. You both should see the electricity here and this is only daytime. I haven't even seen it at night. And no wires in the air to carry the current so I don't know how they do it. When we got up to the street there were so many people and cars rushing I thought great, we're here in time to see the big emergency and Shannon said it was no emergency, just the way things always are here. We took a yellow taxicab because of the bags and Michael sat up front with the driver. We've still not seen the place where Shannon lives so that tells you how long we've been here. An American woman on the ship gave Johanna and me an airmail stamp each when she heard we were gone from home for the first time and told us to write our mother. We would have done anyway but I thought that was nice. Johanna was tempted to tell her we didn't have a mother just to give her something to chew on but in the end she took her stamp and said thank you. Saving Johanna's stamp for news once settled.

Love you both, miss you, God Bless.
Greta

November 7, 1963

Mrs Lily Cahill
Ballyroan
Conch
Co. Galway
Ireland

Mammy,

I hope you are well and not missing us too much. Hello Tom! Shannon is a pure saint. We've been here six nights, myself and Johanna on a bed that folds out of a sofa, and Michael on the floor of another small room she uses for pressing and to hang up some of her clothes. She seems happy to have us though three is a lot and her flat is about the size of our kitchen at home with your bedroom attached. We try to make ourselves scarce and clear out sometimes to give Shannon room, but we don't want to wander too far yet. I never knew places could be this busy and I'm amazed at how everyone knows exactly where they're going and how to get there but that's very stupid of me I suppose. I mentioned the electricity in my first but now I've seen it at night and I think they must have to replace bulbs every day with the brightness all night long. The streets are lit, the shops, the windows of the buildings, and everything is packed in so close together that it makes it so it's bright out all the time. There's even doors that swing open by electricity when they feel you standing there which takes a while to get used to. Michael already found work moving furniture for people switching flats and needing their things carried downstairs and into a lorry. He starts on Monday and found it thanks to a man on the ship whose friend runs the business. Guess where the man's friend is from? Roundstone. He was surprised we don't have much Irish, and we explained a bit about Ballyroan. Michael was smart and said he was from Cork where the man had never been. Shannon wasn't telling tales when she said there's Irish everywhere and every other kind of a person you could think of as well. The moving will earn Michael good wages and he says he will give half to Shannon. Johanna and I will do the same when we find something. First thing we'll do is cook her up a nice supper to have waiting when she comes home. It'll take a while to get used to the shops here though Shannon says they try to be like the Irish shops because that's where everyone is from who lives in Queens. Or lives in Woodside. I keep forgetting if Woodside is inside Queens, or Queens inside Woodside. I don't think they're a bit like Irish shops, though I suppose I only ever shopped in Conch and maybe that's different. I forgot to say last time that within an hour of getting here we saw people who were dark like that man we saw in Galway once, but not the same type of dark. These were Indian. They are lovely looking people and reminded me a bit of home the way the women had their babies in a sling that went over their shoulder and around their backs. Shannon says there's sections of the city all Indian like Woodside (that's Queens) is all Irish. We met two girls in Shannon's building yesterday from Limerick who said they can't go home because they were only supposed to be here thirty days and now it's gone over a year and if they go home they won't be let come back. They said we're lucky we got a sponsor and the right paperwork because that means we can work here without going off the books which means our employer can pay us with a check and nothing is in secret. They had another friend who was illegal and got a job making up the rooms in a hotel. They paid her for a few weeks and then stopped and told her the wages would be delayed. Long story short she worked for six weeks without wages and can't do a thing about it because she's not supposed to be here working in the first place. There are a lot of rules about it and Johanna is already studying them. Send the news from home whenever you have the time.

Love,
Greta

P.S. Some of the *gardai* in America – police, they say, or cops – are on horseback and trot up and down among the cars. I wonder do they ever do a full gallop. They have horse and buggies for hire as well. Johanna says to write horse and carriage and its very dear and she thinks they only do it for a laugh, not really to get place to place. But she is writing you her own letter and should stop butting into mine.

November 8, 1963

Mrs Lily Cahill
Ballyroan
Conch
Co. Galway
Ireland

Dear Mrs Cahill,

I asked the girls to hold their letters for one day so I could stick mine in with it. I should have written earlier, but I think Greta already sent a note to let you know they'd arrived. They were selling postcards on the pier on the day the ship came in, and she was determined to pick one out to send to you, never mind how exhausted she was or that the man was barking at her for exact change. All three of them were wobbly from ten days at sea, and Greta took the longest to adjust to walking on land. She was doing zigzags down the pier and we had to catch her by the elbow. Of course the four of us were dying laughing, and it came to me that anyone else might be sensitive. Not Greta. They're two great girls, and Michael Ward is a very nice kid, and I doubt it will take much time for them to learn the ropes. Poor things are crammed into the pullout together, and Michael sleeping in a closet, but they don't have a word of complaint. This is what my mother must have meant when she always told me to be more like the kids from Ireland. Oh, and one day while I was at work they scraped together ingredients from my pathetic cupboards to make a brown bread. I could get used to that kind of treatment!

The girls do a little walking around the neighborhood each day just to get their bearings (not too far, don't worry), but they are more interested in Manhattan — taller buildings, brighter lights. Johanna especially, and I don't blame her. As soon as I get a free day, I'm going to take them in to see the Empire State Building. Michael has more courage and I get the sense he's traveled quite a bit. Except for that first day when the ship came in, he hasn't been to Manhattan yet either, but he's explored Woodside in and out, and on my way home from work the other evening I ran into him studying the bus and subway map. He asked me to point out where we were, and once I told him, it all made sense. He has it memorized by color and number and has already figured out north, south, east, west. Instead of doing it by the streets, he does it by the river, which is genius if you ask me. He says he can smell which direction the river is, and I can't tell if he's having me on. I don't worry about him getting lost, and some mornings he strikes out on his own even before I've left for work. I don't think he likes being stuck in my tiny apartment all day. He starts a job the day after tomorrow.

Anyway, I just wanted to assure you that your girls are safe and happy, which I'm sure they've told you themselves. They mention you and Tom a lot, different things they wish you could see, and of the three of them I'd say Greta misses home the most. She'll be fine though. Half of New York is from somewhere else and everyone is fine after a while. I hope you and Tom are getting along okay in Ballyroan.

Best,
Shannon O'Clery

November 20, 1963

Mrs Lily Cahill
Ballyroan
Conch
Co. Galway
Ireland

Mammy,

Thanks for your letter and tell Tom not to get too cozy in our room as he'll only have to move his things again when we come back. Mammy, we had no clue you sent Shannon money in advance and have been sick wondering where you got it as there was only one bull sold as far as we know. How did you swing it? But you're right, we'll give her a quarter of what we earn and we can save up the rest so we can get out of her hair – which she'd probably like better than the extra few dollars anyway. Johanna overheard her telling the girls from Limerick that we'd only be with her a few weeks, which is true, I hope, but gave us a feeling like we should hurry. Speaking of Tom, next time he passes the main post office in Oughterard could he leave in a note for Dermot Ward with our address in America? Michael forgot to put it in the letter we did up for him before leaving and thinks his father might check in at Oughterard before Christmas.

Sorry I didn't write sooner, but Johanna has been sick with the flu for the last week. We didn't want to bother Shannon with it but she noticed herself and has brought Johanna to the doctor's office where she works. I'd say just a piece of bad meat that stayed with her. The noise and action here is enough to throw a person into a tizzy. I'm the expert at being sick as I spent the first 24 hours of the Atlantic journey on the floor of the ladies loo. You know Johanna doesn't like being down so you can imagine the mood she's been in. All day and all night there's cars and sirens and people walking on the sidewalk outside. Even at three o'clock in the morning we hear them talking as they pass by under the window. We've been on the subway at least a dozen times now, and it's easy enough as long as you pay very close mind to how many stops you've gone and the name of the place where you have to get out. We only take the one from Woodside, where Shannon lives, and haven't moved on to any others. Sometimes two subways go to the same stop and people race from one train to another even though they're going in the same direction. There are some trains that skip stops and go faster but we decided slow and steady is the way and we've nowhere to be in a hurry anyhow. The first time we went without Shannon there was a woman with the biggest diddies you ever saw and just half a little gansy on her. She had a giant bare belly as well, twice Mr Carmel's who we've long said will need a double-wide coffin when he goes. She was shouting about something and making a spectacle and next thing Johanna looked up and we were gone two stops too many. Then the lights in the trains went out for fifteen minutes so I guess there's a few kinks in the electricity even in America. When the lights came back on a policeman helped us get back. And guess where the policeman's mother is from. Clifden.

Johanna has an interview to work at Bloomingdale's, which is a famous store downtown. Shannon said it would be fabulous to be hired there and is lending her a suit and high heels which she tried on last night and looked like a million bucks. If she gets it she'll have to buy a few nice things because they want their sales ladies to look presentable and they give their employees a discount for that reason. It pays good wages so say a prayer that her flu is gone by tomorrow and she won't have to run out of the room in search of a loo. By the time you get this she'll know either way, and God willing I'll have something of my own lined up soon.

Love,
Greta

P.S. Went to St Patrick's Cathedral and lit a candle each for you, Tom, Jack, and Padraic. Forgot Jack's new bride but will remember next time.

November 22, 1963

Mr Dermot Ward
c/o Post Master
Ballinasloe
Co. Galway
Ireland

Dear Da –

I didn't know whether to try you in Oughterard or Ballinasloe so I'm sending the same note to both. Greta Cahill is putting this on paper for me – you remember, the youngest girl of that house in

Ballyroan – so I don't want to go on too long. I also don't want to give too much gossip to the Post Master who is surely reading this to you. I need to talk to you about something and I want to talk by telephone. As it is November I expect you are heading to Galway City shortly. There are shops around the fisherman's market that will let a person accept a call for a few P. If you could be in a shop in Galway or Salt Hill in a few weeks time I could call you there. Just let me know where and what day. Send a reply to the address on the front of this envelope.

Your son,
Michael Ward

December 5, 1963

Mrs Lily Cahill and Mr Tom Cahill
Ballyroan
Conch
Co. Galway
Ireland

Dear Mammy and Tom,

Sorry it's been a few weeks since you last heard from us. I should have wrote sooner to say Johanna is fine, just a piece of bad meat like I thought. That's me making a big production out of nothing. So don't worry! Johanna would have wrote herself but she's been busy and knows I'm a better letter writer than she is (she only means I can sit for longer without getting antsy). I hope you haven't been thinking of it ever since. Funny thing is she did have to miss that interview she had at Bloomingdale's so I went in her place. Johanna told me how to do it. When they called Johanna Cahill I stood up and told the secretary that Greta is my legal name, Johanna a nickname, and I'd like to go by Greta from now on. She just scratched out Johanna and put Greta and kept me at age seventeen. And guess what? I got the job. I put the price tags on the clothes that come in and hang up clothes after people leave them behind in the changing room and when the store is closed myself and two other girls fold everything displayed on the tables in our section and make sure everything is hung up in the right spot. They give us a wooden board to fold with and you should see how nice it makes the stacks. It's easy and the things they sell there are lovely though very dear. There's a popular navy blue skirt going for 60 USD. The lining is done very well, but the zipper and the button are as simple as could be and to my eye could be better. Then again as you know my eyes aren't so good. I get my first check on Friday and I'm supposed to spend some of it buying clothes to wear to work which Johanna thinks is damn rich that the money will go right back in their pockets. Shannon is going to bring me to a place that sells the leftover Bloomingdale's clothes from a year or two ago and are marked down to almost nothing so I'm going to go there instead. She said it will be easy for me to find things as I'm so slim which is a big thing here – being slim. To think I always dreamed of putting meat on these bones! Johanna's looking around for something else, but she'll tell you all about that when she writes. Mammy, between the new clothes and the dollars I want to give to Shannon I don't know how much I'll have left to send but I'll send whatever I can.

The other delay was President Kennedy getting killed in Texas. I'd say it was big news at home, was it? I didn't know much about him but everyone says he was a great man, and his poor wife has been on the television news every minute. The new man who took over was on the television on Thanksgiving (that was last week – we went to a big parade) and he seems nice enough but not as nice as JFK. His name is Lyndon Johnson but you probably know that already. I know Tom is good about reading the papers. Give him my love and I miss you both very much.

Love,
Greta

P.S. If you do a novena include me and Johanna and Michael Ward. No special reason just because it's almost Christmas and we've been missing home.

December 6, 1963

Mr Dermot Ward
c/o Post Master
Ballinasloe
Co. Galway
Ireland

Da –

   If you've brought this back to camp for Bitty Ward to read for you, take it from her now and bring it into town to a stranger.

   You can forget the letter of a few weeks ago and the plan to talk by telephone. Since I haven't heard from you yet I don't think it would have gone off anyway. Greta Cahill now knows all and so I can write what I need to talk to you about with her putting it on paper for me.

   As I hope you know by now from the letter I sent before leaving for America, when I left camp I went to Ballyroan to visit my mother's grave. I stayed and found work there and enjoyed living in one place even if it ended up being only for a few months. I got to know the Cahill family. Remember how they took Mother in that time? They were very good to me. Most of all I got to know Johanna Cahill, the oldest of the two girls, the one you invited to sit at our fire late at night years ago.

   Johanna Cahill is now expecting a baby. It must have happened on the ship, a ten day journey, because it hadn't happened before or since in that way. It is not the best thing to happen but I remembered how you said a *gasúr* is always a blessing, even if it's a blessing well disguised. Also, since her Mam was so good to me I must be good to her. And I want to be. And Greta will help in any way she can. That's Johanna's sister.

   I know what you think about country people all having money to burn, but I saw with my own eyes that wasn't the case at the Cahills unless you count eggs and milk and hay as cash money. I'm sorry to say so as Greta Cahill is the one putting this letter on paper, but she knows it well herself. We're right now staying with a friend of the Cahill family whose mother was from Ballyroan, but we'd like to get out from under her feet and get our own place. Then the three of us can figure everything out in our own way, plus the child when he or she comes in late July. I wonder if you've anything at all to spare? We've considered going straight back to Ireland, but the truth is we don't have the fare and the girls don't want their mother to know yet. I don't think she's the type that would cast them off, but I'd say she's a worrier and they're barely hanging on out there as is. Johanna is determined to stay in the United States. I've gotten steady work since arriving, and I know I can get more. It wouldn't be long until I could pay you back. If there was anyone else to ask, I would. Please write back to the return address on the front of this envelope. Just have whoever puts the letter down for you to copy the address exactly and your reply will come straight back to me.

Your son,
Michael Ward

December 24, 1963

Mrs Lily Cahill and Mr Tom Cahill
Ballyroan
Conch
Co. Galway
Ireland

Mammy and Tom,

I can't believe I'm only writing this now and you won't get it until after the New Year. I'll say it anyway – Happy Christmas. Johanna was supposed to send a long one from both of us but just confessed that she hasn't gotten to it yet. We are disgusted with ourselves knowing you'll be expecting to hear from us. I hope Jack and Padraic sent long ones from Australia. We got your card yesterday morning and put it up around the door with Shannon's and it is by far the nicest. Did you get it at Mrs Norton's? It was good of you to send a separate card to Michael as he's heard nothing from his family since the day he left them in the Burren. He says their ways are different from ours, but I can tell he would love to hear something from them and my heart breaks for him when he checks our box or asks did anything come for him. He wonders about his sister a lot lately. To tell the truth I'd almost forgotten he had a twin.

Bloomingdale's is mobbed before Christmas, and that's really the reason I haven't written. People stream in all day and leave all my neat stacks of sweaters and scarves topsy turvy. I have to swoop in the moment they turn away and make them neat again. We are not allowed to make the customer feel bad for making an unholy mess but it's a test not to cast hard looks. I'd never go into a shop and leave such a sight after me knowing someone else has to straighten it up. I won't even tell you how much people spend on stockings and belts and that kind of thing because it would make you cry (or laugh, I don't know). Once Christmas passes it will be back to normal and the funny thing is that everything being snatched up this week will be on sale for half off or more. If we're still in America next year I'm going to make a rule that we exchange gifts on the feast of the Epiphany instead of 25 Dec. No one celebrates St Stephen's Day here either. I'd say it would be hard to catch a wren in New York City.

So it looks like we'll be leaving Shannon the first week of January. We found a flat on 84th Street and 2nd Avenue in Manhattan where we can all live with room to spare. Johanna and I will be in one bedroom, Michael Ward in the other, and there's a sitting room and small kitchen as well. It's a nice part of the city, quieter than Shannon's part even though it's in Manhattan which you would expect to be busier. There are a lot of German people living there and it seems like that's the way it goes all over the city – people sticking together until the whole section is full of the same kind. They have a section for Chinese, Italians, Germans, Russians and others I don't know the names of. You can walk through and think you're in another country, then fifteen blocks later you're in another country again. A lot of the blacks and the people who speak Spanish live in awful bad neighborhoods, God love them. And then there's people who don't live anywhere at all not even in camps like the tinkers. They just live in the street or in the parks and Shannon says we're to walk right by them and pretend we don't hear them if they beg. The young ones who are men I don't mind so much but when they're a big age or women with babies wrapped up it's very hard especially when it's bitter cold like it is now. Shannon says there are places that would give them beds and something hot to eat, but I'd say most of them are not right in the head. I pass one woman every morning and sometimes see her fixing herself and arranging her coat on her shoulders when she's lying down on her side and the way she fixes the coat makes me think that's a woman who's used to sleeping in a bed. Michael saw one stuffing balled up newspapers under his clothes and said that's a trick the tinkers should learn.

I work with a girl from Trinidad and the way she talks about home sounds the same as any of us. I don't know how she could have left such a pretty place and her father and her sisters and she says the same about me leaving you and Tom and Ballyroan. We both have the same plan to save for a year or two and then go back. I told her to visit me in Ballyroan one day and she said she'd try.

I know it will surprise you that Michael will live with us even now that we're beginning to get our bearings, but we feel very much like a team here so far and it hasn't been very long. Also, we are only able to live in the apartment because Michael will be the handyman for the building – they call it being a superintendent which is a fancier word than the job really is. We will live there for free and only have to pay for the telephone, which we might not even hook up. Who do we call? Michael told the owner of the building that we are his sisters otherwise he wouldn't have let us live there with Michael. The man is a German Catholic in the old style and said he likes Irish because all Irish are good Catholics. We didn't tell him how long its been since we've seen the inside of a church, but Johanna pointed out that seeing the inside of a church has nothing to do with it when you consider how many miserable cranks never miss a Sunday. Take Lucy Sullivan for example how we've long said she wouldn't give a person the steam of her piss but is up there with her tongue out for communion every morning. The point is that once you start sending letters there, send them to Johanna and Greta Ward. In exchange for the free apartment, Michael will be in charge of repairs and problems for the nineteen other apartments in the building. He'll also take care of the building's rubbish and keeping the steps and entryway swept and clean. The floors of each hall and five flights of stairs have to be scrubbed twice a week. Officially he's the one in charge, but we've already divided up what we'll each do for him since he's absolutely in tatters when he comes home from work.

Johanna got a temporary job taking care of an old woman. She's a big age, close to ninety I'd say, and Johanna doesn't have to do much, just keep her company and push her through the park in her wheelchair. Sometimes the woman likes Johanna to chat just because she likes Johanna's brogue. That's another thing we discovered in America. Everyone seems to like an Irish brogue. In England we've heard of people trying to lose it fast or make it sound Scottish that's how much people hate it. But everyone in America has at least one Irish grandparent. Every single person, honest to God. There must have been an awful lot of people in Ireland once to make grandparents to this many Americans. The woman Johanna minds is very wealthy and lives in a hotel all the time and has an entire floor to herself. Her son who hired Johanna comes in once every few days to check on things. During the week another girl comes in at night and takes over when Johanna goes home, but on weekends Johanna sleeps there, too. It's only for six weeks while the regular woman recovers from an operation of some kind, and she already has three of the six weeks behind her. The wages are very good though, far better than mine or Michael's. We're all hoping the woman will start to love Johanna so much that she won't want to let her go when the six weeks are up in mid January.

That's all the news from here. I'll write again when we're in the new apartment.

Love you, Miss you,
Greta

P.S. These few things are from Johanna and me both. Tom, these gloves are not for mending walls! Mammy, I hope you like the dress. I know I complain about the price of things at work but I got these with my discount and were a great bargain.

P.P.S. Why does the thing I said about Lucy Sullivan look awful when it's written down but doesn't sound so bad when we say it out loud?

January 13, 1964

Mr Dermot Ward
c/o Main Post Office
Galway City
Co. Galway
Ireland

Da –

If you haven't left Galway already I know you're leaving soon and heading to Munster where there's little chance of a letter finding you. We are in a better situation than when I last wrote and now it's not money I need but a little advice. Johanna was making great wages at a temporary job we were sure would turn into something permanent. She's not showing yet but mentioned on the job that she was expecting a baby thinking that a little sympathy would go a long way, but it went in the opposite direction and they showed her the door. I thought they only cared about things like that in Ireland. We can get by thanks to a few other things that have gone our way, but that doesn't help Johanna's mood which has been bad for almost three months now. I understand when she's feeling sick, and when she's worried, but it's something else and I don't know what to say to her. Since the ship we have been like brother and sister and that's all I'll say on that subject as Greta is taking down this letter. I've gotten to know a few men at work but I don't like saying much about my situation and don't want to ask about the mood their women were in while expecting as they'll wonder why I'm asking and no one knows a thing about Johanna or if they do they think she's my sister. Greta, who knows her best, doesn't know what to say to her either. Sometimes she's stone quiet, and sometimes she's mad as a March hare. Mam, God rest her, knew about these things and I wonder if she passed much of it on to you.

Please write back. I'm at a new address. Check the front of the envelope.

Your son,
Michael Ward

February 2, 1964

Mrs Lily Cahill and Mr Tom Cahill
Ballyroan
Conch
Co. Galway
Ireland

Mammy and Tom,

We're in the new apartment and all is well. We figured out quickly that some of the people who live here would bang on the door with a different problem every day and have us running up and down the stairs for every little thing. Most of the people are lovely and have stopped by to welcome us. On our floor there's two older women whose husbands have died and live on their own, and one young couple with two small boys. The young couple is from Hamburg in Germany and their two boys have their accent. The mother of the boys says they'll lose it once they go to school which will be a shame. Whenever I hear young children with accents or speaking another language I think how smart they must be, though of course it's all they know and I might sound smart to them just speaking English though I doubt it.

Mammy, you mentioned in your last that Johanna doesn't write and all I can tell you is that she's busy with her job – she got hired on a permanent basis minding the old woman (hooray!) – and she knows I give you all the news. There is no need to be worried about her. You know Johanna, she's too busy soaking up the sights and sounds. If you remember she was never great at writing the boys either but would add a p.s. to my letters. She sends her love even if I forget to mention it.

About Mrs O'Connor's niece who would like to visit New York. We'd love to have her stay with us but I'm afraid the next few months wouldn't work. We're all busy with our jobs and would have no time to show the poor girl around. We have to be careful, too, in case the owner wouldn't like us having guests. If she's just wanting to do a little sightseeing, maybe she could hold off for a little while and we'll see where we're at in a few months. Will Mrs O'Connor be huffy about it do you think?

Tom, I'm sorry to say I can't say what New Yorkers think of the Beach Boys as we don't chat much with too many New Yorkers except the ones we work with and the ones I work with are all women and think the Beach Boys a bit boring. I know you don't like them either. I looked up a picture of Johnny Cash in the record shop and he's a bit rough looking just like you guessed. He has black hair and a longish nose and looks like you might see him footing turf as soon as you'd see him up on a stage.

Wish I had more news but every day is about the same. Send whatever news you have from home.

Love you and Miss you,
Greta

February 12, 1964

Michael Ward
222 East 84th Street
Apartment 1A
New York, New York 10028
United States of America

Michael,

Bitty is putting this down. Da got your letters but late. He said I can write if I want but hes deciding in his mind if he will or not. Did you steal the bicicle Michael? The *gardai* came and gave us grief and took Nora's Malachy into the station to ask questions and later I put 2 and 2 together that Malachy looks a bit like you with the hair and size of him. We had to stay at camp an extra week and you know how Da hates a delay anyway but even more when its one of us wrongly accused. You took it dint you? It was brand new unless they just said that to make it worse. In the end Da had to pay fifty quid to get Malachy.

It dosnt sound like you got too far away after all did you. Yes, New York City but living with your woman and her sister and a *gasúr* on the way. And you moved how many times since leaving us? Dosnt sound too different from camp. Da is heartsick over it though he wont say it and the purpose of this letter is to say dont write again because it makes him mental for a week and pure useless at the work he has to do and if he makes up his mind to write to you then after that you can send him another letter. Are you coming back to Ireland soon?

The babies are fine, fat, and strong.

Maeve

May 12, 1964

Johanna and Greta Cahill Ward
222 East 84th Street
Apt. 1A
New York, New York 10028
U.S.A.

Dear Greta and Johanna,

Mammy is worried sick that she doesn't here from either of you. First Johanna, then Greta. Your last was a letter from Greta on 2 Feb. Did letters since then get lost in the post? Mammy says she's sent three and will hold off on a fourth until she heres from you and you know the price of an airmail stamp. It's just the two of us now and she's gotten so quiet it's like I'm by myself. Remember when Da first died and she wouldn't get dressed all day? It's a bit like that except once in a while she'll snap out of it and give me a great big speech about how it's wonderful you went, and went together, and are doing so well. There's such a thing as getting on in a new place but not forgetting the old place either, isn't there? Remember what it was like here when she didn't here from Jack or Padraic for a while? You being girls makes it worse.

I'm sorry to be so mean but it's only because we miss you and like to here. I go to the dances now and again but in a few years I'll be too old for them. Once Liam McGuinness stops going I'll be the oldest. He's closing in on thirty-seven and still brings the bottle within in his vest. Let's hope it doesn't get to that. There is a card game starting up at your old boss James Breen's inn and maybe I'll start going for the *craic*.

If you write don't say a thing about this or else she'll think you were put up to it.

God Bless.
Tom

P.S. You'll never guess my good luck but John Gilroy left for Canada a month ago Wednesday and left a Ferguson record player behind for his father to sell. Who did I run into but John Sr at a dairy demo and he asked did I want it and wouldn't accept anything for it as he wouldn't know what price to ask and if he sold it he'd have to send the money to John Jr who should have taken care of his business before he left.

June 2, 1964

Greta Cahill
222 East 84th Street
Apartment 1A
New York, NY 10028

Dear Greta,

Sorry to be so formal with a letter but I couldn't find your number, and then I remembered that last time Johanna was at the clinic for her checkup she mentioned you never hooked up your phone. I hope all is well in Yorkville.

I'm really writing to tell you that your mother called me this morning and I figured out fast that she knows nothing about Johanna's situation. She was calling from a shop in Conch, and honestly

Greta, I could have cried for her because I could hear the worry in her voice, and I know how my own mother used to get when she worried. She has no idea how far Woodside is from the Upper East Side and wondered if she waited in the shop could I run up to get you and bring you back to my place. I told her I'd arrange to have one of you here next Saturday. Greta, please be here or send Johanna, because I don't like the position I'm in. I took the number of the shop and said I'd have you ring around 3:00 Irish time, so be here before 10:00.

Speaking of Johanna, when I see her at the clinic she is nothing like the girl I met in Ballyroan. I realize she comes here because it's cheap and because it's where she first found out, but there are other places in the city that specialize in pregnant women's moods and bouts of depression and that kind of thing and I know there have been cases in the past where bad feeling gets a whole lot worse after the child is born. She mentions Los Angeles and Chicago in a dreamy kind of way that makes me wonder if she realizes she's going to be a mother in eight weeks. I don't want to overstep my bounds, but she is very young, and I wonder if she and Michael have discussed all their options. I know she didn't want to hear anything about that other option we discussed back in November, but there are more for after the child is born. A lot of American couples would kill for an Irish baby and Johanna and Michael might even get a say in picking the parents. This has surely occurred to her, but I wonder since you are the one closest to her if you could feel out what she's thinking or if she's thinking at all. I hope your mother doesn't blame me for all of this happening.

Telling your mother would be a way to lighten the load for all of us, and – who knows? – she might have the perfect solution. Have you thought that it might be time to go back home? New York is wonderful, but it's not for everyone. Just make sure one or both of you are here at 10:00 A.M. on Saturday.

See you soon,
Shannon

June 4, 1964

Shannon O'Clery
39—28 61st Street
Apt. 3D
Woodside, New York 11377

Shannon,

Thanks for your letter about Mother. I have to work all Saturday and
Johanna won't go talk to her on the telephone. We fought about it all
morning since getting your letter. She barely leaves the apartment
except to go visiting with the woman who lives upstairs from us and
who Michael says is a big drinker from the looks of the garbage she puts
out and also we found her sleeping once in the 3rd floor hallway (she
lives on the 2nd floor). Johanna talks to her more than she talks to us
lately and I don't know why. Michael worries would Johanna ever take
a drink with the woman, but I think it's just company she's after that is
not myself or Michael. I hope, anyhow. I sniff her when she comes
home and never smelled anything off her and you told her that time at
the clinic how bad that would be for the baby. I don't have hurt feelings
for myself because I know how Johanna can be, but I feel sorry for
Michael who thinks he's done something wrong when he's been nothing but good-natured throughout all of this. It's Johanna who should
be talking to me about the baby, but instead it's Michael I sit down with
at the end of each day and the two of us have to guess how she's feeling
and how the baby is doing because she doesn't say. Michael and I are the
ones who've started collecting clothes and nappies and she doesn't seem
the least bit thankful for it. She's long stopped looking for work, though
I guess she can't be blamed for that as no one would hire her in her
condition. I've taken on as many shifts as I can and if the ones at home
could see me when I'm working I think they'd barely recognize me.
Sometimes I barely recognize myself when I'm firm with the women
who want a discount, or how fast I can hurry up the aisle to check a
price. I thought it would be harder doing a job in a place where no one
knows me, but it's easier because I can always pretend to know exactly
what I'm doing. The ones at home would know the truth straight away.

189

To Michael Johanna acts like he has nothing to do with the situation she's in and like it's none of his business what happens to her or the child at the end of July. He asked if he could go with her to the clinic and she said no thank you just the same as if he'd invited her to go for a walk. So then I had the idea to go to the public library, the two of us, and look up everything that she was learning from the nurses at the clinic. We looked on our own for a bit with no luck, but then a woman helped us find what we wanted. When we were leaving she wished us all the best and I realized she thought we were thinking about having a baby together. Michael got red in the face but I laughed for the first time since before we got this news.

I'm sorry to ramble but I'm worried, and I'm rushing because I want to post this to you on my way to work. Please just keep it light with my mother and tell her I'll have a long one in the mail to her by the end of the week. Tell her I love her and I miss her and we'll try for the telephone call another time.

Love,
Greta

June 9, 1964

Mrs Lily Cahill
Ballyroan
Conch
Co. Galway
Ireland

Mammy,

I hope the thickness of this envelope will make up for how long it has been since you last heard from me, but I doubt it. I have no good excuse except work and a habit of putting things off. Every night I think I should write and then I think maybe something will happen tomorrow that I'll wish I'd held the letter to tell you about. And then I didn't write for so long that I didn't know how to start up again knowing how worried you must be and knowing I have no good excuse. In the beginning a new thing happened every hour, but now every day is almost the same. We've settled into a pattern of waking up and doing. It's not so different from how it was at home when you think about it except for the wages on every other Friday and the buildings and the people. If you look out the kitchen at home and try to count the blades of grass that's the number of people I swear I pass every day, or who pass me.

Remember the rich American lady I invented when I was five or six and Johanna was at school? I've been thinking of her lately and where I could have gotten her. Some of the women I see in Bloomie's could be my rich American lady. I guess it means I was always meant to come here. I'm glad you made me come.

Remember how we used to say city people don't get up until midmorning because they didn't do real work? In New York that isn't true. The city is awake before dawn. Not everyone, but some. I wonder if it would help you at home to be able to picture my day. I get up around half five to help Michael tie up the trash and bring it outside to the curb. I tie, he carries. It's a big job with twenty apartments including ours, and people leave their trash a mess just throwing it in the bin without the top tied off. We have to make it neat and tidy so the people passing on the sidewalk would hardly notice it at all. The trucks come to collect it twice a week. We try to make this fun by saying things about what we see in the trash, or I make up a story about someone's weekend seeing what they've eaten and bought and Michael says what I lack in muscle I make up for in imagination. When the trash is taken care of Michael goes up ahead of me to the fifth floor and sweeps the hallway and the stairs. I wait a few minutes and then go up after him with a mop and bucket and wash down the hall where he's swept. I follow him down to the first floor and it's a pretty good system if I do say so. We can still talk while we're doing this because the voices carry in the stairwell almost the same as if we were beside each other, but sometimes we get afraid of waking people up. Michael sings songs in that language tinkers have and next thing I find myself humming them even though I haven't a clue what they're about. Then he goes down to the basement to check the mousetraps and the different poisons he has to put down for the cockroaches and other things that get into buildings if you don't keep it up every day, and I get ready for work because I go the earliest. On the weekends we work on the flower boxes outside. If someone has a plumbing emergency they come banging on the door for Michael. He's seen a few flushing toilets in Ireland with all the places he's been – probably more flushing toilets than I've seen – but he doesn't know a thing about how they work. He's figuring it out and says it's perfectly logical the way the water is carried in the pipes and then shoots out in different directions the closer to the apartment it gets. You should hear how we laugh when he comes in after talking to one of the tenants like an expert and little do they know his bathroom for eighteen years was whatever patch of grass he could find. He talks about knobs and levers and they believe every word he says. He fixed Mr Karmel's toilet on the 5th floor and next thing the water in the bowl was boiling hot. Steam coming up out of it I swear to God. He went about fixing it back but the man stopped him and said he likes a warm seat when he gets up in the morning. Next thing the woman down the hall comes knocking that she wants a hot bowl like Mr Karmel's.

Mammy, New York City is not as big or as frightening as it seemed at first, and no where near as scary as when I had bad dreams about it before leaving home. You can't imagine all the people and sometimes when I think I'd like to stay home and curl up in bed it helps to just open the door and step outside because it gives me a feeling like I want to get moving and see where everyone else is going. To get to work I take the train that runs underground like we've told you about in other letters. I walk to 86th Street, just two blocks north, then across Third Avenue up to Lexington which is the avenue we used to hear about sometimes at home like Broadway and Fifth Avenue. It's a longer distance between avenues than it is between blocks. I get on the subway going downtown and you should see the throngs of people who get on every morning. They just shove themselves inside like sardines and this time of year it's hot and muggy and some days the smell is worse than anything coming out of the stable at home. Most of the people look sharp with suits and lovely dresses on them and you'd never know from looking at their faces that they smell what I smell which is each other sweating like pigs. Come to think of it even the pigs don't sweat like this. I get off at 59th Street and if I'm a few minutes early I go stand in the lobby of any office building to soak up the cold air they have forced out of vents and that helps me dry off and cool down and look like I haven't ridden to work on a pack of wild ponies.

Before the store opens I go up to my department which is ladies intimates and hosiery. It's just underpants, night dresses, bras, and that kind of thing. Bathrobes. Slips. Gansies (except they don't say gansies in America). Myself and two other girls unpack any new shipments that have come in. When the shipments come in the things are so wrinkled and horrible you'd never imagine them selling period never mind for the prices they ask for. But we steam them and get them looking lovely and hang them out with the rest. Once a week we make a rack with what's on sale but we don't decide that. Our boss decides, and I think someone else tells her. I've already told you about the wooden folding boards that make folding easy. I've never worked the register but one day I probably will. I've gotten better with American change and am close to being able to pick the right amount out of my purse without laying it out on my palm and trying to see is it a five cents or a ten cents or a quarter. I'm in charge of the dressing room which might sound easy but can get to be a bit of a madhouse depending on the day. There are ten changing rooms in our section and sometimes those fill up so fast a line forms that goes all the way past the racks of clothes, past the register, all the way back to the escalator (the stairs that move). I have to fetch different sizes and take away the clothes they don't like. Women in New York always try the smallest size first, then work their way up. When the smallest ones don't fit they get in awful moods and sometimes take it out on me. One thing I have to work on is how to say the names of some of the brands they have. I try to imitate what I hear the other women say but the boss says I say most things the wrong way and I should practice or else be stuck folding and steaming. I don't mind folding and steaming too much but I think I should practice anyway. Also an Irish woman came in the other week looking for a gift and whispered to me that she couldn't believe the prices they were asking for some things, and I agreed it was all too dear and we laughed about it. Later the boss said I'd been overheard by another salesperson and I said I didn't see what was wrong with having a laugh with a customer and she said if I didn't see anything wrong with what I said then I might not be right for the job. It was only that the woman was about your age and even though she had a Dublin brogue it made me think what I'd do if I saw you come through the door one day.

Don't worry about what the boss said. Another time she told me I was doing a great job, which you mightn't be able to believe, so I think she only said it to scare me a bit. I do think I'm doing a good job and I think it helps being in a place where no one knows me so they don't expect me to make a mistake. I love getting that paycheck every other week.

It's an eight hour day but I usually get overtime which I love because they give you time and a half. That's what you make per hour plus half again. We're saving a fair amount of money and sending Shannon a check once in a while, but she never brings them to her bank so we have to go down there with cash one day soon. Johanna and I have one bank account and Michael has his own.

I get home around eight o'clock and eat the rest of whatever Johanna or Michael has cooked. One thing we didn't know about Michael is he's a brilliant cook. He's also very smart and I swear he could figure out anything if you just gave him thirty minutes alone with it especially things like pipes and tools and wires. After dinner if it's very hot in the apartment I usually make a cup of tea and sit out on the stoop of the building to watch the people going by. Michael likes watching the people too and usually comes out to sit with me. Whenever I've thought I could stay here forever it's been while sitting on the stoop. Whenever I think I'll be back in Ballyroan before 1965 it's been on the subway with my nice ironed blouse soaked through.

Mammy, I know you are anxious to hear about Johanna and it's not that I'm avoiding talking about her but I think it's her business to discuss. I honestly can't tell you if she loves New York or hates it. She says she doesn't want to go back home, but when we talk about staying for good she doesn't seem happy with that either. She's still minding the old lady and getting great wages. She also made friends with a lovely woman who lives upstairs from us. So she's grand! Doing fine, as they say here. We all get on in our own way, and you know Johanna. I'm sure she'll send you a long one before the month is out.

Give my love to Little Tom and tell him Bloomingdale's doesn't sell records or else I'd use my discount to buy him a few for his player.

I love you both very much,
Greta

June 22, 1964

Michael Ward
222 East 84th Street
Apartment 1A
New York, New York 10028
United States of America

Michael,

So that's big news your going to have a baby. If your woman is in a mood now it will be worse after but then it's her who has to push the baby out and have it hanging off her not you. Before all mine were born I would have the same dream about being asked to spell out the child's name or being asked to read something from the signpost and not knowing how. It was the kind of dream I'd wake up with a panic like someone was just after stealing something from camp but I couldn't remember what. It was worst with you and Maeve because you were two coming together. I wonder did you have any strange dreams.

Grandmother died the end of May. She was a great age and had been looking forward to it for a long time so there wasn't much sadness except missing her day to day.

You are a good worker, Michael, and have a good head on your shoulders and you'll get on well in America I know. There are Travellers in the south part of America on the Atlantic side come from Irish Travellers during the famine who still know the language and keep the traditions but I'd say that's a good distance from New York.

Good luck. God Bless.

Your father,
Dermot Ward

July 10, 1964

Greta Ward
222 East 84th Street
Apartment 1A
New York, New York 10028

Greta,

A funny thing happened today that you can help figure out. Mam and I took the horse and cart into town as we needed a few things too big to carry. We left it outside the pub and who is waiting for us when we come out but Mr Riordan the postmaster. He said Dermot Ward left an envelope for us and we thought grand he's finally decided to get in touch with Michael. But the envelope is not for Michael it's for us and inside is the town where he expects to be all of August to get in touch with news of the baby. What baby Mam asks and the postmaster says the baby your daughter Johanna Cahill and the tinker Michael Ward are having together at the end of July. You know what Mr Riordan thinks of the tinkers.

Greta, Mam is beside herself wondering if this is true or not. I'm the only one who wonders why weren't we told. Mam only wonders what you plan to do and says come home and we'll figure it all out in Ballyroan. She is not angry only wants you to come home. You've saved plenty now and must have the fare. You can start over next year maybe in England. I'm writing to you instead of Johanna because we haven't heard from Johanna in months and I'm afraid for whatever reason she wouldn't read a letter from home right now, especially if this is all true.

Write back right away so we can sort this out.

Tom

July 14, 1964

Shannon O'Clery
39–28 61st Street
Apt. 3D
Woodside, New York 11377

Shannon,

I was going to write this for Michael but as I have the same question I thought I'd put it from both of us. Johanna says no one is allowed in the delivery room and that her doctor told her that in America no one is allowed to visit mothers or babies in hospital except the husband and as Michael is not her husband he is not allowed. Is this true? We saw a program on the television at your place once with people visiting someone in the hospital but Johanna pointed out it wasn't after giving birth and that the program was a comedy so they could bend the truth. Very few people know Johanna is expecting so I don't know who to ask in case they'd wonder. We wouldn't put it past her to make up a fib to keep us away. I think she'll want us when the time comes and this baby after all is Michael's child and my niece or nephew and we want to be there. Is there really such a rule? Michael said absolutely not it just doesn't make sense.

The other thing is that I have a small fear of what Johanna might do once the baby comes. We have talked about it at home and we don't want her to give the baby away. I don't think she wants to give it away either, but on the other hand I don't know if she's ready to keep it. That's the second reason I want to keep track of her.

Please write back as soon as you can.

From,
Greta Cahill and Michael Ward

DATE: JULY 23, 1964
  TO: LILY AND TOM CAHILL
     BALLYROAN
     CONCH POSTAL AREA
     COUNTY GALWAY
     IRELAND

BABY GIRL BORN. GRETA WITH JOHANNA IN HOSP.
JOHANNA AND CHILD HEALTHY. PLS SEND WORD
TO DERMOT W.

MICHAEL WARD

July 25, 1964

Mrs Lily Cahill
Ballyroan
Conch
Co. Galway
Ireland

Mammy,

I hope you got Michael's telegram with the news. Johanna and baby are still in hospital. They will keep them for five nights which is the usual in America from what I understand. There was no trouble in delivery and in fact she came faster than expected. I owe you a long one but I'm dead tired. All this writing things down makes things too hard to explain and all I can think of is how I wish I was home. The baby's name is Julia, which was my suggestion.

Johanna doesn't like me telling her business, even to you, and since she has no patience for letters she said after first seeing the baby that she'd like to arrange a time to talk to you by telephone. I had an idea about you coming for a visit and Michael thought that was great but when we looked at our accounts and all the things a baby will need it just seems like we can't swing it just yet. Michael had to buy a lot of tools to look after the building – tools he pretended he already had when he got the job and in fact helped him get the job in the first place. Would you come down the road if we could cover it? Mammy, I think of you all the time how you say a person can do most things they put their mind to but neither myself nor Johanna knows much about babies and Johanna wouldn't go to any of the classes they offered at the clinic. I thought it was because she is so young, but Shannon says there are even younger girls having babies in New York City believe it or not. If they can do it we can do it. Of the three of us Michael knows the most about it as the camp had a new baby arrive almost every year.

I'm sorry we kept it from you. All I can tell you is that now that Julia is here she seems absolutely one of us already and though I suppose it wasn't the best thing to have happened I'm glad she's here and I love her. Johanna said she is goosey like I am the way she looks around and waves her arms in front of her but unlike me I hope she loses it when she grows up. Well, maybe I've begun to lose it a bit because no one at work has commented on it and Michael says I have a light step which is the same as being graceful. Speaking of Michael he came home last night with a second-hand crib that he sanded and painted white as a surprise. Honest to God you've never seen anything as pretty not even at Bloomingdale's. She'll sleep in the room with me and Johanna.

I'm most sorry you had to find out from Mr Riordan.

Love,
Greta

August 23, 1964

Shannon O'Clery
39–28 61st Street
Apt. 3D
Woodside, New York 11377

Shannon,

I have a favor to ask and I'm sure you wonder will these favors ever end. You know how Johanna has been as you've seen it yourself at the clinic. She is no better at home and looks at Julia sometimes like she forgets whether they've met. Johanna's milk dried up early on so Michael and I take turns feeding Julia with a bottle. When she cries Johanna looks at me or Michael and never gets up herself. Johanna is not a lazy person and so I feel it in my heart that something is wrong. The drunk woman upstairs is moving to Chicago to live with a man and has been turning Johanna's head with dreams of other cities. We've just got our feet under us here so I don't know what I'll do if she suggests we move.

The favor is whether you would mind coming by for a visit on Sunday 30 August. I have to work a double shift and Michael is working as well and has to go in the truck all the way upstate to Rockland County and won't be back before supper. It only happens once in a while and we can't turn it down. Neither of us like leaving Johanna and Julia together so long alone. Julia is a good baby but once she starts wailing she doesn't stop until she's picked up and I'd be afraid Johanna wouldn't go to her straight away and next thing the whole block would know we have a baby in here. It's bad enough the tenants know and them totally confused about the baby's father since we said at first we're Michael's sisters. Now we say I'm Johanna's sister and Johanna Michael's wife and act like they just misheard us the first time. I don't know if they believe it or not or if they care. If you came for a visit she'd be better about getting up and tending to the child.

I'll call from work on Friday evening to see if it works for you and if not, no problem, we'll figure it out. If you can't come I'll just call in sick from a payphone. We thought you might like to see the baby again anyway.

Love,
Greta

August 25, 1964

Michael Ward
222 East 84th Street
Apartment 1A
New York, NY 10028

Michael,

Bitty is in Ennis. Paul the butcher is putting this down. You had your girl and named her Julia. The brother with the lip came to tell us in Clonbur. He wanted no part of a place by the fire or a cup of tea. Our fire is as warm as any other and our tea as strong and I regretted offering. But he came and that was good. I was the first one he came upon and he tried to talk to me alone. Its a puzzle understanding him the way he swallows up his words poor crathur but he has his own way using his hands and going slow about it. He made like he was rocking a baby in his arms and we knew yours had come. Bitty was there and gave him a board to scratch the name so she could read it out. He's a good writer. Da called our men off and explained he doesn't know our ways. The brother is called Tom.

Da wont write again as he said his goodbye in his last and wishes you well. I wish you well too Michael tho I dont understand. You are an outsider now but we would want to see you if you return one day. The carravan has got very big so we are splitting in two. Catherine Donavan married a cousin too close and Da said at least there was no danger of that with Michael. The cousin she married is a drinker of the worst kind and shames her every day and night.

You are my twin Michael which is a thing I try to understand when I think how different we are. I hope your girl Julia grows big and strong and has a good head on her shoulders. Here is a length of lace from Mary Ward. Don't send another letter as it only makes us want to be always checking.

Your sister,
Maeve Ward

Greta,

I tried to wake you twice last night with no luck. Then Julia woke and you were up like a shot. Then Michael came knocking at the bedroom door asking if you needed a hand and I knew my chance was gone. You say I'm bad but when you left for work this morning you left the milk out on the counter and you know how fast it will turn in this heat. You have to pay more attention. You will be seventeen before you know it.

You must imagine I'm very thick if you think I don't know you've asked Shannon to come over later today. You and Michael aren't quiet when you talk, and the door of this room is as flimsy as an old sheet. I hear everything. You think I'm a bad mother and I won't argue. I wasn't meant to be a mother yet, but here I am. You had no intention of leaving Ballyroan but here you are in New York City and getting on better than I ever thought you would. Sometimes you hardly seem like the same Greta.

Before I tell you anything else, I want to apologize about the bank account. You will think it's the least of what I've done, but I feel it's the worst. It's the only thing I feel truly bad about because I know how hard you work for it and how you hate making nice to the women who treat you like some at home treat the tinkers. And me with a tinker child sleeping at the end of my bed. Life is strange. I feel most bad because I know it means you won't be able to go home, or at least not until you've saved it all up again which will take a long time, especially now that Julia is here. The God's honest truth is that I don't think you should go home anyway. Yes, there's Mam at home to help you but think of what you can have here that you can't have there. Think of what it would be like for Julia. The poster in the clinic said nothing is greater than a mother's love, but from the moment I had to switch to the big skirts and loose blouses I think you've loved her more than I do.

You will wonder how I can be sorry about the bank account but not about leaving, but it's the truth. I'm going to Chicago with Linda upstairs. She has a car that will bring us and a room at her boyfriend's place where I can stay. She's going to teach me how to drive on the quieter roads. After a few months I want to go to California and see what kind of a life I can make for myself. I left home because I wanted something else but every night looking at you and Michael and now Julia I think I might as well be in Ballyroan. You left because Mam made you and so it's different for you. And don't think I haven't noticed what's happening between you and Michael. I don't mind, believe me. Can you believe it never even crossed my mind to teach him his letters? I never imagined he'd be with us this long, but then again I never imagined being in the position I'm in. I hear the two of you in there every night turning sounds into words, and laughing, and you congratulating him, and him thanking you in that way he has, and it reminds me of how we used to listen to Mammy and Pop talking on the other side of the wall. Unlike me he will never ever leave you stranded. I see him look around for you whenever it's the two of us home and we hear the locks turning in the door and I thought to myself the other week that he is in love with you. And every night lately when you walk in from work, smoothing down your hair and already starting in with the stories from your day I see how much you've changed, and what good leaving home has done you, and also that you might love him too. And then I thought you would make a nice family. Him and you and Julia.

I believe Shannon is due to drop by and surprise me around 11:00 this morning and I will chat with her for an hour then ask her to watch Julia for a minute while I run out to get more milk. Linda will be ready with the car packed. Apologize to Shannon for me. I hope she didn't have big plans for the rest of her day. I figure you'll be home around 4:00 and she'll be in a panic about why I never returned. Then you'll find this letter. Then you'll give it to Shannon to read for herself. Shannon, I'm sorry. To Michael you'll have to read it out loud unless he's gotten further than I thought so please tell him how sorry I am. He is going to be the best father. He already is.

I will get in touch with you when I'm settled, and I'll understand if you are angry, believe me. With Julia, I trust any decision you make. If you want her to call you Mam or Mammy – or MOM – then by all means. Just don't give her away, Greta. I didn't go through all this to have her brought up by strangers and never hear of Bally-roan. I love you and despite everything I've said and done, I know I will miss you very much.

Leaving you is a million times harder than leaving Julia, or Michael, or even home.

Your sister,
Johanna

PART IV

1977

Nine

On a wet February morning in 1977 Greta readied herself for work for the first time since giving birth to Eavan twelve weeks earlier. Julia had soothed her baby sister while Greta showered, and now, as Greta hurried to dry off and change the child's diaper before she started wailing again, she thought of how foolish it had been to expect a baby to be easy now, just because she'd raised one already at a time when she knew so much less. Knowing more might make it harder, not easier, Michael had said when they discovered that Greta was finally pregnant. And though he hadn't been totally serious, there were moments over the past twelve weeks when Greta had wondered if he might be right.

A half hour later she boarded the 6 train headed downtown and realized with a start that she'd been working at Bloomingdale's for more than thirteen years. She calculated the years again as she tugged at the bottom of her coat, which had gotten caught between the closing doors of the subway car. 'Excuse me, please,' she said to the man who had planted himself just inside the door, a massive backpack strapped to his back, and he shifted slightly to let her pass. Yes, she would be twenty-nine soon, and since she started at Bloomie's in December of 1963, this year would be her fourteenth. With her bag zipped tight and tucked securely under her arm, she fought her way to the middle of the car and found a seat between a sleeping woman and a man holding a pair of dress shoes on his lap. She had stepped in a puddle of slush on the corner of Eighty-sixth and Lexington, and as she stared straight ahead at an advertisement for business classes at Lehman College, she tried to move her numb toes inside her soaked sock. As she did so, she also realized that she'd worked in almost every department at Bloomingdale's at one time or another. With her hands warm inside thick wool mittens, she tried to name them all on her fingers while the stops raced by in a blur, and as often happened when Greta was tired and her glasses fogged with the steam of so many damp bodies pressed together, it seemed as though the stops were on a moving track and the train were standing still.

Women's sportswear. Women's formalwear. Women's intimates and hosiery. Men's sportswear. Men's suiting. Outerwear. Beauty. Home. Children's. Ten minutes later Greta stepped off the subway at Fifty-ninth Street and was swept toward the stairs like a piece of driftwood caught in a current. What's left? she asked herself as she passed the display windows along Third Avenue. Shoes? Accessories? The displays had changed more than once in twelve weeks, and the windows were lined with black velvet and featured different scenes starring Cupid with his bag of arrows. The mannequins were set up so that their backs were to Cupid, completely unaware that one among them was about to get shot and wounded. She noticed that one of the female mannequins was wearing a pale pink casual suit, and when she stepped up to the glass to inspect the outfit, she sighed and felt sadness in her throat, as if someone high up in the Bloomingdale's corporate office had made a specific decision to ruin her first day back. Linen. The suit had a single-button jacket and wide pant legs with two-inch cuffs.

'Jesus. And pleats too, I bet,' Greta said as pedestrian traffic rushed behind her. She squinted up at the top of the pants. Her fears confirmed, she turned and pushed through the first of four heavy glass doors at the main entrance. She gave quick waves to each of the women in cosmetics and called over to Lorraine that she'd catch up with her later. Lorraine had once given Greta a collection of hair products to help her tame the frizz and get the curls to sit, as Lorraine put it, where they're supposed to sit. She'd also shown Greta how to powder the end of her nose so that it appeared softer, less sharp, but when she held the mirror in front of Greta's face, all Greta noticed was her same old nose looking back at her with a smudge at the tip, as if she'd spent the day baking.

As she let the elevator lift her to the upper floors, she tried not to think about the baby, whether she'd woken up again and started crying. Whether Michael had woken up and gone to her or whether he'd slept through it until one of the neighbors knocked on the door. Since starting the night shift, he'd either been unable to sleep at all or he slept like a dead person, with no hope of waking him. Julia had probably gone across the street to 225, where she and Pam Cooke, both in the same seventh-grade class, would spend the day trying to think of ways to convince their parents to let them go to a night movie alone.

Greta stepped off on the fourth floor, passed the sign that announced LINEN IS IN, and once she checked in with the other women who worked the floor, she headed to the dim and musty back room, where she ripped open box after box, tore away the plastic and the tissue paper, pulled out pin after pin after pin. This, she'd been told at multiple annual reviews, was where she really stood out. There was no one better at making the garments look presentable for display. They'd even asked her to train the new hires on how to work the handheld steamer. She had long ago decided to believe that expertise here more than made up for her consistent inability to pronounce all those Italian and French names on the labels, and knowing she'd probably get them wrong made her more reluctant to try. Still, she told herself she mustn't be the worst of the lot, because they'd asked her twice now to be a supervisor. Once when Julia was about three and again when Julia started kindergarten. Although she'd declined – the pay was only a dollar more per hour, and she didn't want to be the one all the others hated – it felt good to be asked. She'd written Lily about it straightaway, but she must have forgotten to say that she'd ended up declining, because the next letter that came from Ireland said that Lily and Little Tom were having fun picturing Greta as boss.

She got to work with the steamer. If people knew this is how the clothes come, she thought as she worked. If they knew their pleats and their silk linings were once twisted like old washrags. After each garment was transformed, Greta arranged it on a hanger, placing the shoulders of each linen jacket squarely on the plastic arms, clipping each pair of pants so that the pleats were neat and sharp. She had the new shipment pressed by ten o'clock, and when she emerged, blinking, into the white and gleaming light of the floor, the store was busy with the tinny rasp of hangers being pushed briskly aside as women searched the racks for their sizes. Greta felt her head begin to ache as more and more women passed by with their choices thrown haphazardly over their arms. She imagined the clothes dumped on chairs in the dressing rooms, the wrinkles she'd just worked so hard to press away becoming more pronounced every minute.

'Another round with the steamer, Greta,' Bonnie, the floor supervisor, said at noon as she approached Greta with an armful of garments.

'I wonder how long will linen be in,' Greta said as she opened her arms to accept them. She thought again about the apartment, whether the baby's diaper had leaked, whether Michael had slept enough to go to work again that night. If he had gotten up, he'd likely be chatting away to her as if she could understand and talk back. It's a cold one today, Eavan, he might say as he tied the laces of his boots. Colder than yesterday. Will we warm your milk? Will Daddy have his tea?

'Oh no, Greta,' Bonnie said, stopping abruptly and hugging the garments tighter to her body. She half turned, as if the clothes were a child she wanted to protect.

Greta followed the direction of Bonnie's shocked gaze and dropped her chin to look down at her own chest, which was stained with two damp circles.

Greta gasped. 'I forgot my pads. I'm breast-feeding. Oh, Christ.'

Ignoring her, Bonnie took a quick look over both shoulders to see if any customers had seen. Greta turned and walked quickly toward the employee restroom. 'Cross your arms or something,' Bonnie whispered after her.

In the bathroom, Greta saw that the circles had burst their boundaries and begun to run down toward the waistband of her slacks. Her blouse was blue, and the wet spots were dark, impossible to miss. Inside her shoe, her sock was still wet and cold, and that coldness, combined with the cold spots of her blouse against her skin, were like points of interest on a map, the map drawn on her body, all to show how her day was going so far.

After a few minutes of useless rubbing at her chest with paper towels, she stopped and took off her blouse. She put the whole thing in the sink, turned the knob for the cold water, and watched the sink fill. When it had filled, she went at it with every bit of energy she had and once in a while looked up to find her own flushed face looking back at her from the mirror, her own two breasts swollen and huge, swinging away from her body despite the wired bra she'd bought to hold them back after Eavan was born.

'I don't know what to do with them,' she'd said to Michael just the other morning as she was getting dressed. 'I mean, my God. What do women do who have these their whole lives?'

Michael had laughed. 'Don't look at me,' he'd said, believing she was joking, and then reached out to cup one in his hand. He simply held it, as if testing its new weight, and then let it go.

As Greta was wringing out her blouse and about to walk it over to the hand dryer, Bonnie came in with a sweater set, tags still on, and Greta's bag hanging from her elbow.

'It was in the irregular bin,' Bonnie explained, handing her the sweater set. She placed the bag on the floor and eyed Greta's bare stomach below her bra. Greta straightened her shoulders and tried to act as if it were the most natural thing in the world for your supervisor to see you in your bra, but she could feel her skin heat up and the prickly flush travel from her neck to her leaking chest and down to her stomach, which was threaded with faint pink stretch marks.

'Let's call it seventy-five percent off,' Bonnie said. 'You're not petite, are you? It's a regular small.'

'Thanks very much,' Greta said, accepting the sweater. She felt the pressure mounting behind her nipples. 'I'll be out as soon as I can.' Bonnie took a step toward the door, but at the last minute she turned and looked at Greta again.

'I'll put a note at the register so you don't forget to pay for it.'

'Perfect,' Greta said, and tried to nod Bonnie out the door.

'Has Mr Halberstam spoken to you yet?' Bonnie asked. Mr Halberstam managed the entire store, and Greta tried to block out what was happening to her body for just a few seconds so that she could figure out why Bonnie had asked.

'To me?' Greta said. 'Why?'

'Oh, nothing,' Bonnie said. 'I just thought he might have.'

'No,' Greta said. She could hear the question mark plain in her own voice. She momentarily forgot her bare stomach and dribbling breasts. Just before she had gone on leave to wait for Eavan to arrive, Greta felt sure that Bonnie was going to accuse her of taking a few of the crocheted hats and scarves they'd set aside for return to the warehouse. She had taken two sets – one lavender and one heather gray – but that wasn't the point. Bonnie had no reason to accuse her. At least, no reason to accuse her above any of the others. They weren't even for her. She'd given the lavender to Mrs Cooke to make up for Julia being over in 225 so often, and the gray she'd mailed to Lily.

'What are you so worried about?' Michael had asked at home. 'You've no reason to be nervous. You would never take anything without paying for it. That kind of thing doesn't go over in America like it might at home.'

'No, of course not,' Greta had said, and decided on the spot to pay for every little thing she took from that place, even the sample moisturizers and perfumes Lorraine told her to stick in her bag. It was just that there was so much – not only out on the hangers, but in the back rooms, in the dusty basement that ran an entire city block, tossed in corners and in cardboard bins behind the register, all to be packaged and shipped in different directions. It was hard to see how little things here and there could matter.

Once Bonnie left, Greta locked the door and rooted through her bag for her pump. She knelt on the cold tile floor and pulled the mouth of the bag as wide as it would go. She found the empty bottle and stood it on the floor next to her; then she found the nipple, the nipple cover, but no pump. Finally she turned the bag upside down and let the contents bounce and roll across the floor. 'No, no, no, no,' she chanted as she moved her things back and forth. Then her mind flashed to exactly where she'd left it, freshly sterilized on the drying rack at home.

She took a series of long breaths to keep the tears at bay. Eavan had slept through the night for the very first time, but instead of embracing the sleep she'd been so greedy for, Greta woke up at four A.M., disoriented, feeling that there was something important she'd forgotten to do. When she opened her eyes, she found herself on Michael's side of the bed and noticed that everything in their bedroom seemed drawn on a different scale from his side: the door that much farther away, the window that much closer. Michael was all the way up in the Bronx now, burrowing underground with the other men like rabbits in the fields of Ballyroan. He'd been working as a sandhog for seven years now, and every January he said that year would be his last. Eavan looked like him. The nurses at the hospital had said so just hours after she was born, her face so pinched and red Greta couldn't see how they could tell. Then when they came home, Mrs Strom had said so too. 'And of course, Miss Julia is a mystery,' Mrs Strom had added, clutching Julia at the waist and squeezing. 'You must have been dropped down from the sky.'

'That sort of stinks, doesn't it?' Julia had asked as Greta waited with the baby for Julia to unlock the two dead bolts and open the door. 'Going through that whole thing twice and neither kid looks a thing like you?'

'Do women have babies so they'll have people around who look like them?' Greta had asked. She'd asked the question to be funny, but realized once she'd said it that she wouldn't be surprised. Just the other week she'd seen a woman on Park and Seventy-seventh pushing a baby carriage, and when Greta looked inside, she saw a Labrador puppy dressed in the very same coat as its owner, right down to the fur-lined hood.

Greta's knees were beginning to ache against the hard bathroom floor, and the tips of her nipples had become like two blunt knives. She stood.

'Okay,' she whispered. She reached back to unsnap her bra. She leaned over the sink and tried to relax. There was a song Michael had hummed to Julia when Julia was an infant, and he had resurrected it for Eavan. Greta did her best to remember the tune, and she hummed it to herself in the small bathroom. When she felt calm enough, she placed her right hand on her right breast, her thumb an inch above the nipple, her fingers an inch below, and she pressed straight back. She rolled her breast gently, gasping at how sore it had become in so little time. When the milk arrived, she tried to catch as much as she could in the bottle, but it was spouting in too many directions and she quickly gave up. After a minute or so, the flow eventually became calm trickles that ran down from her nipple and marked paths across the soft fullness of her lower breast. She reached for a handful of paper towels, and as she pressed the towels to her chest, the thought of home came to her as it usually did, without warning: the boys pushing torn tea towels against the rain that leaked down the walls of their bedroom, like using a tissue to stop a flood.

After about fifteen minutes, she patted her left breast dry, put her bra back on, and shoved a few paper towels inside the cups. She ignored the rawness of the rough paper against her sensitive flesh. She pulled the shell of the sweater set over her head. For a moment there, as she'd been scrubbing and wringing the blouse and again when she realized she'd forgotten the pump, she felt sure she was going to cry. She had felt the sobs gathering like thunderclouds at the back of her throat. Now she realized she was in real danger of breaking down into giggles, and she felt the first warnings course through her body on different nerve endings from those that had carried the knifelike pain of her nipples. Once she had the sweater on, it got worse, her breasts even more foreign to her with the additional padding. Looking at herself in the mirror, she pushed them out even farther and put her hands on her hips. She noticed that she'd lost the clip that had been holding her hair in place at the back of her head, and during the commotion the curls had sprung forth. Her face was even rosier than usual, as if she'd just walked a mile in the cold, and her neck was splotchy.

'My God,' she said, and then bit down on her lip and turned away from her reflection. The giggles were bubbling up from her stomach to her chest, and she knew from experience that once they started, they wouldn't be stifled. She took a few deep breaths.

'You're grand,' she said to her reflection, and then splashed her face with water, hung her wet blouse over the doorknob, and was back out on the floor by twelve-thirty.

Eavan was born in mid-November 1976, on a perfect fall day. Julia was at school, but once the nurses assured Michael and Greta that it would be a few hours, they decided that Michael should go over to the school to get her. Michael had recently requested the unpopular midnight shift so that he'd be at home during the day in case Greta went into labor and everyone they knew was at work. It was easier to find people home at night. At the hospital, they didn't have to wait as long as the nurses told them they would; by the time Julia would have been home from school on a regular day, Eavan was born.

In the apartment, they made room for Eavan in Julia's room. They'd stored Julia's old crib in the basement, and when Michael brought it upstairs again, it was even more handsome than Greta remembered it.

She cleaned it; Michael bought a new mattress. Julia made a poster of Eavan's name spelled out in bubble letters and filled with glitter. She hung it where Eavan could look out from her crib and see it. 'E-A-V-A-N,' Julia said to the baby almost every time she passed the crib, pointing to the letters one by one. 'That means you.' At twelve going on thirteen, Julia was interested in everything having to do with babies, and she barraged Greta with questions as they popped into her mind. She wanted to know if she'd been breast-fed and for how long. Did breast-feeding hurt? Did Greta know that she winced and said 'ouch!' every time Eavan latched on? Had it been the same with her? What was labor like the first time compared with the second? Was it better or worse knowing what was to come and how much it would hurt? And did Greta know it would be a girl because the baby had felt the same inside of her as Julia had?

Greta answered what she could, and to the rest she just said, 'Julia, please. Too many questions.'

Julia was taking sex education at school, and unlike the other parents, who complained that talking about sex only made their kids more embarrassed about it, Greta saw that Julia had taken the door her teachers cracked for her and pushed it wide.

'Don't say dick,' Greta had overheard Julia tell Pam Cooke just before Eavan was born. 'It's a penis.' Greta had started her temporary leave two weeks before the baby was due, and all those quiet daytime hours at home were like a peephole that looked into Julia's life when Greta wasn't around. As Greta waited for some sign from her belly, her feet propped up on the kitchen table, propped up on the couch, propped up on a stack of pillows in bed, she listened for Julia. And later, when she was sick of lying down, as she paced the hall, paced in front of the windows of the living room, decided against doctor's orders that the baby was ready no matter what his calendar told him, she eavesdropped on Julia and her friend. Each afternoon from Julia's bedroom, where she and Pam Cooke usually did their homework together, came the sound of glossy heavy-stock textbook pages being turned.

'And those are the testicles,' Julia said evenly on the same afternoon.

'Don't be so disgusting, Jule,' Pam said, and giggled.

'You're the one who's disgusting, with all those dumb nicknames,' Julia answered. 'Prick. Dick. Balls. Nuts.'

Greta, her back aching and her ankles swollen, took one step farther down the hall to peer into Julia's bedroom just as Pam finally laughed so hard she collapsed to the floor. Julia leaned over her, '. . .wang, dong, bat, Mr Floppy . . .' By now Julia was laughing too and was struggling to keep the list going.

'Mercy,' Pam shouted, clutching her stomach.

'Don't get me started on breasts,' Julia said, and dropped to the floor beside her friend.

'Girls?' Greta had interrupted, looking at the textbook, which was abandoned on Julia's bed, and Pam lying on the ground. 'What's so funny?'

'Excuse me, Mom,' Julia said as she jumped up and brushed past Greta. 'I have to urinate.' Pam had a laugh that sounded like she'd been kicked in the belly.

Later, when Greta reported all that she had overheard, Michael said he thought it was good for young people to learn those things. Deep down, Greta thought so too, but sometimes, when the other parents complained about things, especially the loudmouth types, and letters came home needing her signature so that Julia could watch a movie that Greta later learned some parents had refused to sign, and every school meeting was about one more thing the children had been told in sex ed, Greta sometimes felt like she should object, like the other parents expected her to, but she didn't know why. Sometimes she felt like all the other parents had an extra piece of information that had been kept from her – an oversight, most likely – and if she had access to that extra bit of information, everything would be easier to understand.

When Greta's shift finally ended, she rode the subway uptown, climbed up the stairs to the sidewalk, walked the two blocks and two avenues between the subway and the apartment, and was reaching for the knob of her building's front door before she remembered that she'd left her blouse hanging in the employee restroom.

'Shit,' she muttered to herself. They'll throw it out, she knew. An almost brand-new blouse. Just as she turned her key in the lock and pushed the inner hall door open, she heard Eavan begin with the faint, short cries that were a prelude to longer wails. 'Okay, baby. Okay,' she said as she unlocked the apartment door and dropped her bag to the floor. She threw her coat over the back of the couch and was already pulling up both layers of the sweater set when Michael emerged with a roaring Eavan tucked up high on his chest, one broad hand on her back.

'How was work?' he asked, handing Eavan over.

'The usual,' Greta said, and then winced as the baby latched on. 'Why don't you lie down,' she said to him. She looked over her shoulder at the clock. 'Did you sleep at all?' At Greta's breast, Eavan clenched and unclenched her small fists as she rooted and sucked.

'She'll roll over any day,' Michael said, sinking into the couch beside Greta. He rubbed his eyes with the back of his hand. 'I can see her trying when I put her on her belly. She was almost there today, and I thought I might give her little push so she can see what it's like, but then I thought that's cheating.'

As they both looked down at Eavan, they heard the locks sliding in the door once more.

'I'm home,' Julia called, dropping her bag beside Greta's and plopping down on the couch next to Michael. 'Jeez, is she starving or something?' Julia asked, leaning forward to watch Eavan's little mouth move.

'I was just saying she's about to roll over,' Michael said. 'Let's be on the lookout.'

'How many weeks was I when I rolled?' Julia asked, resting her index finger in Eavan's open palm and then smiling as Eavan grabbed hold.

Greta glanced up at Michael. Once in a while, not often, but once in a while she felt as if Julia might be testing them with all her questions about her birth, how it had felt for Greta to be pregnant so young, so on and so forth, worse now that Eavan was here. Michael had long since decided to follow Greta's lead. This fib they'd been keeping up for more than twelve years seemed to mean more to her than it did to him. Not that he didn't care what Julia thought or believed, he had clarified recently, but he really didn't see how it mattered very much. Julia wouldn't care whose belly she started out in, Michael said. She knew who raised her. She knew who loved her most of all. This, Greta felt, was one of the few leftovers of tinker in him, all that handing about of babies for raising by whoever had space and need.

'You rolled right about the age she is now,' Greta said, and Michael agreed.

'Better hurry up,' Julia said to the baby, who opened her small milk-wet mouth and laughed. 'Oh, yeah,' Julia said, jumping up from the couch and walking over to one of the shelves Michael had installed above the radiator. 'Mail for you. Ireland.' She dropped the letter on the cushion beside Greta and then told them she was going across the street to watch TV with Pam.

Michael leaned over and looked at the envelope with interest. 'Been a while, hasn't it?'

'Has it?' Greta asked. Yes, it had been a while, she knew, but whose fault that was she couldn't decide. How often could a person write? There were things to do every single hour that ate up the time, especially since Eavan was born. She had variations on the same thought at least a dozen times a day: I'm so busy. I'm too busy. If only I had the time. Those big blue mailboxes on every corner made her feel queasy. The telegram office across the street from Bloomingdale's felt like a reprimand. Her body stiffened, as if she'd been having an argument and was bracing herself for a sharp response.

Eavan flailed her arms and wailed.

Julia was turning out to look only like herself. Her hair was soft and smooth, pin-straight, and when she wore it loose, it hung down her back like a gleaming curtain sewn with threads of gold, blond, red, brown. At twelve, she was already taller than Greta, and her face – wide-set eyes, a straight, pert nose, a large mouth that revealed upper and lower teeth when she smiled – came from neither of her parents. Only when she was angling for something and wanted Greta to give in did she remind Greta of Michael's sister, Maeve. It was a comparison Michael couldn't understand, considering Greta had seen Maeve only a few times and only when they were children. He once suggested to Greta that she might see Maeve in Julia because she liked the idea of daughters looking like aunts. 'That's not it at all,' Greta said at the time, but the possibility had been wandering in and out of her mind ever since.

The first months of Julia's life had been both the hardest and the easiest. Hard because Greta couldn't quite grasp what had happened, what was continuing to happen every day that Johanna stayed away. Easy because neither could Julia. Julia raised her arms to be lifted, and Greta lifted her. Julia cried to be changed or fed, and Greta changed and fed her. When Greta came home on that hot August afternoon in 1964 to find Shannon O'Clery standing in the middle of the apartment, bouncing Julia in her arms, she guessed what had happened. She needs a break, Shannon had assured her. Gone to the movies, probably. Hot day like today. Who could blame her? Young mothers do strange things sometimes. Yes, Greta agreed, almost shouting over the dumb thumping of her heart, she probably needed a break. Probably went over to the park to cool off a bit, Greta suggested, but she didn't believe a word. The space just below her ribs felt hollow, the flesh scooped away and replaced with worry. Since arriving in America, worry felt to Greta like something tangible, like one more organ, or a person who followed her into rooms and walked beside her on the sidewalk and once in a while covered her face with his hands. Taking the baby from Shannon, she went into her bedroom and found the note on the pillow on her side of the bed.

'She'll turn around when she realizes what she did and take the bus back home,' Shannon said, looking over Greta's shoulder at Johanna's neat print. 'Happens all the time, believe it or not.'

'Home?' Greta had said. 'You mean here?'

'She'll probably sneak in tonight when everyone's sleeping.'

'That's exactly what will happen,' Greta agreed, feeling it was important that Shannon believe this.

'Well, listen,' Shannon said as she gathered her things and took four backward steps toward the door. 'Call me if you need anything, and tell her to come down to the clinic to see me when she gets back.'

'I will,' Greta said, feeling suddenly as if she'd overstayed her welcome, as if she and Johanna were still sleeping on Shannon's foldout bed, Michael in the closet, and all three still making meals out of her cupboards. There was a limit, Greta knew, to people's kindness. Lately it had struck her that Shannon never thought they'd take her up on her offer of New York, that they'd never use the address she gave them when she left Ballyroan. She probably never imagined that good Irish children like the ones her mother had always told her about could be capable of getting into such a mess. 'I'm sorry,' Greta added. 'Your day ruined.'

'She'll come back,' Shannon said brightly, still backing away. 'I know it.' Then she turned, opened the door, and walked briskly into the hall. Through the large double-paneled window of the vestibule door Greta could make out the bright sidewalk beyond, glinting with flecks of mica in the August sun. That's the end of Shannon's help, Greta thought.

After reading Johanna's note many more times and searching for some clue that none of it meant what it seemed to mean, there was nothing to do but wait for Michael to come home. Greta held Julia, fed her, paced with her in silence so that she could hear the sound of his step on the stoop outside, and during this Julia was calm, her inquisitive, round face turned to Greta as if she understood far more than she could communicate. Greta willed Michael back to the city from faraway Rockland County. She conjured the growl of the moving truck, the boss behind the wheel letting him off at the subway, the subway delivering him to Eighty-sixth Street. Or, if the boss didn't want to drive Michael to the East Side, Michael would walk across the park, preferring the power of his own two legs to the crowded city bus, where he hated having to push his way on and off. Finally, just before dark, Greta heard his step, his key in the lock, and she had just enough time to lay Julia in her crib before he walked in and she dove into him, both hands pulling on his shirt, pulling on his neck, commanding him to 'read it' as she indicated with a nod of her head the letter sitting on the table.

Michael, who had not made it two feet inside the apartment, reached back with his foot to close the door before reminding her that she'd better read it out.

'She's left. Gone,' Greta summarized instead, still holding tight to his neck as if she'd fallen and he'd pulled her up and without him there she'd fall again. Julia cooed from her crib, and Michael put his arms around Greta as if he'd done so before and rocked her as she'd rocked Julia an hour earlier. She choked out the rest of the story. Chicago. The woman upstairs. California, eventually. Gone. 'I knew it,' she kept saying, her voice growing more fierce each time she accused herself. 'I knew it,' she said as he continued to sway with her back and forth. Eventually she stopped speaking and stopped clinging so tight, and as they moved gently from side to side like a curragh at sea, Michael thought how it was almost like dancing.

The news was, Michael discovered, a relief to him. A break from Johanna for a few weeks – surely she'd be back in less time – might clear the air in the apartment where Johanna had sat so unhappily for so many months now. He'd been a fool with Johanna: the excitement of the Atlantic crossing, feeling like he'd finally have his dream of settling, even while making the longest journey of his life. He couldn't even think of the crossing anymore without also thinking of Greta's face the day he asked her to put down the letter to Dermot telling the news of the expected baby. He had been certain that Johanna had already told her, privately, as she'd promised she would, but Greta's biro, which had been moving steadily in those careful rows he admired, stopped dead, and she continued to stare at the page. 'Greta,' he'd said as her face flushed and her body sagged, just a little, where she sat. That was the first time he'd wanted to put his arms around her like he was holding her now, to waltz the problem away.

And now that he was holding her, the nest of her hair a place for his chin to rest, her body softer than he'd imagined it to be when he'd watched her, all angles and joints, cross the room to lift the baby, he discovered that for the first time since setting foot in New York, his mind was at ease. He ran his hands down the smooth white undersides of her arms, her ribs, her waist, resting on her hips, and when he felt her pull him closer, he felt joy. Maybe this is what he'd been searching for all along when he stopped to look at cottages with their stone walls and turf billowing from chimneys. Maybe this was what Dermot had been trying to tell him with all those stories of ancestors and how far they'd traveled together. I understand now, Michael wanted to tell his father, already shaping the letters in his mind like Greta had taught him. We don't settle in places. We settle in people.

The first postcard from Johanna came two months later, postmarked Chicago, and said only 'Thinking of You!!' Greta and Michael went immediately down to the delicatessen on Second Avenue, changed a five-dollar bill into dimes and nickels, and with Julia strapped in her umbrella stroller on the other side of the folding glass doors of the phone booth, they took turns calling operators in Chicago and asking for any listing under Cahill. They called motels, hotels, B and B's. Then they tried Ward. They tried the last name of the woman Johanna had gone with, but no luck. As they considered what they should do next, a woman walking along Second Avenue stopped next to Julia's stroller and crouched down.

'Pardon me,' Greta said, pulling on the knob that should have collapsed the folding door. She pulled again and then pushed when it didn't work. Michael reached around and pulled it for her, and Greta stumbled onto the street. The woman had her hand on Julia's belly.

'You're asking for it,' the woman said as she straightened to standing. She turned to look at Greta. 'You know how fast someone could lift up this whole thing and start running? He'd be around the corner and down to the park before you even figured out how to open the door.'

'Pardon me,' Greta said again, louder, the only thing she could think to say. She stepped close to Julia and put her body between the baby and the stranger.

'I'm just letting you know,' the woman said. 'It happens all the time.'

Greta could hear the tinkle of Michael's keys on his belt as he crossed the short space between the phone booth and where the woman was standing.

'Get yourself away from our child right this second,' he said. The woman threw up her hands and continued on down the avenue.

'Do you think she would have taken her?' Greta asked once the woman had turned the corner.

Michael considered. 'No. But why did she touch her? She shouldn't have done that.'

'No,' Greta agreed, and looked closely at him. Whenever he spoke of home, he said he had had trouble raising his voice in public; it had been a problem since he was a boy. Now he was the papa bear protecting his cubs. It was America, creeping in. An older Irishwoman Greta met at the market told her to save her pennies now while she still had the ways of home; too long in America, and the new Irish spend every penny they get hold of. Just that morning, Greta realized, they'd gotten coffee from the street vendor on the corner instead of making tea for themselves at home. They were growing more comfortable with each other every day, small touches as they worked around each other in the kitchen, bodies unnecessarily close when they sat together at the table. Greta often thought of Lily's warning: if he touches you. She had not said anything about what to do if Greta wanted to touch him back. And just like the dimes and quarters they'd stopped worrying about saving, it was America that gave Greta the courage to lean into him one evening as they were washing dishes and press her mouth to his. He had stepped back, surprised, before stepping forward again and placing his hands on either side of her face to kiss her back.

After their failed attempt to find Johanna in Chicago, the Irish postmark, which used to make Greta want to drop everything and eat up the news from home on the spot, now brought only dread. She and Michael went back and forth over whether they should tell Lily what had happened. And if they told, should they go home or should they stay? Should they send Julia home? And then send for her later? The second question was raised only once, and not seriously. They'd both known children at home who waited and waited for parents to send for them from England, Australia, Canada, America. Both knew those children grew up to adulthood in the place where they'd been asked to wait. What happens in these faraway places to make parents forget promises? Plus, Greta pointed out, Johanna wanted Julia to stay in America.

As Lily's worry grew – a worry Greta swore she could feel from three thousand miles away – so did her impatience with letters. She listed dates and times when she'd be at Mrs Norton's shop and wrote to Greta in advance telling her to call during those times. When the first date and time arrived, Greta went down to a store on Seventy-seventh and First Avenue that advertised low rates on international calls. She purposely called an hour too soon. As the man at the front of the store listened to her, and New Yorkers milled around her, shopping for batteries and envelopes, Greta made her voice bright and competent, just like the ladies at Bloomingdale's. As much as anything else, America was a way of speaking. Not the accent, as Greta had first thought, but that way Americans have of pushing their voices out so they're heard without shouting. Michael had shown her that he could do it on the street outside the phone booth. Greta's supervisor at Bloomingdale's told her she'd need to master her interpersonal skills if she wanted to get ahead. Interpersonal meant, Greta figured out, how she spoke to strangers. Mrs Norton was no stranger, but there were strangers all around her, glancing over at her and the tea-stained canvas bag she had trapped between her feet. Mrs Norton's voice carried over such a long distance was even more itself: crisp, like the stationery she carried in her shop, like the sharp corners of the tea and biscuit boxes lined up on the wall under the window. When Mrs Norton shouted into the line that she hoped Greta and Johanna were getting on well in America, Greta mistook it for a question and told Mrs Norton they loved it. Everything they'd ever heard about it was true. Things couldn't be better, really. Just lovely.

Greta could hear the tingle of the bells on Norton's shop door – an Irish tingle, bells sounded different in New York – and Mrs Norton calling away from the mouthpiece of the phone, 'The Cahill girls. From America. Go on. I'll be with you in just a second.'

A female voice in the background of Norton's shop said, 'Ask them is there plenty of work in America now like people say.'

Mrs Norton whispered something Greta couldn't make out, and then came the sound of static rising and falling as if on the wind. Greta kept her eye on the second hand of the clock, which was hanging above the counter.

'And what about Johanna?' Mrs Norton asked in a rush when she came back to the phone, abruptly aware of American cents adding up with every minute. 'And the baby,' she added.

Greta heard a measure in Mrs Norton's voice that told her Johanna's news was big at home. They'd be aflutter with the information: a tinker, a baby, Johanna not even twenty, no ring on her finger, no ring on the way. Their conversation now, Greta realized, would be a prize Mrs Norton showed off to every single person who came into the store that week.

'Oh, you know Johanna,' Greta said, equally rushed. 'She could get on anywhere. Look – can you tell my mother I tried but missed her? I should get off now.'

In the panic often induced by overseas connections, Mrs Norton hung up without another word.

The second time Greta called, Lily had arrived at the shop an hour earlier than planned and was there to take the receiver from Mrs Norton.

'Greta?' Lily said in an overloud voice Greta didn't recognize. 'Hello?'

'I'm here,' Greta said. 'Mammy?' she added foolishly. She could hear Lily fumbling with the phone, pressing it tight to her ear. All the effort it must have taken, Greta realized. Lily's week planned around the possibility of this conversation. Tom's week too, most likely. And how they would have discussed the plan over supper the night before and breakfast that morning. Lily would have boiled water thinking of this call. Milked, swept, seeded, washed, and collected eggs thinking of this call. Fixed her hair against those she might meet in town. Rubbed some of Dr Joyce's Miracle Cream on her water- and wind-chapped hands. Tom would be out on the street waiting for the news from New York, nodding hellos to all who passed.

Lily cleared her throat into the phone and Greta started crying.

'What's happened?' Lily said.

'She's gone off,' Greta said helplessly. 'Chicago. We tried to track her down but couldn't find her.' She hadn't planned on telling, but there was her mother's voice in her ear, somehow brought all the way over the ocean on wire and string. What the boys had once told her was half true: a person could throw her voice all the way from Galway to New York if the wind was pitched in the right direction. They hadn't been able to imagine that New York could shout back.

'Chicago? She doesn't know anyone in Chicago. And the baby?'

'The baby's doing very well. Michael knew a lot and taught me and we're taking care of her.'

Silence. And then in a lowered voice: 'I knew something happened. I've spoken to the bank about borrowing the fare. I could be there by the end of the month.'

It was already the tenth of the month, and Greta felt greedy for her mother. Lily in New York. Lily in the apartment. Lily there at the table with the baby with a plan. Now that the possibility had arisen, all Greta wanted to do was sit down on the ground right where she was standing and wait. The man behind the counter turned the little clock so Greta could see it. She'd paid for ten minutes. No time for extra words. 'To stay?' she asked.

'Just until we see about Johanna, and then all of us will go back home together.'

'And Michael?'

'We can't worry about Michael. He can do as he pleases.'

'What do you mean? Myself and Julia go back and Michael stays?'

A high-pitched buzz came from the other end of the phone.

'What was that?' Greta asked, and saw in her mind the brand-new telephone lines of Conch swinging like jump ropes in the school yard. The connection had gone faint, as if another Atlantic had added itself to the first and doubled the distance.

'Will I try to borrow the fare, Greta?' Lily shouted as if from behind a dozen closed doors.

'I'll call again next week,' Greta shouted, and everyone in the store turned to look.

But Greta did not call next week. Or the week after. The greed she'd felt standing in the store, pressing the phone to her cheek as if to bring her mother closer, had faded to something different. Michael came home the afternoon that Greta spoke to Lily and swooped Julia up in the air. 'Will we go to the park?' he asked, the musky scent of a hard day's work rolling off his body and into the currents of the air. He loved her. He had told her so just two weeks after Johanna left. He knew his own mind, he told her, and there was no doubt about it. And although she did not say so for another full week, she knew immediately that she loved him back. Love, it turned out, was disarmingly simple, straightforward, and there was no better way to put it than the way they already knew. They loved each other, but they didn't know what to do about it yet.

The second postcard from Johanna came four months after the first, from Minneapolis. Greta and Michael went back to the deli with another five-dollar bill and then to the same phone booth. This time they left the door to the booth open, and Julia, now almost seven months old and bundled in her one-piece snowsuit so that only her eyes, cheeks, and nose were exposed, laughed up at them as Greta slammed the phone down. They borrowed a Polaroid camera from a man in their building and took snapshots of Julia. They enclosed the pictures in a long letter to Lily and told her, once again, there was no need to come. They were happy. They were getting on well. They'd be home for a visit one day soon, and there was no sense wasting money. They'd heard from Johanna, they told Lily, and she was working and had a nice apartment in Chicago. No sense telling Lily she'd moved again so soon. They told her it was all working out just fine.

'What would we have done,' Michael asked gently once the letter was sent, 'if we'd gotten hold of Johanna?'

'Told her to come back,' Greta said, surprised. 'What do you mean?'

'I mean, what would happen if she came back? And wanted to take Julia with her? What if she wants to take her to Minneapolis? Or back to Ballyroan? Or even if she came back to New York and stayed?'

'What do you mean?' Greta asked again, feeling a little like she did the few times she and Michael had gone to the movies and she had to step out to use the ladies' room halfway through. Everything about the end, it seemed, depended on those few minutes that she'd missed. She felt her stomach rise and flop the way it used to when she first started using the elevator at work. It had not occurred to her that Johanna would take Julia away with her; she'd only allowed herself to dream of Johanna back again, the way she used to be in Ballyroan – not the silent, spiritless girl she became once her belly grew large. But Michael, she saw, was worried about the very possibility Greta had been hoping for: Johanna's return. She reminded herself that although Maeve was his twin, she was also a girl and he a boy, and things could not be the same between them as they'd been between Greta and Johanna. She had slept next to Johanna every night of her life until Johanna took off for Chicago. Even when they fought, and each girl felt that the other was a millstone that could not be lifted, it was a load so familiar that Greta couldn't imagine not having it to bear. She had weighed every decision and every thought she'd ever had against what Johanna would do and how she might react. And now, three thousand miles from home, she woke up for the first time in her life to a blank pillow beside her, no breath in her ear. Even when Michael began sleeping on

Johanna's side of Greta's bed – first on top of the covers and soon underneath, his body fitted behind hers like the spoons in the kitchen drawer – his company could not replace Johanna's. Nights were easier than mornings, and Greta's heart jumped each evening when they acted out the familiar parts of pretending they didn't both know where he would end up. He'd come in with a pretense of a question, or she'd call him in to look at something – a crack in the windowpane, a small mouse hole in the wall – and next thing he'd be kneeling on the bed, pulling her and pressing her as if it were possible to get any closer.

At night, it was easy to forget. But every morning the absence of Johanna startled her all over again.

The third postcard came a full six months after the second, from San Francisco, and in this one Johanna told Greta to send news from New York and Ireland. It was August 1965, a full year after she'd left. She'd long since left her traveling partner behind. 'She had it bad,' Johanna wrote. 'Worse than I knew. A drink first thing in the morning and sips from the flask in her pocket all day long.' She didn't say whether she was alone or if she'd taken up with someone else. Michael was at work when the mail came, and Greta read the postcard standing next to the row of mailboxes in the vestibule. After reading it through, she flipped it over and examined the picture: a long red bridge with a boat passing underneath. Greta shoved the rest of the mail back into the small box and read the postcard again. This time Johanna had included a return address. 'I love it here,' she wrote. When Greta got to the bottom of the card – the words shrinking in size as they drew close to the edge – she read it once more.

'How's the baby?' Mrs Kraus asked Greta as she squeezed by clutching two grocery bags in each of her arthritic hands. Green cabbage, Greta knew. Ham. Germans seemed to eat the same things as Irish, except noodles instead of potatoes.

'Loud,' Greta said, smiling, shoving the postcard in her pocket and reaching for one of Mrs Kraus's bags. 'Fast,' she added, thinking of how quickly Julia could cross a room on all fours. She could walk a few steps here and there, but when she really wanted to travel, she dropped to the floor and moved those chubby arms and legs. The old women in the building loved her; Greta could feel it. Loved having the young child around. Loved the young couple starting out in America. Loved that Greta welcomed every word of advice they gave her.

Your husband is so young, they told her. A worker. You're a lucky girl. And your sister, they asked. What happened to her?

They were forgetful old women, Greta had noticed. They asked her the same questions again and again.

Back to Ireland, Greta told them.

Now that you've had the baby, they told her, you look more like her. The hair, the face. Pregnancy does strange things to a woman.

Yes, Greta said.

You must be lonesome after her, they said, and didn't wait for an answer.

Instead of getting on a bus and heading west as she always thought she would once she finally had an address for where Johanna was, Greta found herself very calm at the news. Once she was back inside the apartment, after a quick glance at Julia to make sure she hadn't escaped the barricade Greta had made – two chairs and the small kitchen table turned on its side – she read the postcard again. It was chilly in San Francisco, Johanna wrote, and in the winter it got cold. These were the details Johanna offered. She asked a single question: Didn't you think California was warm all year? And then she answered it: It's not.

Greta turned again to the photograph. Maybe there was a message in this bright, candy red bridge. After another few minutes of staring, Greta walked the postcard to her bedroom closet and tucked it in with the others. Later, as Michael sponged himself in the bathroom and called through the crack in the door the news of his workday, Greta started to tell him. She started to tell him again as he peeled potatoes for supper, the dark slashes of skin neat and uniform under his blade. And again as they were falling asleep. But they were all false starts, like mounting a bicycle faced downhill only to find after a few turns of the pedal that the road pointed upward.

I'll not write her any news, Greta thought as she lay awake that night listening to Michael snore. She didn't even ask for Julia, Greta marveled, didn't even ask how we're coping here. She doesn't even wonder whether Julia is growing strong or if she's saying any words.

She expects me to just write and tell everything without even having to ask. Well, I'll not write back, Greta confirmed, shrugging her shoulders and nodding to herself in the dark. She wondered why she didn't think of it earlier. She wouldn't give one bit of news unless Johanna came to her and got it in person. Let her know how it feels to check her mailbox every day, to take in the daily bills and flyers and go back again a few hours later just to make sure that no small piece had gotten overlooked. Let her know what it's like to wait and wonder.

Ten

Eavan eventually fell asleep at Greta's nipple and, with her little belly full with milk, didn't stir even when Greta moved her to her crib. People said she was a laid-back baby, but Greta felt she was crankier than Julia had been, already more demanding of her attention. Michael said that the moment Greta called out a hello when she walked in from work, Eavan's little fists started flying and her legs began cycling in the air. 'She already knows her mother's voice,' Julia said once, and Greta wondered if Johanna had walked in the door when Julia was one, two, five, seven, would Julia have known her?

Back on the couch, the letter from Ireland was still there where Julia had tossed it. Michael's snores were drowned out by the heavy clank of the heat, which had begun coming up for the evening. The sound of the heating system was the one thing Greta had not gotten used to over the years, and once in a while she still suspected that someone was in the basement banging on the pipes with a hammer or a wrench. Their first winter in the apartment Michael had believed the pipes were broken; nothing else would explain the violence of the sound, like cast-iron pans slamming against each other for a full minute every hour on the hour. But after a quick conversation with the super from across the street he understood completely and came home to Greta with a story about steam and water and what happens when they bump against each other inside the pipe. Eavan had already learned to sleep through the noise.

It was Johanna's handwriting on the airmail envelope, a detail Greta had noticed right away. So she was back in Ballyroan, Greta thought as she leaned back to rest her head on the arm of the couch. A holiday, Greta guessed. Vacation. After that first postcard bearing Johanna's address so many years ago, Greta had held out for six whole weeks before she broke down and wrote back, but even then she was stingy with the news. Instead of sending updates about home and Julia, Greta told her about Bloomingdale's and Michael's work in the building and the new coffee shop that had opened on Eighty-sixth. Johanna worked as a waitress in a restaurant she said was very popular, and she sent pictures of the apartment she had rented just outside the city limits. Dissatisfied with Greta's news from home, Johanna started writing home directly for the first time since arriving in America. She explained to Lily that Julia was a situation she and Greta had worked out between themselves and there was no need to worry. She said she was sorry not to have written earlier, to have kept the secret from home, and then to have left for so long without telling where she was, but it was over now, wasn't it, and there was no use digging up old mistakes. Besides, she wrote, Greta doesn't mind. Greta took to Julia straightaway and even signed up for a public library card so she could go reading up on things having to do with babies. She was a natural. And she had Michael to help her.

In Ballyroan, especially after hearing that Johanna had left New York, Lily inquired almost every month about airfares at the small travel desk at the back of the post office. And almost every month she walked out of the office and said to herself, 'Next month.' When she heard that Johanna had gotten as far as San Francisco, she couldn't stop thinking of the day she'd waved at her two daughters from the pier in Galway and how she hoped strangers wouldn't be able to guess there were pound notes sewn to the underside of their skirts. It never occurred to her that they'd split up and that one of them would keep traveling until she arrived at a new ocean. But as long as she kept hearing from them, she felt at ease; they were alive and earning and feeding themselves and had a roof over their heads, which was almost more than Lily could say for herself. The roof over the boys' old room had finally collapsed, but instead of trying to fix it, as they would have, surely, if the other two boys were still in Ireland and Big Tom were still alive, Lily and Little Tom didn't discuss it and didn't go near it. Tom looked at it for a day or two, poked it with an old walking stick, tried to prop it up with long branches and tarp, but the damp was too heavy, and it all came down again.

He tried to buy lumber on credit but was turned away by a man who walked him to the front door of his yard, all the while saying,

'You see the position I'm in. Surely. You see it. You must see the position I'm in.' When Tom began to refuse his dinner and instead of eating or smoking stared into the fire with his hand cupped over his mouth, Lily decided to simply shut the door to that bedroom and stay away from that side of the cottage. She told Tom to do the same.

So the girls were doing well, and once in a while Lily forgot what was worrying her so much about them. Then she'd remember the baby, and the feeling of remembering what had momentarily been forgotten was like hearing the news for the first time all over again. Her little girl had a little girl. And Greta, that goose, left to raise her. There's no use going all the way to America, Lily told herself, when Greta will be home with that child any day. Any day now the post will come with a letter to say look out for the Galway bus. And then it came to her one day that she didn't know a single person who'd been to America and returned. Even Regina Fallon, who at fifty-seven years old only went over because she won the county raffle and wanted to see Niagara Falls, had never come back again. The next time Lily was in Norton's shop, she asked Mrs Norton to name three people who left for America and returned. When Mrs Norton failed to do so, she demanded of Lily, 'What's that to do with the price of eggs?'

Once the lines of communication had reopened between Johanna and Ballyroan, Greta remained as gatekeeper of only one area: Julia. About a year after she arrived in California, Johanna had started mentioning Julia in all of her letters. She did it mostly in roundabout ways – how nice the schools were out in California, how much more room she had in her garden apartment than Greta and Michael had in the apartment on Eighty-fourth. Johanna never mentioned her apartment without also mentioning that it was a garden apartment. Greta finally asked a woman at work what that meant. She imagined rose-bushes and tulips and a vine-covered trellis that Johanna passed under every time she went out. The woman at work said all it meant was grass outside the front door, sometimes no bigger than a doormat. Greta thanked her for clearing up the question, but privately she decided that it must have a different meaning in California, or why would Johanna mention it so much? In every letter, Johanna painted a picture of San Francisco that was calm and peaceful, with elbow room galore. Julia was two at the time, and Michael and Greta decided the best thing to do was to ignore the hints. Then, just as Greta had gotten past thinking of Johanna's garden apartment every time she bumped into Julia's crib, another letter would arrive. Finally, just after Julia's third birthday, 1967, Johanna wrote to set up a phone call. She wanted to hear Julia's voice.

'What harm?' Michael said when he read the letter for a second time, his capacity for reading growing by the month. He didn't have to sound the words out loud anymore. Didn't even have to move his lips. Soon he'll read as fast as I can, Greta thought when he handed it back to her. Faster. It's just a chat on the telephone, Greta agreed, and ignored the hard knot of panic that turned in her belly as the date got closer. The concerns Michael used to have about Johanna coming back and turning their lives topsy-turvy had been steadily wiped away as the months passed and she had not shown up to take Julia away. Greta hoped that Johanna wouldn't tell the child she was her mammy and confuse her. It would be just like her, blurting it out to get a reaction. 'She wouldn't,' Michael said. 'Why would she?' Just to say it, Greta thought. To claim what's hers. Greta held her tongue as she dressed Julia, and she even laughed when Julia cried out that Greta was holding her too tight. Together, Michael and Greta walked with Julia down to the stationery store, and once they got there and paid for their fifteen minutes, Greta held the heavy receiver up to Julia's ear.

'Hello,' Julia said in her child's voice as she pushed Greta's hand away so she could hold the phone herself. 'Who is this?'

Greta couldn't hear what Johanna was saying, but she watched Julia's round face as she smiled and announced that she had a friend named Veronica who had two cats. She told Johanna the cats' names and how they liked to jump up on her lap and up on the refrigerator. When Johanna first left, Greta had thought of herself as taking up a temporary role. She was more than aunt, yes, but not quite mother. Then the months went by, and people in the building and in the shops and even on the street started saying what an adorable little girl, what a young mother, what a good job you're doing with your daughter. Greta watched Julia's face get very serious as she concentrated on aiming her voice at the round bottom of the receiver, and then as it opened and transformed when she noticed a man outside walking dogs. 'Mama,' she shouted, dropping the phone. 'Look at all the doggies!' The man had eight dogs on eight leashes. Michael caught her under the arms just as she was about to run into the street.

'Johanna?' Greta said into the abandoned telephone. 'She's run off.'

'I probably bored her,' Johanna said. 'She's a talker, isn't she?' It was the first time they'd ever spoken on the telephone, and Greta noticed that Johanna didn't raise her voice the way Lily did when she took Greta's calls in Norton's shop. She didn't shout down the line as if she were dictating a telegram. She's used of it, Greta realized. Probably had a telephone installed straight off when she got settled in California. Michael held Julia up in the air as if to ask whether he should bring her back to the phone, but Greta waved him off.

'She's a rip,' Greta said.

'Like her mother.' And then, 'Sorry.'

'No sorries. You are her mother.'

'She calls you Mama.'

'Or Mom, or Mommy, depending on what she hears in the park.'

'She sounds happy.'

'She is happy. And so are we.'

'Good,' Johanna said. 'That's good.' And then, after a pause, 'Strange to talk on the telephone, isn't it?'

'At first, a bit.'

'Same distance you to me and you to Ireland, but I bet you don't get the same feeling like you have to rush.'

That was true, Greta thought.

'Because it's over land,' Johanna pointed out. 'And it's the same country.'

'And not nearly as dear.'

Silence. Greta wrapped the curly cord around her index finger like one of those Chinese finger traps they sell on the street downtown.

'She doesn't know,' Johanna said.

'She's too young to understand anyway.'

'Well, we'll have to decide soon what to tell her.'

Greta chewed her lip as she watched Michael approach the dog walker with Julia in tow.

'Did you hear me, Greta?'

'Yes, I heard you.'

'I'd love to see her. I have vacation time coming and I –'

Julia crouched down to skim a chubby hand down the back of a black Labrador. The other dogs yipped around her, and she kept snatching her hand away and running to the shelter of Michael's legs. Again and again he led her back to the dog, showed her how to pet nicely. 'Gently,' he said, his voice faint through the glass. He ran his hand from the top of the dog's head all the way down its back, and then Julia did the same.

'No, Johanna,' Greta said, surprised at her own firmness. 'Let's talk about something else. You said in your last that you bought a bicycle?'

'When, then?' Johanna asked, the tentative voice dropping away. 'I've asked a dozen different ways in my letters, and you never mention a thing about it when you write back.'

'You said it's up to me and Michael.'

'Well, it is, but Christ, Greta. I'm the child's mother.'

Greta could see her sister's face, three years older, a fringe over her forehead now – she'd mentioned a dramatic new cut in her last letter. These were the things they wrote about: haircuts, new shoes, cars, gained weight, lost weight, noisy neighbors, weather, and home. Home most of all. Have you talked to home? I heard from home last week. And in Johanna's letters, at the very end, a P.S. about Julia. The more they avoided talking about it, the more Greta felt it rise up between them. It was a dumb show, letters back and forth across the country, comments, questions, gestures without meaning. She's careful of me now, Greta thought as she listened to her sister breathe into the connection. She's the one in the wrong. Now she'll backpedal and make nice.

'Sorry, Greta. I didn't mean to snap at you.'

'No bother.'

'But I do want to see her. Not take her, Greta, if that's what you're afraid of. I wouldn't just take her. And I won't ever forget how much you've done for me. For Julia and me.'

There she goes, Greta thought, putting herself and Julia on one side and me on the other. She heard the echo of her own labored breathing somewhere deep inside the phone, miles down the line.

And what about Michael, who belongs on both sides? Ask, she urged herself. Ask her if she's thought for one second about Michael over the last three years. She closed her eyes and saw without effort Johanna standing on the flagstone path outside the front door of the cottage, hands on her hips, wanting something and not wanting to ask for it. Johanna went out in the evenings, Greta knew. Dinners with friends she'd met out there in California. She sipped wine in restaurants just as she'd always dreamed. She went on dates. One time she wrote of being out on a boat with two other girls and getting a sunburn. Greta hadn't been swimming since Ballyroan.

The tug from Ireland was equally strong, and the letters that came from Lily had none of the careful coolness of Johanna's. Time enough now to be coming home, Lily wrote. That child belongs here, in an Irish school, and wouldn't it be lovely for us here to have a child around? Tom will paint your old bedroom, and Julia can take Johanna's old place in the bed. We could make it nice for her, just as it was nice for you, Greta. You've gotten on so far, Lily wrote, but what next? You are not even twenty years old. Greta, you goose, bring the child here to me.

On the rare occasions where their letters arrived on the same day, Greta felt exactly as if her mother had taken her left hand, Johanna her right, and at the same moment decided to walk in opposite directions without letting go. Once, on the Galway Road, two tinkers, men, had pulled a child's arms out of her sockets doing that. Both claimed the child for his own as the mother stood by hiding her face in her apron.

Greta watched through the gritty window of the stationery store as the dog walker gathered his leashes tight around his fist and moved on down the street. Michael plucked Julia up and over his head to his shoulders.

'No, Johanna. Not yet,' Greta said, and without saying goodbye, she hung up the phone.

With Julia across the street at the Cookes' apartment and Michael and Eavan asleep, Greta stretched out on the couch and folded her arms behind her head. It was the perfect time to read the letter from Ireland, but she couldn't quite get up the energy. What was Johanna doing in Ballyroan? She hadn't been home in fourteen years, and to not have mentioned it seemed odd. The letters came and went. Sometimes they wrote as often as once a month, and sometimes four or five months would go by. They'd spoken on the phone a handful of times since that morning in 1967 – Christmases, birthdays – but Julia quickly got too old to talk on the phone to someone she didn't know without asking a hundred questions later. By the time she could talk properly, she was like a sponge for all that was spoken or even felt inside the apartment. She's like a willow witch, Michael said once, except instead of searching for water, she watches us with those big eyes to figure out what's going on. Johanna had eventually stopped asking to see Julia, but Greta felt that she could get the notion in her head again at any moment. Once, out of the blue, when Julia was five, they received a letter from a lawyer who'd been hired by Johanna to pursue joint custody. Littered throughout the letter were the terms custodial, noncustodial, visitation, and something called a parenting plan. Every night for two weeks, after Julia went to bed, Michael and Greta pored over the letter to try to figure out what it meant.

'They mean to confuse a person,' Michael had said. 'That's part of it.'

'Well then, they're doing their job,' Greta said, looking again at the glossy navy blue lettering at the top of the page, the address in San Francisco.

'What do we do?' Greta asked, wishing that Johanna had brought the letter herself so Greta could take her by the shoulders and give her a shake. She had a good mind to write and tell Johanna that even from the other side of the iron gate of the kindergarten playground, she could tell what Julia was feeling by the way she held her shoulders, the way she held her arms at her sides. Every afternoon, Greta stood waiting for her, watching the child's back as she reached with the others for the highest rung of the monkey bars.

'Ignore it,' Michael said, folding the letter into quarters and passing it to Greta. 'She'll come to her senses.'

And he was right. Two weeks later they got another letter from Johanna, apologizing for the lawyer, explaining that she'd been through a rough patch recently, a failed romance, a raise in rent, a job she described as more boring than being cook at poor Mr Breen's.

'I got talking to this lawyer who came in to the restaurant for a drink, and he turned my head a bit about the whole thing,' she wrote. 'I would be a good mother now, but I'll never hire a lawyer again, Greta. Never. That was wrong and I'm sorry. I've always said it's up to you, and it is. And it would be a shock to her now, I suppose. Getting to know another mother.'

'Damn right it would be a shock,' Michael had said when Greta showed him the letter. 'That one must be out of her mind.'

And as usual, Greta moved to defend her sister. She was young when it happened. She was so full of ideas. She was terribly confused. Michael didn't know what a turn it must have been to her.

And you? Michael always asked. Were you not young? Were you not full of ideas? Wasn't I?

It was different for me, Greta said. She said it the night they got the apology letter from Johanna, and she'd said it on a hundred other occasions.

Ah, Greta, Michael always came back, that's what I'm trying to tell you.

Soon after the lawyer incident had passed, they decided it was time to come to some kind of decision.

'Come as an aunt,' Greta said to Johanna over the phone. 'Come as Aunt Johanna and it won't confuse her, and let's take it from there. Can't we do that?' Lately Greta had been dreaming of speeding trains. Sometimes, to stop the train, she hung from the side and put her foot along the ground to slow it with friction. She'd seen that on Julia's Saturday morning cartoons. Sometimes the trains plunged off cliffs into the ocean, the tracks never turning away. Sometimes her train just sat in the station, empty, while all the other trains pulled out. Julia was talking in full sentences and smart as a whip. It was now or never. Michael felt it too. The air inside the apartment had changed. Greta could see the decision pressing down on his features in the quiet way he came in from work and opened a newspaper or stared off into space when he said he was sleeping. Calling Johanna 'Aunt' was the solution she and Michael had discussed and agreed on. Johanna was within her rights when she said she wanted to see the child, but still, having her back in the apartment she'd left so abruptly – returned from a milk errand that had lasted so many years – made both Michael and Greta nervous. Boundaries would have to be erased and drawn all over again.

'You mean not tell her who I really am? That I'm her mother?' Johanna asked when Greta told her the plan.

'Yes, Johanna. Say you're her aunt, and she'll understand that that's why she doesn't see you.'

'Well, how long then until we tell her the truth?'

Greta felt the same white heat travel through her body that she'd felt that night so many years earlier, hiding on the road while Johanna spied on the traveller camp.

'That's what I'm telling you. That will be the truth. That's it. She's starting to notice the trips we take to talk on the phone, and even the letters. It's time we told her something, and this is what we decided.'

'What do you mean will be the truth? It's either the truth or it isn't.'

Greta stayed silent, waited.

'Well, I don't know if I can do that,' Johanna said.

'Then we'll have to wait until you can.'

Greta dozed off on the couch, and when she woke, Eavan and Michael were still asleep. She turned to look at the clock. They'd gotten a telephone installed in 1973, the year Julia started fourth grade, and in a few minutes Julia would call from the Cookes' and ask if she could eat over. Greta would say no, she could not eat over, Julia would ask why, and Greta would say because I said so. That's not a reason, Julia would say. Well, it's my reason, Greta would say, and then she'd think of Lily saying no to the dances in Oughterard because it was no good for girls to be on the road like horse's shite. It happened like this almost every Saturday.

Once, Julia arrived home after a Saturday afternoon at the Cookes' and announced that she'd already eaten. 'It's not a big deal,' she'd added, flipping her hair and skipping off to her room before Greta could say a word.

'Yes it is a big deal,' Greta said, following her in.

'Why?' Julia asked. 'Why is it a big deal?'

But Greta didn't have a reason. It just was. She couldn't say why except that it gave her a feeling like the time she realized she was the one who'd left the gate open for the new calf to escape. Warm in her bed with Johanna grinding her teeth next to her, she had heard the calf bawling into the dark as Big Tom and the boys searched for her. Lately Julia was demanding explanations for everything, and when those moments arrived, Greta felt more than ever that she was playing a pretend game and that Julia would announce at any moment that the game was up. Lily would have given the girl a belt, Greta knew. Two or three smart slaps to the back of the legs, and that would be the end of it. Greta had smacked Julia a few times when she was little, always on occasions when Julia scared her so much she didn't know what else to do. Don't run out into the street. Don't open the door to strangers. Each time, the child's shock was plain on her face, her mouth a round and soundless O until she caught her breath and the wailing started. Good for you, the older women in the building said. And if she starts with the curse words, give her a smack on the mouth.

At five o'clock the phone rang, just as Greta knew it would. Imagine! Only twenty-five steps across the street and using the telephone to ask. And knowing full well Eavan and Michael were probably asleep! Greta jumped up from the couch and ran to the kitchen to catch it before the second ring.

'Hello,' she said, a statement. No question of who was calling.

'That you, Greta?' It was not Julia.

'Yes?' the line crackled.

'It's me. Did you get my letter?' A dog barked in the background. Greta could make out the thin clink of teacup returned to saucer at the other end of the connection. She quickly added the hours ahead and wondered where Johanna could be calling from. Norton's closed at four o'clock in the winter.

'Johanna? Is that you?' Greta said. 'No, I didn't see any letter.' Too much to explain, getting it but not wanting to open it yet. She wondered if Johanna ever had to work up the energy to face things, or if she just plunged right in. 'Is something the matter?'

'It's Mammy. She's sick, Greta. She's had a stroke. She can't talk yet, and the doctor still can't tell how much she'll recover. Are you there?'

'I'm here. Where is she now?'

'Galway. I'm there now at a B and B. She'll be here at least another week.'

'Another week?'

'It's been nearly a week already.'

'A whole week? Why didn't –'

'We wanted to wait and see. We thought she'd be up talking after a few days and tell us what she wants herself. Sorry. I should have called sooner. But I was in Ballyroan for the first two days and you know the phone situation.'

Silence, except for the occasional rush of static on the line. Greta had so many things to ask she didn't know where to begin. Where was she when it happened? Was there pain? Did the doctor come out to Ballyroan or did Tom bring her to town?

'And Tom called you to come home?'

'No. It's a strange thing. I was coming anyway for a visit. It happened just before I arrived. I took the bus from the airport to Galway, and Tom met me there to tell me. I wrote to you right away and dropped it in the post.'

Greta heard the locks slide in the door, the door pushed open, Julia drop her bag on the floor. 'Anybody here?' Julia called out in a stage whisper once she'd gotten past the closed door behind which Eavan was sleeping. She was a good girl.

'You don't seem surprised I'm in Ireland,' Johanna said. 'Anyway, we've gotten in touch with the boys. Padraic is tied up, but Jack is going to try his best.'

Greta waved Julia away from the kitchen.

'His best to what?' Greta asked.

'To come, Greta. What do you think we're talking about?'

'But she'll be all right, won't she?'

'Well, she might and she mightn't. I think he's coming just in case.'

Julia stalled at the open refrigerator and pretended to look for the date on the milk.

'I'm breast-feeding,' Greta said. 'Eavan's only twelve weeks.'

'You could bring them. Bring them both. We'd all love to see them. And Michael too, if he has the time off.'

Michael did not have the time off. There was no such thing as time off. Either you worked and were paid for it, or you didn't work and were not paid. He'd taken a week off when Eavan was born, and with the threat of a layoff always looming, he could not afford to take any more time. She flashed to Julia, tugging down her Lee jeans to do her business in the fields just as Johanna and Greta had. It seemed not only out of place, but impossible.

'So you dashed off the letter before you saw her? Then what's all in it? It's thick enough.'

'I thought it didn't come yet.'

Shit, Greta thought. 'It came today, but I'm just after walking in the door from work.' Julia turned from the fridge and mouthed 'Aunt Johanna?' Greta nodded and shooed her out the door.

'I started the letter on the plane and added to it when I saw Tom,' Johanna said. 'If it's a question of the fare, I'll be glad to help pay for a ticket. Julia will be an adult fare now. We could half it. Eavan can sit on your lap.'

'Wait,' Greta said, and leaned against the counter. 'Just wait a second. I have to think.'

Johanna waited.

'How bad is she?' Greta asked.

'Bad. If she was going to make a good recovery, she'd be partly there by now.'

'How's poor Tom?'

'Worried. He was here yesterday but had to go back to feed and milk. He's looking for someone to look after the place for a few days.'

Julia came back into the kitchen and poured herself a tall glass of juice. She took a fork off the drying rack and mimed eating, then raised her eyebrows. She rubbed her belly and groaned. Greta picked a dishrag off the counter and whipped it at her until she left.

'Why are you home, anyway?'

'I told you. A visit. Look, things aren't going so well in California anymore. The restaurant closed, and I haven't found anything else yet. I needed a break.'

Another failed romance was Greta's first guess. Or maybe she'd just gotten antsy doing the same thing day in and day out. Brush your teeth, rub the washcloth, go to work, make your dinner, go to sleep.

It wasn't what Johanna had in mind for herself when the packet boat carried them across Galway Bay to the ship anchored off the shore. Maybe she'd figured out what Greta had already figured out, that even when you find yourself living in a better place than the one you left, the people around you will still want to be someplace else. Listening to her sister breathe into the line, Greta realized that she might be hearing Johanna admit to failing at something for the very first time. She'd failed at being a success in America. In Conch, she'd be the subject of gossip whispered behind cupped hands. Years ago Johanna Cahill had abandoned a sister and a new baby in America, they'd say. And look at her now.

Or maybe she hadn't failed. Maybe she'd just gotten sick and tired of California the same way she'd gotten sick and tired of Ballyroan. Maybe after a few weeks at home she'd set out for Germany or Australia. Or maybe she'd head back to America and start all over again with a better plan.

'Well then, it doesn't sound as if you should be offering to halve plane tickets. Are you strapped?'

'Not at the moment.' A pause. 'I'll stay here until I think of the next step. Poor Tom, Greta. You should see the cut of him. And the cottage! I barely recognized it. The boys' room and the whole western gable is totally –'

Greta didn't want to hear about the cottage, though she couldn't say why. She declined the information just the same as if she'd plugged her fingers in her ears. 'Aren't there loads of restaurants you could work in?'

'We're not talking about me. We're talking about Mammy. Now, what do you think? Will you come?'

'Look. I just don't know. I could bring Eavan I suppose, but Michael works nights, and I don't like the idea of Julia here alone.'

'I said bring her,' Johanna said. 'Please, Greta. Just bring her.'

Eavan began to cry and then abruptly stopped. Julia had picked her up.

'I'll call you tomorrow,' Greta said. 'Four o'clock your time.' She took down the number and said good night.

'What was that all about?' Julia asked when she returned to the kitchen carrying Eavan. 'Crisis?'

Greta nodded.

'She's always having a crisis. Is that why we never see her?' Julia turned and bounced Eavan out of the room.

It couldn't be a trick, Greta told herself. They wouldn't take it that far. And Lily would never go along. And Johanna would never jinx Lily by making up a story about a stroke. And they weren't a family for tricks or lies. Not toward each other, at least. Okay, once, when Johanna went out to get milk and never came back. And yes, maybe when it came to night fishing or tucking a thing or two into a purse when the boxes in the Bloomie's back room were overflowing. But not when it really mattered. No, the stroke was real. The danger was real. The B and B in Galway and Tom's worry were real. Jack coming all the way from Australia might be real and might not. The most real thing was that Johanna wanted to see Julia. And so did Lily. And now they were together, pulling her in the same direction.

The heat came clanking up through the pipes again. Mr Ackerman knocked on the door to say that his radiator was leaking. As usual, he stood on his tiptoes to look past Greta and into their apartment. Greta told him to put a towel down and promised to have Michael up there as soon as he woke.

'I don't have an extra towel for that. Why should I use my towel? Then I have to do laundry a day early? Is it my fault the radiator —'

'Hang on a second.' Greta let the door close as she rushed down the hall in search of a spare towel. She plucked a damp one from the laundry. 'Use this,' she said when she returned to the door and Mr Ackerman's impatient stare.

Eavan started crying again. Greta changed her diaper. In the kitchen, Julia boiled water for pasta. She broke the spaghetti in half before dropping it in and then twisted the cap off a jar of sauce.

'There's salad,' Greta said, striding into the kitchen with Eavan tucked into the nook of her left arm like an American footballer.

Julia dove headfirst into the fridge to search for that bright orange dressing she poured over anything in the vegetable family. Her bum wagged under the fluorescent light.

'What's the news with Aunt Johanna?' Julia asked as she pulled a mostly empty bottle of French from the back of the bottom shelf.

'Nothing. The usual. Work. Life.' Julia was like Johanna in some ways. She was a perceptive girl. She might notice the similarities first thing if they ever met. Even now Julia was watching Greta as she began to eat. Her fork poised in midair, she chewed her food slowly, her left hand flat against the table, as if feeling for signs of a coming train, some telltale tremor where bodies connected to solid ground.

'Did she want you to go somewhere? You were talking about air-fare. Does she want us to go to California?'

'Ireland,' Greta said as she arranged Eavan in her carry-seat. Julia's face fell. The prospect of California was more exciting than Ireland, which, as far as Julia could tell, was full of rain and cows. California on the other hand was full of music, beaches, suntanned boys. No one in her class had ever been farther west than Ohio, except for one boy who was born in Colorado but moved to New York as a baby. Outside, a car squealed to a halt. A taxi, Greta guessed. Maniacs. When they were finished eating, Greta cleared the table and Julia got out her textbooks and the artillery of colored pencils she used to underline and make small notes for herself in the margins. Greta took Eavan to the couch for another feeding. Once Eavan had her fill, Greta burped her and put her down once more, even though she knew she'd pay for it around two o'clock in the morning. She told Julia she was going to for a quick sleep.

In bed, Michael barely stirred as Greta climbed in next to him. If he had woken, Greta would have told him. Instead, she decided to let him sleep. Sometimes it was difficult to keep track of what Julia knew and what she didn't. It was not strange to Julia that she had a grand-mother and an uncle in Ireland whom she never saw. The few times Julia had mentioned it, all Greta had to do was name all the people in the building, or people they knew from the block, who were from Germany and Poland and Korea and many, many other places, but who hadn't been home in twenty, thirty, sometimes forty years. Sometimes more. Julia was not the only girl in her school who had a grandparent living across the ocean whom she'd never met.

Even having two uncles in Australia that she knew nothing about didn't faze Julia. She often forgot their names. In stories, Greta referred to all three brothers as 'the boys,' and when Julia asked about them, it was always 'the boys.' Australia was a long way away. At twelve going on thirteen, she didn't seem interested in how they ended up there.

What did strike Julia as very strange was having an aunt in California who never came to visit and who never invited them out. Greta pointed out that California was the same distance as Ireland, but Julia kept insisting it was completely different. It was the same country, after all. There were trains that went all the way to California. There was even the Greyhound bus for those who could stick it.

Greta watched the lights from the street play across Michael's legs. One day, if Johanna returned to the States, she might call the apartment while Greta was out, and Julia might answer. They'd get to talking. Johanna would mention the outdoor markets, the trolley cars, whatever else made San Francisco different from New York. And then she'd invite Julia directly. She might even send her an Amtrak ticket. All this, she would do in innocence. There was no harm in getting to know each other, she might say.

'America has made you paranoid,' Johanna once wrote in a letter to Greta. 'You never used to think people were scheming all the time.'

I don't think everyone is scheming, Greta thought, her attention diverted for a second by the sound of Julia's chair scraping against the kitchen floor. I don't think that at all. But I'm no fool either. It was one of the first kind things Michael had said to her after he began living in their hay shed in Ballyroan. 'You're no fool, are you, Greta?' he'd asked, not needing an answer. Something in his voice told Greta that he'd come to this conclusion despite what he'd been told.

Greta's grumbling belly woke her at one A.M. and she remembered that she'd hardly even touched the spaghetti Julia had made. She opened her eyes to find Michael's face an inch from hers and his sleep-stale breath taking over her air. She turned, counted on her fingers one, two, three, four, five hours ahead. Six A.M. in Ireland. She sat up, pushed off the bedcovers, and stood.

The letter was still sitting on the cushion of the couch. Greta tucked it into the pocket of her robe and then looked in on Julia and Eavan, both sound asleep on their backs with their arms over their heads. She went to the kitchen and turned on the flame under the kettle. She propped the letter against the sugar bowl and looked at it as she waited for the water to boil. It was exhausting, all this writing back and forth. Maybe Michael's people had the right idea when they put an end to it early on. What could be in a letter so thick? All that time on the plane, Greta supposed. Nothing else to do. Greta had never been on a plane, but she imagined it like a long bus ride — nothing but staring straight ahead and thinking any thought that presented itself.

I could go, Greta thought as she moved the squealing kettle to one of the cool burners. I could bring Eavan and go and be back in a week's time. Two at most. I could tell them Julia has school she can't miss, because America isn't like home in that way. In America you can't pluck a child out of school for a week here and a week there. And it would be a good time to miss work, because if Bonnie mentioned Mr Halberstam, that meant the hunt was still on for those hats and scarves. Yes, she and Eavan could go alone, and that way Julia and Michael would be here to come back to. That way I would have to come back.

Well, of course I'd come back, she scolded herself in the dark kitchen, lit only by the stove bulb. What an odd thing to think.

Or I could stay right where I am, she thought. She looked again at the letter and began to resent its thickness. Does Johanna think I've all the time in the world to be reading and writing letters of that length?

And Lily would be fine, Greta decided. People recover from strokes all the time. She didn't know the year Lily was born, but she certainly didn't seem old enough to be put down by a stroke. It was impossible to imagine Lily any older than she'd been when Greta and Johanna left Ballyroan. And if she waited until the summer, they could go as a foursome, a family. Michael could get the time from work in a couple of months, provided there was no layoff. In the summer, maybe, when the days were long and the weather was fine.

She moved her mug of tea to the table and sliced the envelope open with the handle of her spoon. Six pages, she counted before she began. Front and back. She took a big swig of tea and began to read.

Dear Greta,

You will be surprised to find out where I'm writing from – an Aer Lingus jet headed direct to Shannon Airport. I tried to write this letter twice before leaving California, and even thought about making a surprise stopover in New York for a visit. Then I decided the stopover might make you nervous as you seem to get nervous every time I mention passing through New York.

Greta, you won't want to face this but I think it's high time we talked seriously about what Julia is to be told about her birth. I've thought a lot about what's fair to everyone and I really believe she should know that I

Greta stopped reading, refolded the letter, and returned it to the envelope it arrived in. Immediately after, she was surprised at how easy it was to pretend she'd never opened it at all, that it had never arrived. Later, she would tuck it into the cookie tin she kept at the back of her bedroom closet along with all the other letters that had arrived over the years, and putting it there, out of sight, sealed tight under the lid, would feel like she'd put a final close to a conversation she didn't want to be having in the first place. She finished her tea and listened to the second hand of the clock tick off the time. It was one forty-five. She had to be at Bloomingdale's in seven hours. Michael would be up any minute, his sleep cockeyed – as he put it – from working so many nights. She got up, rinsed her mug, and left the kitchen to recheck the locks on the apartment door. They were bolted tight. She returned to the kitchen and tried to remember how she felt when she discovered Johanna's plan to go to America. If she could have chained Johanna to Ballyroan, she would have. If it meant chaining Johanna to Greta's own hands and feet, she would have, and would have been happy to do it. But something had changed since then, doors had opened and then closed. New York had turned out to be the place where Greta became a mother, became partner to a man, became an earner of steady wages, a navigator of public transportation, an expert in building maintenance, a maven of local parks and playgrounds, a master of coupon shopping. All of the busy, racket-filled days since arriving in America had risen up between her and

Johanna. Maybe Johanna was onto something – a week in the silence of Ballyroan might put them right again.

Michael would be generous, Greta knew. If I told him all of this, he'd tell me to go home and be back in two weeks and he'd think it's as easy as meeting me at the airport to hear all the news. He was simple in some ways, or maybe it was because he'd never had anyone in the wings threatening to take fatherhood away from him. Let her see the child, he used to say when Johanna's requests got more insistent. It might put an end to all these ideas she has. You are her mother. That's clear a mile away. He'd made few friends since arriving in America. Ned Powers, a man he worked with, was one of the few he ever brought around to the apartment. And only Ned, Greta suspected, because Ned didn't ask too many questions. Michael was protective of even the most innocent information about his life. How he came to live on a nice block like East Eighty-fourth Street. The number of children he had. His age. He was especially careful when he was with other Irish. That way he guarded personal information was another leftover from the camp, and it seemed to Greta that these two sides of him – his increasingly casual outlook on Johanna's role next to his guarded secretiveness toward the rest of the world – were a contradiction. Johanna is your sister, he explained. Your blood. That's all the difference. How many years in America, Greta wondered, until that explanation stops making sense?

At two A.M. Greta heard Michael clearing his throat in the bathroom. It was a practice that was taking up more and more of his routine lately, and it would get worse, he predicted, the longer he worked in the tunnels. Quickly she plucked up the paper where she'd written the phone number of the B and B where Johanna was staying, and she went over to the telephone. She misdialed the first time but got the number right on the second try.

'I just want to leave a message for a guest,' she said when a man answered. 'Please tell Johanna Cahill I cannot be there, but to please give everyone my love.' When she returned the phone to the receiver, she noticed that she felt very calm.

They were waiting for her at Bloomingdale's when Greta arrived at nine o'clock. There was Mr Halberstam and another man Greta had never seen. Mr Halberstam wasn't normally in on Sundays. She nodded hello and made for the back room, but they stopped her and asked her to accompany them to the top floor, where Mr Halberstam had his office. Greta tried to catch Bonnie's eye as they passed, but Bonnie didn't look up, only handed Greta one of the smallest of the famous little brown bags, which held Greta's blouse from the day before.

The three of them rode the elevator in silence, Greta in the middle feeling her heart jumping against her ribs. I'll tell them it wasn't me, she decided. They were just little things, here and there, not nearly enough to matter with all that goes in and out of this place. I'll remind them how many years I've been here and how I've never been late, not a single time. She thought of Lily's old warnings in case Mr Grady should find her alone and ask what she had for supper. She dropped her hands to her sides and tried to keep perfectly still.

'Greta,' the strange man said when Mr Halberstam had closed the door to his office. 'I think you must know why you're here.'

Greta was back on Third Avenue by nine-twenty with a partial paycheck covering what they owed her for that period. Unable to face the subway, with the check still pinched tight between her first finger and her thumb, she turned and walked north up the avenue. They'd been patient. They'd wanted to be sure.

Michael wouldn't understand, Greta knew, feeling the trembling in her legs when she put one foot in front of the other. He didn't like liars. He didn't like thieves. I'll tell him I quit, she decided, but then two blocks later she realized there would be too many questions, and also the chance of him being hurt that she hadn't discussed it with him first. How could she quit with the possibility that he might get laid off? When had she ever been so careless? I'll tell him I was fired because of the milk, she decided, and the way that possibility settled her stomach and calmed her trembling legs meant it was the right one. For the next twenty blocks, she chewed on what she would say. Yes, customers had seen and had lodged a complaint. It offended them, seeing that kind of thing where they shopped and when they'd hoped to have a nice day. Women in America don't know what breast milk is, she'd tell him. They bottle-feed, and even that they hire out to dark-skinned nannies. He would believe it, she knew, with all the stories she brought home about the ladies who bought thousand-dollar winter coats and five-hundred-dollar belts. But Michael, she would say, how could I have helped it?

It was a white lie, she told herself, and recalled Lily sweeping out the henhouse one afternoon and describing to Greta all categories of lies. Little ones, big ones, good ones and bad.

Lily in a hospital bed in Galway. Now she could go to Ireland for a month and not worry about missing work. My pet, Lily might say from the bed, reaching for Greta. My best girl. Their secret. And maybe it would even be fine to bring Julia; Johanna wouldn't be able to pull anything with Lily there to keep things fair. She thought of the weight of Johanna's letter in her hand. She didn't need to read it to know what was in it: Johanna making her case for motherhood so that even a goose like Greta would understand.

When Greta finally got home, she opened the door to find the apartment strangely quiet and Julia sitting cross-legged on the floor with Eavan in the hollow between her knees. It was as if she were waiting for Greta to come home even though she wasn't expected home for another five hours.

'Dad got called in,' Julia explained. 'The pumps failed or something.'

'It happens,' Greta said, tossing her keys on a pile of papers. Julia was not a worrier, but something in her face seemed tense and afraid. Even Eavan seemed not herself — subdued, watchful — as if at almost four months she knew something her mother didn't.

'I have bad news,' Julia said, and at almost thirteen, felt very grown up all of a sudden, more grown up than she was prepared to be that day. 'Aunt Johanna called. Your mother' — Julia sighed as she cast around for the best word — 'died.' She froze, never having broken such news before, not sure what was supposed to happen now.

At first Greta didn't do anything — didn't move, didn't even breathe. Then she made a sound Julia had never heard her make before. It was a sob, throaty and heartbroken. The couch springs creaked as Greta's body sank into it.

'Mom?' Julia whispered. When Greta didn't answer, Julia set Eavan on the floor and crawled over to Greta's knees. 'Mom?' she said again, louder this time.

'So your Nana is gone to heaven,' Greta said, huffing back a wave of sobs in a style Julia recognized as her own. Julia handed Greta the piece of paper where she'd taken down all the information. The time, the doctor's name, and again, the number of the B and B where Johanna was staying. There was no extra information.

'What else did Johanna say?' Greta asked. 'Did you talk for long?'

'No, just a minute or so. She said Tom was waiting for her. She said she hoped to see me. She said that you said we're going over there and I'd meet everyone for the first time.'

'I never said that,' Greta corrected. No point now, she added silently. Mammy gone. That feeling of a fire always warming the kitchen of home abruptly put out. Even though she had had no real intention of going back, the news of Lily dead felt as if that option were stolen from her and that she was in America for the very first time not as a foreigner trying out a new life, but as someone who'd come for good and could no longer return to the life she'd left even if she wanted to. Going home now, she knew, would only mean being reminded of all the years she had not gone. Even when Lily had begged, and Greta knew well what such a return would mean to her, she'd put her off with 'later' and 'soon,' until Lily could hardly get up the energy to ask.

And Johanna, stuck there now because she'd been present for this. Stuck to make decisions about the farm and the cottage and what's to be done about Little Tom, the very last person left in Ballyroan.

'Which one is Tom?' Julia asked softly, and then watched as Greta slid from the couch to the floor and covered her face with her hands.

PART V

1986

Eleven

In the hoghouse of the shaft site in Red Hook, there'd been talk of layoffs for weeks. At the three daily shift changes – 7:00 A.M., 3:00 P.M., 11:00 P.M. – the muck-covered and bone-soaked men who were spit out from the throat of the shaft greeted the clean and shaven group making their way down as if they hadn't crossed paths in years, as if seeing one another again came as a pleasant and unexpected surprise. Before the talk of layoffs, there had been thoughts of layoffs, but superstition held that the possibility should not be spoken out loud until it appeared inevitable. Once the ban was lifted – you'd have to be blind not to see it was coming – men who'd been working the water tunnels since the project began recalled the layoffs of 1978, showing up at work to find the gates closed and locked, returning home with sandwich and apple still in hand. Michael Ward, who had been one of these, knew men who packed up their rooms in the Bronx or Brooklyn or Staten Island and headed for the pipeline in Alaska the very next day.

For Michael, those lean years of the late 1970s had been a onetime thing, a stretch of twenty-six months once survived would never return. If he got through it, Michael told himself then, he'd be rewarded for it. That was the way the world had to work, after all. From August of 1977 to October of 1979 he'd shaped for day labor, he'd gone back to moving furniture three days a week, he'd driven a cab for a friend who owned his own medallion and needed his vehicle on the road twenty-four hours a day. Greta, who'd lost her job just a few months before the layoffs, got a new job at Macy's but had to start over at the minimum hourly pay. And on Sundays, while the Koreans across the street were at church, she worked at their laundromat doing dark load after light, folding and tagging each batch as she plucked the hot clothes from the dryers. Julia usually went with her to help, and sometimes Eavan went along to crawl among the humming machines while Greta and Julia worked. Inside the locked and shuttered store they listened to the radio and played games Julia had learned in school — twenty questions, alphabet trip. If Michael was home for supper, they reported on the various styles of underwear they'd encountered and told him they would decide on the funniest one and bring it home to show him, one of them ones with the string going up the crack. Michael knew that all this talk of underwear was the same as saying they didn't mind the extra work. The bags under Greta's eyes told a different story.

'I'm pregnant,' she told him one night after Julia had gone to bed. 'Eight weeks gone.' That was October 1977. Julia was thirteen, Eavan was about to turn one, and Greta had far less of that astonished joy she'd had when she told him she was pregnant with Eavan. With Eavan she hadn't even been able to wait for him to come home; he'd walked through the gate of the job site one afternoon to find her sitting on the curb, chin on her fist, the bus map in her hands twisted into a tight cigar. She had told him the news as if she'd finally been awarded the title she'd long deserved. Carrying a child of her own made her feel even more like Julia's mother, and the first thing she noticed about herself when her belly began to grow larger was that she loved the unborn baby no more and no less than she already loved Julia. Michael was surprised to see that the realization came as a relief to her, when he knew all along that she could not possibly care for Julia any more than she already did. When the baby kicked and turned and Greta gasped at the pain of her ligaments stretching, her bladder being pressed, it was not only anticipation of the new baby that made her suffer these discomforts without complaint, it was also the knowledge, finally, of how Johanna had felt all those months when she curled up on the bed she and Greta shared, a pillow between her knees.

Michael knew that despite the brave face she wore, Greta had been feeling unmoored since Lily's death, and to have lost her job the same day and for such a silly reason, and for weeks after to have had to face Julia's endless questions about why they didn't go to the funeral, why Aunt Johanna had not returned to California, why Greta didn't seem to miss her brothers — all of it had quieted Greta in a way Michael had never seen before. He suggested to Greta a few weeks after Lily died that telling Julia might make her feel better. He'd brought up the possibility many times before, but this was the first time he'd pushed the matter, made it clear that telling Julia felt to him like the right thing to do. Not just for Julia, but for all of them. To Michael, the details surrounding Julia's birth seemed insignificant compared with the work Greta had put in since then. And not only the work, but the love as well. Julia would see that, surely. Dermot Ward always said that too many secrets would turn a woman old before her time. Men, yes, they could handle secrets, but a woman with a secret was a woman turned inside out. And she missed Johanna. That much Michael knew without being told. She missed Lily, of course, but she missed Johanna more. She either rushed to the mailbox when the mail came, or she made sure not to rush to it. In the first few weeks after Lily died, she picked up the phone and returned it to its cradle half a dozen times a day, and even now, so many years later, he still caught her at it now and again, looking at the silent phone, then picking it up to look at the lit up numbers.

There had been no calls from Ireland since Lily's funeral. No letters. Nothing. Nine years, and still nothing. Right away Michael had felt a finality about the silence that he was afraid to point out to Greta, and then he realized that the silence might have started on Greta's side of the ocean. Maybe over in Ballyroan they were also looking out for the postman. He urged her to tell Julia their secret, shine a little light on that cobwebbed old news. But Greta had lashed out at the suggestion, thrown it up in his face that he wasn't the one who had to worry. No one was out there threatening to say he wasn't Julia's father.

'But I am her father,' he'd made the mistake of saying, and then had to watch as Greta's eyes swam beneath her glasses and two fat tears slid down. He saw that she was smart. He saw it long before she and he and Johanna had left as a threesome for America. She'd taught him to read and write, after all. She'd figured out how to raise a baby. She'd always found steady work. Yes, she was smart, but still, once in a great while Michael saw that thing in her that they used to talk about in Ballyroan. That quality of being apart from other people, of veering left when everyone else veered right. Not to be rebellious, like Johanna might have been, not marching in the opposite direction with defiance, but simply wandering away without noticing there was another choice.

God loves a doer, the first Julia Ward used to say. And Greta was a doer. She tried. Lord, did she try. When she cooked dinner for them, she was either so careful not to burn it that they ate everything nearly raw, or she was so careful to cook everything through that it all came out burned. And at Eavan and James's school, Michael could see some flicker pass through the teachers' faces when they saw her coming. Amusement, maybe. Harmless enough, Michael supposed, as long as they answered the questions she asked. How do I help them at home? What kinds of things should I do? When they show me their home-work and their figures are wrong, am I supposed to correct it or make them figure it out? What if I don't know the answer myself?

God only knows how Julia turned out so smart. With her, they were so green they didn't even know there were questions to ask.

In the late 1970s, all of these feelings were carried along the drafts of the apartment like seaweed on the ocean. And when the tunnel work started up again, finally, after twenty-six months, things finally began to feel as if they would return to normal. The silence from Ireland continued. Michael stopped nudging Greta to let the secret out. Life went on.

But here they were again, 1986, another big layoff on the horizon, not much smarter now despite having been through it before. Julia was almost through with college — just three weeks until graduation — and at almost twenty-two she, at least, was old enough to fend for herself. As for the others, Michael tried not to think about it. Eavan was nine and James was seven, and every week they seemed to need something new — clothes, sneakers, books for school, ten dollars for teacher, twelve dollars for a class trip, money to buy a gift for some-one's birthday party. He didn't remember Julia ever needing so much.

Michael went along with the others who said they had seen the lay-off coming for ages, but privately he was surprised. Mayor Koch — who'd been all for the construction of water tunnel number 3, who'd put on a yellow rain slicker and a hard hat and stepped into the mud-caked and rusted cage and descended seven hundred feet under the sidewalk, who'd beamed out from his seat on the roofed railcar below as if he were admiring purple mountain majesties instead of soggy walls of mud, who'd hopped off the train three miles down the track to run his hand along the weeping rock face where the tunnel ended, who'd clapped his palm on the broad backs of the workers and told them the end result of all their labor would be as important as the Panama Canal – could lately be seen on television talking about the federal tax bill and what cuts would mean for public works in New York City.

'Public works,' one of the West Indians said in the hoghouse on a Monday afternoon just before the start of the three o'clock shift. 'That means water tunnels.'

One of the Irish corrected him. 'It means apartments for the blacks.'

'No. It means everything that gets money from the city,' another said.

'Including tunnels,' Malcolm, one of the Haitians added, and the rest shrugged. If it was going to happen, it was going to happen. All they could do was keep working until it did. Almost sixty years old, Malcolm was the oldest sandhog on the job and had worked the oil refineries of New Orleans, the shipyards of Baltimore, and, for the past sixteen years, the tunnels underneath New York City. Once, years earlier, Malcolm had saved Michael's life. There was an electrical fire down in the tunnel, and Michael had never seen smoke so black or a fire that moved so fast. Some men dropped their tools and ran down the narrow mile of tunnel that stretched north. Three men who'd been on break ran down the tunnel that pointed south, only a hundred feet long at that point, and were chased by the toxic smoke, eventually cornered by it. Michael, who'd been standing closest to the two huge power boxes when the fire was sparked, started to run south just like the men nearest to him, but he felt himself being tugged back, knocked to his stomach, pushed facedown into the murky five inches of water that were always present at the bottom of the shaft.

'Let it pass over your head,' a voice said, and Michael looked over to find Malcolm drawing a long breath and plunging his face into the muddy water. Just that morning, as they were pulling on their boots, Malcolm had said to Michael, 'I hear the Irish say tinker. It means black?'

By the time they'd lifted their faces from the water and pushed themselves onto hands and knees to begin the long crawl to the cage, one man was dead and another had inhaled so much smoke that he'd never work again. As Michael stopped crawling to tear off his shirt and tie it around his face, he decided that if he made it to the top, he'd find another job, something at street level. Even above street level would be better – the men who did the repairs on the George Washington Bridge, suspended high above the glittering Hudson, only had to fall through air if something went wrong. If Michael was going to die on the job, at least he would do it out in the open, not crushed under a thousand tons of rock and dirt or smothered by air that couldn't be recycled fast enough. Six more months, he decided as he and Malcolm crawled onto the lift. That was 1981.

As Michael tried to stuff the cuffs of his jeans down inside his boots, he listened to the other men on his shift discuss the possibility of a layoff. At least a layoff would shut them up about a strike. He'd been through one strike already, six long weeks of sitting at home while the powers that be held out for some detail of a pension plan that Michael could hardly see had the slightest thing to do with most of them, retirement being as distant and as impossible to imagine as picking the numbers of the New York Lotto. At least in a layoff you weren't refusing good work that was sitting there waiting for you.

The bell that signaled the ten-minute warning rang out, and Michael's friend Ned Powers hung back as the rest of the men filed out of the hoghouse and made their way to the cage that would lower them underground in groups of five. Michael noted the stubble on Ned's face, the way he kept rubbing it roughly with the palm of his hand, up and down, as if he'd already worked his shift and was trying to scrub himself clean.

'What'll happen?' Ned asked as he waited for Michael to hang his street clothes in his locker. Ned, like the rest of the men, stuffed his good clothes in as if it were a hamper.

'Don't know,' Michael said. 'Wait and see, I guess.'

'But what'll we do if it does happen?' Ned asked. 'I can't sit around like last time, not knowing.'

'We can shape for day labor doing something else. The odd day might get us through. Might only last a month or two.'

'You must be fucking joking,' Ned said, striding ahead of Michael through the rows of hoghouse lockers and pushing on the bar of the

262

heavy fire door. Michael patted his back pocket for the third time, confirmed his flashlight and folded ruler. They'd be measuring and laying down fuses that day. Greta always said that Ned Powers was typical Irish. He drank big. He talked big. He claimed to know everything there was to know about building tunnels, or building anything for that matter. He'd seen it all. He'd done it all. He told lies a mile long.

He was not typical Irish, however, in his attitude toward Michael. He didn't care whether Michael was raised by the side of the road or on a raft floating in the middle of the Indian Ocean. Michael worked hard, and that's all Ned cared about. Plus, Michael didn't go in for a lot of the Catholic stuff like the rest of the Irish. Sure, the others might talk rough once in a while, but that didn't prove a thing. They bowed their heads on Sundays just like they'd been taught. They fingered their rosaries and prayed on the inhaled as well as the exhaled breath. Michael didn't participate in the rough talk, but not for any religious reasons. For Ned, it was enough that a man *was* Catholic; he didn't have to believe on top of it. For Michael, it was clear that Ned would have fitted in nicely at Dermot Ward's campfire. He might have been the only country person Dermot invited in.

'I'll go home is what I'll do,' Ned said as they walked side by side across the lot to the check-in board, and Michael got the sense, as he often did when it came to Ned, that he'd be having the same conversation with himself even if he didn't have an audience. In this respect Ned was like all the Irish Michael had ever met in New York City; they all claimed they were just six months or a year away from going home. Some men had been in America for thirty years and still, when they spoke of the future, it was always set in Ireland.

Ned was rambling on. 'I'll get a construction company going at home. Modern houses. Modern plumbing. We could have it up and going in no time.'

'We?' Michael smiled. There was no sense pointing out to Ned that a business building houses meant there had to be people willing and able to buy the houses that were built. There was also no sense in reminding Ned for the millionth time that Michael had no intention of going home. Besides, he and Greta had just had an offer accepted on a house thirty minutes upstate, a fact Ned knew perfectly well. The closing would be scheduled any day.

'I know, I know,' Ned said. 'Well listen, there are rumors about a project in Boston. Something huge. Something to do with the highways. They'll need sandhogs if they're digging under the river. They're doing the planning now, and construction might start any day.'

'You'd rather wait around in Boston than wait around in New York?'

'Christ, Michael. What are we going to do?' Ned asked, angrier this time.

'Take it easy,' Michael said, under his breath now that they were getting closer to the men waiting for the cage to come back up for another trip. There was only one way down to the tunnel, and most of the sandhogs were already below. The three men waiting were engineers, and Michael knew better than to mix Ned with the engineers if he was already in a mood.

'We'll wait,' Michael said when the cage came to a stop and the rusted gate swung open.

'Already three oh two,' one of the engineers pointed out, looking at his watch. Michael stepped slightly in front of Ned, his right shoulder overlapping Ned's left. If Ned made any kind of stupid move, Michael would block him, have him on the ground before the engineers knew what had happened.

In silence, he and Ned watched the engineers arrange themselves inside the narrow cage so that their shoulders wouldn't bump on the way down.

'Three oh three,' the same man said, smirking, just before the cage dropped and they disappeared from view. 'You wouldn't want to get docked.'

Ned's chest puffed out and his broad hands became fists. 'Fucking cunts,' he shouted down the shaft.

'Jesus, Ned. Are you drunk?' Michael asked, taking hold of the back of his friend's shirt and pulling him away from the mouth of the shaft. All at once Michael took in the slackness in his friend's face, the volume at which he'd been speaking all afternoon, the smell, barely detectible but there, definitely, even over the primal smell of blasted-out rubble and muck, eighty tons of it so far that day, waiting in a container at the edge of the site to be transferred to a landfill in New Jersey. Each afternoon, Michael's first whiff of this dirt, so recently excavated from the bowels of New York City but so deep it was untouched by the city, reminded him of home. There are six kinds of dirt, Dermot Ward used to say. Easy, hard, dry, damp, clean, and dirty. The mountain at the edge of the site mixed all of them, plus, Michael guessed, some types Dermot didn't know about, never having spent time underground.

Ned gave Michael a guilty look, but he didn't answer.

The thing about a lot of these guys, Michael thought a half hour later as he stepped up onto the back of the huge pneumatic drill, is that they react to things before things actually happen. There might be a layoff, but there might not. And here they were getting worked up already. Ned stood beside the drill with a ten-foot wooden pole and waited to tamp in the dynamite when the holes Michael drilled were ready. There was a word for that kind of person, Michael thought, and he told himself to ask Julia what the word was when he got home. She knew the names of everything, and the two little ones – Eavan and James – were quickly catching up. Someone behind Michael switched on the power, and he felt his bones knock against each other each time the tip of the drill touched the ancient rock where the engineers had marked it with a blast of bright purple paint. He drilled one hole, slowly drew back, drilled another, drew back, kept at it for almost two hours, reaching and drawing away until there were forty holes in all.

The thing about Ned in particular, which was not true for the other guys, was that something had happened to him. So while he was reacting in advance to a layoff that may or may not happen, Michael had to remind himself that his friend was also reacting to a tragedy he never saw coming. Who am I to say what should help a person get through these things? Michael thought, and then cringed at the idea of 'these things,' as if all tragedies – in this case, the death of a child – could be swept into the same drawer and labeled. After the dynamite was planted, Michael and Ned worked together to wire the web of fuses. Michael double-checked the placement and the length of Ned's work while Ned stood by and pretended not to notice.

'You'll be fired before you're laid off anyway,' Michael mumbled when the web was almost complete.

'I know it,' Ned said, hugging himself tight in the damp air. 'Jesus Christ, don't I know it?'

For a second, Michael was afraid he would look up to find Ned crying, and this too reminded Michael of the camps of home. Sentimental men, all of them, brawling one minute, crying the next, while the women looked at each other and rolled their eyes. In Ned's case, it had happened once before, and Michael wouldn't know what to do this time any more than he'd known then. But it was only for a second, because next thing Michael heard the train approaching and the men climbing out and Ned saying 'Lazy sons of bitches' under his breath.

A few minutes later they covered their ears and closed their eyes for the blast. As planned, the wall in front of them collapsed in on itself, and an area sixteen feet wide and eleven feet deep was reduced to a pile of rubble. As always, Michael's eyes began streaming as soon as the dust cloud reached him. Even though he'd made sure to press his lips together, he could taste the dust on his tongue. He took off one of his work gloves and held his palm out to catch some of the water that never stopped dripping from the top of the tunnel. Once his hand was wet enough, he wiped his eyes. Ned, who had just done the same, began the noisy process of clearing his throat. When he spit, his saliva was darker and dirtier than the rock it landed on.

As Michael and the others began the long process of clearing the rubble from the blast and loading it onto the train that would transport it down the tunnel to the belt that would carry it up to the top, Michael thought about the house he and Greta had settled on. They'd seen bigger houses for the same price, but this house had a big square yard that disappeared into rough brush and bramble. The brush extended only about thirty feet and then faded on the far side into another stretch of manicured lawn – their neighbor at the back. Their plump and powdered real estate agent suggested that they could clear it and cultivate it to blend into their lawn so they wouldn't lose those thirty feet of acreage. 'Yes,' Michael had said to the woman. 'The yard is bigger without it.' But when he and Greta asked for a few minutes to talk it over, they walked up to the top of the yard and took a closer look. Greta reached down and pulled apart some of the bushes that had grown into each other. 'Blackberries,' she said, drawing her hand away and popping her finger into her mouth. She looked at him over the top of her glasses as she sucked at the thorn.

'Careful, Mrs Ward,' the real estate agent called out from the kitchen window, which looked out over the deck and into the backyard. 'They might be poisonous! I haven't identified them yet!' She shouted this in the most pleasant tone of voice. It no longer sounded strange to either of them to hear Greta called Mrs Ward. They had long ago decided that it felt exactly the same as it would have felt had there ever been a ceremony to make it official.

Greta smiled, looked back at Michael, popped a single blackberry into her mouth. 'I like it,' she said finally. 'It's time these little ones of ours learned a bramble from a briar.'

'Yes, it is,' he said, wanting to put his arms around her but conscious of the woman observing them. Greta chewed her blackberry, picked another, held it out to him in the palm of her hand.

'Ah, go on,' she said, her teeth black with juice.

At lunch, Michael unwrapped his sandwich – a thick slab of ham between two slices of brown bread – and tried not to get goaded into the conversation shouted around him over the roar of the fans and the pant of the water drainage system that never stopped pumping. Who was good for nothing. Who was injured. Who was faking. Who was stepping out on his wife. They brought up this last for the benefit of Mick Twomey, who was a Catholic in the old style and who Michael had never thought would last as long in the tunnels as he had. He prayed as he swung his pick, he prayed as he plunged his heavy rake into the gravel, he prayed as he heaved sandbag after sandbag over his shoulder to keep the underground streams at bay. 'You shouldn't talk that way about a man and his wife,' Mick said, as they knew he would, and they cupped hands to ears so he would say it again.

The wood benches that had been lowered down the shaft years before were slowly rotting in the damp and the dark, and Michael, who was at the very end, could feel the wood plank under him begin to soften and give way. He wondered what kind of evening it had turned out to be up top.

'Aren't you eating, Powers?' Michael asked. Ned had taken a bite of his sandwich, turned it around in his mouth a few times, and gagged as he swallowed. He's getting worse, Michael thought. Maybe a layoff would be good for him. Maybe he'd do better if he went home. Maybe I should say it to him. Later, when the shift has ended. Maybe I should say, Ned, have you really thought about going home? Maybe I should say, Ned, you're not getting on here at all anymore. He would have said something, definitely, if they were still at home and Ned were one of his camp, but they were not at home and Ned was not of his camp, and this was something Michael had tried to explain to Greta recently – the question of how to behave toward a friend who is nothing more, no blood, no ties beyond having the same employment and looking forward to seeing him in the morning when he got to work.

'I forgot something,' Ned announced suddenly, standing up. 'Anyone need anything from the top?'

'You're going to the top?' Michael asked, and then felt his cheeks burn as the others glanced at him.

'I am,' Ned said, speaking only to Michael. 'I'll be back in a minute.' There was no such thing as being back in a minute if you had to go to the top and back down again, so the whole row of men watched as Ned sloshed off through the mud to ask the bellman to signal for the cage. The bellman shook his head, pointed up the shaft, jerked his thumb toward the belt that was still transporting the rubble blasted out that morning. Michael looked away as Ned put his shoulders into the request, stepping up close to the bellman and nodding toward the phone that only reached one destination, the cage operator on top.

After lunch Michael and the three others who were charged with fixing the mighty mole – the engineering miracle that promised to bring tunnel digging into the twentieth century – rolled up their sleeves and decided to get on with it, no use in putting it off any longer. Ned was supposed to be with them but had not yet returned from his errand. The mole, a monstrous machine that weighed three hundred and fifty tons and was nineteen feet in diameter and seventy feet long, had changed the way the tunnels were bored. Shaped like a cylinder, like a rocket turned on its side, it excavated twice as fast as the drill and blast method, but it had been broken now for more than a week. The engineers had glanced at it, said it was 'on their list,' but the walking boss told Michael and the others that since they used the machine and knew it best, they should have a look at it that afternoon. Maybe it was something as small as a loose hunk of granite jammed between the blades. It had taken a full week of twenty-four-hour shifts to lower the mole down the shaft in its many parts, and another week to assemble it below.

The train, sounding its horn three times to signal a man load, brought them to the opposite end of the tunnel from where they'd blasted that morning, and there sat the mole, the sleeping beast, its trailing gear eerily silent and empty of rock and dirt, its lights blinking red in a rhythm that reminded Michael of a pulse. It filled the tunnel so completely that they could walk beside it only in single file, and even then they had to suck in their bellies and press up against the slippery rock face. Michael, first in line, inched his way around to one of the giant arms that gripped the rock in front as the machine's head drove forward. Attached to the head were twenty-seven cutting blades of three hundred pounds each.

'See anything?' one of the others called from the back of the line.

Michael reached up to run his hand along one of the blades and used it to pull himself forward. He reached around for his flashlight and, switching it on, ran the light over the rest of the blades. Standing on tiptoes, he shone the light over his head at the pointed nose of the machine and in the central lock where the blades came together. Turning, he swept the light up and down the front of the mole and then at the wall of rock that faced it. If the mole was truly stuck, they'd have to build a second shaft directly over her to bring her out. This would take weeks. Whatever Michael found, he'd have to discuss it with the rest of them before they reported to the engineers. Would the company be more likely or less likely to lay off men if the mole was stuck and needed to be brought out?

'Nothing,' Michael answered finally, ducking his head as he pushed around to the far side of the machine. 'Why don't you clear out and try starting her up. I'll take a look at what's stopping her.'

'You sure?' Mick Twomey asked as the rest of them edged backward.

'Is it you these lazy fuckers stuck in there, Ward?' Ned Powers shouted from the way back. He had finally caught up.

Michael and the rest ignored him. 'I've seen the engineers do it a hundred times,' Michael assured Twomey. 'I know where to stand.'

A minute later, once the other men had cleared out from beside the machine, the alarm sounded, and Michael could hear them running up and down the trailing gear and calling out to one another, shouting instructions. Just as it should, the mole began to vibrate, first gently and then with more speed. Michael, his palms pressed hard against his ears, could feel the rock at his back trembling as the enormous cutters started to spin. The head drove the nose forward, and sparks flew as it made contact with the granite. Michael, already in a crouch, tried to make himself even smaller and listen to what the machine was telling him. Something in the rhythm of the cutters' spin did not quite match the vibration coming from the body, and after a moment the whole contraption sighed and began to slow down.

'Turn her off,' Michael shouted when the noise subsided enough for him to be heard. He made his way forward on all fours. Using his hard hat as a shield, he kept his head down against the bits of rock that might chip off and fly at him. He heard his instruction shouted down the line like a game of telephone.

'The head is fine. The nose is fine,' Michael shouted. 'It's the cutters.' As he shouted, the spin of the cutters came to a complete stop.

Michael's legs ached from crouching. His left calf muscle began to cramp, and he put his hand on the now still machine to pull himself up. 'You there, Twomey? I said it's the cutters. There's something wrong with the spin. Powers?'

He could hear voices in the distance, one of the advantages of being so far down the tunnel and away from the roar of the fan, the generators, the constant bells and whistles signaling what was going up the shaft, what was coming down. The mole hummed gently, as if to remind them that she was still alive. Michael could hear that the men were arguing and getting louder. 'Goddamn it,' he said aloud, and wondered what could be keeping them. After a minute or so of trying to make out what they were saying, he decided it wasn't his problem.

If they could waste time, so could he. He straightened his legs, first the left, then the right, as far as the tight space would allow. He stretched his arms. He tucked in behind the blades and rested against the head where they were rooted. The head alone was more than ten feet around, weighed more than two tons, and felt smooth and comfortable against his back. He leaned back farther and let his spine match the gentle curve of the solid steel cylinder. I could go to sleep right here, he thought, brushing away a drop of water that landed on his cheek.

A moment later he heard the purr before he felt the vibration, like a car engine switching gears. Too surprised to call out, he jumped up to scramble back to his corner, but something stopped him and the shock made him stupid and slow. He tried to reach behind himself, over his shoulder, to swat at whatever was caught. The hood of his rain slicker, he realized, hurrying to unzip it. A split second later, in a mighty display of power, the mole did its job exactly as it was supposed to, exactly as it had not done just a few minutes before. The accumulated strength of three hundred and fifty tons drove the nose forward toward the granite, and the two tons of steel holding the blades in place – and against which Michael had decided to rest – became the axis at which all that power was transformed from something indefinite and haphazard into a driving force, centered and efficient. Michael envisioned the terrible spin before he felt it, and a single breath later, body limp as a rag doll, he went along for the ride.

When Greta learned that Long Island College Hospital was not on Long Island, where she'd never been, but in Brooklyn, where she had, she began to cry. 'Long Island!' she'd shouted at the cab driver when she jumped in, leaning her head over the partition to add, 'Please hurry.'

The driver sighed. Please hurry, please hurry, that's all he ever heard. 'I'll never get a fare back,' he said. If she was in such a rush, she'd offer to pay for the return trip. 'Where on Long Island?'

Greta, not used to taking taxis, was surprised that he had not zipped away from the curb upon hearing her destination and panicked that he would reject her request and ask her to get out. She'd never seen anyone hop into a cab and then hop right out again. Did she even have her purse? Yes. Wallet? What buses went to Long

Island? Did the Long Island trains leave from Penn Station or Grand Central or both? When she spoke again her brogue was as thick as the day she arrived, a phenomenon that occurred whenever she was nervous or angry or very happy, and she had to repeat herself twice. Taking a deep breath, she told herself what her bosses had told her at Bloomingdale's all those years: slow down, enunciate. Think before you speak, Greta. Greta, try to act as if you understand.

'Long Island College Hospital,' she said for the third time, and just like that, he understood the situation.

'Hey, good news,' he said. 'That hospital is in Brooklyn. We'll be there in twenty.'

'Miss,' he added when he saw that she had begun to cry – big, heavy sobs that transformed her face so much that he could no longer have guessed her age. 'I'm sure it'll be fine. I got an aunt who went to that hospital. She had the big C. Breast. Turned out healthier than ever. I'm going over there for dinner day after tomorrow.'

Greta wiped her face with the sleeve of her shirt and realized that she'd forgotten to ask Julia what she should give him in the way of a tip. Quietly, and out of the view of the rearview mirror where the driver kept trying to catch her eye, she slid a crumpled ten from her purse and smoothed it out against her thigh.

Once in the emergency room, Greta leaned over to place her mouth directly in front of the circular hole cut out of the glass partition at the information desk. 'There's been an accident,' she said. 'The water tunnels.' The woman behind the glass told Greta to take a seat, a doctor would see her shortly. Like an obedient child, Greta stepped carefully around the waiting patients, people clutching their heads, people cradling their arms, and found an empty chair. Once seated, she wondered if the woman had heard her right. Wake up, she told herself, and putting on her most businesslike expression, she went back up and explained that she wasn't injured, her husband was, he was a sandhog and had gotten injured on the job.

'A what?' the nurse asked. 'A hog?'

'Construction,' Greta explained. 'Water tunnels. Please. His name is Michael Ward. I don't even know what happened.'

'The tunnel worker,' the lady said, and her expression softened.

'Okay, I'm sorry. Step through that door and go up to the third floor. Tell them who you are, understand? In the meantime I'll call up and tell them you're on your way.'

From the moment Greta had sat down on the backseat of the cab, she'd felt short of breath, like someone much stronger than she had his hands around her throat, and now that pressure spread to her chest, her stomach, and her legs, which were becoming heavier with every step. 'Third floor,' she repeated as she pushed through the swinging door. She should have taken Eavan and James up to Mrs Kraus and had Julia come with her. Julia was always calm. Julia always knew the right questions to ask. The display above the elevator door said that the car was on the eighth floor and rising. She looked around the corner for the stairs, and when she found them, she clutched the banister and took the three flights two steps at a time. Once on the third-floor hall, she looked left and right for the nurses' station, took a few quick steps in one direction, and, changing her mind, turned around and went the other way. When she found it, she announced herself before she'd even stopped walking. 'The tunnel worker,' she said. 'I'm his wife.'

She heard her name being called and turned to find Ned Powers walking down the hall toward her. He was still in his work clothes, mud dried and caked to the middle of his thighs. It was difficult to tell where his boots ended and his jeans began. His top half was cleaner where he'd removed his jacket, but his neck and face were filthy. My God, she thought with a lurch, there must have been a rock fall, a collapsed wall, Michael buried and crushed. Then, spying the flashlight still in Ned's back pocket, she remembered that this was normal, this was how they all looked after work before they showered and put on their street clothes again. It didn't mean anything more.

'Ned,' she said, rushing up to him. 'What happened?'

'I've been here the whole time, Greta. He's just out of surgery. Surgery is downstairs and then they bring him up. In the ambulance they said he has a broken arm and a cut in his leg that goes almost to the bone, and they had a question about his ribs. The doctors won't talk to –'

'Can I see him?' she asked Ned, and then turned and repeated her question to the nurse.

'No, dear, not yet. But I'll send the doctor out to speak to you. You can wait for him in the lounge, and I'll send him right in.'

'Greta,' Ned said, leaning up against the wall and taking a deep breath as the nurses cringed and looked at one another. 'I'm a fucking eejit ninety-nine point nine percent of the time and I know it full well. Michael, he always says no, Ned, you're not a fucking eejit, but I –'

'I just want to see him, Ned,' she said, walking past him, but he reached out his enormous hand, which was as knotty and rough as Michael's, and pulled her toward his chest.

'He'll be fine,' Ned insisted to the top of Greta's head. After a few seconds Greta managed to wriggle away. Filthy pig, she thought. I could kill him. It was his fault somehow. She felt it. What did Michael see in this man, his only friend? All the nice Irish who work in the tunnels, and this is the one he lands home with every other Friday to eat up all the meat she'd gotten on sale at Spice'n Slice. And gab in the living room, gab and gab, Michael barely saying a thing, only smiling and nodding and adding his two cents now and again. That Ned Powers could talk to the wall. She had to kick him out half the time, dropping hints about the children and bedtime and them not used to cursing and shouting stories and laughing all night when, of course, they were well used to it, Ned being over so often since Kate went back home with their baby. Jesus, the shock that day when they heard about his little boy.

Remembering, Greta became immediately kinder. She put her hand on Ned's arm and squeezed. It was a wonder any child made it to school age with all the things that could happen. But still, Greta thought as she sniffed the air around him, drunk at four o'clock in the day. If there was one type of person Lily couldn't stand, it was a drinker, and Big Tom used to want to kill her for giving coins to Nell Bourke in town, whose husband had it bad. Every time Greta laid eyes on Ned's big red drinker's face she thought of Lily turning her back on Mr Bourke when he passed her on the road. Lily, gone by now except for bones. Greta often wondered what dress they'd buried her in and if the land next to Big Tom had held up well enough for Lily to be buried beside him.

'I'll show you to the waiting lounge,' the head nurse said, and Greta turned her back on Ned to follow the nurse's brisk pace down the hall, past patient rooms, to a corner door that led to a room with a pair of mismatched couches and a stack of magazines.

'Mrs Ward,' the nurse said as Greta looked at the couches and decided she didn't feel like sitting. 'That man has been drinking.'

'Drinking?' Greta said, looking around the empty room as if trying to figure out what she could possibly be talking about.

'That man,' the nurse said, tilting her head toward a vague spot somewhere over Greta's shoulder. Greta turned to find Ned making his way down the hall toward them, touching the wall every few steps to find his balance, his boots leaving dried pieces of dirt behind him like a trail of bread crumbs. 'We suggested he go home, but he wouldn't listen. Now that you're here, perhaps . . . ?'

'I just want to see Michael,' Greta said, lowering herself to the very edge of the closest couch, her back to the hallway.

'Of course,' the nurse said. 'I'm sending Dr Medina right in.' The nurse pulled the door closed behind her.

Greta had tried to picture the tunnels many times, but always, when she imagined Michael going about his day, she came up against a blank that represented a piece of information she didn't have. Where did the men change their clothes? Were there stalls or were they all naked together? Did they have so many lights going down in the tunnel that they forgot they were underground? Where did the lights plug in? Were there hills and valleys underground, or were the tunnels built level so it always felt like a flat surface? What would happen if the cage didn't work one day? Did the water ever get so deep or rush so fast that the men got afraid it might fill up the whole tunnel? And if it did, would they be drowned? Or could the water possibly sweep them out of the tunnel and up the shaft to the top, like the piece of potato that sits at the bottom of the pot but rises to the top again when you fill the pot with water?

Michael had answered all of her questions, amused that she found it so interesting, amused that she forgot his answers sometimes and asked the same question a few months later. Some of her questions were about details so small she didn't even know what to ask. Others were so familiar to him that he didn't know how to explain. No, he'd said just a few weeks earlier, throwing back his head and laughing. They never got afraid the water would fill up the tunnel, but then they both remembered him wondering about this very possibility his first week on the job, 1970, Julia sprawled on the kitchen floor practicing her letters, trying on the ink pen Greta had given her as if it were a new accessory, tucking it, finally, between her first and second fingers and holding out her hand to admire it from a distance. Michael, who'd been to Bloomingdale's many times and then to Macy's where Greta now worked, knew exactly what Greta's day looked like, where her register was, what an impression the racks of clothes made hanging there in the wrong season — wool coats in August, bathing suits in March — the piles upon piles of garments that went in and out of the dressing rooms every day, most of which had to be inspected, turned right side out, returned to the correct rack. The disagreements over how to dress the mannequins.

Now and again, hearing of some politician or writer who went down into the tunnels for a look, Greta would get it into her head that they should have a day when family could go down to see what's what. 'Never,' Michael always said. 'It will never happen.'

'Because the bosses wouldn't allow it or because you wouldn't allow it?'

'Both.'

Now, waiting for Dr Medina to come in and tell her what Michael's injuries were, Greta wished more than ever that she could fill in the blanks of his day. He'd been to sixteen sandhog funerals in sixteen years, all men killed on the job, but the details of those accidents were as vague to Greta as the details of the construction, digging the shaft, bracing the walls, mixing the concrete and laying it down. All of this before the first foot of tunnel was blasted. Suddenly, in this quiet room that had a distinct whiff of oranges, Greta became furious with herself. Like an idiot, like the soft-minded goose that she was, she'd just packed his lunches, sent him off, bought him new long johns and thermal socks faster than he could go through them. Worse, she'd often reminded Michael that they were lucky to have the tunnels to depend on. The Carpenters Union, the Scaffolders Union, even the Bus Drivers Union — all notoriously difficult to penetrate without a connection, and none paid as well as the tunnels. So he'd stayed on, year after year. And now this. Again she thought of calling Julia and telling her to bring the little ones up to Mrs Kraus and take a cab to Brooklyn. She looked around for a phone but found only more piles of magazines. She sat down once more and began to feel as if she'd already spent a week in that room, a month, that her whole life had been pointing to this moment – alone in a room with blue walls, blue carpet, the sickening smell of oranges gone too ripe – expecting a doctor to walk through the door. A thought skittered through her mind: I've known him my whole life.

'Mrs Ward?' Dr Medina said, crossing the room in two long strides. He held out his hand, but instead of shaking it, she squeezed it and let go. He looked around the room. 'Are you here on your own?'

'Yes,' she said, flashing briefly to Ned, who was still in the hall.

'Your husband was lucky,' the doctor said, and Greta felt the invisible man who'd been choking her all afternoon loosen his grip. 'He broke two ribs, and one punctured his lung. Considering the amount of time it took them to get him down the tunnel and up the elevator – is it an elevator? – he was very fortunate. He has a large tear in the rotator cuff of his left shoulder. He also has a very deep cut on his left leg, which we're going to have to keep a close eye on. He's scheduled for shoulder surgery tomorrow morning, and I'm keeping him under until then.'

'Can I look in on him?'

'I already have the nurse getting you a mask and a gown. I'm worried about that leg. It should be fine, but I want no chance of infection. Traffic in and out of his room must be kept to the absolute minimum. You understand, I'm sure. Listen,' he said then in a different tone, and placed a hand on her shoulder. 'The bottom line is, if all goes well, he could back on his feet in no time. He'll need therapy, of course, on the leg and the shoulder, but he's strong as an ox, your husband. Is that a brogue I hear?'

Greta nodded.

'Him too?'

Greta nodded again.

'Beautiful place,' Dr Medina said as he escorted her down the hall to the nurses' station. 'It's completely untouched, isn't it? Like a time capsule.'

'If this happened in Ireland,' Greta said, 'he'd be dead. I'm sure of it.'

Michael filled the narrow bed from corner to corner. He was naked to the waist except for the bandages around his ribs, and from the navel down he was only partially covered, the sheet twisted and tucked around his injured limbs in such a tidy way that Greta realized there must be a point to the arrangement. He was bruised above his bandages and below, and though she cringed to see it, she reminded herself that it could have been worse. He could have been broken in two. He could have been crushed to bits. The room was warmer than the hall, much warmer than the waiting lounge, and Greta figured this must be because they couldn't put a proper blanket on him. It was disorienting to see him sleeping on his back, which he never did, and to see him so neat in sleep, which he never was. His uninjured arm lay parallel to the right side of his body, his injured arm folded across his chest. His right leg was covered by the sheet, but his left leg was uncovered except for the bandages that circled his thigh from knee to hip. Even from the door of the room Greta could see that they'd stripped him bare, and when she approached the bed, she saw that his entire hip was exposed on his left side, his skin almost the same sterile color as the sheet, a few dark hairs underlining his basic whiteness and drawing her eye forward like signposts that grew darker and denser as they gathered at his crotch. She bent to look closer and saw that there were more angry bruises on his hips and legs. She took the very edge of the sheet between her first finger and her thumb and lifted. His good leg was black-and-blue from the hip to the knee.

She looked back at the nurses through the window in the door and saw them watching her.

'Hello, Michael,' she said, standing clear of the bed as she'd been instructed. 'It's me. Greta.' Just as the words were out, his lips parted and his jaw fell open. He never slept with a pillow, but they'd tucked a pillow under his head. They'd cleaned him up for surgery and cleaned him again after. His face, she noticed, had been completely untouched. Not a scrape, not a single bruise. Apart from the bruises and the bandages and the sling, he looked scrubbed enough to step into a freshly ironed shirt and go to a party.

'Michael?' she said, stepping closer and placing her hand on his chest. She pressed down lightly and felt his heart beating wildly in its recently repaired cage.

The knob turned on the door, and a young nurse pushed it open. 'Please don't touch him, Mrs Ward. It's just a precaution for these first few hours. The doctor –'

'He's cold,' Greta said, holding her hand out to the nurse as if she were holding up the evidence. 'He doesn't like to be cold. He slept outside all his life and doesn't deserve to be cold now. He slept out in the cold and the wet, then he worked in the cold and the wet, and now this. Please, isn't there a blanket?'

'I'll get him a sheet,' she said. The nurses at the station were listening to every word. 'But we ask you . . .' she added before turning away, looking at Greta's culprit hand. When she departed, another nurse took her place.

'Is there anyone you'd like to call?' the second nurse asked. 'Someone to keep you company?'

Greta remembered Ned, asked if the nurse had seen him.

'That gentleman left. Would you like to use our phone to call someone in the family?'

Greta shook her head and turned back to Michael. She should call Julia, she knew, but she couldn't get herself to walk out the door into the hall. He'll be fine, she told herself, fighting the urge to take off her jacket and drape it over him. He once asked her what she would do if anything happened to him. It was just after that electrical fire where one man had died and another was left not right in the head. 'Do?' Greta had asked, never once having thought of the question herself. 'I wouldn't do anything.'

'I mean,' he'd said, 'would you go back?'

But Greta had refused to answer, had refused to even let the possibility settle into her thoughts. And now, looking at Michael's chest rise and fall, she unbuttoned her jacket in the warm room and knew she had been right not to let herself think about it. He was – as she had told him so many years before while they sat on the front stoop with Julia on her lap – her best friend. She had never said that to anyone, not to Johanna, not to any schoolmate. Johanna had left, and Greta had survived. Had thrived, even. But Michael was different. Without Michael she'd be like the child on the low end of the seesaw, no partner to lift her up toward the sky.

When the nurse came back with the sheet, she also had a metal folding chair that had been sterilized by the cleaning staff, and she opened it for Greta in the farthest corner of the room. No sooner had Greta sat down on the chair and slid down so that her head rested against the wall behind and her legs extended out in front of her, than she began to feel the tension of the day drain out of her. Out in the hall, a monitor beeped in a steady rhythm that Greta found soothing, the wheels of a gurney rattled as they passed. He would be fine. Up and about in no time. The temperature of the room really was very warm, Greta thought as her head lolled down toward her shoulder. I can't go out now and ask if it might be too warm, not after the stink I made about him being cold.

Just a few seconds later Greta was surprised to hear Michael laughing at her, laughing with her, telling her to shush so he could listen to a patient playing a fiddle down the hall. Ned Powers was at the nurses' station doing a jig, waving to Greta from the other side of the window to get up, do a dance, live a little. Didn't Greta know the Seige of Ennis? Didn't they teach them anything out there in Ballyroan? He pulled an amber bottle from the gap in his wellies, but Greta discovered that she didn't mind, poor thing, all he wanted was a nip. It was the old habits brought to a new place that made them seem so wrong. The smell of salmon cooking on a grill Dr Medina had set up in the waiting room set her stomach rumbling. Will we go for a swim? Michael asked as he bent and straightened first his right arm, then his left, to test them out. Last one in is a three-legged donkey, he shouted, leaping up from the bed and, still naked, his bandages unwinding with every stride, he ran down the hall, down the stairs, out the front door of the hospital, and using that sixth sense of his, lifting his nose to the air and taking a long sniff, he turned and made for the river.

Twelve

Because Michael had come so close to dying but had lived instead, Greta felt that he would be safer in the tunnels from now on. It wasn't rational, exactly, but it felt like the truth. Greta and Michael discussed it, sheepishly at first, it was such a silly idea, but then with more conviction. Where sixteen others had died, death had taken its shot at Michael but had missed. The next accident on the job would be someone else's turn.

The day Michael came home from the hospital was hot, getting hotter every minute, and felt to Greta more like August than June. Even the sidewalk outside was quiet in that August way, older children in groups and younger children with their mothers or their nannies over at Carl Schurz park on the East River or, if they had the energy, west to Central Park, where there was more room and where they imagined they felt a breeze stirring the leaves of the trees. The only sound from outside was the beat of a ball being bounced along the sidewalk, the supple smack of rubber against concrete moving closer and closer despite the handler's drowsy pace. Greta listened as it passed, counted one Mississippi, two Mississippi, kept listening as the sound faded away toward Third Avenue. The smell of spoiled milk wafted up from the garbage piled on the street and slipped through the iron bars of the Wards' first-floor window gate. For twenty years now, the tenants of 222 East Eighty-fourth had been promised a large container for the garbage cans, something made of wood with a hinged door on top to trap the smell and hide the cans from view. For twenty years Greta had been wondering when the handsome wood container was going to arrive.

She stared at the tiny kitchen she'd used for twenty-two years – first the rack of drying dishes, then the sheer cotton curtain as it moved toward her in the humid air. Her look fell upon the calendar, and with her index finger guiding the way, she ran her eye down the column of Wednesdays. June the twenty-fifth. Not possible. Was she looking at May? No, there it was at the very top, June 1986, month and year correct. She pushed her glasses up on her nose and leaned against the counter. Somehow, that afternoon, she had to accumulate as many boxes as she could carry from twelve different liquor stores if she walked down Second Avenue to Fifty-ninth, then back up along Third. Liquor store boxes were best for moving – they were strong, the right size, and they were unlikely to carry roach eggs. If only she'd learned how to drive. There was Michael's car, just sitting there at the curb until Julia came home and moved it to one of the Tuesday/Friday spots on the other side of the street. Julia could drive her from stop to stop, but only if Greta waited until after six o'clock. No, Greta thought. I've already left it too long.

In the next room, Eavan and James were constructing models of their new house out of Legos. Twice now Greta had heard faint sounds of demolition, pieces bouncing and skidding along the scuffed hardwood floor. Twice she'd heard Eavan tell James to cut it out or else. On Saturday, when she lifted the mattress in there, she would find red and yellow Legos along with socks, clips, hair bands, notices from teachers meant for Greta to read and sign. Eavan's voice came through the thin wall again. 'You think I'm kidding?' she said, then a thump, something hard – a knee, a head – against the floor. 'Oh, go tell,' Eavan said a few seconds later, and then whispers, silence, back to the business of building houses.

'What's going on in there?' Greta called, rapping her knuckles on the wall. 'If I hear any fighting you're going to be sorry. Your father is trying to rest.'

'We're not fighting!' Eavan called sweetly, and then – Greta imagined the nudge – James shouted, 'We're being quiet!'

In the dim living room, Michael lay sweating on the soft velour of the couch they'd inherited from a woman who used to live down the hall. His leg was propped up on pillows, his injured arm in a sling across his belly. When James had come along seven years earlier, Michael had cut the room in half with a wall of Sheetrock to make a third bedroom. He didn't see why it was necessary; they could have just put a cot in Julia and Eavan's room, but Greta had insisted. At home, he'd pointed out, the girls and the boys were often mixed and

282

nothing wrong came of it. Plus Julia was so much older, it was like having a parent in the room. You're not at home, Greta told him, as she'd told him a million times before. He reminded her of the same fact just as often. Sometimes they joked about making a tally, who mentioned home most often. Since Lily died, and after getting over that first year or so of silence, it seemed that Greta had decided to fill the mute space left behind with more stories than ever, stories he'd never heard, about the boys, about Big Tom, about raising chickens and selling salmon. And somehow, the more she talked about it, the farther away home seemed to both of them. For Greta, home was not a place that coexisted with America, a place that went on and grew and changed at the same time New York was growing and changing. It felt more like Ireland had ended where America began, as if it were something out of America's past.

Even the children had caught on, saying the word home to each other but meaning Ireland, a place they'd never seen. 'They don't have pizza at home, do they, Mom?' James had asked on his seventh birthday. He held the slice at an angle so that the oil formed a current down the center, leaked onto the plate, and made the thin paper almost transparent. 'No, love,' Greta told him. 'They have delicious pig's feet.'

'Home,' James said, 'sounds disgusting.'

The side of the living room that became James's room got the larger of the two windows, so the portion of the room left over for the couch, the armchair, the television, and the low table they called a coffee table, though they usually drank tea, was at its brightest a rose-tinted gray. While it lasted, the light was perfect in its pinkness, in the way it airbrushed everything in the room, in the agile way Greta imagined the rays must have bent and turned to avoid the tall buildings up and down Eighty-fourth Street just to shoot an arrow into the Wards' ground-floor apartment. For roughly thirty minutes each day – slightly longer in the summer, slightly shorter in the winter – the living room was awash with pinks and reds. At all other times the room was a black-and-white photograph – the maroon couch, the deep-piled beige rug, the blue-and-white-flecked armchair, the navy-and-green-striped curtain – all reduced to a palette of grays.

They had a single lamp in the corner, but Julia had told Greta recently that it wasn't enough; it would do more harm than good. Who ever heard of a reading lamp that only held a forty-watt bulb? It was this lamp that Michael inched closer to as he listened to Greta move back and forth in the kitchen, the girls' room, the hallway, his newspaper tilted to catch the light. Two weeks of physical therapy in the hospital had done wonders, but a dull ache still ran down his limbs when he craned his neck to catch sight of her. He had three more weeks of therapy to go, and those would be held in the suburbs, at a hospital he'd never seen.

'Did you take your pill?' Greta asked as she crossed the living room to James's room, a single memory of a toy wagon becoming sharper with every step.

'I did. Didn't you give it to me yourself?'

'Oh, right,' Greta said, pausing her search to rest her hand on Michael's forehead. She'd asked him to explain it to her a dozen times, where he'd been standing, the size of the cutters, how, exactly, his hood had gotten caught. No, he wouldn't get paid while he was laid up, but he was alive, he would walk, he would be back at work within two months if all went well. The walking boss had come to the hospital with his cap in his hands and said he never should have asked them to look at the mole, that was for the damn engineers to kill themselves over, he should have let those good-for-nothing engineers get injured for a change. The man pointed out that the company always needed someone to supervise the pumps, no matter what the funding situation. 'You can read a paper, Michael. You can bring down one of them portable TVs. As long as you're there if the pump stops.' Without the pumps, all their years of work would be washed away. It was as Michael had always believed: with the bad must come some good to balance things out. As the rest of the men got laid off, Michael tried to hurry himself to health so he could go back to work.

'We could put off the move,' Michael said as Greta took her hand away and he shifted to find a cool spot on the couch. 'We could call and ask them if we can stay another month. After twenty-two years, what's another month? They could check with the new tenants to see if that works for them.'

Greta smiled, tried to remember what she'd been about to do when she asked Michael about his pill. They couldn't put it off; Michael knew that as well as she did. The new owner had the apartment scheduled to be gutted the day after they moved out. Plus they'd signed something saying they'd be out by July 1 and they'd have no further claim on the apartment. The management company, retained by the new owner, had already taken on all maintenance responsibilities. If they stayed now, after giving up their rent-controlled lease, they'd have to pay four times what they'd been paying since 1964. That – combined with the mortgage they were already paying on a house they hadn't spent a single night in yet.

'I know we signed, Greta,' Michael said as if reading her thoughts. 'But most people are decent, and when they know what happened –'

'We've put it off long enough, and we've a lovely house waiting for us, and we always said we wanted to be out before the heat of the summer. Julia and myself can handle it, and Eavan and James will do their part and that's that. And I've asked that lunatic Ned Powers to help if he's doing nothing else. He agreed in a heartbeat, which I suppose means he has the guilts about the accident though I didn't say a word. You can supervise. In fact, your first job can be to tell me how in the world I'm going to get all those boxes I've coming to me in one trip. I have to be at work at three o'clock and if I don't get them today they'll throw them out.'

They'd looked into hiring movers after Michael's accident, but the men Michael knew from the days of working as a mover had all gotten steadier work in different fields – construction, the phone company, heat and electric. Greta called a moving company she found in the phone book, and they sent a man over who looked in all the rooms of the apartment, opened and closed closets, got out his tape, and measured the apartment door. Greta was so shocked by the price he quoted that she felt her whole body flush. She stood speechless, staring at him, and he lowered it by fifty dollars. Just having him in the apartment made her panic, and she ushered him out the door as quickly as she could. She could fill the new house with furniture for the price he was asking. It amazed her to think there were people who would have agreed.

'You need the old grocery cart,' Michael said, trying to make out

Greta's features in the dim light. Her dark hair was in a low ponytail. It had been a warm spring, and her arms were already brown from walking to work. She was still rail thin, and unlike Michael, she felt no temptation whatsoever when she passed a bakery with money in her pocket. More than twenty years in America, and Michael still hadn't gotten over all the different things there were to eat and how cheap so many of them were. At home he'd been beaten many times for being caught with his licked finger in the sugar sack, but in America he could pour packet after packet into his tea at no extra charge and no one would look twice. Down on Spring Street a man could eat like a king with just two dollars if he got his toasted cashews from one vendor, his paper box of noodles and pork from the next, a sweet bun from the next, and so on, until his belly felt tight as a drum.

'I stored it in the basement,' he told Greta. 'The keys are on the ring behind the kitchen door.' Sometimes he was struck by how much she had changed since she was a girl, how lost she'd seemed then, how adrift in the wide-open landscape of home and then the immense backdrop of New York City. More often he suspected that she'd only pretended to change, had memorized the pace and language of a new place and had learned to mimic it so well that she forgot she was only playing a part. He'd caught himself at it hundreds of times, barking his breakfast order across delicatessen counters in all five boroughs, pressing his fist against the car horn the instant the light turned green.

Greta bent to kiss his elbow above the sling. She went to get up, but he grabbed her hand with his good arm.

'It's not Ned's fault, you know. It's just the job. You've got to get that idea out of your head.'

'Well, then tell me how many had he on him when he met me at the hospital.'

'He never drinks on the job.' He'd said the same to the walking boss when he'd come asking questions at the hospital.

'But he drinks every hour of the day except the hours he's on the job? And didn't he come straight from the site to the hospital?'

'He stopped off, and I don't blame him. He's been through enough.' It had been just three years since Ned Powers's three-year-old son had fallen off the roof of their building in the Bronx. Up the stairs the boy went, up, up, ahead of his mother, who was weighed down with bags and an infant daughter in her arms. 'Go easy,' Kate Powers had called up the stairwell to her son, and then stopped to swap the baby from her left arm to her right. As she bent to pick up the groceries, she heard the roof door slam shut.

After, she woke up at night after night and accused Ned of watching her sleep, of plotting revenge. Eventually, because he couldn't think of anything else, they decided she should go back to Ireland, to her mother's house, until she felt better. She and the baby had been gone for two and a half years.

'Anyhow, he quit the drink. He told me when he came to the hospital. He's given it up.'

'But Michael,' Greta started, but then she noticed that he was wearing that expression he always wore when he was bracing himself for something, and she stopped. She freed her hand and crossed the room in three long strides, and a moment later the jangle of her keys could be heard moving down the hall to the apartment door, to the hall outside, to the door leading to the basement. A few minutes later Michael heard the tinny rattle of lightweight metal as she opened the cart in the hall.

'I'm off!' she called into the apartment, and pulled the door closed. Michael listened to the squeal of the rusted wheels as she pulled the flimsy cart down the steps of the stoop, then turned right toward Second Avenue. I hope she remembered twine, he thought. I hope she knows enough not to be tempted by grocery stores or restaurants, however strong their boxes might look. He didn't want to carry roaches to the new house in the suburbs. In the suburbs, they would never peer under a cabinet to find a trail of egg cases, its cargo hatched and gone. In the suburbs, they would slide their feet into shoes without giving it a second thought. In the suburbs, they'd have 0.39 acres of rich brown dirt and green grass all to themselves.

Back in late April, on the day Greta and Michael told Julia that they'd made an offer on a house in a town called Recess and that the offer had been accepted, Julia had spent a week's worth of tips on three pairs of shoes. One pair was absolutely necessary, black flats, slip-ons, easy to walk to and from the subway, easy to slip into her bag once she got to work or campus and wanted to switch to a pair of heels. The second pair, black leather ankle boots with a slim silver chain running along the top of the foot, would go with a lot of outfits and would be great on bare legs or with tights or with sheer black stockings or with anything, really, pants or jeans, short skirts or long. The third pair was the one Julia couldn't get off her mind as her parents were describing a sidewalk, a deck, a large front window, neighbors named Diane and Bill. They were cherry red patent leather peep-toe stilettos, and they'd cost seventy-five bucks. Why had she done it? Jesus, seventy-five dollars? That was a whole semester's worth of books, a jacket, an interview suit – all things she actually needed. She'd done a slow lap around the store in them and then stopped to stare at her transformed lower legs in the mirror. Cherry red! There were her toes, looking right at home and ready to be noticed. There were her slim ankles above the impossibly narrow spike of a heel. They seemed like things to show off under a spotlight, things to be propped up on a table and discussed. 'You walk like a natural,' the saleswoman had said. 'You know how many girls can't go three steps in those babies?' And like that, one throwaway comment the woman had probably quoted from her sales manual, and the shoes were hers.

'Julia,' Greta had said, taking her hand and squeezing, 'we decided you can have the bedroom downstairs. There's a separate entrance, and now that you're almost twenty-two, we thought you'd like that. You'll have to use the upstairs bathroom to shower, because downstairs only has a toilet, but look, it's a million miles better than what you have now, isn't it? Julia?'

Julia blinked.

'If you want to stay in the city, you can do that too,' Michael said. 'Visit on the weekends. We would understand. The bus leaves from the Port Authority every nineteen minutes during rush hour and every fifty minutes on weekends. You could come for dinner and be back here the same night.'

'Why would she want to stay in the city?' Greta asked. 'She wants to come. Don't you want to come?'

From Eavan and Julia's room came the sound of bedsprings, followed by the rasp of bare soles on the wood floors. Eavan should have been asleep hours ago, and Greta had taken the extra precaution of looking in on her before she and Michael told Julia the news. They wanted to wait until school was finished for the year to tell Eavan and James, but Eavan was quick, one of those children who noticed everything, and she had been quietly observing her parents for a full week, while Julia, thirteen years older than her sister, had daydreamed about new clothes, a boy in her accounting class named Ben, whether she should throw herself a birthday party when the time came.

Julia watched her mother walk across the room to shut the hall door. As Greta returned to her spot on the couch, keeping wide of the side table that held the crystal lamp for fear she'd knock it with an accidental sweep of her arm, Julia saw it, one of those rare glimpses of her mother as she imagined a stranger might see her. Greta was young, only thirty-eight. She was young also in the sense that went beyond age, young in the way she moved and held herself, self-conscious of her thin limbs, as a teenager might be, holding her elbows to her side as if she was afraid of what might happen if she unpinned them and let them free. She was young in the way she glided carefully across the room in her strappy sandals, each step landing on the ball of her foot rather than her heel and giving the impression of a stealthy march, a creeping prowler, a person trying to sneak out of Mass before Communion. She was young in the way she flipped her dark mop of curls over her shoulder with one quick twitch of her head. Young in the way she looked at Julia and shrugged in that manner that asked, What can you do?

'What do you think?' Michael asked his daughter.

Julia almost asked, About what? But instead she nodded. 'Yeah, okay.' And then: 'Wait, are you saying you're thinking about moving, or have you already bought a house?'

'We made an offer!' Greta said, reaching over to squeeze Julia's knee. 'And they accepted! We have to drive out there on Friday to talk to the man in the bank, and we thought you might want to come for the ride and take a look around. It'll still be a while before a closing. Maybe not until June.'

'I have a paper due Friday.' It was an old reflex, mentioning school to close the door on further conversation. School was a fenced area of her life that neither Greta nor Michael ever tried to breach, and the reverence they had for the thick pile of books by her bed, the pads covered with rows of her slanted script, were like shields she could use whenever they wanted her to do something she didn't want to do. Only once had she wielded this power in a more tangible way: sophomore year, New Year's plans at a club with a steep cover charge, a party dress she'd seen at B. Altman that she absolutely had to have. She'd told Greta that she needed fifty dollars to buy a new biology textbook and had prepared a whole list of reasons why certain textbooks cost more than others, how she couldn't get a used one because the professor was using an updated edition, how the library copy had already been checked out for the semester. But her preparation proved unnecessary; Greta handed over sixty dollars and told her to get whatever book she needed to do her best in the class. Julia hadn't even been taking bio that semester, but she told herself that if they didn't have the money, they wouldn't have been able to give it to her, so it was no more deceptive of her to have made up a story than for them to always claim they didn't have it to give. Even the next day, the morning of New Year's Eve, when she heard Michael cancel an appointment to get new brakes on the car, she still managed to brush off the timing of her father's call and believe it had nothing to do with her. It was only when she kissed them goodbye, her new blue-sequined dress folded in her bag until she got to her friend Mary's apartment, and Michael handed her a ten-dollar bill and told her to be safe, did she swear to God she'd never do it again.

'Next time, then.' Greta had released Julia's knee. 'We have all the time in the world.' Greta turned to look at Michael. 'Don't we, Michael? Don't be saying she mightn't want to come. Of course she wants to come. Who wouldn't want their own door to go in and out that no one else can use?'

All Julia knew about the town called Recess was that it was considered by many people to mark the beginning of that vast wilderness known as upstate. What did people do upstate? She'd been upstate a few times, once to Binghamton to see a friend who went to SUNY, and in high school on a class trip for honor students to see Niagara Falls. She'd been to the suburbs in New Jersey a few times when a new Macy's opened in Paramus and Greta, with her many years of retail experience, had to take the bus out there twice a week to train new hires. Julia knew moving day was approaching, and fast, but it existed on a calendar entirely separate from her own life. The idea of leaving the city to live somewhere else, somewhere north, was impossible to digest. There was too much that had to happen in the interim, and her days were just too fixed and familiar to believe they'd soon be gone. She rode the subway, muttered along with everyone else about the ten-cent increase now six months old, highlighted her textbooks, bought her usual coffee from the stand on Eighty-sixth, starched her blouses for work, washed her clothes for class, waited in the bakery for the day-old rolls, listened to the upstairs neighbors clack back and forth on their new hardwood floors in heels, hurried by the dry cleaners with her head down in case the owner's son asked her for another date, waved to the barber who spent his days framed in the door of his shop and called out each and every morning, 'Julia! You are a sight for sore eyes!' And if Eavan and James were with her, 'Eavan! James! How tall did you grow overnight? Your papa must put fertilizer in your shoes!'

The rest of the family talked nonstop about the move, Greta and Michael describing the house, even collaborating on a rough sketch so Eavan and James would understand. Eavan colored the sketch with crayons to show the green grass her mother told her would feel like velvet under her toes, the black shutters, the white shingles, and then she stuck it under a magnet on the fridge. There was a driveway, a garage, five windows facing front. The sketch gave no hint of neighbors, and when Julia came home from work late at night, winded from a hurried walk from the subway with her keys clenched tightly in her fist, she'd sip apple juice at the kitchen table and wonder how far the next houses were. If they'd drawn the sketch from a slightly greater distance, say ten feet back, twenty, would she be able to see the start of their new neighbors' houses at the very edges? How much grass did one family need? The driveway, as Eavan had rendered it, was jet black, shiny with the wax of the crayon, and empty. Where did people walk to when they stepped out their front doors? Her father would no longer have to circle every block from Ninety-sixth to Seventy-sixth in search of a parking spot. No more planning days around alternate side of the street parking. No more yelling at each other to decide which of them would run out to Second Avenue with dimes if no street spots could be found.

Julia didn't know the first thing about buying a house, but she was sure, after the accident, that moving would be called off. She couldn't say exactly what one had to do with the other, but they were connected, she was positive. She'd been the one to get the call from her father's friend Ned Powers, and she ran to the park on East End where Greta brought Eavan and James most evenings she was off. Julia, Eavan, and James watched Greta rush off, arm raised for a cab before she even reached the curb. Julia had seen her mother hail a cab only a few times in her life, and the idea of her taking a cab all the way to Long Island brought home the seriousness of what had happened. People died where her father worked. She'd seen the documentaries of men covered in mud and operating machinery a hundred stories under the sidewalk. You can't call an ambulance when you're that far underground. First you had to be brought down the tunnel to the shaft. Then you had to be lifted to street level in the cage. She'd taken a class on the city's infrastructure at City College. 'Hogs,' her professor had called these men, and his abbreviation of what they called themselves, as if he were more familiar with their work than Julia was – Julia who brought her father's mud-caked clothes to the Laundromat once a week and tiptoed around the apartment all day when he worked the graveyard shift – was infuriating.

'What happened?' Eavan had asked.

'Nothing,' Julia said to Eavan. 'She forgot to turn off the stove.'

'She's taking a cab?'

'Yeah, she's tired. Long day.'

With a cross glance at Julia, Eavan kicked up some sand with the toe of her sneaker and marched away. A few minutes later she marched right back and said, 'I'm nine years old, you know.'

'I know, kiddo.'

That night, after putting Eavan and James to bed, Julia had slept on the couch and waited for Greta to come home. At a little after one o'clock the locks turned slowly in the door, giving out two soft clicks. Greta pushed the door open. Without speaking, she jerked her thumb over her shoulder to ask if the other two were really asleep.

'They're out cold,' Julia said, and sat up to listen. 'How is he?'

'I don't know how long they'll keep him,' Greta said. 'Maybe all week. Maybe more. My God, he was lucky. You should see the cut of him, Julia. A matter of two inches, and he would have been killed.'

But he would be himself again, that much Greta was sure of. And as Greta went on about how lucky they were, Julia's thoughts floated beyond the day's emergency to the month ahead. Her father was safe in a hospital that turned out not to be on Long Island after all. He was strong. He'd be fine. But surely a scare of this size meant that they wouldn't be tackling any other major change. They'd stay in the city. They'd go on the way they always had. They'd been happy in this apartment. Now they'd been lucky as well.

'What will happen with the house?' Julia asked, interrupting Greta as she described the union's complicated policy on workman's compensation.

'The house?' Greta asked.

'Moving. Will they be angry now if we change our minds?'

Greta blinked, tilted her head toward Julia as if she'd missed part of the question. 'Why would we change our minds? Don't you want to get out of the city?'

'Why would I want to get out of the city?' Julia asked. From the moment her parents had broken the news about moving, getting out, getting something of their own, it was as if they had confessed to leading secret lives, complete with secret dreams, secret preferences. She'd given serious thought to staying. If she found two roommates, they could divide the rent three ways, and if she got a good job, she might actually have some pocket change left over. For a whole week she had passed time on the subway thinking of who she might ask to move in. There were girls in her classes she'd become friendly with, there were girls who used to live in the neighborhood but had moved away, there were girls from high school who still lived with their parents and might jump at the chance to move out. They could decorate the place in their own style, paint the walls bright blue and red. They could spread a huge zebra-print rug on the floor where Greta's old rugs had been.

As Julia tried to decide who to ask, she pictured different faces sitting across from her at the table, on the other end of the couch. She rotated the faces of her girlfriends in a way that reminded her of James popping the heads off Eavan's Barbies, rolling them across the kitchen floor, and then reattaching them at random so that Malibu was wearing a business suit and Disco was wearing a formal gown. Every time she settled on someone, she got a feeling in her stomach that she'd regret it. It was one thing sitting next to someone in class. It was another thing to come home to them every day and have conversations about whose turn it was to clean the toilet, who'd forgotten to chain the door.

For months now, her friends had been striking out in navy suits, low-heeled pumps, pearl stockings, résumés in hand. Julia, in all her rushing about, finishing papers for class, waitressing five nights a week, deciding whether to stay or to go, hadn't even started looking.

And what would her mother do? The question came to Julia at the oddest moment – as she was finishing up the last essay of an art history exam and her No. 2 pencil broke, the jagged tip leaving a faint trail across the page of the blue book before falling to the floor. Who would watch Eavan and James if Greta got called in to work an evening shift and Michael was already at work? Where do you go for favors in the suburbs when the neighbors are so closed off in their own set of rooms, their own square of velvety green lawn?

'I thought everyone wanted to get out of the city,' Greta said, rubbing her eyes. 'I always thought of this as temporary, I suppose. Until we got on our feet. Well, it took a little longer than we thought, but we're on our feet.'

'I didn't know it was temporary,' Julia said. 'Twenty-two years isn't temporary.' She didn't feel like arguing. She wondered if the house in Recess would ever give her that feeling of coming through the door and being settled, of all the frustrations of the day seeming suddenly minor the moment she inserted her key in the lock. 'It just surprised me, is all,' Julia said. 'Did you ever think of moving back home? That would make more sense to me.'

'No, love. Now go on in and go to sleep. I'm sleeping here.' Greta patted the couch. 'The hospital might ring very early in the morning.'

Anyone who might have entered the Ward apartment in late June 1986 would not have guessed that they were moving in a matter of days. Everything was the same as it had always been, or at least as long as Julia could remember. Framed photos covered every flat surface, and inside the frames of those photos were stuck more photos, wallet-size snapshots of Julia or Eavan or James, or all three together. The closets were stuffed with old coats, appliances in need of attention – a blender without a lid, a juicer without a cord, a food processor Greta had never learned how to use. There were also shoeboxes filled with odds and ends, souvenirs from special occasions, matchbooks, candles, ribbons, letters, pamphlets, more photos. There were some boxes that held old lipsticks, buttons, shiny hair combs lined with crystals, bracelets, compacts, scarves, even old stockings wound up and tied into balls. Julia's grammar school papers and projects were crammed on the top shelf of the hall closet, while science projects, book reports, and artistic endeavors by Eavan and James were mixed together and divided between their bedroom closets and the closet in the kitchen. Long before news of any move Julia often wondered if her mother had ever thrown anything away.

Once Greta had the boxes from the liquor stores she'd called – close to thirty in all, uniform in size and strength – she took a week off from work and got down to business. Julia, she said, was off the hook until her finals were over. School was, after all, the most important thing. She gave Eavan and James busywork – line up Mama's shoes in a neat row, organize the Tupperware so they all fitted into each other – while she dumped drawer after drawer and shoebox after shoebox onto the floor of the living room and separated what should be thrown out from what should be packed and brought to the suburbs. When Julia came home from her last exam at City College, she found that the stack of packed boxes lining the hall had grown tall since morning. Empty, the closets and cabinets revealed themselves as Julia had never seen them – expansive, naked, squares and circles of shelf liner bright and dust-free where the cartons of pasta and cans of soup were once stored.

'Jesus,' Julia said as she watched her mother, who was sitting cross-legged on the living-room floor with a bandana tied around her hair. 'Why don't we get a shovel and just throw it all out.'

'It's not garbage,' Greta said as she stood to hug Julia. 'College graduate! How does it feel? How was the last exam? Are you hungry? You should be very proud of yourself, all those tests. I made a cake, and Eavan's icing it, so don't go in the kitchen.'

'It's really not a big deal, Mom.'

'Of course it's a big deal. You think everyone graduates from college?'

'Pretty much. It's not like I went to Harvard.'

Michael, listening from his bedroom, propped himself up on his good elbow and called down the hall, 'Is she home? Was the test very hard?'

'I thought you were asleep,' Julia said, walking down the hall to perch at the edge of her parents' bed. 'Feeling better?'

'Forget about me. Tonight, Miss Ward, we're going to eat steak and spuds and then we're going to have cake your sister is icing with pure sugar, I think, from the taste on the spoon she brought in for me to lick. Just one little spoonful she brought me, no more. That was awfully hard of her, wasn't it? After supper we're going to have a toast. How do they do it? To Julia. How do they put it? City College graduate, class of 1986.'

'But before that,' Greta said, coming up behind Julia, 'you'll give me some help, won't you? I don't want to face this pile after the celebration.'

Once Julia had changed into sweats and a T-shirt, she sat down on the opposite side of the pile from Greta. She'd quit her job at Jackson's Bistro earlier that week, and now, with the last exam behind her, the immediate future was beginning to look like a place she wouldn't mind checking out. She was twenty-one going on twenty-two. She had a college degree. She had nowhere to be in the morning. She would soon have an entrance all to herself. Recess was only a short drive away. Her parents had gone a lot farther from home when they were a lot younger than she was now.

'How about a rule?' Julia asked. 'How about if you haven't looked at something in over ten years, it gets tossed.'

'Just because I haven't looked at it doesn't mean I don't know it's there. And ten years isn't so long.'

'Mom,' Julia said as she opened a plastic bag and peered inside. 'This bag is full of coloring books. Old coloring books, but,' Julia took one out and flipped through the pages, 'never used.'

'So they're good. They come with us.'

'James is too old for coloring books.'

'So what? We just throw out a dozen perfectly good coloring books?'

Julia sighed, reached for another fat plastic bag. 'Are these what I think they are?' she said, shoving her arm elbow-deep into the bag as if searching for a winning ticket. She pulled out a long strip of glossy paper, torn on one side. She held the paper to her nose. 'I think these are old perfume sniffers. Like from magazines.' She dumped the bag into her lap. 'The whole thing!'

Greta's features drew together in a scowl, the way they always did when she was thinking seriously about something. 'Those can go,' she said finally.

Julia rolled her eyes and threw the bag into the trash pile. 'What about this?' she asked a moment later, tilting the mouth of the bag toward Greta so she could see the tiny balls of yarn inside. Some balls were smaller than marbles, few were bigger than golf balls. Every color of the rainbow was represented in multiple shades.

'Put that aside for now,' Greta said.

'I feel I should point out that you don't knit.'

'I do knit. I mean, I know how to knit. I used to knit. Crochet too.'

'Mom —'

'Listen.' Greta put down the box she was sorting and put her hands on her hips. 'I have my own way, and if you're going to argue about it, maybe you should go and clean out your own closet.'

'My closet's clean.'

'Then bring your brother and sister to the park.'

'Okay, I'll shut up,' Julia said, and did shut up, pressing her lips together every time she felt an objection forming in her throat. The garbage pile was growing, but very slowly. The pile marked to come with them had grown into a mountain and had spilled over the couch and onto the floor in front of the armchair. At the top of the pile to make the journey to the suburbs were little bundles of Polaroid photographs held together with rubber bands, bags of half-used jars of cold cream and lotion left over from promotions at Bloomingdale's and Macy's. Julia picked up a bright red cookie tin of a brand she knew could only be bought in the Irish parts of Queens and the Bronx. Once in a while, usually before Christmas, Greta took the train to one of the shops that sold these cookies and bought enough to last through all the special occasions of the year.

Julia used her nails to claw at the tin's top, which was jammed tight. She tried to twist the top off, tried to pull in different places in search of a weak spot. Finally, with the help of an old nail file stuck in with the junk Greta had cleared out from under the sink in the bathroom, she finally pried off the lid. Two dozen or so letters were bundled together; others were loose inside the box. Julia plucked out one and looked at it. It was the only piece of paper that did not have an envelope, and she recognized her own handwriting as it had looked almost ten years earlier. It was an old phone message, written on paper from a pad magnet that used to be stuck on the fridge.

'I remember this,' Julia said, trying to remember more details of the day. She'd been at school, Mrs Olarski's class, eighth grade, and had just come home. No, she'd been home sick. No, school had been canceled because of a burst pipe in one of the classrooms. No, it was a Sunday, Greta was at work, Michael had gotten called in, Julia was minding Eavan. James wasn't born yet. Pam from across the street had just buzzed to see if Julia wanted to take turns doing each other's hair in fishbones. She'd just learned how. Then the phone rang, and this was the message Julia had taken from Aunt Johanna, who had not called since. Breaking the news was the first time in her life Julia had felt the same age as her mother.

'Hmm?' Greta said absently, her back turned to Julia as she held some old blouses to the light of the window and searched for stains or pulls beyond repair.

Yes, Julia remembered now. That afternoon they prayed the rosary for the first and last time in Julia's recollection, and when Michael came home, Greta sent Julia to her room so she could tell him. 'Does he know her?' Julia had asked. It was confusing enough imagining what her parents had looked like and how they'd acted before she was born. It was harder still to imagine how they came together, who had said what, when they had known they were in love. How did her father know her Nana if he and Greta met on a ship on their way to America and had never gone back home? Instead of answering, Greta had just pulled Julia close and hugged her, squeezing and rocking until Julia could feel her hair weighed down with her mother's hot breath and runny nose.

Julia refolded the note along the old creases and reached for another of the loose letters shoved in beside and on top of the main bundle.

'What's that?' Greta asked, stepping away from the window and wading through the clutter on the floor toward Julia's side of the pile. 'What are you reading?'

'I think they're old letters,' Julia said, sliding a piece of lined blue paper out from an envelope that was postmarked October 16, 1966. 'This one is –'

'Give it here,' Greta said, stopping in front of Julia and holding out her hand.

'Why?' Julia smiled. 'Is it a love letter?' She cleared her throat as if to begin a dramatic reading. She had unfolded the letter to the first crease when Greta snatched it out of her hand.

'Does it have your name on it?' Greta asked, grabbing hold of Julia's upper arm and squeezing hard. 'Does it? No. It says Greta, doesn't it? Did I raise you to poke your nose in places it doesn't belong?'

'Jesus, Ma. I was only joking around.'

'It's fine,' Greta said, calmer now that she had returned the letter to the box and jammed the lid on tight. 'I'm just exhausted. And that cake, Christ Almighty, the kitchen was so hot with the oven on. You keep going here, but leave out anything for the garbage so I see it first. I want to see how Eavan is doing with the icing.'

She left the room with the cookie tin tucked under her arm.

After this first stage, the process of moving swung in the opposite direction, and it seemed as if something major disappeared every day. First the rugs were rolled up tight and leaned up against the growing stack of boxes in the hall. Then the vases and knickknacks, the extra bedding, the pictures that hung on the wall, all the dishes, glasses, mugs, utensils. The large pieces of furniture – the couch, the armchair, their beds – seemed frank and lonesome as they waited in bare rooms. Julia's bed, a twin, would be the only one left behind on the curb. A new full-sized bed would be there to greet her in Recess when they arrived. This is our whole life, Julia thought, staring at the pile in the hall and then at the dusty and cobwebbed corners of her bedroom. As Greta had happily informed them the day before, they would need only a medium-sized truck.

On June 29, the evening before moving day, Greta walked into the living room, where Michael was on the couch watching *All in the Family*, Eavan and James on the floor in front of the couch, begging him to change the channel.

'No way I'm turning on that oven in this heat,' Greta said. 'I'm getting a pizza.' At the news, James pumped his little fist in the air and Eavan clapped her hands together. 'I need Windex as well. Anyone need anything?'

Michael shook his head. 'Need help?' he asked out of habit, and then shook his head as he remembered.

James and Eavan looked at each other. 'Ice cream?' Eavan ventured.

'Yes,' Greta said. 'I think we can do ice cream on our last night ever living on Eighty-fourth Street.' James and Eavan turned back to the television and were very still, as if afraid one false move might disrupt their streak of good fortune.

'Julia?' Greta called toward the kitchen, where Julia was on the phone with her friend, saying how easy it was to get from Manhattan to Recess, how often the buses went back and forth, how it wouldn't feel like she'd left the city at all, how she could still do a birthday party if she wanted to, maybe in the country, on her new deck, why not give her friends a chance to get out of the city for a day. The girls could bring bathing suits and lie out on the grass.

'Yeah?' Julia answered, covering the mouthpiece of the phone with her hand.

'You want anything from the store while I'm out?'

Julia shook her head. 'You want me to go?'

'No, I'll go. I need the walk. The house will be clean, I hope, when we get there. Do you think? No one said anything about that at the closing. Or if they did, I don't remember. They looked like decent people when we met them. They looked like clean, decent people.'

'We can always buy what we need when we get there, can't we?' Julia pointed out. 'Worse comes to worst, we'll just clean it ourselves.'

'That's true,' Greta said. 'Yes, that's good. Wait and see.'

Julia finished her call right after Greta left, and she sat in the kitchen listening to Archie Bunker yell for Edith from the other side of the door. Her clothes had all fit in one large black plastic bag, the same type of bag Michael had used for the building's garbage cans before his duties had been passed over to the new management. In another large garbage bag were her makeup bag, her hair dryer, hot rollers, hairbrushes, and random pairs of shoes that had not fit in the box with Eavan's. In her backpack, which she would keep with her in her father's car, which she was in charge of driving, she had a few of the books she hadn't returned to the university bookstore, her wallet, the hand-carved wooden box an ex-boyfriend had brought home for her from New Mexico, and a framed photo of herself holding James on the day he was born, his face wrinkled under the cotton blue cap, Eavan beside her on tiptoes, peering up to see the bundle in her big sister's arms.

Greta had reserved a truck for eight A.M., and Ned Powers was supposed to arrive at the apartment by seven-thirty for tea and bagels. Julia looked up at the wall where the clock had been for so long and then at the watch on her wrist. It was already past six, an hour later than they usually ate dinner. All day she'd been waiting for the fact of leaving the city to hit her. She waited for the tears, even stared at herself in the small bathroom mirror and instructed herself, once again, on what was happening. Sitting in the kitchen, she tried it again. They're going to knock down the walls of your home, she thought sternly, as if reprimanding herself for something. Someone else is going to pee in your toilet, look out your window.

She left the kitchen and passed through the living room, where Eavan and James had climbed up on the couch and tucked in by Michael's feet. All three were staring at the flickering TV screen in perfect contentment, smiling at Dingbat, smiling at Meathead, smiling at Lionel Jefferson, who'd just come to the door. She passed James's room, his clothes for tomorrow already laid out on his bed, and headed down to her parents' room, which was still, with just a few hours to go, littered with odds and ends: new linens in their plastic cases, new undershirts for Michael, socks without mates, underwear, hangers, old cooking magazines stuffed under the bed long ago and recently rediscovered, presents received for various occasions too dear to ever be displayed. Julia picked up one of the smaller boxes and opened it to find a sterling silver baby spoon.

'She's hopeless,' Julia said, sighing. There was probably a name for this thing her mother had, this impulse to collect and collect but never let anything go. Without deciding to do so, after a few minutes Julia found herself sorting what was on the floor, making neat piles, shoving anything that looked like something her mother would never miss into an empty grocery bag hanging from the knob of the door. She took the last unused box from the hall and taped the bottom. Then she filled it with anything that would fit. Finally, when most of the floor was clear, Julia noticed at the back of her mother's closet the red tin cookie box. She picked it up and, moving over to the edge of the bed, held it in her lap.

Once, when Julia was a senior in high school, Greta had forbidden her to go out with a boy she'd met in a pool hall on Seventy-ninth. They'd fought about it, Julia telling Greta she was going to a movie or shopping or over to the park to meet a girlfriend, Greta finding out about it each and every time, saying to Julia 'You're grounded,' though they both knew she had only a vague idea of what that meant. Greta disconnected the phone; Julia used a pay phone. Greta walked with Julia to and from school; Julia made up after-school activities and forged her teachers' names. 'He's a bad one,' was all Greta could say. 'I can see it in his face.' Back then, that was reason enough to go out with him, or at least to be seen going out with him. Four years later Julia knew what her mother meant. He was mean then, and he was still mean, what little Julia had heard about him. Once, as he was kissing her, he put his thumb against her throat and pushed, stopping Julia's breath in her lungs and trapping it there. Julia coughed; he pushed harder. Julia slapped his hand away, and he laughed. 'You're an asshole,' she said as she walked out, and he laughed her all the way out the door.

Maybe here, Julia thought, looking at the box on her lap, is the answer to how her mother knew he was bad with one glance. There couldn't be too many secrets. She already knew that her mother had had her at sixteen. There would be no references to smoking up, dropping acid, all the things she should have been doing when she was new to America in the 1960s. Her mother, Julia decided, was underestimating her.

Julia listened for the dead bolts of the apartment door, and once she was sure it was safe, she pried the lid off the box, easier this time, and reached for the same letter Greta had snatched out of her hands. October 16, 1966. She took it in first as a whole, with one glance, her eyes sweeping over the penmanship and the length before she absorbed any of the words. It was from her Aunt Johanna, her mother's only sister, the one who happened to be in Ireland when their mother got sick and had never left.

This is going to be good, Julia thought, but before she let herself read the letter slowly from beginning to end, she lifted the tied bundle from the center of the box and broke the aging string.

Thirteen

Julia, right hand on the wheel at six o'clock, left hand out the window to feel the force of the air as it rushed by at seventy-seven miles per hour, eased the car left, left again, and left once more, onto the ramp that would bring them across the upper level of the George Washington Bridge. Greta, who'd adjusted her seat to the most upright position, sat on the passenger's side of Michael's Chevy Cavalier with her right hand gripping the handle of the door, her left in a fist that pushed into the worn vinyl of the bucket seat. Julia was a good driver, but aggressive, like a long-distance runner determined to pick off the runners in front of her one by one. She was a rare thing in the city, a lifelong Manhattanite with a driver's license and occasional access to a car. But she was out of practice and more used to the quick and jerky movements of city driving than the relaxed, we'll-get-there-when-we-get-there style of the highway. Eavan, holding tight to the single Barbie Greta told her she didn't have to pack, was quiet in the backseat. James had gone in the truck with Michael and Ned Powers. 'All boys in here,' James had said as Greta took the end of his lap belt and pulled it tight, 'girls in there.' He'd pointed at Michael's car parked across Eighty-fourth Street. Julia had braided Eavan's hair for the occasion, but with the open windows up front Eavan could already feel pieces coming loose.

'Hey!' she said after a while, dropping Barbie and using both hands to hold her hair in place. 'Hey, Jule! The window! Mom!'

But the same wind that plucked so many strands out of the tight braid and whipped them around her head also turned her voice into something small and soundless. She gave up on shouting and bent over to tuck her head between her knees. Don't cry, she warned herself. Do not cry. Thirty minutes, Greta had said when Julia first turned the key in the ignition. Twenty more to go. Then Eavan remembered: there were kids living on the block. An eight-year-old, an eleven-year-old, and who knows what others she hadn't heard about yet. They'd see her with her hair a strealy mess and think that's what kids were like who lived in the city. She held her breath against the pressure that was building behind her eyes and her nose, but like a dam where one small log breaks free, when the first tear came, the flood followed quickly in its track.

'How many people were there?' Greta turned her head and shouted at Julia, whose long ponytail was lashing her headrest. Without waiting for an answer, Greta rattled off names, called them over the roar of the wind and the car's diesel engine. She ticked them off on her fingers. 'There was Mr Ricci and the other barber. What's his name? The assistant? And there was the five of us, of course. Ned Powers. There was Mrs Strom, and Jackie, and Jackie's son Mel. Mrs Kraus. Everyone on the first floor came out, didn't they? Was anyone missing? The Morgans from 220, and the Magstaniks from 216. Remember when their girl used to babysit you? She's all the way in Minneapolis now. Did you know? Who came from Eighty-fifth Street? Mrs Levy and Mrs Schmidt. Did I tell you Mrs Levy found a lump in her breast? Is that it? Am I missing anyone?'

'That sounds like everybody,' Julia said, swatting at a tendril of hair that had gotten stuck in her lip gloss, swerving right to the ramp that led to the Palisades. She eased her foot off the gas as all three of them leaned into the curve. Her friends Bernadette and Mary had planned on coming to see them off as well. Earlier in the week, Julia had picked up two crisp copies of the Red & Tan bus schedule, stuck old Christmas bows on top, and planned on giving one to each of the girls. But after getting through more than half the letters in the red tin box before hearing Greta's key in the door, and then sitting through pizza and ice cream that the rest of them ate with plastic forks while Julia looked on in silence, she'd called her friends and told them not to bother, they were leaving earlier than expected. They had all summer to see each other and would see each other, Julia had insisted. Definitely. Lots of people commuted into the city from Recess every single day. Upon being uninvited, each had asked, 'You okay, Jules?' Julia said she was just sad about leaving all of a sudden.

After pizza Greta had to go out a second time for more packing tape, another box of plastic bags. When she went out the second time, Julia was tempted to go back to the box and finish what she'd started, but she stopped herself and plopped down with the others in front of the T V. Since then she'd felt in a daze, as if she were hung over, not sure if what she'd read meant what she thought it meant. How could it? Not possible. She'd misunderstood. There were other Julias in the family. Her paternal grandmother. A cousin, maybe. But the thought felt feeble upon arrival, and she'd felt dizzy all night and all morning.

'It was lovely, really, for them to come,' Greta said.

'What?' Julia shouted, tilting her head to the right.

'Lovely!' Greta shouted back, cupping her hands around her mouth as if shouting across a field.

Julia reached down and turned the knob that brought up the window. 'What?' she said again, quieter.

Greta rolled up her window as well. 'I said it was nice of them, wasn't it? For everyone to see us off?'

'Oh,' Julia said in the abrupt quiet, the trees outside rushing by silently now, the blue twinkle of the Hudson glimpsed between the branches somehow more removed without the roar of the wind.

'Mom,' Eavan said after a moment, her voice husky and miserable. She tried to lean forward to present her head between the two front seats, but her belt stopped her. 'Look what happened.' She took her hands away from her head and her hair fell in limp tendrils around her cheeks and neck. 'I tried to tell you,' she began bravely, but found she could go no further, and instead dipped her chin toward her chest and let the tears flow once more.

'What's the matter with you, *mo ghrá*?' Greta said, turning as far as possible in her seat without taking off her belt. 'Julia will do it again. It's not a tragedy. It's nothing to cry about. Isn't that right, Julia? Won't you do it again?'

'Sure,' Julia said, searching for the top of Eavan's head in the rear-view mirror. 'But why didn't you kick the seat or something? Why'd you let it get so bad?'

In Recess, outside the white shingled house with black shutters, the medium-sized U-Haul was parked in the driveway with its nose facing the street. Ned and James were sitting on the step outside, and Greta wondered for the first time if people did that in Recess, if they sat on their front step like it was a stoop, like there would be people passing to whom they could say Good morning, and Hot one, isn't it?

Only thirty minutes north of the city, Recess was a kind of in-between world. In Manhattan they called it the country as often as they called it a suburb, but it was quieter than the country as far as Greta could tell. There were no animals to snuff and grunt and squawk and bellow into the wind. There was the occasional bark of a dog, the meow of a hungry cat, but together these calls only empha-sized the silence that fell in between. All paths and hedges were neat and trim, and there was a general tidiness about the town that had no relation to the shaggy, overgrown, rock-strewn country in Greta's mind. But it was lovely in its own way, like a picture of America she might have seen at home, posted up in a shop or in the church hall, sent by someone who'd left a generation ago and wanted to keep in touch. She tried not to think about what it had cost, what it would continue to cost for the next thirty years. Michael hoped to pay it off in twenty years, citing all kinds of factors Greta didn't quite under-stand and didn't believe Michael completely understood either. 'Look it,' he'd said the morning they decided, running one of his chapped fingers down a column of numbers, and Greta had nodded, keeping her eyes on his cracked and blackened fingernail. 'I see,' she'd agreed.

But now, considering the house from the curb, she wondered if there had been anything in that long contract with the teeny print about a person getting laid up for weeks without pay. Though Greta put in as many hours per week as Michael, when they put their two paychecks together every other Friday and walked them up to the bank, hers came to only a third of his. He made a good salary when there was work, but when he was sick or when the equipment failed or when there was a layoff, he got nothing. And a man couldn't do that kind of work forever. It was a young man's job.

'Michael's set up in the back,' Ned said as he stood to greet them, and Greta got up close to him, pretending to peer at some part of the house glimpsed over his shoulder as she sniffed the air around him, inhaled the wake he'd left after him in his short walk over to where they now stood. To Julia, who took it all in from the driveway, it looked as if Ned had let himself be sniffed, had actually stood still for it, waited for the inspection to wrap up before moving forward. That morning Greta had been even more obvious about it, standing behind his chair as he sipped his tea and moving her head in a circle behind him as she filled her lungs with his scent. She'd watched with a grave expression as he poured the milk, dumped in two spoons of sugar, brought the paper cup to his lips and sipped.

'You can handle the truck?' she'd asked.

'No problem.'

'And don't forget James is going with you.'

'Aye-aye, Captain.'

Greta didn't smile, and later, after bringing out some of the heaviest boxes, Ned had peeled off his sweat-soaked shirt to work in his undershirt, and Julia had caught her mother plucking the shirt from the wood floor of the apartment and burying her face in its folds. When Greta saw that she'd been observed, she offered the shirt to Julia for a second opinion. Julia refused. 'He's fine,' Julia had said. 'It's working its way out of his system.'

Greta still looked skeptical, but when the time came for the men and women to part for their separate vehicles on Eighty-fourth Street, Michael had put one hand on James's shoulder, the other on Greta's, and assured her they'd be fine.

'Okay,' Greta said now, clapping her hands, the inspection over. 'Where do we start?'

'A tour,' Julia suggested. She had seen the house only once, a week after Michael's accident, when she'd driven Greta up to Recess to pick up papers and drop off something from their bank. The previous owners had invited them in, urged Julia to look around, but the house was full with their things, their kitchen table laid out with their place mats and cutlery. There were strangers smiling out from frames on the wall, and the smell of something sweet mingled with steam issuing from a pot boiling on the stove settled on her skin like a baby's faint breath.

'Come on,' Greta had urged, pulling Julia downstairs to see what would be her bedroom, her separate entrance.

'Next time,' Julia had said, turning her body into a statue Greta couldn't budge.

Inside, after greeting Michael, who was settled in a lawn chair the previous owners had left on the deck, Greta led the group from room to room, announced which of them would sleep where, opened closet doors, lifted and lowered windows, pulled the string that brought down the folded ladder that led to the attic. First Eavan dropped off the tour to examine her bare room from corner to corner, then James went outside in search of caterpillars.

'How will we do this?' Greta asked, back out on the driveway, as she, Julia, and Ned stared into the dark mouth of the truck.

When they'd loaded the truck in the city, the men who'd gathered to see them off had all pitched in, taking an arm of the sofa, one side of a dresser. Here, it was just the three of them. They took all the small boxes out first, Greta inside the truck handing boxes to Julia, and Julia hurrying back and forth between the truck and the garage. The plan for bigger, heavier things was that Greta and Julia would take one end while Ned handled the other. In theory, the plan was perfect. Two women, Ned estimated, equaled the strength of one man. In practice, the plan was a failure. Two bodies couldn't carry the same end around corners, through doors. Greta couldn't find a good grip. She nearly fell down the steps and had a bookcase land on top of her.

When only the heaviest pieces remained, they convened again at the mouth of the truck and stared inside. All three of them were soaked through, and dark streaks of dust and grit smudged Greta's face where she'd pushed her hair out of the way. Of the three, Greta appeared the most spent, and she sagged against the side of the truck so completely that she had to stop herself from sliding to the ground. 'If I sit down,' she said to Julia, 'I'll never get up again.' Then she slid down, her back against the wall of truck, until her legs folded and her backside hit the black tarmac of the driveway.

'Will we knock?' Ned asked, nodding toward the house next door and then the one across the street. From the back of the house came James's voice shouting, 'Dad! Dad, look at me!'

'Will we?' Greta repeated, staring hard at her new neighbors' houses, their windowed, perfectly proportioned faces impassive in the early summer sun. None of them had seen any signs of life in these houses, not even a passing car.

Greta struggled to her feet, peered once more into the darkness of the truck, and considered how many things were still left to go. Her shoulders were drawn up in an exaggeration of the posture she had whenever she came home from a double shift. Her thin limbs appeared even thinner against the bulky load that remained.

'No,' Julia said, turning her back on the other houses and pushing up her sleeves. 'We'll do it. Ned and I. You go in and check on Dad.'

Ned raised his eyebrows, sized her up from head to toe. 'I better knock,' he said to Greta.

'I said I can do it,' Julia said, squatting beside Greta and Michael's dresser and feeling along the base for a good grip. When they lifted it, Ned brought his side up faster, and the lion's share of the weight tipped toward Julia. She let go, and the dresser fell the two inches she'd gotten it above the floor of the truck, landed with a thud, and missed her fingers by a hair. 'Again,' she said, this time using her legs, the length of her back, locking her arms in position and willing herself to step outside her body, think of something else, anything else, while every muscle from her calves to her neck burned and strained.

'Do you have it?' Greta asked, hovering around Julia as they moved slowly down the ramp of the truck, Ned walking backward, Julia forward. 'Don't hurt yourself. It's only a dresser. Don't hurt your back. Let go if –'

'The door,' Ned said, and Greta rushed forward to open the screen door of the house.

Two hours later, all six of them were on the deck eating the ham sandwiches Greta had bought that morning on the corner of Eighty-fourth and Second. Michael gobbled his down as if he'd been lifting all day, while next to him, Ned picked and nibbled, turning the food around in his mouth and forcing himself to swallow. Julia's legs and arms were trembling, a detail James found hysterical as she tried to bring her soda to her lips. 'You've got a workhorse here,' Ned said, clapping Julia on the back as if she were a man his own size. He pushed his sandwich away, and Michael eyed it as he brushed crumbs from his lap.

'Fair play to you, girl,' Michael said, squeezing Julia's aching shoulder with all the strength in his good arm.

'Who wants an ice cream?' Ned asked when the rest of them had finished their sandwiches. He feigned weakness when James and Eavan threw themselves on him, pulled him by his thick arms, shouted their requests.

'I guess I should run up to the shop to get a few things, but I thought I'd wait until tomorrow,' Greta said.

'I'll run up,' Ned volunteered. 'I'm sure there's a market up on the main street.'

'Oh no,' Greta said, looking pointedly at Michael. 'They don't need ice cream. They had ice cream last night.'

'Yessssss,' James cried. 'Yes I do need it. I really neeeeed it, Mom.'

Michael shifted on the lawn chair, answered Greta's look with one Julia couldn't quite read. More secrets, she guessed. They seemed capable of anything now. Come to think of it, they were always asking and answering questions of each other with looks thrown across tables and rooms. Theirs was a language of facial expressions and widened eyes. She wished she'd read the rest of those letters. Maybe her memory had embellished what she'd read, blown it all out of proportion. She tried to remember portions of the letters word for word but suspected herself of adding words and sentences – sometimes to make things better and sometimes to make things worse. She probably misunderstood.

'You see?' Ned said, and turned to Julia to ask where she had put the keys to Michael's car.

Greta was silent for a full hour after Ned drove away. No, he hadn't smelled of drink or had the look of drink in his face, but a drinker was a drinker. And she'd let James ride with him that morning. Jesus. Michael had said that Ned was fine to drive and he'd never put one of his own in danger, but Michael had some strange liking for the man and maybe didn't want to insult him by questioning him behind the wheel. Travellers had a casual attitude toward drinking anyway, or at least that's what Big Tom used to say. Wouldn't be the least bit ashamed to be caught drinking at twelve in the day. Earlier. And sitting above on the stone wall that led to town, where everyone would pass them. Maybe Michael didn't realize the danger. Not to mention the talking the man got up to when he was drinking. He talked enough the rest of the time, but with a few in him he got weepy on top of it and talked about the old days when Kate was still in New York, before they had any babies, and meeting up with Michael and Greta, and the occasional dance or two, not that Greta and Michael went in much for the Irish dances. Once, at the apartment, late on a Friday night, after listening to him pour himself another from the brown bottle he'd brought with him – still in the paper bag, as if she couldn't tell what was inside – Greta heard him reminiscing about the days when he first met Michael, when they were still movers. That night, with Greta in kitchen fetching ice, he'd asked Michael loud and clear whatever happened to that sister of Greta's who used to live with them?

What if Julia had been home, Greta demanded of Michael after Ned finally left. Or Eavan, who could put two and two together faster than most adults. They'd never told the children anything about Johanna living in New York. As far as the children knew, Johanna had gone straight to California and then gone home again when Lily got sick.

'You're making too much of it,' Michael had said. 'Poor man,' he'd added, and Greta saw red.

'Poor man?' she sputtered. 'I don't see what's so poor about him.'

'Greta, it was your own mother who told me we have to watch out for each other here. We're from the same place, Ned too. So what harm if he does his drinking here instead of in a pub with strangers who don't care whether he lives or dies?'

How dare he use her own mother's words back at her, as if he knew Lily as well as Greta did. 'She meant you and me,' she corrected him. 'Not us and any drunk Irishman who comes along. And truth be told, she really only meant me and Johanna. In fact, she once wanted to pay my way home and leave you here. Mine and Julia's way home. She said you could do as you liked.'

That had shut him up so good he was still turning it over the next morning, until over oatmeal in the kitchen she told him she'd made it up. Lily had loved him. She was sorry. He'd just made her so mad.

'I thought that might be it,' he'd said, and hunkered over his bowl and dug in.

Now Greta felt sure that Ned Powers was about to go on a bender, in their car, in their new town, and she'd done nothing to stop him. And when he came back he'd be full of memories and all sorts of blather, and all three of the children around to listen – nothing else to do. Greta busied herself with sweeping, vacuuming, scrubbing the already spotless bathtub, toilet, underneath the kitchen sink. After two hours she strode out on the deck, pink rubber gloves dripping, and announced to Michael, 'I knew it.' Back inside she muttered, 'I knew it, I knew it,' until it started to take on the rhythm of a song.

Thankfully, James and Eavan had put ice cream out of their minds the moment a young girl knocked on the screen door and introduced herself as, 'Jessica, two houses down, going into fourth grade.' After a quick introduction, but before agreeing to go outside to play, Eavan had raced from room to room in search of Julia, and once she found her, dragged her by the hand to the bathroom, where Eavan sat perfectly still on the closed toilet seat as Julia redid the braid of that morning. 'I'm coming!' she shouted as soon as Julia snapped the rubber band tight around the end.

'Wait,' Greta said, grabbing Eavan mid-flight before she disappeared out the door. 'Just wait,' she said again, feeling that there was something she should say or do here but not sure what was called for. 'Where are you going?'

'Outside,' Eavan said, nodding toward Jessica, who was waiting on the front step.

'Are Jessica's parents home?' Greta asked. Eavan shrugged. 'You can go as far as Jessica's house on that side and the house next to us on the other. And don't cross the street unless you come back here and ask me.'

'Mom, there aren't even any *cars* on this street. We don't even –'

'Eavan,' Greta cut her off. 'Don't start. And bring your brother.'

Another two hours – sheets on beds, curtains on rods, Eavan and James full of stories of above ground swimming pools and sprinklers that spit water in circles that could follow a person around a yard, all glimpsed – they swore with fingers crossed – from within the boundaries they had been given, and Greta was unable to speak. They needed that car. Between the closing fees and the lawyer and the real estate agent and the rental truck and Julia's new bed and the first mortgage payment, they needed that car to return safe and sound.

'You have to understand –' Michael began when Greta went to help him inside, but she held her hand in front of her face and closed her eyes.

Finally, around nine o'clock, Michael, Greta, and Julia all heard the sound of Michael's diesel engine coming up the block. Eavan and James had fallen asleep watching television in Greta and Michael's room. 'Greta,' Michael said, grabbing her wrist. 'Not a word. You let me handle this.' He dropped Greta's wrist, and she walked over to the couch and sat with her two hands pressed between her knees.

'I see it now,' Greta said. 'It was him all along. The accident at work. He nearly killed you. Him and the drink. I knew it. Didn't I say it? He's like a wrecking ball that thinks it –'

Michael hushed her and then said to Julia, 'You stay here.'

Whenever Eavan or James did something wrong, Greta often told them about an old dog she'd had at home. Julia had never heard of this dog before Eavan and James came around, so she listened closely whenever Greta told the story. It was Greta's older brother's dog, really. Greta had known him only when he was very very old, but one thing she remembered was that when the dog did something wrong, they could tell just by looking at him that he was guilty. Just one look at his lowered head, and Julia's grandmother would send Greta to check whether he'd dirtied the drying laundry with his paws or shit in one of the bedrooms. This is the story Julia thought of when Ned Powers opened the screen door and stepped inside.

'How's it goin'?' he asked, closing his eyes against the strength of the overhead light.

'Ned,' Michael said. 'Julia's going to drive you home tonight. How does that sound?'

'Ah no,' Ned said. 'Not with the way that girleen worked today. Have you got your driver's license, Julia? Well, that's grand.'

'I drove up here this morning, remember? I'm almost twenty-two.'

'I was twenty-two once,' Ned said. 'We all were,' he added, and burst out laughing.

'You set, Ned? She doesn't mind.' Michael turned toward Julia with a look that said he was sorry.

'I couldn't,' Ned said, and then a long pause as he scratched his neck. 'I'm dead tired to tell the truth.'

'Ah, go on,' Michael said. 'All that hard work you did today. I'd drive you myself if I could.' One hand clutching the banister for balance, Michael reached toward his friend with his right hand outstretched.

'I don't mind,' Julia agreed as the men shook hands.

'Let him take the bus,' Greta said from her perch on the couch. 'Let him sober up on the damn bus.'

'I'll drive you home, Ned,' Julia said again.

'Well then, I'm going with you,' Greta said, standing up.

'Leave it, Greta,' said Michael.

'Come on, Ned,' Julia said, and was out the door and into the car before Greta could make it outside.

Julia didn't know how to get to the Bronx from Recess. From Manhattan, yes, they'd been to the Powers's apartment a few times for dinners, two Easters, an occasional Thanksgiving, and for the Christening parties of Ned's two babies. One dead, Julia reminded herself. Dead for years now.

Instead of running back inside to ask her father what road to take, what bridge, she decided to drive back into the city and go the way she knew. Ned, awkward in the small bucket seat, seemed to have trouble finding a comfortable arrangement for his shoulders, and he kept pulling on the portion of the belt that crossed over his chest. 'Jesus,' he muttered after a while, and pressed the button on the buckle that set him free. He tugged at the crotch of his jeans, pulled at the collar of his T-shirt.

'Well, thanks a million,' Ned said as Julia eased the car away from the curb. The interior smelled of cigarettes and the sharp, musky smell of whiskey once it has made its way down the hatch and out again through the pores of the skin.

Julia turned onto the main road and maneuvered the car forward through the dark tunnel of oak and evergreen trees that lined the road on both sides. Greta was usually so calm, but something about having Ned Powers around made her crazy. It wasn't the drinking, Julia felt. It couldn't be. One of the newer tenants in 222 was a drinker, and Greta had felt so sorry for her, told everyone to be kind to her, how she used to spiff herself up the day after being found, once again, locked out of the building and asleep in the vestibule. Then, as Ned cleared his throat beside her, Julia remembered that Ned was one of the few people who'd known her parents from the beginning, all the way back to a furniture moving job her Dad had when he first arrived. They lost touch for a while, but had run into each other again when they were both shaping for day labor at a construction site in Queens. After another few years of seeing each other off and on, Ned had called Michael one morning in the mid-1970s and asked if he could help him get on as a sandhog.

'I knew your Dad before he had any *gasúir*,' he once said to James, picking him up and swinging him over his head. This was before he had any children himself, no little boy to love and grieve, no wife to accuse him at night and cry to go back home. 'Even Julia?' James had asked. To James, Julia seemed almost as old as his parents. 'Oh, Julia,' Ned had said. 'Yes, Julia. Julia was there almost since the beginning. I wasn't counting her.'

'No problem,' Julia said now, reaching over to turn on the radio. 'I like driving.'

'And you did college, didn't you, Julia?' Ned said, leaning his forehead against the cool glass of the window, then abruptly shaking himself upright, rubbing his face vigorously up and down, up and down, as if scrubbing it with a washcloth.

'I just finished.'

'Good for you,' he said, and leaned forward to squint at a faint light in the distance. 'I was useless at school myself. The times tables and seven goes into ninety-nine how many times and all that.'

'I hated math too,' Julia said, seeing what he was seeing, finally. She wondered if they'd been wrong about him. Maybe he wasn't so bad after all if his eyes were sharp enough to have caught that light in the distance, sharp enough to have recognized it for what it was from so far away.

'I'm out of fags,' Ned said, eyeing the small store where it sat glowing, twinkling in the middle of the parking lot, growing bigger and brighter the closer they came to it. 'Would you mind stopping? I'll run in.'

Julia pulled in, parked in the spot closest to the front door, unbuckled her seat belt. She could hear the rush of cars on the highway just beyond the row of trees at one edge of the lot. The entrance ramp was just a stone's throw away.

'You don't have to get out,' Ned said. 'You stay.'

Julia ignored him, and inside the overbright store she looked at the magazines and the newspaper headlines while Ned paced up and down the aisles, pretended to search for something he couldn't find, finally walked up to the refrigerated beer section and pulled the door open. He took out a six-pack of Budweiser and then another. He walked over to the register and placed them carefully on the counter. 'And a pack of Camels,' he said to the young, pockmarked man behind the counter.

'And a 7-Up,' Julia said, sliding the single can across the counter.

'And a 7-Up,' Ned repeated without looking at her.

Back in the car, as he cracked open the first can, Ned pointed out how weak American beer was compared with other beers, how watered down, how American beer could hardly be called alcohol at all, how despite its weakness Budweiser was a good union beer, a well-made beer, as good as any German or British or Irish beer, and how he'd never drink Coors, not if he was dying of thirst in the desert and someone handed him a cold Coors in a chilled glass.

'So, Ned,' Julia said after the third pop and hiss. He had placed the two empties neatly in the pockets he'd taken them from, and each time, in the careful manner he placed them and secured them, he seemed to want Julia to notice this courtesy. 'You and my Dad go way back, right?'

'Way back. Green as grass, the two of us. Poking our noses inside every room of these fancy apartments, and the cut of us, my God, they'd be holding their breath before we even touched a thing, afraid we'd smudge cushions and cloth things, lampshades, I dunno, them things they hang over the windows that aren't curtains – I called them curtains once and the missus of the house corrected me. You know the ones, long things from the windows and the see-through

317

part underneath. Anyhow, whatever they're called, it was great *craic* altogether.'

'And you knew my mother too? Back then?'

'The tunnels is nothing like moving furniture. Better work, some would say, better money anyhow, but not like the moving, when you could be inside and outside all day long and every job was during the day, and even when you were inside, there was light coming in through the windows, and nine days out of ten you'd be home by supper and the evening news and that's the end of it.'

'You met them when – 1963 . . . 1964?' From the passenger seat came a fourth pop and hiss.

'The problem with the tunnels is the dark. Some say the damp. Some say the dust. I say the dark. I'll be working away, and all of a sudden I think to myself how I'd like to just look out the window and see what kind of a day it is at all, and of course there is no window, because there you are hundreds of feet under the sidewalk and by the time you call for the cage, it's ten minutes later and four minutes up and four minutes down and they'll dock your pay and mightn't let you on the next day. And to go up on break takes too long and they don't like to be sending the cage up and down like that, so it's eight hours straight in the pitch dark except for the lights they string around, which is fine when you're standing right under them, but not a mile down the tunnel. That's the trouble I have.'

'I know,' Julia said, trying her best to make her voice warm with sympathy. 'But listen for a second, Ned. Just listen. Do you remember meeting my mother in 1964? Back when you and my father were still movers? Do you remember meeting her when she was expecting me?'

'Expecting you?'

'Pregnant.'

'Your mother is a good-looking woman. Not at first, but you come around to it after a while.'

'Jesus, Ned, concentrate for a second. It's important.'

'I remember her pregnant, and you ten or twelve following her around.'

'Earlier. Pregnant with me. Do you remember?'

'I had two myself,' Ned said, reaching again for the supply tucked neatly at his feet. 'One died, God rest him. An innocent child, so no worries where he is now and the priests say I should be happy about that. I should be happy about that. I should be. Up in heaven flyin' around with the other babbies.'

'I know, Ned. I'm very sorry.'

'Ah, it's all right. My wife, though, she's having an awful time since then.' Ned turned a little in his seat to look at Julia. 'You're an educated person.'

Julia waited.

'So tell me this, is my boy any wiser now that he's in heaven? Is he looking down and understanding things like he's still three years because time stopped for him at three, or in his mind is he wiser than three?'

'I don't know, Ned.'

'And when I meet him, will he know me? From watching me all the time? Or does time go by there the same way it goes by here, when you get on to other things and start to forget?'

Julia, full to the brim with her own questions, let his questions float in the air between them without answering.

After circling every block in Woodlawn between the cemetery and East 240th Street, Ned finally stopped talking long enough to remind Julia which turns to take to get to his apartment.

'Will we go for a pint?' Ned asked gamely after popping the car door open and placing one foot on the street outside.

Julia considered it for a few seconds. A pub could be the setting that set him on course again, got him to focus on what she was asking, but when she looked over at him, he blinked once, slowly, and when he blinked again, his eyes stayed closed. The way he was now, there would be too much to wade through, too much of his own static to get a clear picture on hers.

'Oh, thanks,' said Julia. His eyes flew open. 'I'm wrecked from today.' She rubbed her arm from her bicep to her shoulder to remind him. When he still didn't get out, she turned her polite smile to the front windshield and pretended to squint at something in the distant dark. She could feel the warmth of her face from the sun of that afternoon,

and she knew her skin was glowing in that way she'd been compli-
mented on in the past. Her ponytail had loosened in the course of the
day, and there were pieces framing her face. She reached up and tucked
one of the loose pieces behind her ear. She could feel something happening, that same stirring in the air that always signaled when a guy was
about to touch her or kiss her or ask to be touched or kissed. But this was
a first. As she got older, it seemed the difference in age between herself
and her parents was shortening, and it was her friend Mary who'd
recently asked if she had a crush on any of her father's friends. Ned, two
years younger than Michael, was Greta's age, thirty-eight.

'You're lovely looking,' Ned said, reaching his hand across the
space between the seats, and instead of leaning away, Julia became
fixed where she was, one hand on the wheel, the other resting, palm
down, on her own thigh. She waited to feel where his hand would
land, but after half a dozen thunderous heartbeats she looked over to
see it resting on the gearshift, his chin tucked into his collarbone,
Ned sound asleep.

'Ned,' she said, squeezing his hand. 'Wake up. You're home.'

Ned's head snapped up, and he looked surprised to find one leg
already outside. 'Well, thanks again,' he said, smiling brightly, and
slowly, slowly, pulling himself by the frame of the door, he got out of
the car.

Julia had an easier time finding her way back to the Bronx River
Parkway than she expected, and when the bridge loomed for the third
time that day, she turned the wheel and the car dipped quickly down
the ramp, then back up, and she was suspended over the Hudson, her
headlights pointing north, the lights of Manhattan bright over her
shoulder and in her sideview mirror. For the second time that evening, Julia looked at the clock – not quite midnight – and recalled one
of Greta's stories of home. This time it was of a woman – an old
woman, Julia had always assumed, Greta had never said – who didn't
know what to do about some of the sad things that had happened to
her, so she stopped doing anything at all, just sat in a chair and stared
out the window or lay flat on her back in her bed looking up at the
ceiling while the world kept turning underneath her. Years went by,

and the woman stayed like this, solemn as a tree, not seeing with her eyes, not hearing with her ears, just breathing in and out. 'She was coping, you see,' was how Greta always put it. Then, without warning really, without those little pushes or sparks that always come first when you read about such people in books or see them in the movies, the woman had started to come around again, seeing and hearing and doing the way she used to. Soon after she came around, another sad thing happened – someone she loved had to leave her, and she knew she mightn't see this person again, or at least not for a very long time. But instead of locking herself away as she did before, she met this new sadness head-on, walked up to greet it, stepped into its fold, and wore it like a shawl she could put on or cast off at her own choosing.

'So what's the moral?' Julia had asked once at fifteen or sixteen, feeling cheeky and impatient with this story she'd heard a million times. 'Is there a point?' Greta had shrugged, seemed genuinely stumped, but days later, after the storm had passed and the tension between them had disappeared – at least until the next time Julia asked to do something and got a negative answer – she'd taken a seat at the tiny kitchen table across from Julia and her bowl of cornflakes and said, 'I think it's that we don't know what we're capable of. None of us. Until we get up and try to do it. If there's a point, that might be it.' Forty-five minutes later, after Julia had packed her bag, walked the twelve blocks and three avenues to school, and taken her seat in first period, she finally remembered what in the world her mother was talking about.

Before Julia knew it, she was in New Jersey, and the cars heading home after an evening in the city fell into place in the lanes beside her. How long until she got used to going through New Jersey every time she traveled between the new house and the city? 'It's on the other side of the Hudson,' she told her friends, and just about all of them had said in one way or another, 'but that's New Jersey' or 'but you're moving north, upstate, and New Jersey is south.' If you couldn't get there on the subway, it just didn't make sense. Julia went with two of them to the bookstore to look it up on a map, and tracing the route with her finger, she showed them.

For the rest of the drive home Julia wondered what her parents might be capable of. There could be no mistake. The letters were that clear, her

Aunt Johanna's name all over them – Johanna's pregnant belly, Johanna's apologies, Johanna's pleas to send Julia to California. Letters from Greta's mother – who sometimes signed Lily, sometimes Mam, sometimes Mother – saying enough is enough. She wanted Julia to come to Ireland. James and Eavan's birth certificates had been in there too, listing the parents as Greta Cahill and Michael Ward. Julia's eye had run over them at first, greedy for what else she would find about herself, but it was as if her mind split into two directions, one half poring over as many letters as she could process, the other half stuck on some detail of those certificates. Cahill, she realized. Greta Cahill. When had they ever celebrated an anniversary? 'Oh, 1966,' Greta always said when Julia asked, as if it was a nuisance to look back so far. 'You were two and cute as a button.' But winter or spring? Summer or fall?

Michael and Greta, the pair of them, had embraced a lie and swallowed it whole. Julia imagined walking into the kitchen as soon as she got back to the house in Recess and accusing them. Then, just as clearly, she saw Greta scowl, scratch her head, try to remember, oh yes, that rings a bell, haven't thought about that in years, and then lean forward in that Greta way and ask if it mattered so much, it was nothing to get upset about. And then later, Greta and Michael alone in their bed would talk about it all night, the way they talked about everything, his low tones answering her high tones as if it was something to get through, not something that was.

Which of them is more guilty, Julia wondered, glimpsing a deer bounding across the road at the very limit of her headlights' reach. She pressed lightly on the brake. She moved over to the slow lane, rolled the window down, noticed for the first time that she hadn't had the radio on since she and Ned got back in the car after buying beer and cigarettes. Like all things Greta and Michael did, Julia guessed that they were in on the story fifty-fifty, had agreed on every detail before going forward, just as they talked and talked and talked and eventually agreed on everything. Even when they argued, they did so in a code only they understood, with looks and chopped-off sentences and the occasional closed door that was usually kept open. As Julia's friends' parents began leaving each other – the first, Patricia Scott's parents in first grade, Julia hadn't known such a thing was possible, all the way up to the previous week, when her friend Mary's parents sat their children down, all grown, and announced they hadn't loved each other in years – Julia was absolutely certain that it had never crossed Greta's and Michael's minds. How could her Aunt Johanna – she revised the thought before it was fully formed – have competed with love like that?

And then, for what felt like the hundredth time that day, Julia wondered how Greta could not be her mother. It just seemed impossible, not with the way she watched her from across rooms, and all those years looking at her homework and putting it aside to show Michael, and the two of them shaking their heads in wonder at her book reports and science fair projects and saying things like, 'Where did you come from?' And 'Where did we get you?' as they squeezed her and rubbed her head and beamed. Just last month Julia had met a friend at a diner on West Thirty-fourth Street and, as she was coming out, had seen Greta in the distance, leaving Macy's and turning east for the long walk home. 'I can't believe it!' Greta had cried when Julia caught up, grabbing Julia's arm and hugging her as if they hadn't seen each other in ages, as if it were nothing short of miraculous that they'd found each other like that, at just the right moment, odds one in eight million.

But somewhere under all the evidence to the contrary – a mother's love, a mother's pride – there was a place in Julia's gut where all of this felt true. Johanna, Tom, the two other brothers in Australia – it wasn't that anyone had ever forbidden mentioning them, but they weren't mentioned except in Greta's recollections of some day a long time ago – and never by name. Johanna used to write, and even call once in a while, but all of that had stopped once Lily died. There was no word about what they were all doing now. And in these recollections Greta's siblings were never more than background figures, beside the point. Julia could pinpoint the day, the moment – Christmas, she was fifteen – when she realized with a lurch that all these people were still alive, lived just a plane ride away.

Julia drove two houses past her own before she realized her mistake and turned around. The windows were dark except for one in the middle and a light outside the front door that Julia hadn't noticed that morning. Unwilling to get out of the car just yet, she sat and considered how she would put it. I know. Or, Mom I have something to tell you. Or, Mom I think you have something to tell me. Or, Dad, is there something you want to tell me about my mother? But in answer to each of these tries she saw only Michael's raised eyebrows, Greta's face open and interested, as if she was about to hear good news.

After twenty minutes or so in the dark car, Julia saw movement in the one lighted window, then the front door of the house opening and the screen door pushed ajar by a long, pale arm as a collection of moths fluttered around the light.

'Hello?' Greta called in a stage whisper. 'Is that you, Julia?'

'Yeah, it's me,' Julia whispered back, elbow resting on car door, chin resting on fist. The suburbs were dead silent at night.

Greta nodded, relieved, and, leaving the front door wide open, turned to retrace her steps down the hall. She switched off the lamp beside her bed, and after postponing it for so long, after pinching herself awake for a good hour and a half or more, with her daughter finally home safe on the driveway outside, opting, no doubt, to use her own private entrance whenever she finished thinking about whatever she was thinking about out there in the utterly mute dark, nothing like the dark of the country, Greta closed her eyes and waited for sleep. Beside her, Michael grumbled indistinctly, grunted something that sounded like a reprimand, and then sighed. He turned, rearranging his wounded body under the thin cotton sheet.

'She's home, is she?' he said, reaching out to rest a sleep-warm hand on Greta's hip, and then, asleep again, he snorted, flinched, tugged at Greta's nightshirt as if it were a rope pulling him forward.

PART VI

2007

Fourteen

On the morning of the day of Michael's retirement party, or *party day,* as Greta and the children had been mouthing over Michael's head and behind his back for going on six weeks, Greta stopped sweeping the front step to watch a black cat emerge from behind a tree, walk across the neighbor's lawn, across the sidewalk, across the sun-warmed tarmac of the street, hop up the curb on Greta's side, prance across the Wards' lawn, and brush against Greta's bare shin as she passed by (it was a she-cat) to settle herself on the Wards' welcome mat. Good luck or bad luck? Greta couldn't remember. Good luck to see a black cat on moving day. Good luck on a wedding day. Bad luck to see one by moonlight. Bad luck to have a black she-cat look at you if she's just after licking her paws. But what about on party day? The cat purred, stretched herself across the mat, settled in for a sleep. Step over her, Greta told herself as the cat's soft belly rose and fell. Glad none of the children had arrived yet, and with a suspicion that the neighbors were looking out their windows and laughing at her, Greta turned and walked around the house through the dew-wet grass. She felt younger than fifty-nine today, as if she could run ten times around the block without getting winded or turn a cartwheel on the lawn if the mood took her. She climbed up the back steps, left wet footprints across the dry boards of the deck, and entered the house by the back door. The morning weather report had called for heavy rain, but so far the sky was blue and the day unseasonably warm.

Her stomach had done flip-flops all night. Lying there beside Michael, who snored so loud that she had spent most of the night peering over at him in the gray and chilly dark to see if he was having her on, she wondered if everyone who'd been invited would come, if they'd expect a big spread, if James would remember to pick up the cake, if Eavan had remembered to buy a few music CDs. 'Mom, are you serious?' Eavan had nearly shouted the week before when Greta suggested they just play the radio, as they always did at home. Julia, swamped at work, was expected only to show up, relax, turn off her cell phone and the thing she punched messages into when she thought the rest of them weren't paying attention. After working in merchandising for Polo and Kenneth Cole for a combined fifteen years, Julia was now head buyer for a new clothing label that had started up in New York. She kept calling to ask what she could do to help and then telling Greta to hold on, she'd call back, would Greta be free in two hours?

The children tried to talk her into doing an RSVP date, but it seemed so formal to Greta, so pushy. Respond by this date or else. People liked to be able to change their minds, Greta explained. They liked to feel they were being spontaneous. It seemed to Greta that RSVPs had come into fashion only in the last decade or so. At how many weddings had she simply slipped into the back of the church? An RSVP date also implied something about the party that Greta didn't want to imply. Without one, she could get away with doing the food herself, having plastic plates, playing the radio instead of worrying about music. There would always be enough room. There would always be enough food.

How? Her children asked, each in their separate ways – Julia with a sigh, James with raised eyebrows and a shrug, Eavan with the same question over and over and over: 'But how do you know?'

'I just know.'

'But how?'

'It always works out.'

'But how does it work out?'

'It just does,' Greta said, and then reverted to the line she'd been using with each of them since they started school and began to question how she knew things, how she came to her decisions. 'Some things you know in your brain, and some things you know in here.' Greta placed a hand on her chest.

'Your rib cage?'

'Don't be fresh.'

'I'm not. Your upper intestines?'

'That's not where your intestines are, is it?' Greta looked down at herself and saw that her hand had migrated south.

'But Mom, we've sent out close to eighty invitations. How will you know how much food to buy?'

'I'll know to stop buying when I have enough.'

Early that morning, before Michael's alarm, Greta had stared at the clock, its neon orange numbers two inches high and casting a glow over Michael's face, their bed, Greta's bare arm. It was 5:13. She sighed, thinking, I've not had one single wink of sleep this night. But then she turned gently, careful not to let the cool air under the covers, and felt her pillow wet with drool. Well, maybe for an hour or so, she thought. Maybe a few minutes here and there. Michael shifted, threw his heavy arm over her, trapped her arms at her sides. The alarm woke up, sent its shrill wail directly down Greta's spine. Michael closed his eyes tighter.

'Ay,' she'd whispered into the dark as she tried to free one of her trapped arms. 'Last day.'

'Last day,' he'd repeated, and held on tighter while the alarm continued to sound. He moved closer, nestling his chin against her shoulder until they were like one of those prize eggs at Easter, where the smaller egg is tucked inside the larger. Slowly, slowly, she pushed back with her elbow until she made contact with his stomach, and then she kept pushing. He sat up abruptly, threw back the covers, swung his legs over the side of the bed, and pressed every button on the clock until it went silent. Greta watched the shape of his back as it bent, began to lean, his head drooping off toward his pillow. Outside, the sky was as dark as midnight.

'Five-eighteen.' She nudged his rear with the ball of her foot. When he was finally standing, she threw back the covers on her side, stood up, felt her way across the room until she laid her hand on the thick cotton of her robe. 'I'll get the kettle,' she told him. He was stretching, extending his arms like wings and then tucking them back in beside his body.

'Stiff,' he muttered, clenching and unclenching his fists. Yawning, he reached down and rubbed the muscles at the front of his thighs, rubbed his hips, put his hands on his waist to drive his thumbs into his lower back. He cursed, coughed a few times to loosen the dark phlegm in his throat, hopped up and down once, twice. Above the elastic waistband of his boxers his stomach curved to meet his broad chest. A good stomach, Greta thought. Full. Healthy. Well fed. Not like the gaunt 1960s or the fat '80s, when he seemed unable to pass a bakery without stopping in for a slice of pie. Every hair on his body was gray.

'Bacon and eggs,' he said, pausing his kneading fingers to listen for her response. When she didn't answer, he looked over and smiled at her. 'Last day,' he said.

She switched on the lamp next to him.

'Oh, you're mean,' he said, shielding his eyes.

'Five-twenty-one,' she said.

To be at work in time for his shift, Michael had to leave their house in Recess by 5:45. Without traffic, he'd be at Thirtieth Street and Tenth Avenue by 6:15. This would give him forty-five minutes to park, change into his gear, get over to the cage, and get down the seventy stories to the tunnel. It didn't used to take so long. Years ago, he could get out of his street clothes and into the tunnel in twenty minutes. Less. Lately, he couldn't shake the feeling that he was forgetting something. Once he was dressed in his work clothes, he'd have to look himself over, bend to confirm the boots on his feet, wiggle his toes to feel the thick socks beneath. He'd pat his chest for his folding ruler, his back pocket for his flashlight. Three times in the last few months he'd gone over to the supply shed to get another hard hat, only to have Donahue, who kept track of everything, reach over and rap on the hard hat that was already on his head. Each time, he had put his hand to the top of his head, astonished to feel the hard plastic, the knob at the back that tightened the strap. The first time, Donahue had laughed and laughed, shouting after him from the door of the shed as Michael made his way across the site to the cage. The second time, he'd just looked at Michael with eyebrows raised and told him to get more sleep. The third time, he didn't laugh, didn't smile, only placed his hand on Michael's back as he walked with him across the yard.

The first two times Michael forgot about his hard hat, he saved up the story to tell Greta when he got home. 'That Donahue,' she'd said, rolling her eyes. Exactly, thought Michael, smiling along with Greta as if it were Donahue who'd put the hard hat on his head and then caused him to forget it. Greta urged him to go to bed earlier and stop falling asleep in front of the TV. She started getting up when his alarm went off to make oatmeal for him to eat before he left. Eavan mentioned something about ginseng, so Greta began laying out one ginseng pill next to his multivitamin and his cholesterol medicine. The ginseng made his piss smell strange, he complained. Piss is piss, Greta said.

He didn't tell her that it had happened once more or that one morning, just two weeks before his last day, he'd taken the train with the others down to the dead end of the tunnel, a twelve-minute ride at the train's slow pace, and had looked above him and beside him at the tunnel walls and couldn't for the life of him remember where he was going. He sat up to look around the shoulders of the man in front of him and saw that the tunnel narrowed to a point and then disappeared. He looked behind him and saw the same thing. They were going on a trip, he decided. A journey. It was nighttime. It was raining. He looked over his shoulder once more to find Ned Powers, his friend. 'Where to?' Michael had asked, and Powers laughed so hard he nearly fell out the side. Michael laughed too, and the joke spread up and down to every member of the crew. When the train finally stopped, Michael was relieved to discover that he knew exactly what to do, where to stand, which tool to reach for. Still, the entire shift seemed off, like a picture that was always slightly askew no matter how many times he walked up to the wall and nudged it at this corner, that corner, a little here, a little there. Later, back on the train that returned them to the shaft, he kept his mind fastened on the movement of the machinery, the work they'd just done. He focused on the cage, its rust recently covered with another coat of reflective yellow, emerging in the hazy distance.

'Don't expect this treatment every day,' Greta said as she slid two eggs onto his plate and placed it in front of him. The clock in the kitchen read 5:37, and Greta reached over to snap up the blinds. 'It'll start getting light soon,' she said as she brought the saucepan from the stove and spooned out the beans. She reached for bacon that was resting on paper towels on a plate on the counter. 'Another few weeks and the sun will be up at this hour.'

'As of tomorrow morning, I won't be up at this hour, so the sun can stay where it is.'

Greta watched him work across his plate, his head bent so low he could have stuck out his tongue and lapped up the stream of egg yolk that had gotten away. 'So,' she said. 'Will they have something planned for you, do you think? Something at lunch?' From the fridge she took the lunch bag she'd prepared the night before. She placed it on the table next to his plate so he wouldn't forget it.

Michael coughed, reached for his mug, sipped the steaming tea. 'Of course. The whole shift goes to Tavern on the Green, and after lunch they present me with a cake with one candle for every year on the job. And a gold watch.'

'That's it, wise guy. You've had enough.' Greta took the plate out from under his nose and jerked her head toward the clock. He pushed his chair back, stood, rubbed his belly, reached the hall closet in three long strides.

'What are you doing?' Greta asked as she watched him pull his heavy winter coat off the hanger.

'My coat,' he said.

'It's supposed to get up near eighty today.'

Michael frowned, put the coat back on the hanger, patted the pockets. 'Fine. My keys, then,' he said. 'I'll just take my keys.'

'Michael,' Greta said, taking his hand in both of hers and bringing it to her mouth, 'you haven't worn that coat in months.' She squeezed his fingers as hard as she could, then repeated what she'd already said. 'Okay? Months, Michael. Now go on. You'll be late.'

She reached around to the wall where he'd hung his keys the day before, and pressed them into his hand.

Greta began preparing the moment the taillights of Michael's car disappeared down the block. There were a lot of things she had meant to do, but the days had gotten away from her. She meant to figure out a way to get Michael to paint the shutters outside before party day. She meant to get a new mailbox. She meant to buy a potted plant for the front step. She meant to get Michael to put a fresh coat of tar on the driveway to cover up the oil stains and the crack. She put a pot of water on the stove to boil the potatoes for potato salad. She took down the kitchen curtains and put them in the washing machine. She stripped her bed and dug out her best quilt, usually brought out only for Christmas Eve, when they had Ned Powers and a few other people over. She brought every mat and throw rug out to the deck and beat them one by one against the railing, pressing her lips tight against the dust that flew back at her. As usual, the rugs were heavier than she expected, and as she leaned against the railing, panting, she noticed that the sun had come up. She swept the driveway, the flagstones of the walkway, the steps leading up to the front door. By midmorning, taking the black cat as a sign, she decided that she needed a break, and she sat down at the kitchen table to write the card she'd picked out for Michael. No sooner had she composed her first sentence – 'Dear Michael, Thirty-seven years!' – than she spilled a glass of juice across both the card and the new tablecloth. When she bent to mop up the mess, her glasses fell off her nose and cracked. It took forty minutes to dig up her old pair.

Eavan, the swelling in her belly just beginning to become obvious, arrived at eleven o'clock with a bag of fruit and four long baguettes for making the sandwiches. When Eavan walked in, Greta was sitting at the kitchen table wearing a pair of James's old track shorts and a T-shirt she'd found at the bottom of a dresser that said THE STONE ROSES across the chest. Before Eavan had even said hello, Greta explained that she didn't want to get anything on her party clothes, which she had folded over the back of a chair in the living room and would put on just before people started to arrive. Eavan hadn't even noticed. It was common to come home and find her mother in clothes she or Julia or James had discarded more than a decade before. Once, when Eavan brought a friend home from college, Greta, after a morning spent weeding, had come in to meet the guest wearing a T-shirt that said SCUMBY RIDES THE BIG WHITE WAVE.

When they laughed, Greta had asked, 'What's a Scumby?' pulling the front of the shirt away from her body and trying to look at it upside down.

Eavan set the bag down on the counter, and Greta began to unload the melons, oranges, cherries, grapes, apples, paring knife, peeler, butcher knife, melon baller. She placed the baguettes on the table. Eavan forgot the wine she'd tucked in behind the passenger seat and went back out to the car. She returned with a bakery box. 'Shit,' she said, leaving the box on the doorstep and turning back. On the way in she nearly stepped on the box, which contained Michael's favorite: caramel apple pie.

'You losing it?' Greta asked, rushing forward to take the pie from harm's way and standing by to follow Eavan's ample behind down the hall. Greta had already predicted that her daughter would be one of those women whose arse looked as pregnant as her belly.

Eavan put her hand on her forehead, as if checking her own temperature. 'Julia has a meeting at Saks at two o'clock,' she said. 'She'll leave as soon as she can.'

'I have knives, you know,' Greta said, reaching for the paring knife Eavan had brought.

'Not good knives.' Eavan shrugged. 'Sorry.'

'Okay, well, I have spoons. I have very good spoons,' Greta said, nudging the melon baller.

'That's not a spoon,' Eavan said, whisking it away and putting it back in the bag. 'Did you get the meat for the sandwiches? Are the potatoes in the fridge? Cooked? Jackets on?'

'Yes, boss,' Greta said. 'But first we need a cup of tea and a snack. Don't we?'

'Mom, we have a lot to do between now and four o'clock, and you know when James comes, all he'll do is distract –'

'It's a lovely day, isn't it? Perfect.'

'It's supposed to rain later.'

'You have too many worries, girl,' Greta said, taking the peeler out of Eavan's hand and tossing it into the sink. Facing her daughter, Greta took Eavan's hand and waltzed her across the kitchen.

'You're out of your mind,' Eavan said, laughing, placing her hand on her mother's shoulder and letting herself be led across the room.

'Party day. Let's hear some of that music you worried so much about.' Greta leaned over to speak directly to Eavan's belly. 'Wanna hear some music in there? Let's see if your Mama picked out anything with a fiddle.'

After a short break for tea, they rolled up their sleeves and got to work. They peeled, chopped, diced, turned melon after melon into perfect bite-size balls. Greta looked on as Eavan cut slices of bacon, wrapped each around a pitted date, and drove a toothpick through the middle. They made a team in the bathroom, where Greta scrubbed the tub and the toilet while Eavan polished the mirror, scrubbed the sink and the counter, and stashed away Greta's jars and lotions, Michael's razor and shaving cream. Eavan placed a candle behind the toilet while Greta searched under her bed for the little soaps shaped like seashells she'd picked up at fifty percent off weeks earlier. When they finished, Greta put out the good towels, the new bath mat. My girl can clean, Greta thought as she glanced at the sparkling sink. My girl is a good worker, a fine, strong, capable girl.

'The fumes don't bother you?' Greta asked. She'd been crippled with nausea when she was pregnant with James, and sometimes the sight of a pregnant woman still made her stomach turn.

'Nah,' said Eavan, and reached up on tiptoes to brush away a spider-web. Greta saw that she had already begun to thicken at the shoulders, the neck. Head to toe, her whole body was getting ready for the baby. Greta hadn't been that kind of pregnant woman. People used to say they couldn't tell she was pregnant unless she stood in profile. Eavan would have looked pregnant in a head shot at only five months along.

'You know what my mother used to say about expecting a baby?' Greta said.

'That she could squat down in the field in the morning and be up again to get the tea?'

'So I told you already.'

Eavan looked at her.

They teamed up again on the deck, where they hoped people would gather. The weather was warm for May. The rain would hold off, Greta assured Eavan, and commanded that Eavan look at the sky, acknowledge that it was blue, stop worrying. Greta swept and then went down to the spigot at the side of the house to fill bucket after bucket of water to wash down the planks of wood. Eavan scrubbed two seasons' worth of grit from the white plastic chairs, six in all, and then stood aside as Greta splashed them clean. They used their hands to flatten the creases in the vinyl outdoor tablecloth. As they worked, they talked about names for the baby. Greta suggested good, strong names like John, Patrick, William. Mary, Ann, Kathleen.

'We want to do a family name,' Eavan said as she used her finger-nail to scratch a stubborn piece of dirt from the window.

'Michael is a family name.'

'We thought Maeve is pretty for a girl.' Eavan watched her mother reflected in the glass. 'Or Lily,' she added. 'Gary likes either of them.'

Greta, down on her haunches, with the sponge dripping water down her shin and into her sock, looked up toward the back of the yard and shrugged. All these years later, so many miles from home, and still the children felt a connection to these people they'd never met. It was a fad now, she'd noticed. Family trees and tracing ancestors. There was big money in it. Money spent mostly by Americans, Greta guessed. She could probably count on one hand the number of times Maeve Ward was discussed by name in their house. Lily was right. Blood is thick. Greta wondered briefly how Maeve Ward had turned out, whether she was still alive, still traveling, or whether the government had settled her in a flat outside Dublin.

'How did she spell it? Do you know?' Eavan asked.

'She didn't spell it, love,' Greta said, and ignored that bereaved look all the children got when they remembered that their father's people could not read or write. The fact that Michael had learned as an adult in a matter of months made him a genius in their eyes. They were fiercely proud of him, that much Greta could see, but she never got the impression that they truly knew how much work it had been or how much it meant to him to stand in line at the deli and read the headlines of the paper just like everyone else did. The children would never be able to understand that some days, when he'd been frustrated and Greta didn't know how to explain some aspect of putting words together in a way that made sense, it was less humiliating for him to not be able to read at all than to go to the library and check out a book intended for a first grader, or to be quizzed on the sidewalk beside a new street sign as strangers passed by. Somehow, through the years, the detail that Greta was the one who taught him had gotten lost. In the children's version he'd simply buckled down and taught himself.

'But if you go that way,' Greta said, looking up at Eavan, 'I'd pick the one Americans will make sense of. Otherwise she'll be correcting people her whole life.'

'And Lily?'

'Either one, really. Either one and you can't lose.'

'So you wouldn't mind Lily?'

'After my mother?' Greta asked. 'Why would I mind?' And she wouldn't mind, she realized as she spoke. Another Lily in Greta's life to fill that long-empty chair would be welcome, and for the first time since she learned that Eavan was pregnant, it hit her that there would be another person in the family soon. Not just an idea, a name tossed back and forth, an empty bassinet, but a person who ate at her table and felt as at home with her as her own children had.

Eavan turned back to the window and, in a habit recently formed, pressed her hand to her belly, spread her fingers wide like a starfish, took a deep breath.

They spoke at the same time. 'Will I run into town for flowers?' asked Eavan.

'Do you think your father has any idea?' asked Greta.

'I think flowers would be nice,' Eavan said, and turned so fast she knocked the Windex off the ledge and sent it flying over the railing and onto the grass.

Greta stepped up close to her daughter. 'You're flushed,' she said, pressing the back of her hand to Eavan's cheek.

'I just hope it goes okay,' Eavan said.

'Why wouldn't it go okay?' Greta asked, squeezing Eavan's hand. 'We have food, don't we? And music, thanks to you? We have a crowd of people all bent on keeping the surprise. Don't worry so much. It's bad for the baby.'

James arrived at one o'clock with a cup of coffee in one hand, an oversize cake box in the other, and, tucked under his arm, the pictures he had blown up at the copy shop and mounted on cardboard.

'Jesus,' Eavan said when she saw him, and rushed to hold open the screen door. 'Ever hear of making two trips?' she asked, taking the cake from him.

Unlike Eavan, who seemed worried and distracted, James was keyed up. Looking him up and down, Greta was glad to see that he owned an iron after all. He'd pressed his khakis and his button-down shirt. He'd also gotten a haircut and bought a new belt. As usual, from the moment he stepped through the front door, it felt as if the house were on tilt and everything within it sliding toward him. 'Listen up,' he said, as if he were talking to his class of fifth graders. 'We have some work to do.' He wanted the party to be perfect and had put himself in charge of what he called the extra touches. The blown-up pictures, along with a giant diagram of the tunnel as it would appear when finished in the year 2020, with a sticker that said YOU ARE HERE, to mark where it stood on Michael's last day. The sheet cake had Michael's caricature done in icing.

The pictures were of Michael at a union picnic playing tug-of-war, Michael lying on the couch in the old apartment with his leg and arm in a cast, Michael outside a site in the year 1982, Michael in his work gear, barely recognizable in his blackened, mud-drenched clothes, the dark hole of the tunnel stretched out behind him. When Eavan and James were little, they loved that one, thought it was hysterical, and Greta gathered from listening to them talk that they thought it was something that had happened only once, the day Daddy was covered in mud, Daddy filthy dirty, Daddy with muck all over his face.

'He mightn't like that one,' Greta said, pushing it aside. 'Maybe we better leave it.'

'Mom, stop,' James said, pushing it back where it was. 'People will think it's funny.'

'You know, never once did your father come home with a speck of dirt on him,' Greta said, taking up the picture and bringing it close to her glasses. 'Never once. He's a very clean person.'

James cleared his throat, nodded at Eavan to put the pictures away. 'We know that, Mom. That's exactly why it's so great.'

'Yes, but –'

'Okay,' James interrupted. 'So I called last night – did he mention it? – and asked him some B.S. about how to fix a hole in Sheetrock, and I don't think he suspects a thing.'

Eavan pulled up a chair and sat down. She put her head in her hands.

'Will he be mad?' James asked. 'Mom? What do you think?'

Greta stood behind Eavan and pulled the hair away from her daughter's face. 'I feel sick,' Eavan said, then shook her head when she saw James and Greta glance down at her belly. 'No, not that.' She groaned into her hand. Greta couldn't think why the kids should be so nervous.

She, after all, had thought up the idea, and she was the one he'd take it out on if it turned out that he was being serious all these years when he forbade them to ever throw him a surprise party. He issued the warning whenever they went to a surprise party thrown for someone else. It's cruel, he insisted. What was fun about giving a person the shock of his life? It's not to honor the person, it's to laugh at him. And is reaching a particular age really a cause for celebration? Just breathing in and out for a certain amount of time? He'd reminded her after the last surprise – a sixtieth birthday thrown for the wife of a former sandhog – that he didn't even know exactly when he was born, as if she weren't already well aware. That's how silly birthdays were. Probably in early April. Maybe in late March. Probably in 1945, but possibly 1944. It was a circumstance the kids would never in their whole lives get sick of thinking about. 'How can you not know when you were born?' they'd demand, the tone in their voices changing little from childhood to adulthood.

But this wasn't a birthday party. It was a retirement party, the first among their small group of friends, and so something Michael had not specifically outlawed except under the general umbrella of surprises. Also, Michael just wasn't that intimidating. At worst he would smile through it and take a week to recover. If he got presents, he'd refuse to go near them, putting his hand to his forehead and shaking his head. 'All that money,' he'd say, looking at the pile. And then one by one the kids would coax him to pick just one and open it. Then another. Then another, until the whole pile was unwrapped and at his feet.

They had the food prepared by three o'clock, and anything that didn't have to be refrigerated was left out on the dining-room table. The refrigerator was packed to the brim, so James brought the cake down to the garage, the coolest room in the house. Eavan put out a few photo albums next to the blown-up pictures and Greta's gift – a nine-piece gardening set complete with seeds for starting an herb garden. At three-thirty Greta changed into her party clothes: white slacks, red sandals, a short-sleeved black cotton sweater with a red stitch along the collar. They had another half hour to kill before people would start to arrive. Michael – with Ned Powers's help – wouldn't be home until five.

Back in the kitchen, sitting at the table and eating the ends of the soda bread and waiting for the hands of the clock to move, Greta began to take more notice of how odd Eavan and James were behaving. Twice now she'd seen Eavan look at her brother with widened eyes, as if urging him forward. It was as if they were teenagers again, trying to send each other messages with kicks under the table.

'Nicole is coming, right?' Greta asked. Nicole and James had been dating almost two years, making it James's longest relationship by a year and ten months. As Michael put it, she was a sound girl, and Greta wouldn't mind if all this looking and signaling each other had to do with some engagement plan they wanted to let her in on.

James pulled his eyes away from his sister. 'Oh, yeah. She'll be there.' Same as always. No extra look of significance. No flutter of surprise.

'And Gary?' Greta asked, looking at Eavan.

'Of course,' Eavan said, and Greta noticed it again, how she tossed the words out casually, then looked straight back at her brother. Go on, the look said, tell her.

'Stop staring at me,' Eavan said to Greta without taking her eyes off James. 'Your eyes in those glasses bug me out.'

'I'm not staring. Maybe that's your conscience making you think I'm staring. Keeping secrets from your mother.' She turned to James and stared at him instead. Of her three children, he looked the most like her. She'd never thought of herself as pretty, but her features on his face had turned out to be quite handsome.

'Cut it out,' he said. 'Seriously. Didn't you get glasses that don't make your eyes look so weird?'

'They broke. This morning.'

'They just broke?' Eavan asked.

'Yep, just broke. Don't change the subject.'

Eavan looked at James. 'Let's just tell her.'

'No! Are you crazy?' James pushed away from the table. 'Nice, Eavan. Nice going.'

Greta looked back and forth between them as they glared at each other. Eavan, the middle child. Her sensible, dependable girl. James, her unshaven, bed-headed boy. Julia, the oldest, the absentee daughter, the workaholic, the one who called in the middle of the night not realizing the time.

'That's enough,' Greta said, putting on her most serious expression. 'What's going on?'

'Okay, well, we wanted it to be a surprise –' Eavan began.

'Eavan, you are such a pain in the ass,' James interrupted.

'Easy now,' Greta said, taking hold of James's wrist.

'Well, this is crazy, James. It's too much. We shouldn't have done it.'

'Done what?' Greta asked. They ignored her.

'Something like this' – Eavan pleaded with her brother – 'it's not the surprise that's the big deal. It shouldn't be a surprise. Plus –'

'Plus what?' James demanded.

'It's not our business, really. I was talking to Gary last night, and he agrees. It's not really our business.'

'I'm going to kill you. I'm serious,' James said.

'James, your sister is expecting a child.'

'I think we should tell her, and if she thinks it's a bad idea, we'll cancel the whole thing.' Eavan turned to Greta. 'I don't know if we can cancel, really, but we'll figure something out. We'll handle it. Well, Julia will have to handle it I guess. At this point' – Eavan looked at her watch – 'she's the only one who can handle it.'

As Greta waited for her daughter's long preamble to end, as she looked back and forth between her children's flushed faces and the excitement that played in the air between them, she decided two things. First, whatever it was, they'd taken a big chance. It was something they'd thought about for a long time, argued about, probably decided on and re-decided a number of times before going through with it. Second, they were afraid.

'Spit it out, girl,' Greta said. 'I never heard such a speech in all my life.'

'Seriously,' James said.

'You shut up,' Eavan said to James. 'This was your big idea. It's your head if they hate it. Not mine.'

'And if they love it,' James pointed out.

'The Lord save us,' Greta said. 'Will someone just tell me what it is?'

Eavan got up and walked across the kitchen to where she left her purse. She drew out a long envelope. Even from across the room, even wearing glasses she was no longer used to, Greta could make out the airmail stamp on the upper-right-hand corner. She recognized the Irish postmark.

'What's that?' Greta asked, looking at the envelope as if she'd never seen one before.

'It's a letter,' Eavan said, placing it on the table. Greta crossed her arms and leaned over to inspect it. She peered at it as if it were a specimen in a cage. She pushed her glasses up on her nose and leaned closer. Everything in her body, every nerve, every vein, every ounce of blood felt in that moment like it began and ended in the pit of her stomach. It's not what I think it is, Greta thought. Silly woman – now their nerves have gone and rubbed off on me. It's not what I think it is, because there's no way they would be that brazen. Had they found out somehow? Done an investigation behind my back? No. Not possible, not after all these years. It was the first big decision she and Michael had made as parents, and they'd stuck to it. Their story was simple. Michael had helped Greta and Johanna with their luggage when they boarded the ship in 1963. He and Greta quickly fell in love. They were careless, and Greta got pregnant with Julia. When they realized what had happened Greta and Michael moved in together, and Johanna went on to California. They've not regretted it a single day since. If the children wanted more information – too bad. There were things parents didn't have to explain to children. American parents explained everything to their children – why they're angry, why they're hurt, why they make every little itsy-bitsy decision. They explain and explain until the child is satisfied. Greta and Michael had explained only as much as they wanted to explain, and placed the rest firmly off limits. The children had an aunt and an uncle in Ireland and two uncles in Australia. Michael and Greta had emigrated from Ireland and would never go back.

'I can see it's a letter, Eavan. Why was it sent to me at your address?'

'We got in touch with them,' James said, more tentative now that he'd seen Greta's reaction. 'In Ballyroan. Johanna. Aunt Johanna, I guess. We wrote a letter, and she wrote back. So we wrote another letter to tell her about the party. We thought it might be a good excuse to, you know –'

'Excuse me?' Greta felt as if she were treading air. 'I've told you a thousand times about your Aunt Johanna and Uncle Tom. They don't travel. Haven't I told you all of that? They can't leave the farm. And the house is tiny, so they can't have visitors. It's just the two of them there, and they don't have –'

'It's not the two of them, actually,' Eavan said. 'Johanna is married and has two sons, twenty-five and twenty-three. And Tom is still there. And you know, Mom, we're old enough now to have heard of B and Bs. Inns? Hotels? Come on. Besides, they built a new house more than fifteen years ago. Johanna says they have plenty of room.'

'How do you know all of that?'

Eavan nudged the envelope closer to Greta. 'We just thought we'd make it easier for you. Don't you think it's time? I mean, this is silly, isn't it? She's your only sister. Our aunt. Those boys are our cousins. There are flights between Shannon and New York half a dozen times a day. What could have happened that you can't get over?'

'Nothing happened. I've told you. They're busy with the farm, and we're –'

Eavan held up a hand to stop her. 'Mom, please.'

Johanna with two sons. Greta looked at the curtain and thought, That's a curtain. She looked at the clock and thought, That's a clock. Where had they moved the barn to? Greta wondered. And then: Why would they have moved the barn? Had they put the new house in the place of the old one or built it right alongside?

'So what does all this mean?' Greta asked, picking up the envelope and turning it over in her hands. It was addressed to Mrs Greta Ward at Eavan's home address. The name on the return address said Mrs Johanna Rafferty. I don't know any Johanna Rafferty, Greta wanted to say.

'Open it,' said James. Outside on the street, a car slowed to a stop, and a moment later two car doors slammed.

'Has Julia been writing to her too?' Greta asked.

'It was a joint effort,' James said. 'Now open it.'

'No,' said Greta, and she held the envelope out for him to take. The light coming through the window dimmed and brightened again. She noticed a small drawing on the back flap of the envelope. Blue pen. A constellation. Orion's hunting dogs. Big Tom's nighttime map when the sky was dry enough to see the stars. Without wanting to or trying, Greta pictured the others: Monahan's whaling ship, the

343

fisherman's beard, the donkey's tail. Not one of them real, Greta had learned long ago when Julia was taught about the stars in school. There are no constellations by those names, Julia had informed her plainly. Not in America, Greta had corrected her. Not that you can see from America, maybe, but in Ireland, yes. In Ireland they have the donkey's tail and Monahan's ship and Orion's hunting dogs. Stars were stars, Julia had said, no matter where you're standing. And besides, the constellations were made up anyway. Made up long ago by people who didn't know any better.

'Okay, Ma. Then I'm going to open it for you,' James said. And as easily as he might have picked up a book in a bookstore and turned to the first page, he slid his finger under the flap and ripped it open. He removed the lined page, only one, and unfolded it.

'Here,' he said, smoothing it out before he handed it over.

Greta took it without looking at it. 'So they'll be here at four? Like the others? All of them? The sons and husband and all?'

'No, just Johanna and Tom,' James said. 'Julia's at the airport waiting for them as we speak.'

Greta turned to find Eavan crying. Big, silent streams ran down her plump cheeks. She dabbed her face with one of the CON-GRAD-ULATIONS party napkins Greta had picked up on clearance at the party store, not realizing until James told her that when they spelled it with a *d,* it was for a graduation, not a retirement. A play on words, he'd called it, and Greta had suggested that since there was only one word, it was more of a play on letters.

'We shouldn't have,' Eavan said, pressing carefully around her eyes to avoid smearing her makeup. 'I knew it, and I went along with it anyway.'

'No, you shouldn't have,' Greta agreed, and handed her a tissue.

Greta sank back in her chair and tried to absorb what she'd been told. Johanna was in New York, on her way to see them. Julia was picking her up at the airport. There was no meeting at Saks. Greta reached out for the water jug and filled a paper cup with water. She swallowed it in one long gulp and poured another. All the youthful energy she'd felt that morning shriveled, and now, feeling James's and Eavan's eyes on her, she felt far older than fifty-nine.

'You'll be happy, we think,' Eavan stuttered. 'You know. After.'

Greta couldn't think of a single thing to say in response, and she felt she couldn't have responded anyway, her tongue as heavy as it was, her jaw as brittle. She ran her hand along the edge of the table as she stood. She could be back in Ballyroan, blind but ignorant of her blindness, Johanna just a blur bouncing up ahead, telling her to hurry it up, for God's sake hurry it up.

As the walls of her kitchen seemed to expand and contract, Greta's thoughts flew back, way back, to the day Padraic, Jack, and Little Tom had let her and Johanna join in on their game of dare. One by one they'd stood with their backs to the lip of the high sea ledge, the waves slamming against the rocks far below, and were directed by the others to move back, back, farther back. The challenge was in believing there was enough room behind for yet another step. When it was Greta's turn, she stood at the marked spot and waited for her brothers and sister to instruct her. 'You've loads of room,' they called as they urged her to take another step, but they couldn't control the wind, pushing her this way and that with no more effort than it took to push the tall grass, to bend it flat on its back. 'That's the wind all the way from Canada,' one of the boys had called, and another had corrected him: 'No, from America.'

And when she did fall – fear and dizziness overtaking her – the long journey from standing with her two feet planted on the hard ground to landing on her rear felt for split second like she'd really gone over. When she realized she was safe, she looked over her shoulder to face how close she'd been to death and saw that there were still a good ten feet between her and the edge. They'd been telling her the truth after all, and knowing she'd been safe all along made her feel as if her mother had swooped in and wrapped a blanket tight around her shoulders. She loved them then, felt guilty for not trusting them, for not knowing in her heart that they'd never let her fall.

Of the five of them, the Cahill children, the last family left in Ballyroan – Jack, Padraic, Little Tom, Johanna, and Greta – Johanna was the only one who wouldn't have stopped on her own. Barely bigger than Greta, a full eight years younger than Padraic, she'd taken every step backward as confidently as she'd taken the first. The rest of them had refused the final step, not believing they could back up farther without falling over the edge, except Johanna, who they had to call back.

'That's it,' Jack had had to say at the final point. 'You're at the edge. Now walk back toward us.'

Fifteen

'Just a minute,' Greta said. She felt both James and Eavan watching her as she put one foot in front of the other, detected something grainy under her sandal, bent to sweep a few stray crumbs together and then press them against her fingers. When she turned, they were still looking at her – two ruddy faces next to each other, bodies too big for the delicate legs of the chairs they sat on. She brushed her hands over the sink and then started to walk out of the kitchen. The letter still sat on the table, and as she moved away from its neat rows of blue ink, its precise folds, she felt it reproaching her. In those first few years, when Julia was an infant and then a toddler, with Michael and Greta timing their shifts around the baby but never each other, it would occur to Greta what a terrible thing her sister had done, and her fury toward Johanna would become a cold hand that had gotten its numbing fingers around her heart. But as Julia got older and Eavan and James came along, unexpected thoughts began coming to Greta, thoughts that made old furies stumble and fall into a thousand scattered pieces, and no matter how badly Greta wanted to catch them in her arms and put them together again, they would not be reassembled. Strange questions would stop her as she walked down the avenue or reached for her wallet in the grocery store or riffled through the children's clothing racks at Macy's with one of the kids in tow, holding shirts or jeans up against their bodies to gauge their ever-changing sizes. Who had really done the leaving behind? Who had done what to whom? And when these questions struck her, it felt as if she'd been walking along a pitch-black road, only to have the spotlight switched on at the very spot where there was nowhere to duck and hide. And the spotlight followed her wherever she moved and amplified everything she did. She tried to close her eyes and ignore the feeling, but it was still there, for years it had been there, crouching at the edge of her conscience, just as the letter was still sitting on the table, waving at her as the ceiling fan beat the air overhead.

'Where are you going?' Eavan asked, jumping up to follow close behind.

'Eavan,' Greta said simply, walking down the hall and slowly closing her bedroom door on her daughter's bewildered expression, Eavan's two fat cheeks pulled long and taut by her gaping mouth. With her hand tight around the knob, Greta pressed until she heard the click of the bolt. Earlier, after they'd tucked the sheets tight at the corners of the bed and tugged at the quilt until it hung evenly on both sides, Greta had raised the blinds to the highest point and Eavan had opened the windows. Now the room was full of sunlight, full of fresh May air, fragrant with the smell of a neighbor's grass cuttings. After so many years, Greta had gotten used to the noiselessness of the suburbs, the neat and ordered quietness of each house in its place. The sounds Greta did hear were always distant, the next block over or farther away, and it had taken her a long time to stop looking up, looking around, waiting for the noisemaker to appear. Car engines roared. Dogs barked. Lawn mowers coughed and grunted. But rarely on the Wards' block, or so it seemed. Rarely where Greta could look out the window and find the source.

'What are you going to do?' Eavan asked, her voice closer, somehow, than it had been with the door open. Greta could tell that she'd put her mouth to the narrow slice of space between the door and the wall, just as she used to do as a little girl.

The doorbell rang. The screen door squealed.

'James,' Eavan said, a command, her voice thrown away from the door and down the hall to her brother. James called out a welcome to the first guests.

'Mom?' Eavan said, quieter now that someone might overhear. When she was little, she used to crouch down until she could rest her chin on her knees, purse her lips, cup her hands around her mouth, and stretch her neck toward the crack beside the doorknob as if it were a microphone, a walkie-talkie, a tin can pulled tight at the end of a string. It was usually Julia she was trying to speak to on the other side of the door. When they first moved to Recess, Julia took no time getting used to having a room to herself. She closed her bedroom door when she read, when she spoke on the phone, when she changed clothes. At night Greta and Michael discussed the change in Julia since leaving the city. She'd grown up, they decided. Eavan, unused to sleeping in a room by herself, unused to having only her own things about her, spent every night for weeks creeping down the stairs after midnight, pillow clutched tightly to her chest, whispering, 'Julia? Can I sleep with you?' As far as Greta knew, Julia always said yes, because there they'd be in the morning, one a fully grown woman, one just a girl, twisted up in the sheets, their arms resting on each other's hair, as if they'd walked miles upon miles upon miles and then collapsed where they stood. During the day the door would stay closed to Eavan, so she'd crouch, press her lips against the slim gap where the door met the wall, and ask Julia what she was doing, ask to be let in, ask if Julia would like to come up to her room and color. At those moments Eavan always reminded Greta of herself, whispering Johanna a message through the weathered planks of the stable door.

'Just give me a minute, will you, please?' Greta said. After a moment she heard Eavan move away.

Greta listened as the guests greeted her children, asked for Julia, mentioned Eavan's growing belly, offered congratulations. She heard the pop of a wine cork pulled free, the thin tap of three glasses being set down, one by one, on the kitchen countertop, the thud of more car doors, more greetings, the rasp of gift bags stuffed with tissue paper, the heavy tread of male footsteps, a woman's voice imbued with the long o's and u's of Donegal, scolding, 'Pick up your feet, Oran, Jesus. You think you're down in the tunnel?' The guests were hurrying, quieter than they'd normally be at a party, no gales of laughter, no hellos shouted outside from the ones who were already in. 'Is he on his way?' they asked in their separate ways, voices lowered, a surprise party in the hour before the honored's arrival the most serious kind of party there is. The crosscurrent from all the open windows rattled the bedroom door in its frame. Greta walked around the bed to her side and sat down.

The longer she sat, the farther away the party seemed. Through the window, which looked toward the western half of the street,

Greta could see that the curb was almost completely lined with cars. Soon they'd have to park on the next block. Surely Michael would see these cars and know. Surely Michael would figure it all out before even arriving at the house, and on he'd sail, pressing his foot to the gas, pulling his cap down over his eyes. Up to town he'd go, Greta figured. Up to Sweeney's for a hamburger and a pint. An idea came into her head and settled across her thoughts like a balm: maybe she'd go join him, order up her own burger, her own pint, call the house after a few hours to ask if the coast was clear.

'Ma.' James opened the door just enough to peek in. 'People are asking for you.'

'Any sign?' Greta asked without turning around.

'Not yet. Julia called to say they –'

'Not them. Your father. Any sign of your father yet?'

'No.' James waited a few seconds and then shut the door.

There were things the children didn't know. At some point in the past year, without ever deciding to do so and without telling a soul, Greta had begun taking an inventory of moments when Michael didn't seem himself. First, he could never manage to find his keys. This was common, Greta told herself. It happened to everyone, look at the people on the TV comedies. What was less common – and this was the difference that gave her a feeling in her gut like a mugger had come up to her on the street and shown her his knife – is for a man who can't find his keys to sit in his car for more than ten minutes before realizing what he was missing. It had happened only a handful of times, but each time, Michael had looked at Greta with anger, as if she'd hidden the keys on him, as if she were playing a joke, as if it were her fault he couldn't make the car go. Second, after forty years of refrigeration, Greta had recently caught him looking for the butter in the cupboard or on the ledge above the stove. Third, he kept forgetting that Eavan was pregnant. Fourth, he sometimes referred to Julia or Eavan as Maeve, a name he hadn't mentioned in years. Fifth, once in a while, usually on a Sunday afternoon, he would go downstairs to the basement bedroom to look for James. 'James cleaned his room finally,' he'd say to Greta when he came back upstairs. 'Went out, did he?'

'Michael,' Greta would say, some mechanism in her throat causing her voice to go tight and serious even as she tried to sound light and pleasant. 'James moved out, remember? James lives in Brooklyn now.' She'd look right in his eyes as she reminded him. If she was carrying something, she'd put it down. She'd touch some part of his body. If she was standing and he was sitting, she'd knead his back and shoulders as she corrected him in a loud and clear voice. Remember this, she would add silently as she dug into his flesh. Pay attention.

'Well, I know that, Greta,' Michael would say. 'I just thought . . .'

Greta would wait, hoping for a perfectly sound explanation for why he thought his son who moved out six years earlier might be staying in the bedroom downstairs. None came.

The list went on and on. Sometimes she could convince herself that they were all little things, really, until you looked at them all together, and why do that? Once, when she couldn't manage to convince herself, she mentioned something vague to Eavan and asked her to look up about forgetfulness on the Internet. A few days later Eavan had shown up with the ginseng tablets and a few loose pages about Alzheimer's disease. The pages described people who forgot where they lived, the names of their children. People who didn't know what to do with a toothbrush, a comb, a bar of soap. People who had to be watched like kindergartners lest they wander off one afternoon and never come back. People who forgot everything except for their earliest memories, which came back to them with the clarity of far more recent history.

According to the pages, printed on the backs of first-draft garage sale flyers Eavan was crafting to post around town, there was no treatment, no cure. Diagnosis, yes. And pills. And careful observation. And advice on how to make life easier – locks on the dials of the kitchen stove, bracelets engraved with home address and phone number.

'This is bad,' Greta had said after absorbing the information.

'Exactly,' Eavan had said. 'He's not even close to anything like this. He's probably tired is all. And did I already tell you that Gary locked himself out of his car twice last month?'

Greta folded the pages into quarters and tucked them in among the canisters of flour, sugar, and oats on the top shelf of the cupboard.

'Did he really?' Greta asked, and as Eavan went on and on about all the little things everyone, young and old, forgets every day, Greta thought about the people described in the pages and wondered how it had happened. Had they simply opened their eyes one morning to find large swaths of memory rubbed out, or had it happened in bits, standing at a party and insisting that someone's name was on the tip of the tongue, stopping halfway through a story and asking, What was I saying? Had they realized something was missing, or had they just pushed forward, filling in the blanks with whatever fit.

For years Michael had been talking about how much he wanted to go to North Dakota to see the Badlands. He wanted to go to Alaska. He wanted to see the Rocky Mountains. He informed Greta one night as he was getting into bed that all of Yellowstone National Park was in truth an enormous volcano that could erupt at any moment, so that was added to the list. He wanted to go to South Carolina to see if there really were travellers living there, still speaking the Shelta of home. 'There are Wards there,' he'd said recently. 'Since the famine. I saw it on the television.' When he first mentioned the possibility of retirement, he sat across the table from Greta and pitched these places one after another. They would trade in his sedan and get a bigger car, more suitable for cross-country driving. He would be at the wheel. Greta would navigate.

'Me in charge of the map?' Greta had laughed. 'You're dreaming.'

And then, as the months went by and he still hadn't set a last day, she saw that he really was dreaming. She noticed that instead of looking forward to what came next, he'd begun looking back, way back, to the camps and the tents and the tinsmithing trade he'd cycled away from one day in the Burren. More and more he mentioned Maeve and the made-up language they spoke as children that only they could understand. There's not a thing wrong with this man's memory, Greta convinced herself as she listened to the details.

'A turf fire is warmer than a wood fire,' he swore one day, and wanted to show her in the backyard.

'Fire is fire,' Greta told him lightly, hoping to God he'd stay where he was and at the same time trying to think of a way to stop him if he marched outside and began splitting wood. Authentic turf was impossible to come by in America, so whatever happened, one side of the demonstration would be built entirely upon imagination.

'Hah,' he'd said, sitting back in his chair, satisfied by some mysterious point he'd just proven. 'That's country people for you. That's what country people know.'

He remembered the ship, his berth on the floor, sleeping with his hand in his pocket to protect the few pounds Lily had given him to exchange for dollars on the other side.

And once, only once, just a week or so before he set a firm last day, he mentioned Johanna. Not Johanna as Greta's older sister, as she had been referenced over the years, but Johanna in relation to himself. It was early March, the morning after the last snowstorm of the season. They were shoveling the driveway. Michael plowed through his half in no time and came around to help Greta.

'She was lovely,' he said. 'Brazen, but lovely. Wasn't she?' Greta nodded, wiped her running nose with her glove, thought of Johanna as she was then, especially in the months before they left for America. As Lily used to say, there was no holding her. There was no keeping her. Then Greta thought of herself as she was during that time – like a day-old chick that couldn't manage to grow out of its box.

'But I loved you,' he said simply. He stopped shoveling, as if the thought had taken him by surprise. After fourteen inches of snow the street was even quieter than usual. The air was sharp and brittle, the world made smaller and brought closer by the thick blanket now holding everything together. As far as Greta could tell, she and Michael were the only two who had ventured outside so far that morning, and it seemed to her that the other houses were empty and she and Michael were completely alone. Under a ski jacket James had grown out of, under her thick wool sweater and her long johns, Greta flushed.

'You had a funny way of showing it,' she teased, lifting a mound of powdery snow and tossing it into the wind.

But he didn't even look at her as the snow blew back in his face. He just leaned on his shovel and continued to stare off across their brief stretch of property, everything a thick, downy white except for the trees, whose branches were weighed down with glinting ornaments.

'I was very young,' he said.

'I know that, Michael,' Greta said, dropping her shovel and closing the distance between them. She could no longer feel her toes inside her boots. 'What's gotten into you?'

He shrugged, blinked back to the present, surveyed the work left on the driveway. 'Isn't it good luck we never had snow like this at home?' He filled his shovel with a massive heap and walked down the length of the driveway to the curb, where he dumped it. Greta watched him do it again.

'Why are you bringing it all the way over there?' she asked. For the past hour they'd simply tossed the shoveled snow to either side of the driveway. In some places the piles they made were more than four feet deep. From past years Greta knew that these hills that marked the boundary of the drive would be the last white patches to disappear once warmer weather returned.

His eyes were hidden by his cap, but she could tell by the set of his mouth that he was completely baffled. 'Well, where do you want me to put it?' he asked. He held a third shovelful aloft with both arms as he waited for her answer.

The tunnels were a worry. He'd be okay, she told herself. The others would watch out for him. Then he came home that day – a rainy Thursday, he'd dripped a path from the garage all the way to his chair in the kitchen – and told her about going up to the supply shed for another hard hat only to discover it already on his head. He'd told her to make her laugh, and she did laugh, even as her heart became a cup that ran over.

At a quarter to five, there came a knock on the bedroom door. 'Hey, Mom?' James said in a low voice. 'Can I come in?'

Greta stood to open the door for him and looked over his shoulder and down the short hall to glimpse the crowd in the living room. An old neighbor from Eighty-fourth Street saw Greta and waved. James held up his cell phone. 'It's Julia. What should I tell her? They're stuck in traffic. Should I tell her to stay stuck? Then we could meet up with them later? Or tomorrow?'

Greta took the phone out of his hand. 'Julia?' she said, and then quickly, 'Don't say it's me.'

'Yes?' Julia said. Greta could hear a woman's voice in the background, brought close by the small space inside Julia's car. The woman's voice was low, continuous, despite Julia's being on the phone, as if she was telling someone a long story and couldn't be interrupted. Greta imagined her pointing out the car window, Tom nodding, the muscles around his mouth too tired after the excitement and the long flight to shape any words. Then she heard a male voice say 'George Washington Bridge' as clear as day.

'Are they with you?' Greta asked, and then scolded herself. 'Who's there? Just Tom and Johanna?'

'That's it.'

'Not another man? You didn't pick up anyone else?'

'Mom, what are you talking about?'

The voices in the background went silent. 'I told you not to say it was me.' Greta sensed them listening, heads tilted toward Julia, eyes on the world outside the car windows but taking in every word. 'Well, how long do you think it will take?'

'Forty minutes, I'd guess. Maybe more. It depends on whether they clear this accident. We haven't hit the bridge yet.'

'Julia,' Greta said, 'I can't believe you kids did this. I just don't understand how you would do something like this without telling me. I can't believe —'

'Yes,' Julia said, laughing lightly. 'We're excited too. Can't wait.'

Greta heard a click on the line, took the phone away from her ear and examined it where it sat in her palm. The screen was glowing, but as she watched, it went dark.

'What happened?' she asked.

James took it from her and pressed a button. 'She hung up,' he said.

'Hung up?'

'Or got disconnected. The signal here is spotty.'

'James,' Greta said, sitting again at the edge of the bed, 'are my sister and brother really in that car? Are they really coming here? It's just not possible.'

'What are you talking about? A few years ago two guys circled the whole world in a balloon. Why can't they get on a plane and come to New York?'

'You think I'm joking?' Greta said, struggling to keep her voice down. 'I should give you a good belt, is what I should do. I should get your sister in here and belt her too. And Julia too, when I see her. Mind your business. I thought that's what your father and I always taught you. There are things you know absolutely nothing about. It's just not as easy as buying a ticket and getting on a plane.'

'Well, it is that easy, actually, because that's exactly what they did. And the minute you see them, you're going to be happy they came. I mean, it's silly – whatever this is between you. Is it because you left? Is it because they didn't like Dad? No, don't look at me like that. I'm not really asking. I'm just saying that they seem to be over it, so you should start getting over it too. You've been talking about home all our lives. I don't get it.'

'You're not meant to get it. It's none of your business.' Greta stood as tall as she was able. She pointed her finger in her son's face but couldn't think of anything else to say.

'Okay. I'm done here. I'm going back to the party. Remember the party, Mom?'

As he left, he pushed the bedroom door open further. 'Mrs Quinn?' he called. 'Still looking for my mother?' He turned, stepped aside, and pointed to Greta, who had returned to her perch on the bed. 'Right in there. Peek your head in and get her moving. I don't think she realizes it's that time.' He looked at his watch and shouted so everyone could hear him, 'The guest of honor will be here any minute.'

'Greta?' Maude Quinn said as she entered Greta's bedroom. 'Everything looks wonderful. Eavan said you spilled on your good blouse. Isn't that just the way? Well, listen, you look like a million bucks. Now tell me how you did those figs wrapped in bacon, will you?'

Sixteen

For Julia, the morning at work glided by like a series of floats in a parade. She sat rooted to the desk chair in her bright and cluttered office, halfway between the company's two largest conference rooms, as the familiar pageant played out on the other side of glass walls. Having arrived early, only to find herself completely incapable of making her thoughts focus on the e-mails waiting for her from vendors in Italy, Turkey, Hong Kong, she observed for the first time that the morning rush tipped in only one direction, from the elevators in the south corridor to the row of cubicles and conference room A in the north. The steady current of arrival, clusters of threes and fours, moved from left to right, as did the scurry to morning meetings, the storming forth with files, swatches of fabric, mugs of coffee clutched in fists, laptops tucked under arms. They must circle the whole floor, Julia decided, like runners on a track.

An hour or so later the pace of the parade slowed to accommodate calm midmorning strolls, everyone finally settled in, elbows resting on cubicle ledges, asses thrust out into the aisles as the assistants whispered about each other, about their bosses, about their accounts. They planned their Friday and Saturday nights.

The phone on Julia's desk gave two quick blips. Silence. Another two blips. An internal call. Julia reached over and tapped a small red button.

'You still leaving early today?' David's voice filled the room. His office was three doors farther down the parade route.

'I've only told you fifty times.'

'I have some things for you to look at before you go. And we have to come up with a plan for next week. If Marshall Field's —'

Julia picked up the receiver. 'Okay, I took you off speaker. Can't we just pretend I'm not here today? I'm leaving at lunch. If I'd taken off or called in sick, you wouldn't need me to look at anything, right? You'd just go ahead and make all these decisions on your own.'

David was silent, and as she waited for him to speak, she recalled their argument of two nights earlier. He was hurt, he'd said, by the way she treated him at work sometimes. 'What did I do?' she demanded, taking another sip of the wine he'd opened for her as he breaded the lamb chops he was preparing for their dinner.

'Nothing, exactly. It's your tone. It's like –'

She had felt the alcohol warm in her belly, under her ribs. Just a few sips into her third glass and she could already detect the predictable heat in her cheeks and the pliant muscles of her arms as she set down her glass and folded them across her chest. 'My *tone*? You're reprimanding me for my *tone*?'

He placed the lamb chop carefully on a plate. 'Well, it's bitchy a lot of the time. And the thing is –'

'It's bitchy? Did you just call me a bitch?'

He stared at her in a way that refused the possibility that she had actually misunderstood. Fine, his posture said, you want to go down that road? Fine. 'No. I didn't. But since you mention it . . .'

She'd gathered her things and was out the door before he could rinse the bread crumbs off his fingers. When she got back to her apartment, she turned the ringer off on her phone.

They'd known each other for nine months and had been sleeping together for four. There was an office policy that prohibited inter-office relationships between any director-level employees who work closely together, but Julia swore to herself that she'd never let it get out of hand. It began as a cliché: too much to drink, the last two left at the bar, the bright idea to share a cab, both knowing perfectly well the cab would make only one stop. The following Monday she'd arrived at work determined to avoid him, and with the hope that he'd have the common decency to avoid her. She blocked out her calendar, sent her phone straight to voice mail, pulled the blinds on her office's glass walls, took a two-hour lunch, kept her door closed. She made it to four o'clock and then made the mistake of checking the second coffee station on the floor when the first was out.

'Hey,' he'd said, coming up behind her. 'Avoiding anyone?' He looked at his watch. 'I was going to give you until five, and then I was going to bust down your door.'

'I'm swamped,' Julia said, stirring her coffee as she tried to step past him.

'Friday,' he said. 'Let's go to dinner.'

She put the stirrer in her mouth as she considered the offer. It was not normally how these things turned out, and she wondered if this was his way of avoiding awkwardness around the office. If they pretended they were interested in each other for more than a minute, maybe that first night wouldn't seem so bad. He was handsome, yes, in a well-pressed blond sort of way. He had very white, very straight teeth – a characteristic Julia knew Greta would approve of, since she was always remarking on the teeth of people born and raised in America. Greta had been nudging Julia toward love for a long time now. You have an education, Greta pointed out. You have a career. You have good looks and good sense. Now it was time to find a partner for life. Did Julia want to be lonely? Did she want to go home to an empty apartment at the end of each day? Greta was, as James had once put it, a true believer, and years back, when Julia was shopping for a new therapist, the woman had asked her to list a few of the priorities she'd been taught growing up. Julia listed love for one's family in ten different ways, and the therapist, after taking a few minutes to look at the page, seemed at a complete loss.

'Look,' Greta always said whenever Julia pushed back, tried to change the subject. 'A girl has to eat, right? So go for a few dinners. Let someone take you dancing.'

But Greta and Michael had never gone dancing, as far as Julia could tell. They worked and they talked and they slept and they got up each morning and did it all over again. Oh, and they worried. Or at least Greta worried. Would ends meet? Would the kids be able to support themselves? Would the oil tank leak before the winter was out? Would Julia find someone to love her soon (Eavan had found her match, and Greta didn't worry about James; it was different for boys). Was Julia a happy person? There were all these worries, plus the unspoken fear that Julia had been able to detect in Greta ever since that last night in the old apartment. Julia often wondered if Greta still had the old tin cookie box hidden somewhere in the house. It wasn't in her bedroom closet; Julia had spent an afternoon looking for it once when Greta and Michael were at work.

For a long time Julia had prided herself for what she considered a carefree, take-it-as-it-comes attitude toward life. As a teenager, she had decided that she would not be like Greta, bogged down with details of daily existence that she couldn't control or understand. Then she'd discovered the contents of the tin box and realized that she would not have to be – little of Greta was written into her DNA. Julia had been born out of a personality so different from Greta's that she'd never even seen the woman whose blood she'd inherited. Her birth mother's crime was something Greta would have never been capable of, and this knowledge made Julia more interested in her own limits and simultaneously terrified of what she might discover about herself.

'Julia?' David had asked, waving a hand in front of her face. 'Earth to Julia? Dinner Friday?'

'Sure,' Julia said. 'Everyone has to eat, right?'

Now, four months after their first proper date, David wanted to go to the party. He didn't understand why she hadn't invited him. He had never met Eavan, who was often in the city for shows or shopping, or even James, who lived just one stop away from Julia in Brooklyn. She had met his brother one evening when he was in town overnight to meet a client, but it wasn't until halfway through dinner that Julia realized the night was less spontaneous than it had been billed by David. She was being formally presented as the girlfriend, considered and evaluated by a representative from David's faraway family. Julia had not asked to meet anyone in his family – it had barely occurred to her that he had a family – and now here he was expecting to be presented to hers.

'It's just a thing for my dad,' she'd explained more than once. 'It's his friends, not mine. You'd be bored.' It wasn't that she wasn't interested in him, she insisted, and as she insisted, she realized it was the truth. It wasn't that she was hiding him – or worse, hiding someone else. She'd even agreed with him when he suggested that it might be time to come out at work about their relationship. She just didn't want to bring him to the party, and that was that. At some point, Julia noticed, he seemed to decide that the best thing to do was to act as if he didn't care.

'Who are you picking up?' he asked now. 'I know you told me, but –'

'An aunt and an uncle. My mother's brother and sister.'

'It's been years, right?'

'It's been forever. I've never met them.'

'Really? How will you know each other? Maybe you should make a sign for when they come through customs.'

'I think I'll just look around to see if anyone else is looking around. Anyone else who looks a lot like me. Or my mother.'

'Family resemblance is tricky, Jules. I have an uncle who looks Arab. I swear to God. He gets stopped for random checks at La Guardia just about every –'

Julia sighed.

'Okay, okay,' David said. 'I'm just making conversation, you know? Call me over the weekend. It's supposed to rain, but if today's weather holds and if you want a day at the beach . . .'

I'm almost forty-three years old, Julia thought. Then, annoyed with herself as well as with David, she wondered what that had to do with anything. She'd been thinking about her age more and more, ever since James had come over to her place one Saturday morning to tell her about the idea he and Eavan had cooked up. 'Wouldn't it be great?' he asked. 'After all this time, for them to see each other again?' Julia had never told anyone what she'd discovered that last night in the apartment. Not Eavan. Not James. None of her girlfriends. Not a single boyfriend. Not even Donald MacEwan, who she was eight weeks away from marrying once.

Julia was resistant to the idea at first. It's not our business, she told her two younger siblings. We shouldn't stir the pot. 'But wouldn't you love to meet them?' Eavan had asked, and Julia had immediately felt her resistance cracking. She finally agreed it would be perfectly great, and she agreed again two weeks later when Eavan reported that Johanna had written back. At almost forty-three years old, she told herself, she should be ready. She'd done all the growing up she was going to do. She wished it would stop occurring to her whenever the three of them were together that neither Eavan nor James would ever reach into a box one day and discover that they were not the people they'd always been told they were.

*

When the digital numbers on the screen of Julia's office phone read 12:30, she set her e-mail to an automated reply and picked up her bag. She dialed the garage downstairs and told the attendant she'd be down in ten minutes. She pressed the code on her phone that sent messages directly to voice mail. She pushed the papers on her desk into a neat pile. She walked out into the hall, pulled her office door closed after her, and, like everyone else, turned north. Thankfully, David's office was empty when she passed.

'I'm out of here,' she whispered to her assistant, who was on a call. Rebecca nodded, waved her away, mouthed the words 'Have fun.' Julia continued north along the corridor, turned left, left again, and left once more, until she'd completed a lap and found herself at the bank of elevators.

'Going down,' she said to the crowd pressed inside the first elevator that opened, and determined to find room where there wasn't any, she maneuvered herself inside.

Coming from her apartment in Brooklyn Heights, Julia usually took the subway to work. Two subways, in fact. She had to transfer at Union Square. So, on a day when she already felt a little peculiar – as if her mind were tethered on a short leash and trailing slightly behind her body – taking the elevator straight to the basement of her office building and getting into her car was just one more aberrant drumbeat in an arrangement that was already out of tune.

It was the warmest Friday New York had seen in months, and for this reason she expected a lot of traffic leaving the city, pasty-faced apartment dwellers heading full speed for the sandy beaches of Long Island and New Jersey. Instead, she shot out onto empty highway, open road. Foot pressed to the gas pedal, she reached over to dig the E-ZPass tag out of the glove compartment and sailed through the tollgate. Up and down exit ramps she flew, barely tapping the brake, hurtling along the Grand Central, the Van Wyck, the car washes, dance clubs, and low-slung houses of Queens all standing at attention, all shifting in their foundations a little to twist from left to right as she passed.

She arrived at JFK an hour and twenty minutes before the flight was due to land. Alone, holding her purse close to her body, she sat at a table in the Euro Café and ordered a glass of white wine. Not ten seconds later she got up, tapped her waitress on the shoulder, and changed the order to a vodka tonic. By the time she returned to her seat, the notice on the arrivals monitor said that Aer Lingus Flight 107 was running forty minutes late.

After her second vodka tonic – which she rationalized by figuring the flight would be further delayed, and counteracted by also ordering a cheese plate – she asked herself, for perhaps the thousandth time that week, the millionth time since that last night in the old apartment in 1986, why she'd never gone to Ireland. There had been chances. A bike tour organized by a friend in 1994, cheap flights advertised in full-page ads in the *New York Times* every winter. She'd been to France, to Spain, to Italy. She'd been to London more than a dozen times for work. On one of the more recent London trips, on a walk through Hyde Park with Francis Brown, a British colleague who liked to talk about the kingdom past and present and never once mentioned his wife or young child, she learned that there was a bus that went from Victoria Station to Galway City.

'A bus?' Julia had asked at the time, checking her knowledge of geography. 'Isn't there a little thing called the Irish Sea?'

He'd laughed, touched her arm. 'It travels up to Liverpool and drives right onto the ferry. On the Irish side it stops in Dublin and Galway City. It's a long journey, all told. Twelve, thirteen hours.'

'You're kidding,' Julia had said, astonished. This mundane fact made Ireland seem closer. Getting to an airport and boarding a plane was a project, an event to be planned, coordinated, arrived for in the correct socks and shoes. But a bus was a different story. A bus never left the ground. People hopped on buses without thinking twice. She'd passed Victoria Station almost every day she'd been in London.

'Ever been?' Francis had asked.

'My parents are Irish,' Julia said. 'From the west. Galway.'

'Oh,' Francis had said. 'So you know.'

The next morning, a Friday, Julia had walked over to Victoria Station to see if it was true, how long the journey took, how much it cost. Twenty-two pounds sterling, the board said. She had more than a hundred in her wallet. I could do this, she thought. I could go. I could roll right into Galway City and take a local bus to a place named Conch. From there I could ask people to point me in the direction of Ballyroan. Maybe I wouldn't even have to ask. Maybe someone passing by the bus stop – coming out of a pub, perhaps, or on the way home from Mass – would recognize me as a Cahill. Maybe that person would offer me a lift, or at least lend me a bicycle. In Ballyroan they'd know me before I even reached the front door. 'It's Julia come home,' they'd shout. Johanna would take one look at her and know that Julia knew everything and had come anyway.

Standing in the middle of Victoria Station, Julia had looked down at herself: a dark gray gabardine suit with a pencil skirt that just hit her knees, bare legs, pointy-toed slingbacks that had pressed her toes into a single throbbing unit by the time she'd crossed the lobby of her hotel.

She'd waited until the bus passengers boarded. Men, women, and children with their backpacks slung over their shoulders. I could get on that bus, Julia told herself, but she stayed rooted to her spot. She stayed long enough to watch the bus pull away, the exhaust pipe billowing dark smoke that hung in the air long after the bus disappeared.

After a third vodka tonic, the three untouched hunks of cheese before her shiny with oil, Julia reminded herself that she had the advantage: Johanna and Tom didn't know about the night she'd feasted on the bundle of letters until Greta returned with a pizza box in her hands and a grocery bag dangling from her middle finger. In all the writing back and forth they'd done over these past weeks, no one had come anywhere near mentioning daughters and mothers, and who belonged to whom.

It would be kind of funny, Julia thought, if we died together today. If there was an accident and we died. And then when they examined the bodies and had to draw their conclusions, the doctors would discover that the driver of the 2001 Honda Accord and the female passenger were daughter and mother. Julia saw them sailing over the guardrail on the George Washington Bridge. She saw the nose of the car hitting the water. If they survived the impact, she saw them struggling with the doors, the windows, not immediately realizing that the electricity in the car had shorted out. That's the trouble with power windows, Julia might say, sighing, as the car sank to the bottom of the river.

The thought was the opposite of funny, Julia knew very well as she pushed her glass to the other side of the small table. It was just that an accident, a death, would represent very neat bookends in Julia's life. That's all. Johanna there when Julia began her life, and there again when she died. And no day in between.

Then Julia said to herself what Donald MacEwan used to say to her all the time: Julia, you are a very strange person sometimes.

Julia signaled her waitress. 'Excuse me? Can I please get a burger and fries? And a very large glass of water?'

As Julia watched the stream of people coming out of customs and through the doors, she was sure she'd spotted them half a dozen times. In some instances the woman convinced her, in others the man. Each time, Julia either heard them address each other by name or watched as they were claimed by another person. Just once she went as far as saying 'Johanna Rafferty?' to a woman in brown tweed, steel gray hair coiled at the back of her head.

'Sorry,' the woman said, an American, shaking her head and turning away from Julia as she scanned the crowd.

After twenty minutes of standing on her tiptoes, keeping her eyes fixed on the double doors that all passengers had to pass through, Julia began to worry. The stream had been reduced to a trickle. A customs officer closed one of the doors.

'Is that you, Julia?' a woman's voice came from somewhere to Julia's left. For a split second she thought it was Greta. Eavan and James had spilled the beans, and Greta had come to the airport to put a stop to it somehow. But the accent was the slightest bit thicker, and there was a certain quality in the pronunciation of her name that made Julia turn around.

'Johanna?'

Johanna released the handle of her small suitcase, grabbed Julia, and pulled her toward the warm softness of her wool cardigan. Julia could feel Johanna's heart beating against her ear as the woman clutched her.

Then Johanna pushed her away as abruptly as she'd pulled her close, pushed her as far as possible without letting go. She looked at Julia's face. She let her glance skitter quickly up and down Julia's body, and then land, again, at her face. As Julia let herself be examined, she noted that Johanna was taller than Greta. She wasn't fat, but she didn't have Greta's airy lightness, that impression Greta gave sometimes of being a collection of bones arranged and attached so precariously that a strong wind could blow them apart. If Johanna had two feet planted on the ground, it would take a lot to knock her down. Her coloring was the same as Greta's, and both women had stayed away from dyes when their hair began to turn gray. She looked, Julia supposed, exactly as she expected Johanna to look. She was wearing navy pants, very well cut, and a long, belted tunic-style blouse under her cardigan. Her earrings matched her necklace, and her nails were painted a muted pink. She is an attractive woman, Julia thought, and she is perfectly aware of her appearance. Without meaning to, Julia conjured up Greta and placed her beside her sister. Greta, who just a few weeks ago, after walking through Prospect Park with Julia, plopped down on a bench, looked at her feet, and said, 'Are these the shoes I'm wearing? Well then, it's no wonder.'

'You look like yourself,' Johanna announced. 'No one else but yourself. Doesn't she, Tom?'

Tom stepped forward, held his hand out for Julia to shake.

'Good God, Tom, will you not hug her?' Johanna asked, giving him a small shove. 'All this time, and you put out your hand like she's a neighbor from up the road?'

Julia stepped up and hugged him as he blushed, patted her back, squeezed her shoulder, and then let her go. Unlike Greta and Johanna, who still had large sections of dark hair, his hair was completely white. Julia had forgotten how much older he was than his sisters. Ten years, at least. Maybe more, she couldn't remember. His face was windburned and shadowed with stubble except for one pale line extending from his top lip to his nose. A scar, Julia realized, wanting to reach up and run her finger along it. She remembered something about a cleft palate, telling Greta the proper name for when, as Greta put it, a person's mouth was twisted up toward his nose.

'Were you waiting very long?' Tom asked, pronouncing each word slowly and carefully, as if he were unused to the sound of his own voice. 'They stopped me because I checked the box to say I work with farm animals. I was thinking of you out here wondering where we could be, and everyone else out before us.' As he spoke, Julia noticed that he was careful about the placement of his tongue, the shape of his lips, the rhythm of his breathing as he exhaled through his nostrils. How difficult it must be, Julia thought, to teach an adult man to speak with a new mouth. How difficult it must have been to learn.

'They thought you had that mad cow disease, Tom,' Johanna said. She turned to Julia. 'You get wise to them, I suppose, after a while, going back and forth to America. They give no such trouble going to Australia.'

To Australia, Julia noted. To visit the other brothers, she supposed. She almost laughed at the lengths Greta had gone to in explaining why Johanna and Tom couldn't travel. What a good job she'd done when Julia, at forty-two years old, even after knowing all the other lies Greta had told, found herself surprised to learn that they could manage to leave Ireland at all. So it was only America they avoided. She pictured them at home, a generic seaside scene, waiting for the post and for their invitation.

'We can't have been the only country people on that flight,' Johanna said. 'The only ones who came into contact with a cow in the past month – or however they put it. It's still Ireland, for God's sake. It hasn't changed that much. You should have seen the cut of the boots on the man sitting next to me.'

And then, before Julia could comment, Johanna asked, 'How's your mother and father?'

'Oh, fine,' Julia said, reaching to help with the bags, surprised to see that her hands were shaking. The pleasant buzz she'd had in the Euro Café had worn off mostly, but she could still feel the heat of the alcohol in her blood.

'Fine,' Tom repeated. 'That's an American word. I suppose Greta speaks American now too.'

As they left the terminal and strode out into the sunshine, Julia excused herself for a moment and dialed James on his cell phone.

'All set,' she said when he answered.

'Good for you,' he said, 'because we're up shit creek on this end.'

'What?' Julia asked, trying to keep the alarm out of her voice as Johanna and Tom ambled along beside her. They stopped at the crosswalk. Julia overheard Johanna remind Tom to always look left first and then right when crossing a street in America, and then she watched as Johanna reached over and fixed his collar. She did not look nervous, Julia noted. Or guilty. Or ashamed. Or the least bit worried about what Julia would think of her. They were well dressed for a seven-hour flight, and at first Julia chalked this up to being old-fashioned. Then she remembered that they'd come prepared to go straight to the party. They'd gotten ready for the reunion three thousand miles ago.

'Little Miss Hormonal told Mom about the extra surprise, and she's not happy.'

'Okay, well, what do we do? Do we still come?'

Tom and Johanna both looked over at her and then at each other.

'I guess,' James said. 'I don't know. Your call.'

Julia turned and took a few steps back toward the terminal. She smiled at Johanna and Tom, holding up a finger to show it would just be a minute. Johanna was watching her, saying something to Tom that made him shrug. As James waited for her decision, Julia watched Johanna take off her sweater, fold it, unzip her suitcase to place it on top. She watched Johanna undo the brown suede belt cinching her long blouse. She watched Johanna try to smooth out the wrinkles of her blouse with her hands. She watched her redo the belt. She watched her say something else to Tom, and she kept watching as they walked off a few paces to look at something in the distance. Maybe I should tell her that I know, Julia thought. Just to see her face.

'We're coming,' Julia said. 'Unless we hit serious traffic, we'll be there in less than an hour.' She flipped her phone closed and rejoined Johanna and Tom.

'Anything wrong?' Johanna asked, again letting her eyes search Julia's body from head to toe. Julia was glad she'd gone out and bought a new outfit for the day, something more flattering than the conservative suits hanging in her closet.

'Not a thing,' Julia said. She scanned the rows of cars and tried to remember where she'd parked.

'You're very tall,' Johanna said. 'Very good-looking. You have a lovely face, like your father. I'm sure he's still handsome.'

Julia was prepared to be protective of Greta, but she had forgotten that Michael would need protecting too. Not from insult – it was already clear that Johanna would be careful not to hurt them – but from claim. Earlier, when Johanna first asked for her parents, Julia imagined herself standing in front of Greta in a defensive stance, feet apart, hands on hips. Now she saw herself reach forward and pull her father back to stand beside her mother, to huddle together behind the boundary Julia had drawn, a limit that would not be passable.

'I thought we just decided she looks like herself,' Tom said.

'Greta knows, doesn't she?' Johanna asked abruptly. 'About us coming?' She looked intently into Julia's face.

'Of course,' Julia said. 'She can't stop talking about it.'

'Can she not?' Johanna asked softly. It was a gentle admonishment, but one Julia did not miss. The message was clear. Johanna would do this – walk into a party where she was not invited – but she would not be spoken to like a fool. Julia felt as if she'd been slapped on the wrist. Don't tell me about my sister, Johanna's tone said. I know her better than you think.

But then, as soon as the moment began to feel too awkward to slip by without acknowledgment, Johanna nodded, resumed her story about the movie they'd watched on the plane. It was not indifference to the enormity of the day, Julia realized. It was determination to keep the moment light. If this woman ever cried, Julia concluded, she did so privately and made sure the tear tracks were gone before she saw another soul. 'The main woman is just recently divorced and puts a notice in the paper advertising herself . . .' Julia watched as the woman who gave birth to her chattered on, ran her hand through her thick hair, tried to puff it up a bit, switched the pull handle of her case from left hand to right.

This is my mother, Julia thought as she tried not to stare. This woman with impeccable posture who keeps looking down at her pants as if to make sure the crease is still sharp carried me in her belly and pushed me out through the birth canal. She pushed and pushed and tore and bled until I landed in Greta's lap. And then she went away.

Greta, who was only sixteen. Greta, who once told Julia that having a baby so young felt a little like playing pretend and how impressed she was with herself when she realized that she could buy Julia's clothes at the secondhand stores on the Upper East Side, where the quality was better than buying new clothes at the cheap stores. Figuring that out, she once told Julia, gave her courage. Not because of the clothes, but because it was a good idea and she'd thought of it. Greta, who'd laughed as she recalled how she used to mash up whatever she and Michael were eating for dinner and try to feed it to Julia, until Mrs Kline down the hall told Greta the baby was too young, far too young. That child needs breast milk for another four months, the old woman had said, and then frowned when Greta explained to her – and later explained to Julia – that her milk had dried up early on. How on Sundays she and Michael used to take Julia on walks around the neighborhood and fold back the hood of the carriage so anyone who wanted to could have a look.

'How long has it been, exactly?' Julia asked as she opened the trunk and Tom stacked their cases one on top of the other. While sitting at the café, Julia had calculated the years almost to the day.

'A long time,' Johanna said, and daintily held the belt of her tunic as she climbed into the backseat of the car.

'But how long?' Julia pressed. 'Have you added it up? You must have. All those hours on the plane. Forty years? A little more than forty years?'

'You know . . .' Tom said as he climbed into the backseat beside his sister. He was most of the way in before Julia saw where he was going, and she decided not to point out that he should sit in the front. 'A farmer once found a pig in the bogs of Ballyroan that had been there for more than five hundred years. At first he thought it must be one of his own, sunk down the season before, that he'd never noticed missing, and the people who saw it said it looked no worse off than a pig who might've died the day before. Scientists came to look at it and everything.'

'And?' Julia said as she turned the ignition of the car. In the rear-view mirror she saw him give Johanna two quick pats on the knee before clasping his hands in his own lap.

'And that's it. End of story. Time is a funny thing.'

Seventeen

The plane had been delayed. There was traffic on the bridge. Johanna called James to say that they might make it before the end of the party, and they might not. Greta dreaded the thought of them walking in like everyone else, having to see each other for the first time in front of so many people who had no idea what it meant. She also dreaded having them walk into a near-empty house, with no one there for her to hide behind. She stopped herself from looking out the window every minute. She tried to keep busy. Once in a while she walked down the hall to her bedroom, shut the door, and looked again at the constellations Johanna had drawn on the back of the envelope Greta still had not opened. The envelope was light in her palm, and Greta doubted it was more than one page. There's nothing in here that won't be said in person this weekend, she thought each time she replaced it on her nightstand. Nothing here that won't be said a hundred times.

As far as Greta could tell, everyone who'd been invited to the party had come. The sandhogs were all freshly scrubbed, shaved, tucked into slacks and dress shirts. Some were wearing sport jackets despite the warm day. The wives kept sizing up their husbands, as if searching for that last unsightly gash across the knuckles he'd forgotten to bandage, that patch of dried mud he hadn't gotten out of his hair. The rest of the party was made up of people they'd known from Eighty-fourth Street and people they'd met at socials at various Irish cultural centers over the years. They'd made friends in Recess — mostly the parents of James's and Eavan's classmates — but those friendships had faded as soon as the children grew up and moved away. None were so close that Greta felt she should invite them to the party, and none of them would have fit in. As James once pointed out, all anyone talked about at these parties was Ireland. When they'd last been home. When they were going home next. They bragged about how much home had pulled itself up and dusted itself off since they left. Paul McCartney had gotten married at home. Some famous actor had been looking to buy a derelict castle in Connemara. All the Hollywood types went golfing at home now. Best golf courses in the world. No need to leave home nowadays, these exiles said. No way. No better place in the world. No more Irish pouring into New York without two pennies to rub against each other. The ones who come now go straight to Wall Street or to some other job in downtown Manhattan.

'I have a job in downtown Manhattan,' one of the older sandhogs pointed out. Most of the men had partial hearing loss, so they turned and asked each other, 'What? What did he say?' The joke was repeated, louder.

The younger sandhogs, and the grown children of the older sand-hogs, and the friends from Eighty-fourth Street who'd all emigrated from somewhere else, if not Ireland, listened closely to the talk of home, watched as the men and women who'd lost very few notes of their accents seemed to swagger as they regaled each other with stories of million-dollar condos at Salt Hill, an article that said Dublin restaurants were now as good as those in New York or London. Not as good, Mrs Quinn corrected. Better. Far better.

It was the kind of talk Greta didn't always understand. She thought of home too, but not in the America versus Ireland way the rest of them seemed to. Greta had never been to Dublin, had never been to Cork City, had never even left Connaught before she placed her bag on the berth she'd stayed curled up in until the ship docked in New York City. She didn't follow Irish politics except to send fifty dollars a year to help the children orphaned by the troubles in the north. She'd lived in Ireland for sixteen years. She'd been living in New York now for almost forty-four. When she thought of home, it wasn't a country she thought of, but a cottage, a turf fire, the sea, tea leaves at the bottom of the cup, the flowers of the hawthorn bush that looked so pretty but smelled not unlike a piece of meat left to rot in the sun. Every spring they bloomed like a nasty trick. She thought of that tin box she used to keep under her bed. Her box of treasures. Bits and pieces she'd hoarded just to have a collection of something, of anything. And Johanna, of course, in the foreground of every single memory. Johanna in bed beside her, Johanna striding ahead of her to school, Johanna naked on the beach, the brine turning to salt on her skin, which she always licked once before dusting off. At home, time had stopped in 1963. Greta couldn't picture new construction, paved roads with lines painted down the middle, the Catholic Church without its power. She saw only the cottage, still trying to keep from being swallowed up by the sea.

And now, she supposed, she should erase the cottage too and replace it with a big modern house. Maybe a two-story house. Maybe a built-on section for Little Tom to find peace and quiet. Maybe they'd left the cottage where it was, turned it into a stable. Maybe Johanna's two boys had the run of the place. She wondered if the two Rafferty boys had walked all the way to Conch to go to school, if they'd heard of their aunt in America, if, when they were growing up, they'd ever heard Julia's name whispered after they'd been sent to bed. She wondered if people passed through Ballyroan now and said to each other, 'That's the Rafferty place.'

Greta didn't think of herself as an American, but America had been good to her. It bothered the others, Greta had realized a few years earlier, that Ireland ended up doing so well. They were proud, of course, but also taken completely by surprise. They'd worked so hard to bring Ireland to America as an intact place that they could live inside, and they had succeeded, keeping their customs the same as they were in the year they'd left, making the preservation of the old ways a new kind of religion. They didn't realize until it was too late that home had moved on, grown up, left the old customs behind. It was as if these exiles had used every last dollar to bet on a horse they didn't own, didn't love, weren't interested in loving, but one that had promised to give them the best return. It was as if that horse had been winning, as expected, for the entire race. Winning by yards, in fact. A seemingly untouchable distance. And just as they bent their heads to calculate their earnings, that horse was left behind by the wild card, the underdog, the one they'd have preferred to lay their bet down for in the first place.

The questions they put to one another were always the same. If you'd known, would you have left? If you had to wait thirty years for the boom to arrive, for the Celtic Tiger to stride across your land, would you have stuck it out? Or would you have still gotten on that ship or that airplane and headed for New York City?

And if you did leave for America, would you have stayed? Knowing about the boom to come? Or would you have worked for a few years and then taken your American dollars and gone back home to stretch those dollars out until prosperity arrived?

I would have gone back, almost all of them said, shaking their heads, describing to one another what they would have done instead. How they would have waited out the hard years. The kind of patience they would have been capable of had they known there was an eventual end.

I would have stayed here, Greta always said. Michael too.

Even if you could have gone back to a good job in Ireland?

Yes.

Even if it meant you would have been able to build a house in Ireland like the ones in America? Could have sent the children to university?

Yes. Yes.

Once in a while Greta turned the question around. Why not go back now? she asked. There's nothing stopping you. Go build yourself a house in the old country. You can get your American pension and the dole on top of that.

And this was another thing she noticed. The moment Ireland became possible again was the very same moment most of them accepted the fact that they'd never move back for good.

'Do you love America as much as you love Ireland?' Ned Powers asked her once. They were sitting on the deck, and before answering, Greta glanced down at the foot of his chair and counted five amber bottles. Michael had gone up to the store to buy a piece of meat for the grill.

'Love?' Greta had asked, smirking, hoping to tease him out of this seriousness Ned had about him lately. Sometimes he and Michael would sit out on the deck for hours, not saying a word.

'I don't know America any more than I know Ireland,' she said. 'New York, New Jersey, yes. But the rest might as well be another country altogether.'

'Yes, but if you had to choose.'

'What do you mean if I had to choose? I did have to choose. So did Michael. So did you.'

'I don't understand you,' Ned had said. 'Neither of you.'

'Come here to me now,' Oran Quinn said to Eavan, putting a heavy arm around her shoulders. 'Will you take that *gasúr* home to see where she's from, or will you do like your mam and da and only tell stories?' He stood back and sized her up. 'You have, let's see now, four months left? Five? She's due in – no, let me guess – September? Your mam's people are from the west, aren't they? Plenty of room to run around.'

'Oh,' Eavan said, looking first at Greta and then at James. 'I –'

'Eh?' Oran Quinn said, leaning in to hear her better. 'Didn't they ever bring you home at all? I suppose when you have the map on your face like your mam does, you don't need to go home too much. I've gone home every year for the past twenty years. Did you know that?'

Eavan shook her head, looked at James, closed her eyes, and hoped that Gary would hurry up with the extra bags of ice he was emptying into the coolers outside so he could come in and stand beside her.

'Don't you young people want to go see where you're from?'

'We're from New York,' James piped up from across the room. 'The Big Apple.'

'That's where you live,' Oran Quinn corrected. 'Only where you live, boy. My Frank thought the same as you, and then he brought his little boy over to Donegal last summer. Do you know what they said to him in the shop right there in Killybegs? They said "Welcome home." Now look, Frank had only been over a few times, and it was the boy's first time, but that's what they said to him. Welcome home. They knew by his face and his name that that's the only place he could be from. Four hundred years the Quinns were in Killybegs. Four hundred years of being reared and married and raising a family in Killybegs. Until July tenth, 1968. The day myself and Maude left for America. You think four hundred years can be erased in forty?'

'No,' Eavan said, as if she were ten years old again, being lectured by an adult for some childish indiscretion.

Maude Quinn turned to the woman next to her and said in a loud voice, 'It's a new thing with him. He likes to give long speeches at parties. Must be old age.'

Oran wagged a finger at his wife, but stepped back, smiled, freed Eavan from the iron trap of his arm.

'Now tell me this, Oran,' Greta said, circling the group, a glass of white wine in her hand. As Gary once pointed out to Eavan, Greta didn't walk, she crept. Careful, deliberate, like an animal trying not to make a noise. She glided through the small dining room, around the clusters of people gathered in the living room, her drink held out in front of her so she could be sure not to tip it onto the carpet, her other arm raised slightly, as if she was trying to make a space for herself, the stem of a ship leading the body through water. Though it was too soon to be possible, Eavan could almost swear she felt the baby move in her stomach as her mother cleared her throat. Outside, the street was quiet. The cars had stopped arriving. James was holding his cell phone in his hand, waiting, glancing at it now and again to make sure there was a signal.

'Tell me just one thing,' Greta said, walking up to Oran Quinn, setting her drink down on a side table, and putting her hands on her hips. 'You tell me how you know it's a girl. Have you been consulting the cards?' she asked. 'Because I think it's a boy.'

Everyone looked at Eavan's belly.

'He has the gift,' Mary Monahan called out, and everyone roared laughing. James hushed them, and they tried to laugh more quietly. 'Isn't it true, Oran? Wasn't your mam or your grandmammy one of the walking people?'

'You're completely daft, Mary,' Oran said, smiling thinly. Everyone laughed harder when they saw that he was offended. 'Didn't I just say the Quinns have always been Donegal people?' He raised his glass to toast himself.

'It *is* a girl,' Eavan said, smiling into her cup of ice water. 'I found out yesterday.' Those within reach clapped Oran on the back as if he had something to do with it. Eavan looked over at Greta and shrugged. 'I was going to tell you later.'

From the back door, Gary stood on his tiptoes and grinned over at his wife.

'Okay, people,' James shouted, snapping his cell phone closed. 'Get away from the windows. He's coming. He's two blocks away.'

Laughter breeds more laughter, Greta thought. It was something she'd learned in church as a girl when the teacher would march everyone in the schoolhouse across the square, two abreast, for first Friday Mass. Only in church would she giggle at something that wouldn't have even made her smile if she hadn't been stuck in such a solemn situation, if so much hadn't depended on good behavior. Johanna once laughed so hard during the consecration that the priest looked down from the altar and singled her out. It wasn't the laughter that gave her away so much as the loud gasp for breath she had to take after struggling for so long to stay silent. Father kept both Johanna and Greta after and wrote a note for Johanna to show their parents. As he scribbled Johanna's crime on thick cream-colored paper that looked and smelled to Greta like Mass itself, he used the time to point out that even though Lily and Tom Cahill had put themselves in mortal danger by not attending Mass every week and showing a bad example to their children, if they had any sense at all, they'd take Johanna's behavior seriously. Not showing them his note, he warned Johanna, would be a grave sin.

'But not a mortal sin,' Johanna had chirped on the way home. Later, after the note had been read aloud, Big Tom demanded to know what she'd found so funny. Johanna couldn't remember exactly. 'Nothing,' she'd said finally. 'Only the bench squealed a little when Sister Agatha sat on it.'

Big Tom had taken a big puff from his pipe, leaned back in his chair, and said, 'You're a silly sort of a girl, aren't you?' He said it as though he'd diagnosed something fatal, and just like that, as if he'd reached over and flipped a switch, Johanna started giggling again.

Now that the laughter had started, it was impossible to trap and stifle. Hands were clapped over mouths as everyone, old and young, crouched down and squeezed into the back half of the house. 'I have to tinkle,' one of the women said, and someone snorted. 'I always have to tinkle at these parties. As soon as we have to hide.'

'Why do only women tinkle?' a male voice whispered. 'Men don't tinkle; they only piss.'

'Some men tinkle,' another man said, and Greta shushed them. The engine of Michael's Toyota drew closer and closer. It turned into the driveway, which they'd made sure to keep clear of cars. Even without seeing him – without seeing much of anything in fact, she was squeezed so tight between two sets of tweed-covered shoulders – Greta could feel him hesitate. She could see him standing in the driveway and surveying the cars lining the curb, listening for the sounds of a party somewhere on the block. Greta had planted a seed a few days earlier, looking up casually from her toast and jam and commenting, 'The graduation parties will be starting soon, I suppose.'

He'd nodded. 'That time of year, isn't it?'

The crowd, with its collective held breath, began to grow impatient. 'What's taking him so long?' a woman whispered. 'Is he out there having a sleep?'

'I might have a sleep if he doesn't come in soon.'

'Hush,' another said.

Had he figured it out? Greta wondered. It had been a strange week overall. A strange few months. At first he'd been so happy with his decision to retire, so excited to make plans to rent a car and drive west. But then as the day got closer, he seemed troubled by his decision. People asked him what he'd do with all his free time, and he seemed at a loss. Back in 1970, when he'd first gotten a job in the water tunnels, he'd signed on with the belief that he would stay only six months. It was an in-between kind of job, he told Greta. Not the kind of job a man could do for life.

'Should you go out, Mom?' Eavan whispered from somewhere behind Greta. 'Should I?'

'No. Just give him a minute.'

They gave him a minute, but still nothing.

'Okay,' Greta said, pushing her way out of the cluster. 'Everyone stay where you are.' Greta walked quickly to the living-room window and looked out. She saw his car, saw that it was empty, but she didn't see Michael. She walked down the steps to the screen door. She pushed it open and stepped outside.

'Michael?' she called. 'Is that you?' She walked down the front path, taking one glance back at the house and noticing how quiet it seemed, how empty. Maybe he'd be fooled after all. She peered in the passenger's window of his car and saw the plastic bag filled with his dirty work clothes.

'Where are you?' she called.

'Over here,' came the answer, closer than she expected. She whirled around, saw him crouched at the side of the house. He was holding a small Phillips-head screwdriver, one of the many tools he kept in his car, and was using it to clean under his fingernails. He held his hands up to her for inspection. She held her palms out flat, and he put his hands on top.

'They're fine,' she said, looking at him carefully. She licked her thumb and reached over to smooth down an errant lock of hair at the back of his head. 'You're grand,' she said. He tucked in his shirt at the back.

'How did you know?' she asked.

'Greta,' he said, looking up at the blank face of the side of the house, the single window, their bedroom. He tilted his head up further as if to examine the line of the roof. Greta followed his gaze, searched for whatever he was searching for. They hadn't outgrown the house. When the value of the houses in their town had gone up, other people on the block had cashed out, moved away to bigger places. But the Wards had stayed, year in and year out, and the house always seemed just enough to hold them.

'What will I say?' Michael asked.

'Just smile and say hello to everyone. They'll do the talking. They're keyed up already. It's only people you know. Only people you'd want to see. Trust me. It's only your friends, Michael. They know you.'

'Who?'

Greta rattled off the names as they came to her and watched as the worry lines around Michael's eyes relaxed. A few more names, and she wondered if he was paying attention; he seemed preoccupied, distant, as if he'd moved on to thinking of other things.

'So,' she said, cutting the list short when she saw that he was no longer paying attention. 'Are you right?'

'Right as rain,' he said, and took her slim hand in his. 'I'll act surprised, will I?'

'They know I'm out here telling you.'

'Fair enough. Plan foiled.'

'There's one more thing,' Greta said. 'And this is a surprise to both of us, believe me.'

Michael looked up, gently dropped her hand, waited. He looked like his father now, Greta noticed once again. Better-looking, but still, his features were becoming an inheritance he had no choice but to accept. Greta remembered Dermot on the day he took his wife's body away from their little cottage. It was shocking to think he was probably twenty years younger on that day than she was right now.

'It's the children. They did something.'

'Threw me a party.'

'Well, yes, that. But they did something else. They wrote to Ballyroan. To Johanna. Asked her to come today. To the party. Are you following? Johanna wrote back to say yes, and where do you think Julia is right this moment but transporting them from the airport. Tom too. They're on their way, Michael.'

'Johanna and Tom?' Michael repeated. He whistled, shook his head. 'Well, that is a surprise,' he agreed. 'There's traffic. A jackknifed tractor-trailer just before the bridge.'

Greta put her hands to her head, pressed her first two fingers to her temples. 'Is that all you have to say? We don't know what they've been writing back and forth about. Julia too. Julia and Johanna have been writing back and forth. For weeks now. Maybe for longer. I don't know. I've just learned of all this myself.'

'So you think she's told Julia? Is that it?'

'What if she did?'

'She wouldn't. Besides, Julia is more than forty years old. No one's going to take her away from you now. No one's going to put a claim on her but herself.'

'What does that have to do with anything? I don't know what you're talking about. How can we say what Johanna would or wouldn't do? I haven't spoken to her in nearly thirty years. Jesus, thirty years. Think of Julia, finding out something like this at her age.'

'Maybe she forgot. It's possible, isn't it? I never think about it.'

Greta looked at him closely, but couldn't tell if he was serious. 'No, Michael. It isn't possible.'

'Greta, love,' Michael said, reaching down to pick at some weeds. 'Let's just go in to the party. They're waiting for us.'

'I don't understand you,' Greta said. Michael put his arm around her shoulder, led her toward the front of the house and the door.

'A shame Lily couldn't have come,' he said. 'It would be lovely to see her again.' Greta stopped, turned to face him. 'Lily? My mother?' she asked, struggling to keep her voice down. She put her face just an inch from his.

'Michael,' she said, gently slapping his face. Once, twice, three times — the slaps got a little harder each time. 'Lily is dead. Lily has been dead for a long time. Don't you remember Lily dying and Julia taking the message and me telling you when you got home?'

'Jesus, Greta.' Michael caught both of her wrists in one of his hands. 'I was only saying if she was alive, she would have loved to come for a visit. Remember how we used to say we'd pay her way out? It's a shame we never did that. She would have seen Julia was ours if she'd come. Would have seen Julia was happy and all the talk about sending her home would have stopped. Maybe. I don't know. She would have liked to see where you live and the children and the city and all that. I was only just saying.' He released her wrists and rubbed his arm where she pinched him. 'Jesus Christ,' he muttered. 'Are you crazy?'

'Sorry,' Greta said. 'I'm so sorry, Michael.' She reached and touched his face again, this time to soothe it. 'I misunderstood.'

As they stood there, Ned Powers pulled into the driveway, hopped out of his car, walked across the lawn with his car keys swinging on his index finger. 'Cat's out of the bag, is it? Well, we tried.'

'Ned,' Michael said, 'I watched you in my rearview the whole way. I went through that light on Central so I'd lose you. Didn't you think it odd I sped through that light?'

Inside, the welcome was thunderous. Some stayed on script and shouted, 'Surprise!' Many others just shouted, or roared, as it sounded to Greta. Wineglasses shook on their stems, the liquid inside lapped at the rim of each glass as if the house had suddenly taken sail on a blustery day. The floor trembled. They attacked Michael one by one, and Greta hung back as he was swept away from her. They clapped his back, grabbed and shook his hand. The women banged against his cheekbone as they leaned in for a kiss. He was pulled into the kitchen, pushed out onto the deck, called back into the dining room to be patted and prodded some more. You knew, they accused him. They recalled stories of running into him in town, on the job, at a card game, and almost but not quite mentioning the party. You knew all along, did you? they asked, and he explained about the cars, about Ned staying so close, and they smacked their heads and laughed. Through all of this, Greta stayed rooted where she stood. Then, as she knew he would, she saw him looking for her. 'Greta?' he called over the tops of his friends' heads. 'Has anyone seen Greta?'

The party went by quickly once the guest of honor arrived. Michael shut the door on the last of the guests just before nine o'clock. Greta waved from the window, but she couldn't see them wave back, as bright as the room was lit, as dark as the evening was outside. They might have stayed longer if Ciaran Hughes hadn't started singing. Greta had heard him clear his throat, had observed as he threw out his chest, closed his eyes. He wouldn't, she thought. Would he? 'Oh Lord,' someone said, winking at Greta before sneaking into the next room. He ignored his wife, who snatched his glass out of his hand, and started with something lively that Greta couldn't place. People stamped their feet through the chorus. He sang another after that, and everyone joined in. Michael, Greta noticed, knew both. But of course the performance had ended up where all vocal performances seemed to end up in Greta's experience – by a lonely prison wall, the low-lying fields of Athenry. When he finished, the guests began placing their small plates on any surface they could find. They tipped back the last drops left in their glasses. Those who'd arrived wearing jackets asked Eavan where they might find them. On their way out, the sandhogs told Michael they'd be seeing him soon.

'Well,' Michael said, sinking into his familiar armchair. Eavan and Gary were sprawled out on the couch, Greta on the armchair opposite Michael. James was stretched out on the floor. Nicole had already gone back to Brooklyn to walk the dog she and James had gotten a few months earlier, a puppy prone to peeing on the carpet if not walked on a precise schedule.

'Well, what?' Eavan prompted him. Greta tilted her head to read Michael's expression. During the course of the night she'd had to remind him of quite a few names. Wives, mostly. He only saw them once a year, if that often. Perfectly understandable. She could barely remember everyone's name herself. But once, as Greta was coming up the stairs with two more bottles of wine, she'd caught him standing between two groups, looking left and right at the broad backs of his friends, his brow wrinkled in confusion. He looked stormy, ready to lash out, as he did on those mornings when he sat staring at the steering wheel of his car until Greta rushed outside with his keys clutched in her fist. He'd never been an angry person. Only rarely had she ever heard him shout at the children, and this new side of him, the Michael that snapped and grabbed and spoke over her in cross tones, was another inheritance he couldn't refuse.

She'd kept watching him, clutching the bottles in her hands until, like a child, he lifted his arm, buried his face for a moment in the crook of his elbow, then wiped his mouth with the entire length of his sleeve. 'Ah!' he said when he saw her, the storm clouds passing, his face breaking out in a broad grin. He crossed the room, took the bottles from her, and placed them on the floor by the wall. He took her by the hand and led her along with him as he moved from cluster to cluster, thrusting his head into conversations, squeezing her fingers now and again as if to remind himself she was still there.

Greta had also noticed that Ned Powers paid close attention to his old friend. He made sure to use names when he brought Michael up to speed. 'Burke was just saying . . . Dunleavy claims . . .' Watching them interact, these men who had labored alongside each other, argued with each other, thrown punches at each other, defended each other for years, Greta got an idea about how their solution to Michael's increasing forgetfulness might have worked down in the tunnels. No one would have mentioned it, she saw. Not to Michael and not to each other. But every single one of them recognized that same blank look that Greta thought she alone could see. 'Ward,' one of them said, 'remember the time you set the fuse too short and nearly blasted everyone up to the sidewalk?'

Michael stared at the speaker, watched his friend's mouth shape the words, grinned vacantly when he sensed it was his turn to react. He's winging it, Greta saw.

'Yes,' another said. 'It was the afternoon shift, five or six years ago . . .'

One by one they filled him in until Michael's face came alive again and he grabbed hold of some detail and ran with it, adding his part of the day.

Ned Powers had become a surrogate uncle to the children over the years. His wife had never returned from Ireland, but he'd never divorced her. He claimed he'd stopped drinking but didn't believe beer counted as real alcohol. It wasn't unusual to listen to him reflect on the days before he quit drinking, just as he was twisting open a bottle. Michael claimed he never smelled booze on him on the job anymore. Ned flew home to see his daughter twice a year.

'Ned,' Greta had said soon after Michael's arrival, catching Ned alone by the buffet. His small plate was already overloaded with shrimp, cocktail sauce, crackers, cheese. 'Have you noticed anything off with Michael in these past few months?' Longer, she added silently.

'No,' Ned said without taking his eyes off the spread before him. His answer was firm, resolute. He would not elaborate. The thought came to Greta so plainly it almost made her laugh: he knew before I did. She looked around at the rest of the men, their faces red and raw from the cold and damp of their workplace, the skin around their eyes grooved from squinting in the dark.

'I can't send back the gifts, can I?' Michael asked finally, eyeing the pile on the coffee table.

'No, Dad,' Eavan said.

'You can re-gift them,' James said. 'You'll probably go to a zillion of these over the next year or so.'

'Re-gift?' Michael asked.

'You know, wrap up the ones you don't want and give them to someone else.'

'That's rude,' Eavan said.

'Why?' Michael and James asked at the same time, Michael's

expression honestly curious about why this would be considered rude, James's expression fully aware of the etiquette but calling it ridiculous.

Greta half listened to Eavan explain. She thought she heard a car stop outside the house, and she was tempted to cup her hands around her eyes and press her face to the glass. She tuned back in when she heard the car pass by.

'They're still coming,' James said to Greta, interrupting Eavan. He leaned up on one elbow, bent one leg at the knee. 'When they finally got over the bridge, they decided they'd be better off going to the hotel first, freshening up. Then they figured they'd better get something to eat rather than show up starving.' James looked at his watch. 'Julia called about an hour ago and said they were still coming.'

'They're staying at a hotel?' Michael asked. 'But why? With three empty beds here?' He looked at Greta. 'Seems like a shame, doesn't it?'

For Greta, it seemed as if no time had passed since her whispered conversation with Michael at the side of the house. Just like that, the party was reduced to a noisy flash, a scene she'd walked through to get from there to here. 'Michael,' Greta said for the second time that day, 'I don't understand you.' She stood and began collecting the refuse of the party. Napkins and plates left on tables, pieces of pretzel on the floor. When she couldn't hold any more in her hands, she went to the kitchen and got a plastic bag.

'It would have been better,' Greta said after a few minutes, 'if they'd arrived during the party. If they'd just walked in like everyone else.' Now that this possibility had disappeared, she decided it would have been best. She looked up at the clock on the wall. 'It might be midnight before they come.'

During the party she kept finding errands to bring her down to the basement. More soda, more beer, more paper plates. Once down there, she stood in the dark and looked out the single basement window that was so high she had to stand on a chair. The window was level with the ground outside. When no cars passed, the world outside as dark and still as it was on any Friday night, Greta found herself staring at individual blades of grass just inches from her nose, the few stray dandelions that had popped up here and there. Once in a while the grass would sway and bend, the blanket of lawn rippling in a pattern that swirled toward the house and then away. In America they call that a breeze, Greta thought. In Ballyroan they never said the word breeze. The wind coming up from the ocean was either so strong you had to put your shoulder to it or it wasn't worth mentioning. 'Tie up that hair,' Lily used to shout at them in the mornings. And at night she'd sit Johanna and Greta in front of the fire and tug at knots twisted by the wind, pulled tight by the heavy salt air.

'So what if it is midnight?' Michael said, addressing the whole room.

Eavan sat up. 'Oh, I almost forgot,' she said to Michael. 'You weren't here yet when we told everyone that we found out the baby is a girl. Mr Quinn guessed it, and he was right.'

'Oh, that's right,' Greta said, glad of the distraction. 'He wasn't here.' She turned to Michael, 'So what do you think of that?'

'A girl,' Michael repeated, and rubbed the faint stubble on his face. His family waited as Michael accepted the information like a puzzle piece that had no matching shape on the board. If he were drowning right this minute, Greta thought, and I threw him a rope, I wonder would he know what to do.

Eavan took a breath and seemed to consider what she would say. She put her hand on her belly and spread her fingers wide. 'Gary and I are expecting, Dad. You know that. I'm due in October.' There was no pain in her tone, no surprise, only patience and determination. 'Gary and I are going to have a baby girl, and you're going to be a grandfather.'

When Eavan stopped speaking, she reached over and pressed her hand against Gary's leg. They've talked about it at home, Greta saw. They've pushed away their dinner plates and said to each other, something is wrong.

'Yes, that's right,' Michael said. He placed his arms precisely along the arms of the chair. He brought his knees together. He straightened his back. He cleared his throat. He gazed at the wall behind Eavan as if the plaster and drywall had been torn away and replaced with a vision that drained him, left him in a stupor. Greta braced herself for the list of excuses he always presented whenever he felt backed into a corner, whenever she held her breath and pointed out that he was forgetting an awful lot lately. He was exhausted. He was preoccupied. He was distracted. He was too old to be working down in the tunnels anymore. When he stopped working, he'd get better. She'd see. When he didn't say any of this, she looked closely at the baffled expression that was becoming more familiar to her with each passing week. As clearly as she saw it on the sandhogs' faces, she saw it on Michael's as well. He knows.

Gary excused himself to go out to the deck for a cigarette.

Michael brought one hand to his shirt pocket, felt for his handkerchief. Leaving it where he found it, he ran the same hand through his hair, smoothing it down at the back. Then he stood and walked toward the kitchen. 'Are there any more of them bacon things?' he asked. Greta, Eavan, and James listened as he pulled trays from the fridge and unwrapped them to see what they contained. They heard him punching buttons on the microwave and a faint whir as the appliance sprang to life.

'I like to touch him when I remind him of something,' Greta said. 'I think it helps. Sometimes I pinch him or step on his toe. Sometimes I make him repeat what I've just told him.'

'I wish you wouldn't do that, Mom,' James said. 'It won't help. Julia knows a neurologist in White Plains. We were thinking he should go in the next few weeks, you know, now that he's finished working.'

'You were thinking? How long ago did you notice?' Greta asked James. He shrugged, looked over at Eavan.

'How long ago did *you* notice?' Eavan asked as she roused herself from her nest on the couch, one hand canvassing her belly, the other firmly planted in the cushion to give her leverage. She headed toward the back door to follow Gary, saying as she walked, 'You'll need help, Mom. Not yet, but in a little while.' James jumped up from his position on the floor, said, 'She's right,' waited a few seconds with his arms folded across his chest, and then yawned and left the room. A moment later Greta heard the television spring to life in his old bedroom.

I'll need help, Greta repeated to herself. How grown up these kids have become. How like adults, though they've never had a thing to worry about in their lives. For the first time in many years, she thought of her father's body laid out on his bed, his limbs gone slack like a drunk she'd once seen being carried through Conch, moaning, his cap pulled low on his face. She knew when she first heard the gunshot. She knew when they carried him inside. She knew the next morning, when the air in the cottage felt a touch too dense, like a great storm was coming even though the sky was blue. In the years between then and now, she'd added details – not a single leaf left on the trees, the fire cracking and popping as if it wanted to say something, unnerving her so much that she refused to sit by it even when Lily begged her, even when her toes and fingers felt as cold as the iron hooks of the old net, left all night to soak up black water while the salmon and the minnows swam all around.

What they must have said about Lily at home after she and Johanna left. How the Cahill girls had run off with a tinker. It's no wonder, they would have said, without faith, without schooling, backward as they'd grown out there alone in Ballyroan. How Lily must have steeled herself against their talk whenever she went in to town.

'Do you really think they'll still come tonight?' Greta asked loudly, calling the question out to the corners of the house where they'd disappeared to wait. If not tonight, then tomorrow. If not tomorrow, then the next day. If not the next day, then the one after that. It would not be possible to avoid them, and as Greta listened to Michael move about the kitchen, open and close cabinets, riffle through the cutlery drawer for something he would not find, Greta began to want to see them. Not talk, not yet, but see. Little Tom as a man in his seventies. Johanna as a mother of young men.

'Greta?' Michael called. 'I need you a minute.' Greta was tugged out of her chair by his voice, drawn into the kitchen by the whiff of panic in his tone.

'What do I eat this with?' he demanded, waving his arm over the table, where he'd laid out and unwrapped every leftover Greta and Eavan had packed away. Above his feast he held two knives, one in each hand.

'I guess all the forks are dirty. You can use –' Greta meant to reach above the refrigerator for the container of plastic cutlery, but out of habit she opened the drawer instead. There, clean, shining, were more than a dozen forks. She plucked one out and handed it to him. In return, he handed her his extra knife.

'Perfect,' he said, and began fishing strawberries from the fruit salad.

'Did you not look in the drawer already, Michael? Did I not hear you rooting around?'

He looked up with a full mouth, not quite sure what she was asking him. 'You're tired, Greta,' he said. 'Sit down. Have something to eat.'

As Michael chewed, he remembered a little girl standing by a river, arms raised, eyes closed tight. The girl's name was Greta, he knew very well, and she was the same as this Greta whose two eyes watched him eat from behind glasses he didn't recognize.

'I hear something,' James called through the house. 'Julia's car. It's stopping. It's them.'

Greta took a breath and stood.

'A bit late, isn't it?' Michael asked as he reached across the table for more fruit. He saw that Greta had gone pale, that her lips had become a single thin stroke of red in the middle of her face. He watched as she stood and swept her hands over the front of her sweater, her hips, the thighs of her pants, as if she were brushing away crumbs only she could see. He watched her walk away from the table. He watched her walk across the kitchen. He leaned back in his chair and watched her walk down the hall to the door, which jingled when she pulled it open.

'My God,' he heard her say. 'Oh my God.'

'Greta,' they said together, then Johanna alone, then Tom alone, then together again. They shouted the word at her, as if they were telling her her own name. He heard Eavan and James emerge from their hiding places, stand together in view of the door, where they'd be seen and acknowledged.

'Come in,' Greta said in a strange voice. 'Please. Is it raining? I didn't realize it had started raining. You're pure soaked. Let's get you tea. Let's get you dry. Let's get you something to eat.'

Raining, Michael repeated to himself, tapping his fork against the rim of his bowl. That was it. That was the sound of running water he'd been hearing since the party ended. He held his breath and listened for it. Water charged through the gutters of the house, down the pipes, raced out to the sewers on the street with the speed and din of a great rushing river.

'Aren't we well used to the rain?' Johanna asked, and Michael listened to the click of her heels as she took a few steps inside the house.

'Michael?' Greta called to him. 'Are you there?'

He got up from the table to join her.

Acknowledgments

I sought out a number of people and organizations for help while writing this novel, and I extend my thanks to the Irish Centre for Migration Studies for their Breaking the Silence project, which added new dimensions to those narratives I'd heard all my life; the staff at the National Library of Ireland for their guidance and, most of all, for their assistance with the microfilm; the M.F.A. faculty at the University of Virginia for their support and encouragement even after I graduated from the program; the Alumnae Association of Barnard College for the AABC fellowship; the men of the New York City Sandhogs' Union (afternoon shift, August 2006, Thirtieth Street and Tenth Avenue), particularly Chris Fitzsimmons, for allowing me down into the tunnel and for answering my questions.

In addition, I must acknowledge the following sources, each of which rounded out my knowledge of the period and helped me imagine what these characters were up against: *Irish Travellers: Culture and Ethnicity,* published in 1994 by the Institute of Irish Studies, The Queen's University of Belfast; *Nan: The Life of an Irish Travelling Woman* by Sharon Gmelch; *Irish Travellers: Racism and the Politics of Culture* by Jane Helleiner; and *The Quiet Revolution: The Electrification of Rural Ireland, 1946–1976* by Michael J. Shiel.

I'm very grateful for the support of the following people: my agent, Chris Calhoun of Sterling Lord Literistic – I could not have found a better advocate; Mary Gordon, for help both tangible and intangible; my readers, Marty Hickey, Eleanor Henderson, and Callie Wright, whose feedback kept me on track through the early drafts; Jane Rosenman, for her editorial feedback on the later draft; Adrienne Brodeur, for shuttling *The Walking People* toward publication with so much care; my parents, Willie and Evelyn, and my sisters, Annette and Catherine.

Finally, and most important, thank you to Marty. You are the one person I know I could not have done this without.

If you loved *The Walking People*,
read on for an extract from *Ask Again, Yes*

'A novel of great compassion and understanding . . .
rich with story'
John Boyne, *Irish Times*

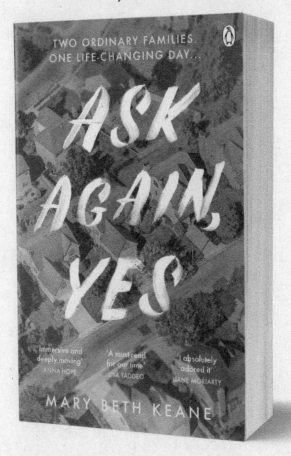

Prologue

July 1973

Francis Gleeson, tall and thin in his powder blue policeman's uniform, stepped out of the sun and into the shadow of the stocky stone building that was the station house of the Forty-First Precinct. A pair of pantyhose had been hung to dry on a fourth floor fire escape near 167th, and while he waited for another rookie, a cop named Stanhope, Francis noted the perfect stillness of those gossamer legs, the delicate curve where the heel was meant to be. Another building had burned the night before and Francis figured it was now like so many others in the Four-One: nothing left but a hollowed-out shell and a blackened staircase within. The neighborhood kids had all watched it burn from the roofs and fire escapes where they'd dragged their mattresses on that first truly hot day in June. Now, from a block away, Francis could hear them begging the firemen to leave just one hydrant open. He could imagine them hopping back and forth as the pavement grew hot again under their feet.

He looked at his watch and back at the station house door and wondered where Stanhope could be.

Eighty-eight degrees already and not even ten o'clock in the morning. This was the great shock of America, winters that would cut the face off a person, summers that were as thick and as soggy as bogs. 'You whine like a narrowback,' his uncle Patsy had said to him that morning. 'The heat, the heat, the heat.' But Patsy pulled pints inside a cool pub all day. Francis would be walking a beat, dark rings under his arms within fifteen minutes.

'Where's Stanhope?' Francis asked a pair of fellow rookies also heading out for patrol.

'Trouble with his locker, I think,' one said back.

Finally, after another whole minute ticked by, Brian Stanhope came bounding down the station house steps. He and Francis had met on the first day of academy, and it was by chance that they'd both ended up at the Four-One. In academy, they'd been in a tactics class together, and after a week or so Stanhope approached Francis as they were filing out the classroom door. 'You're Irish, right? Off the boat Irish, I mean?'

Francis said he was from the west, from Galway. And he'd taken a plane, but he didn't say that part.

'I thought so. So's my girlfriend. She's from Dublin. So let me ask you something.'

To Francis, Dublin felt as far from Galway as New York did, but to a Yank, he supposed, it was all the same.

Francis braced for something more personal than he wanted to be asked. It was one of the first things he'd noticed about America, that everyone felt at ease asking each other any question that came into their minds. Where do you live, who do you live with, what's your rent, what did you do last weekend? To Francis, who felt embarrassed lining up his groceries on the checkout belt of the Associated in Bay Ridge, it was all a little too much. 'Big night,' the checkout clerk had commented last time he was there. A six-pack of Budweiser. A pair of potatoes. Deodorant.

Brian said that he'd noticed his girl didn't hang around with any other Irish. She was only eighteen. You'd think she'd have come over with a friend or a cousin or something but she'd come alone. It seemed to him she could have at least found a bunch of Irish girls to live with. God knew they were all over the place. She was a nurse in training at Montefiore and lived in hospital housing with a colored girl, also a nurse. Was that the way it was for the Irish? Because he'd dated a Russian girl for a while and the only people she hung around with were other Russians.

'I'm Irish, too,' Stanhope said. 'But back a ways.'

That was another thing about America. Everyone was Irish, but back a ways.

'Might be a sign of intelligence, keeping away from our lot,' Francis said with a straight face. It took Stanhope a minute.

At graduation, Mayor Lindsay stood at the podium and from his third row seat Francis thought about how strange it was to see in person a man he'd only ever seen on TV. Francis had been born in New York, was taken back to Ireland as an infant, and had returned just before his nineteenth birthday with ten American dollars and citizenship. His father's brother, Patsy, had picked him up from JFK, taken Francis's duffel from his hand and thrown it on the backseat. 'Welcome home,' he'd said. The idea of this teeming, foreign place as home was mystifying. On his first full day in America, Patsy put him to work behind the bar at the pub he owned on Third Avenue and Eightieth Street in Bay Ridge. There was a framed shamrock over the door. The first time a woman came in and asked him for a beer, he'd taken out a highball glass and set it down in front of her. 'What's this?' she asked. 'A half beer?' She looked down the row at the other people sitting at the bar, all men, all with pints in front of them.

He'd shown her the pint glass. 'This is what you want?' he'd asked. 'The full of it?' And understanding, finally, that he was new to the bar, new to America, she'd leaned over to cup his face, to brush the hair off his forehead.

'That's the one, sweetie,' she'd said.

One day, when Francis had been in New York for about a year, a pair of young cops came in. They had a sketch of someone they were looking for, wanted to know if anyone at the bar recognized him. They joked around with Patsy, with Francis, with each other. When they were leaving, Francis mustered up some of that American inquisitiveness. How hard was it to get on the cops? How was the pay? For a few seconds their faces were inscrutable. It was February; Francis was wearing an old cable sweater that had been Patsy's, and felt shabby next to the officers in their pressed jackets, their caps that sat rightly atop their heads. Finally, the shorter of the two said that before becoming a cop he'd been working at his cousin's car wash on Flushing Avenue. Even when it all went automated, the sprayers would get him and in the winters he'd end the day frozen through. It was too brutal. Plus it was a lot better telling girls he was a cop than telling them he worked a car wash.

The other young cop looked a little disgusted. He'd joined because his father was a cop. And two of his uncles. And his grandfather. It was in his blood.

Francis thought about it through that winter, paying more attention to the cops in the neighborhood, on the subways, moving barricades, on television. He went to the local station house to ask about the test, the timing, how it all worked and when. When Francis mentioned his plan to Uncle Patsy, Patsy said it was a sound idea, all he needed was twenty years and then he'd have his pension. Francis noticed that Patsy said 'twenty years' as if it were nothing, a mere blink, though at that moment it was more than the length of Francis's whole life. After twenty years, as long as he didn't get killed, he could do something else if he wanted. He saw his life split up into blocks of twenty, and for the first time he wondered how many blocks he'd get. The best part was he'd still be young, Patsy said. He wished he'd thought of it when he was Francis's age.

After graduation, his class had been split into groups to do field training in different parts of the city. He and thirty others, Brian Stanhope among them, were sent to Brownsville, and then to the Bronx, where the real job began. Francis was twenty-two by then. Brian was only twenty-one. Francis didn't know Brian well, but it was comforting to look across the room at muster and see a familiar face. Nothing, so far, had happened the way they'd been told things would happen. The station house itself was the exact opposite of what Francis had imagined when he decided to apply to the police academy. The outside was bad enough – the façade chipped and peeling, covered in bird shit and crowned in barbed wire – but inside was worse. There wasn't a surface in the place that wasn't damp or sticky or peeling. The radiator in the muster room had broken in half and someone had shoved an old pan underneath to catch the drips. Plaster rained from the ceiling and landed on their desks, their heads, their paperwork. Thirty perps were pushed into holding cells meant for two or three. Instead of being paired with more seasoned partners, all the rookies were sent out with other rookies. 'The blind leading the blind,' Sergeant Russell had joked, and promised it would only be for a little while. 'Don't do anything stupid.'

Now, Gleeson and Stanhope walked away from the smoldering building and headed north. From the distance came the clang of yet another fire alarm. Both young patrolmen knew the boundaries of their precinct on a map, but neither of them had seen those boundaries in person yet. The patrol cars were assigned by seniority, and the eight-to-four tour was heavy with seniority. They could have taken the bus to the farthest edge and walked back, but Stanhope said he hated taking the bus in uniform, hated the flare-up of tension when he boarded through the back door and every face looked over to size him up.

'Well, then let's walk,' Francis had suggested.

Now, with rivers of perspiration coursing down their backs, they made their way block after block, each man with stick, cuffs, radio, firearm, ammo, flashlight, gloves, pencil, pad, and keys swaying from his belt. Some blocks were nothing but rubble and burned-out cars, and they scanned for movement within the wreckage. A girl was throwing a tennis ball against the face of a building and catching it on the bounce. A pair of crutches lay across their path and Stanhope kicked them.

Any building with even a partial wall left standing was covered in graffiti. Tag upon tag upon tag, the colorful loops and curves implied motion, suggested life, and taken together they looked almost violently bright against a backdrop that was mostly gray.

The eight-to-four tour was a gift, Francis knew. Unless there were warrants to be executed, there was a good chance all would be quiet until lunch. When they finally turned onto Southern Boulevard, they felt like travelers who'd crossed a desert, grateful to be on the other side. Where the side streets were nearly empty, ghost-like, the boulevard was busy with passing cars, a menswear store that sold suits in every color, a series of liquor stores, a card shop, a barber, a bar. In the distance, a patrol car flashed its lights at them in greeting and rolled on.

'My wife is expecting,' Stanhope said when neither of them had said anything for a while. 'Due around Thanksgiving.'

'The Irish girl?' Francis asked. 'You married her?' He tried to remember: were they engaged back in academy when Stanhope had told him about her? He counted toward November – just four months away.

'Yup,' Stanhope said. 'Two weeks ago.' A city hall wedding. Dinner on Twelfth Street at a French place he'd read about in the paper; he'd had to point at his menu because he couldn't pronounce anything. Anne had to change her outfit last minute because the dress she'd planned on wearing was already too tight.

'She wants a priest to marry us once the baby comes. We couldn't find a parish that would do it quickly, even seeing her belly. Anne says maybe she'll find a priest who can bless the wedding and baptize the baby on the same day. Down the road, I mean.'

'Married is married,' Francis said, and offered his hearty congratulations. He hoped Stanhope didn't see that for a second there he'd been trying to do the math. He didn't care, really, it was just a habit brought from home, a habit he'd lose, no doubt, the longer he stayed in America. People went to Mass in shorts and T-shirts here. Not long ago he'd seen a woman driving a taxi. People walked around Times Square in their knickers.

'You want to see her?' Stanhope asked, taking off his hat. There, tucked inside the lining, was a snapshot of a pretty blond woman with a long, slim neck. Next to it a Saint Michael prayer card. Also tucked in the lining was a photo of a younger Brian Stanhope with another guy.

'Who's that?' Francis asked.

'My brother, George. That's us at Shea.'

Francis had not thought to put any photos in his hat yet, though he, too, had a Saint Michael prayer card folded in his wallet. Francis had asked Lena Teobaldo to marry him on the same day he'd graduated from academy, and she'd said yes. Now he imagined that would be him soon, telling people there was a baby on the way. Lena was half-Polish, half-Italian, and sometimes when he watched her – searching for something in her bag, or peeling an apple with her knuckle guiding the blade – he felt a shiver of panic that he'd almost not met her. What if he hadn't come to America? What if her parents hadn't come to America? Where else but in America would a Polack and an Italian get together and make a girl like Lena? What if he hadn't been at the pub the morning she came in to ask if her family could book the back room for a party? Her sister was going to college, she told him. She'd gotten a full scholarship, that's how smart she was.

'That'll be you, maybe, when you graduate from high school,' Francis had said, and she'd laughed, said she'd graduated the year before, that college was not in the cards for her but that was fine because she liked her job. She had a head of wild curls, brown shoulders above some strapless thing she was wearing. She was in the data processing pool at General Motors on Fifth Avenue, just a few floors above FAO Schwarz. He didn't know what FAO Schwarz was. He'd only been in America for a few months.

'People keep asking me if we're going to stay in the city,' Stanhope said. 'We're in Queens now, but the place is tiny.'

Francis shrugged. He didn't know anything about the towns outside the city, but he didn't see himself in an apartment for the rest of his life. He imagined land. A garden. Space to breathe. All Francis knew was after the wedding he and Lena would stay with her parents to save money.

'You ever heard of a town called Gillam?' Stanhope asked.

'No.'

'No, me neither. But that guy Jaffe? I think he's a sergeant? He said it's only about twenty miles north of here and there are a lot of guys there on the job. He says the houses all have big lawns and kids deliver the newspapers from their bicycles just like in *The Brady Bunch*.'

'What's it called again?' Francis asked.

'Gillam,' Stanhope said.

'Gillam,' Francis repeated.

In another block, Stanhope said he was thirsty, that a beer wouldn't be the worst idea. Francis pretended not to hear the suggestion. The patrolmen in Brownsville drank on the job sometimes but only if they were in squad cars, not out in the open. He wasn't a coward but they'd only just started. If either of them got in trouble, neither of them had a hook.

'Wouldn't mind one of them sodas with ice cream in it,' Francis said.

When they walked into the diner, Francis felt the trapped heat wafting at him despite the door having been propped open with a pair of bricks. The elderly man behind the counter was wearing a paper hat that had gone yellow, a lopsided bow tie. A fat black fly swooped frantically near the man's head as he looked back and forth between the policemen.

'The soda's cold, buddy? The milk's good?' Stanhope asked. His voice and the breadth of his shoulders filled the quiet, and Francis looked down at his shoes, then over at the plate glass, which was threaded with cracks, held together with tape. It was a good job, he told himself. An honorable job. There'd been rumors there wouldn't even be a class of 1973 with the city slashing its budget, but his class had squeaked through.

Just then, their radios crackled to life. There'd been some morning banter, calls put out and answered, but this was different. Francis turned up the volume. There'd been a shot fired and a possible robbery in progress at a grocery store located at 801 Southern Boulevard. Francis looked at the door of the coffee shop: 803. The man behind the counter pointed to the wall, at whatever was on the other side. 'Dominicans,' he said, and the word floated in the air, hovered there.

'I didn't hear a shot. Did you?' Francis said. The dispatcher repeated the call. A tremor jumped from Francis's throat to his groin, but he fumbled for his radio as he moved toward the door.

Francis in the lead, Stanhope right behind him, the two rookies unsnapped the holsters on their hips as they approached the door of the grocery. 'Shouldn't we wait?' Stanhope asked, but Francis kept moving forward past a pair of payphones, past a caged fan that stood beating the air. 'Police!' he shouted as they stepped farther inside the store. If there'd been any customers there when the robbery was taking place, there was no sign of them now.

'Gleeson,' Stanhope said, nodding at the blood-sprayed cigarette cartons behind the single register up front. The pattern showed the vigor of someone's heartbeat: blood that appeared more purple than red reaching as far as the water-stained ceiling, settling thickly on the rusted vent. Francis looked quickly to the floor behind the register, and then followed the grisly path down aisle three, until finally, lying in front of a broom closet, a man sprawled on his side, his face slack, an astonishing amount of blood in a growing pool beside him. While

Stanhope called it in, Francis pressed two fingers to the soft hollow under the man's jaw. He straightened the man's arm and put the same two fingers to his wrist.

'It's too hot for this,' Stanhope said as he frowned down at the body. He opened the fridge next to him, removed a bottle of beer, popped the cap off by striking it against the end of a shelf, and chugged it without taking a breath. Francis thought of the town Stanhope had mentioned, walking in his bare feet through cool, dew-damp grass. There was no predicting where life would go. There was no real way for a person to try something out, see if he liked it – the words he'd chosen when he told his uncle Patsy that he'd gotten into the police academy – because you try it and try it and try it a little longer and next thing it's who you are. One minute he'd been standing in a bog on the other side of the Atlantic and next thing he knew he was a cop. In America. In the worst neighborhood of the best known city in the world.

As the dead man's face turned ashen, Francis thought about how desperate the man looked, the way his neck was stretched and his chin pitched upward, like a drowning man craning for the surface of the water. It was only his second dead body. The first, a floater that had risen to the surface in April after a winter in New York Harbor, was not recognizable as a person, and perhaps for that reason it was barely real to him. The lieutenant who'd taken him along told him to get sick over the side of the boat if he wanted to, but Francis said he was fine. He thought of what the Christian Brothers had said about a body being merely a vessel, about the spirit being the pilot light of one's self. That first body, a water-logged piece of meat hauled up, dripping, onto the boat's deck, had parted with its soul long before Francis had laid eyes on it, but this one – bit by bit, Francis watched it depart. In the old country someone would have opened a window to let the man's spirit fly out, but any souls let loose here in the South Bronx would be free only so far as they could bat around four walls until, exhausted, they wilted in the heat and were forgotten.

'Prop that door, will you?' Francis called. 'I can barely breathe.'

Then, Francis heard something and froze. He placed a hand on his gun.

Stanhope looked at him, wide-eyed. There it was again, the whisper-soft sound of a sneaker on linoleum, listening to them as Francis listened back, three human hearts pounding in their cages, another lying still. 'Step out with your hands up,' Francis called, and then, all at once, they saw him: a tall and gangly teenager in a white undershirt, white shorts, white sneakers, hiding in the narrow space between the refrigerated case and the wall.

An hour later Francis was holding the kid's hands, rolling each finger in ink and then on the card, then four fingers together, then the thumb. First the left hand, and then the right, and then the left again, three cards total – local, state, federal. After the first card there was a rhythm to it, like an ancient dance: grasp, roll, release. The kid's hands were warm but dry, and if he was nervous Francis couldn't detect it. Stanhope was already writing up his report. The grocer had died well before the ambulance arrived and now here was the killer, his hands as soft as a child's, his fingernails well tended, clean. The kid's hands were loose, pliable. By the third card the kid knew what to do, began helping.

Later, after all the paperwork, the older cops said it was customary to take a guy out for his first arrest. The arrest had been credited to Francis, but they took Stanhope, too, bought him round after round while he told the story differently each time. The kid had stepped out and threatened them. The blood was dripping from every wall. Stanhope had blocked the exit while Francis wrestled the perp to the ground.

'Your partner,' one of the older cops said to Francis. 'He's creative.'

Stanhope and Francis looked at each other. Were they partners?

'You're partners until the captain tells you otherwise,' the older cop said.

The cook came out of the kitchen carrying plates piled high with burgers, told them it was on the house.

'You going home already?' Stanhope said to Francis a little later.

'Yes and so should you. Go home to your pregnant wife,' Francis said.

'The pregnant wife is why he's staying out,' one of the others cracked.

It took an hour and fifteen minutes by subway to get back to Bay Ridge. As soon as Francis walked in, he stripped to his boxers and climbed into the bed Patsy had crammed into his living room for him. Someone had called the kid's mother. Someone else had driven him to Central Booking. He'd said he was thirsty, so Francis had gotten him a soda from the machine. The kid gulped it down and then asked if he could fill the can with water from the tap. Francis went to the bathroom and filled it. 'You're a fool,' one of guys in plainclothes had said. He still had to learn everyone's name. Who knew? Maybe the grocer had done something bad to the kid. Maybe he deserved what he got.

Patsy was out somewhere. Francis called Lena, prayed she'd pick up and he wouldn't have to go through her mother.

'Did something happen today?' she asked after they'd chatted for a few minutes. 'You don't usually call this late.' Francis looked at the clock and saw it was near midnight. The paperwork and the beers had taken longer than he'd thought.

'Sorry. Go back to sleep.'

She was silent for so long he thought she had.

'Were you afraid?' she asked. 'You have to tell me.'

'No,' he said. And he hadn't been, or at least he hadn't felt what he understood fear to be.

'What then?'

'I don't know.'

'Try to keep it outside yourself, Francis,' she said, as if she'd been listening to his thoughts. 'We have a plan, you and me.'

He just wanted a decent book to read ...

Not too much to ask, is it? It was in 1935 when Allen Lane, Managing Director of Bodley Head Publishers, stood on a platform at Exeter railway station looking for something good to read on his journey back to London. His choice was limited to popular magazines and poor-quality paperbacks – the same choice faced every day by the vast majority of readers, few of whom could afford hardbacks. Lane's disappointment and subsequent anger at the range of books generally available led him to found a company – and change the world.

'We believed in the existence in this country of a vast reading public for intelligent books at a low price, and staked everything on it'
Sir Allen Lane, 1902–1970, founder of Penguin Books

The quality paperback had arrived – and not just in bookshops. Lane was adamant that his Penguins should appear in chain stores and tobacconists, and should cost no more than a packet of cigarettes.

Reading habits (and cigarette prices) have changed since 1935, but Penguin still believes in publishing the best books for everybody to enjoy. We still believe that good design costs no more than bad design, and we still believe that quality books published passionately and responsibly make the world a better place.

So wherever you see the little bird – whether it's on a piece of prize-winning literary fiction or a celebrity autobiography, political tour de force or historical masterpiece, a serial-killer thriller, reference book, world classic or a piece of pure escapism – you can bet that it represents the very best that the genre has to offer.

Whatever you like to read – trust Penguin.